# The
# BOLDNESS
## of Betty

Anna Carey

THE MEMOIRS OF BETTY
MARGARET RAFFERTY, AGED 14

THE O'BRIEN PRESS
DUBLIN

First published 2020 by The O'Brien Press Ltd,
12 Terenure Road East,
Rathgar, D06 HD27,
Dublin 6, Ireland.
Tel: +353 1 4923333; Fax: +353 1 4922777
The O'Brien Press is a member of Publishing Ireland.

E-mail: books@obrien.ie
Website: www.obrien.ie

ISBN: 978-1-78849-123-5

10 9 8 7 6 5 4 3 2 1
24 23 22 21 20

Layout and design: Emma Byrne, The O'Brien Press Ltd.
Cover illustrations: Lauren O'Neill

Printed in the UK by Clays Ltd, Elcograf S.p.A
The paper in this book is produced using pulp from managed forests.

Published in:

**DUBLIN**
UNESCO
City of Literature

*To Susan Houlden, who had to wait a long time to read this book,*
*and in memory of my great-grandfather Robert Carey, dock worker and 1913 striker*

## Acknowledgements

Thanks most of all to Susan Houlden, my editor at The O'Brien Press, who was very patient with me when this book ended up taking much, much longer to write than any of us expected. Many thanks to Helen Carr, whose idea it was to write about the 1913 Lockout, to Louise Lamont for all her help and to Aishwarya Subramanian for kindly taking the time to read the manuscript. Thanks to Jane Casey, Harriet Evans, Sarah Hughes, Sarra Manning and Aoife Murphy, aka the Lord Peter Casting Club, for the serious literary discussions that provided cheer and intellectual stimulation in stressful times. I send a beaming Hiddlesun to you all. And special thanks to Lauren O'Neill for what might be my favourite cover ever, and everyone at The O'Brien Press.

Thanks to the extended Carey and Freyne families, especially my nephew Arlo, who is a very discerning reader, and my cousin Elaine, whose house I borrowed for Betty. Thanks and all my love to my husband Patrick Freyne, who offered very helpful and necessary advice and support.

Several historians and librarians were kind enough to respond to my requests for research help. Mary Jones and Theresa Moriarty were generous with their time. Thanks too to Katherine McSharry and Eoin McCarney of the National Library, who sourced a crucial and incredibly helpful pamphlet by Manus O'Riordan on the cultural life of Liberty Hall in its early years.

But most of all, this book could not have been written without Pádraig Yeates, who not only wrote the definitive book on the lockout, *Lockout: Dublin 1913*, but was incredibly patient when I kept emailing him with more and more questions over the course of many months. I named a union-supporting bakery after him in the book, which was the very least I could do. I did my best to make the book historically accurate, but it's a work of fiction not a history book, and I am not a historian. Any historical errors are, I can assure readers, entirely my own.

# Chapter One

I thought I'd begin these memoirs by writing down my name and where I live and how many brothers and sisters I have (one too many if you ask me), but right now I'm so annoyed I'm just going to write down what happened a few minutes ago. I was sitting down at the table with this new notebook and a bit of old pencil that Ma had left behind the kitchen clock, getting ready to write down all these fascinating facts, when who should come into the kitchen but my stupid big brother Eddie.

'Is that the notebook Da got for you?' he said, because our da had come home from the docks yesterday with a big notebook full of empty blank pages that had been found on the quay after they'd unloaded a load of crates that morning. It really had fallen out somewhere and the cover was all damp so the foreman said he could take it, just in case you were thinking that was another way of saying he'd pinched it. Da's the most honest person in the world. Besides, you'd lose your job down the docks if you tried any of that thieving business so you'd have to be pretty stupid to try nicking anything, and Da isn't stupid. Da gave the notebook to me after tea last night. He knew that I was going to miss having something to scribble on now I've left school.

I hoped Eddie would leave me alone if I answered his question.

'It is, yeah,' I said. And then I looked back at the page because I was trying to think of the most dramatic way to introduce myself. Eddie, being Eddie, didn't take the hint.

'What are you writing in it?' he said in a smirking sort of voice, as if the idea of anyone writing anything down was utterly ridiculous.

'My memoirs,' I said, without looking up from the blank page.

Eddie stared at me as if I was talking Russian.

'What's a memoir when it's at home?' he said. You can tell he's never set foot in Charleville Mall Library even though it's only down the road. He does *not* have a good vocabulary, mostly because he barely listens to a word anyone else says. I, on the other hand, have an excellent vocabulary, as you will discover in these memoirs.

'It's when you write about yourself,' I said. 'Like the story of your life.'

And of course Eddie, the big stupid lump, laughed as if this was the funniest thing he'd ever heard. When he could finally speak he said, 'I'm fairly sure no one is going to want to read the story of your life.' He put on a stupid high-pitched voice. 'I went to the library. Then I came home. Then I took my stupid-looking dog for a walk. Then I went to bed.' He went back to his usual voice. 'Very exciting, I don't think.' And he laughed again at his own 'wit'.

'Well, maybe I'll be rich and famous by the time it comes out,' I said, ignoring his mockery. 'Then lots of people will want to read about my early years.'

Eddie ruffled my hair in that annoying way he has and said, 'If you say so, kiddie' in a very condescending way (that's another word I learned from the books in the library).

Then he wandered off to the front room, which is where he sleeps on the sofa, to draw the curtains and change out of his work uniform. He works for the tram company, in their parcel delivery department. I can hear him singing from my spot here in the kitchen. There's never any peace around here, even though Da's still out at work and Ma is down the road having tea with Mrs Connolly so technically I have the kitchen all to myself.

But anyway, now that he's out of the kitchen and I've calmed down a bit, I can introduce myself to my future readers. My name is Betty Margaret Rafferty. Actually, my name is Elizabeth Margaret Rafferty, after my grandma who died before I was born, but everyone always calls me Betty. I was born in May 1899, which means I turned 14 a few weeks ago. I also left school yesterday, but more on that later.

I live at 48 Strandville Avenue in the North Strand in Dublin, with my ma and my da and my stupid brother Eddie. The house has one window at the front, and from the outside you'd think it was only one level, but when you come in the front door you realise that only the front room and the hall are on the ground floor. There's one set of stairs going up to the two bedrooms and another set of stairs going down to the kitchen and the scullery. Ma and Da have the bigger room upstairs, I'm in the little one and Eddie sleeps on the sofa in the front room on the ground floor. And we've got the toilet out in the back garden, of course.

Until two years ago I shared the small room upstairs with my sister Lily, but then she married Robert Hessian. We always call him by his full name, Robert Hessian, even Ma. I don't know why. There's not much to say about him apart from the fact that he works down the docks, same as my da. He's the most boring person I've ever met. You forget whatever he's said the minute after he says it. If you asked me to describe what he looked like, I don't think I could do it, even though I've known him all my life because he's the same age as Lily and he grew up just around the corner from us, on Leinster Avenue. He's got brownish hair – or is it more mousey coloured? And an ordinary sort of nose … see, I can't do it.

Even though Robert Hessian is extremely boring, the day Lily got married was the happiest day of my life. Not because I was particularly delighted for her (in fact, I was more sorry for her than anything else, having to live with the most boring man in the world), but because that night I finally got to sleep in a bed by myself for the very first time. Me and Lily had shared the narrow little bed (which is all that fits in that tiny room, that and a bockety old wardrobe Da got in the pawn shop) ever since I was tiny.

When we shared the bed, we slept top-and-tail, which means Lily's pillow was at one end and mine was at the other, but it was still an awful squash, especially as Lily made me sleep on the side closest to the wall, which meant that whenever I bent my legs I bashed my knees against the wall. And of course I had her horrible smelly clodhopping feet next to my face all night, which I wouldn't wish on my worst enemy.

If Ma ever read this, she would say I was being ridiculous and that Lil's feet are very dainty and don't smell at all, and that she's always had a bath once a week and is perfectly clean, but Ma didn't have to share a bed with Lily for twelve years. I did and I know. Lily didn't go very far when she moved out, but as long as she moved out of that bed I didn't care. She and Robert Hessian moved in with his ma and da in Leinster Avenue. Mr and Mrs Hessian turned the front room into a proper bedroom for them, and they have a big brass bed and everything.

Of course, Eddie didn't approve of me getting a whole bedroom to myself after Lily left. He thought he should have it 'as the son of the house' and I should get the sofa in the front room, but

Ma said she couldn't have her daughter sleeping in the front room where any Tom, Dick or Harry can see in the window, even with the lace curtains.

'What if someone walked past and saw her in her shift?' she said.

'What if someone came by and saw me in my vest?' said Eddie, very annoyed, but Ma said no one would want to look at him in his vest, and if they did see him, they wouldn't care, and I think she's right and said so. Eddie was very insulted and walked out of the room in a huff.

Anyway, I have the bed all to myself now, but Eddie's clothes and things are in the wardrobe and I only get a tiny corner to put my belongings in. Not that either of us have a lot of clothes. We can't afford them. But the clothes we *do* have are all made by Ma, which means my frocks are beautifully put together even though there aren't very many of them.

Ma is very good at making clothes, and she does a bit of dress-making for ladies in Drumcondra and Clontarf. When she's busy with her sewing we can't go into the front room because she'll have bits of material and patterns and things spread out all over the floor. When it comes to our own clothes we all help out with the cutting and all that, but she'd never trust us to cut out one of her rich ladies' frocks. When she's not doing sewing she looks after the house and all of us.

So that's Ma. Then there's Da. He works on the docks, like lots of the men around here, which means he's been on strike a lot recently. If you don't know what a strike is (and maybe they'll have stopped having them by the time anyone reads these memoirs), it's when workers walk out of their jobs because they feel they're not being treated fairly. They refuse to go back until the employers agree to change things. Sometimes this works and sometimes it doesn't, but as Da says, you've got to try, haven't you? Da doesn't talk much, but when he does, he usually says something sensible and he knows how to make me feel better. Sometimes, though, even he can't do anything to help. Like yesterday, which was one of the worst days of my whole life.

It was the last day of the school term, but for me it was the very last day of school ever. Same for all my classmates. I don't know anyone whose family can afford to pay the fees for secondary school. Ali – he's my friend Samira's big brother – once told me that in America children don't have to pay to go to secondary school, but even if that's true there's no chance of that happening here in Dublin. Only rich boys and girls get to go to secondary school. The rest of us have to go out and work. I learned that a long time ago.

Most of my class in school were delighted to be leaving forever, but I wasn't and neither was Samira. We spent the whole walk home trying not to cry and not quite succeeding. We were so miserable we didn't even want to talk to each other about how bad we felt, and when I got home I certainly didn't want to talk to any of my family, but I couldn't avoid seeing Ma because she let me into the house.

'There you are!' she said cheerfully as she opened the door. 'Oh come now, Betty, what are you looking like that for? Most girls would be glad to be rid of school.'

Well, that did it.

'You *know* I'm not!' I said, so loudly that our dog Earnshaw stuck his head out of the kitchen to see what was going on.

Ma folded her arms across her chest, the way she does when

she's about to give out to you.

'Don't take that tone, miss!' said Ma. 'I never thought a daughter of mine could be so ungrateful.'

'I'm not ungrateful!' I said.

'You're going to a decent job in that cake shop,' Ma went on as if I hadn't spoken. '*And* when your work is done you'll be sleeping in your own bed at night, which is more than I was able to do when I was your age.'

'You don't understand …' I began, but Ma interrupted me.

'You're right,' she said. 'I certainly don't. And if you can't be more cheerful …'

Well, I couldn't. And I suppose she knew it, because she didn't try to stop me when I ran through the scullery, out the back door and right to the end of the garden. I sat on the grass with my back against the door of the lavatory, where you couldn't see me from the house. And then I cried and cried.

After a while I could hear Ma calling me, but I didn't answer. I just sat there with my arms wrapped around my shins and my head buried in my knees. Earnshaw finally found me, of course, but Earnshaw would never give me away. He just lay at my feet and went to sleep. Every so often a train rumbled past on the line that runs just a few yards from our house.

It must have been hours later when I heard someone walking around the back of the toilet. Then someone sat down beside me. I knew without looking up that it was my da. He put his arm around me, but I didn't lean into him. I just huddled up stiffly with my face buried in my knees and Earnshaw curled up on my shoes.

'I know it's hard for you, Betty,' said Da. His voice is gruff, but there's something warm about it too. It's how you'd imagine a nice warm coal fire would sound like if it could talk.

I hadn't planned on saying anything at all, but when he said that I found the words exploding out of me. 'It's not *fair*,' I said. Well, I say said, but it was more like a yell. 'It's just not fair! I'm good at school. You know I am! It's stupid that I have to leave.'

'Life isn't fair, pet,' said Da, which is the sort of irritating thing parents say whenever you complain about everything, but he sounded as if he really meant it this time.

'I could have got a scholarship,' I said fiercely. 'Somehow. And then I could go to Eccles Street or Loreto on George's Street, or one of them places. You *know* I could have.'

I don't even know if those fancy schools give scholarships, but no one had even tried to check for me and I had no way of checking myself.

'And *you* know that we need a wage coming in,' said Da gently. 'We can't afford to have anyone not working who could be working. Things are rough in this city these days. For all I know, they might sack all of us dockers tomorrow.'

I know this is true. And I know I have to do my bit for the family. All the girls and boys around here do. But it doesn't stop me wishing I didn't have to, and I couldn't pretend I didn't mind.

'If I stayed in school, I might earn more money in the end,' I said. 'I might even be a teacher, or something. They must earn more than I'll earn in that cake shop place.'

Da sighed. 'Look it, if you work for a while and save up a bit of your wages, you'll have enough money for one of them typewriting classes. You could get yourself a fancy auld job in an office.'

I didn't say anything.

'And it's not as though you'll be going into service,' said Da, forcing some cheerfulness into his voice. 'We won't be sending you out to scrub floors. You'll work in that shop for a while and then once you've learned to use those typing machines you'll go and work in a nice warm office wearing a silk frock and typing out some rich fella's letters. That doesn't sound too shabby, does it?'

He was being so kind I couldn't stay angry with him. When he put his arm around me I gave him a big hug back, and then I went back into the kitchen where Ma had a slice of cake ready for me as a leaving-school-treat. She gave me a hug too, and she was very nice to me for the rest of the evening. But I knew they didn't understand, not really. I wanted to stay at school so I could learn things, even the boring things like geography, because then maybe I could go to college and read lots of books about things I *am* interested in. And maybe after that I could become a teacher or, I don't know, anything at all. Even a writer. Something other than being a servant or working in a shop or a factory like most girls around here.

Because here's one thing I haven't ever told anyone else, not even Samira: what I want most of all is to write stories, and in fact the main reason I've started writing this memoir is to prac- tise writing something. And if I'm being perfectly honest, I don't see why I couldn't write a book when I grow up. I mean, lots of people write books, so why shouldn't I? Charles Dickens was sent out to work in a factory when he was even younger than I am, and he went on to become one of the most famous writers ever. And when I become a famous writer I'm sure people would find it very interesting to read about my early years.

But I'd never say any of this to Ma and Da. Every time I tried talking with them about staying at school we had a big row because they thought I was just being silly. And maybe I am. It's not like having to leave school was a surprise – I always knew it was going to happen. So I've made the decision not to say anything about it again. Anyway, those are my ma and da. They don't really understand me but they're all right I suppose.

The last but most important member of the family is the aforementioned (another fancy word!) Earnshaw. Earnshaw is not a person, of course, he is a dog. Da found him on the docks when he was a puppy and took him home because they couldn't find his mammy, and Lily and I wrapped him in a blanket and fed him out of a bottle until he was old enough to eat scraps.

'If I'd known what he'd grow into,' says Ma sometimes, 'I'd have drowned him in a bucket back then when I had a chance.' It's true that he's a peculiar-looking sort of dog, but I think that makes him more interesting. Sometimes people stare at him in the street, but I'd rather have a dog that people stared at than some boring old terrier who looks like all the other dogs and who no one even notices. Anyway, whatever Ma says about Earnshaw, we all know she loves him really. She even sings songs to him when she thinks no one can hear her. Everyone loves Earnshaw, even Eddie who pretends he doesn't care about anything.

And that's our family. In comparison to some people round here there aren't very many of us, only three kids (and we don't all live in our house anymore). There are some families with even fewer (that's good grammar, the nuns would be proud of me). The Phelans only have two kids (though they have two policemen lodgers, Mr Carroll and Mr Ward, who sleep in the front room).

There should have been more children in our family, but Ma had two babies who died. I never saw them. One was called

Thomas and he was born two years after Lily. Another was called Mary and she was born a year after Eddie. They only lived for a few weeks each. Most families on our road have had at least one baby who died.

There are still lots of big families though. The O'Hanlons have ten kids, in a house the same size as ours. Lily and Robert Hessian only have one so far, and it's to be hoped they don't have any more, if my nephew Little Robbie is anything to go by.

I forgot to mention Little Robbie when I was listing all my relations. That's because I try to pretend he doesn't exist. You wouldn't think a baby could be so terrible but he is. He was born a year ago and when he was tiny he just cried all the time, which lots of babies do, I suppose, so I can't blame him for that (see how reasonable I am?). But once he got a bit older and started showing some personality, his true nature was revealed.

He's all smiles to his mammy and daddy and to my ma and da, and he doesn't seem to care much about Eddie one way or another, but as soon as he gets anywhere near me he turns bright red and starts roaring. Practically the minute he got teeth, he bit me. I told Ma I should go to the doctor because I was worried I'd get poisoned, like when people get bitten by mad dogs, and she told me to go on out of that. No one in our family ever goes to the doctor, I think they'd only get you a doctor around here if they thought you were in danger of dying and probably not even then. They're just too expensive. Then she said that I wouldn't get poisoned by a beautiful baby like Little Robbie.

'He's not a beautiful baby, Ma,' I said. 'He looks like a tomato in a wig.' Because as well as going bright red whenever he's angry, which is most of the time, he also has a shock of black hair. He was born with it, and if you ask me he just gets hairier and hairier as the days go by. It doesn't seem normal for a baby to have so much hair, or such a red angry face. Ma doesn't agree, of course.

'He looks nothing like a tomato!' she said. 'Actually I think he looks just like you when you were his age. You were a very hairy baby too.'

Me, looking like Little Robbie! I think this might have been the most insulting thing anyone has ever said to me. Anyway, Ma says I have to stop being horrible about him.

'You can't say that about your own nephew!' she says, whenever I give out about him biting me or getting sick on me or head-butting me in the face. 'He's a little dote and an angel-love!' But he really isn't either of those things. He's a monster in disguise. And not a very good disguise either.

Right, Ma just got home from the Connollys and started giving out to me for not starting on the potatoes, so even though I haven't written a word about Samira yet, or the new job I'm starting in a few days, I'm going to stop writing now and hide this notebook under my mattress. I wouldn't trust Eddie to leave it alone if I left it in the kitchen.

# Chapter Two

This time tomorrow I will officially be a working woman. Well, a working girl anyway. I've had a few sweet days of freedom, which I spent sitting in the back garden with Samira reading library books and talking about all the things we'd like to do with our lives if I didn't have to go and work in a cake shop and tearoom and she didn't have to go to work in the shop at the top of the road. But now, as Eddie has been delighting in telling me, I have to 'enter the working world'. Whether I like it or not.

The cake shop and tearoom where I'm going to be working is called Lawlor's, and it's on Henry Street. I actually got the job because one of Ma's dressmaking clients is the wife of the owner, Mrs Lawlor herself. Ma is very good at making clothes. Before she married Da she worked in a drapery in town called Whyte's which is quite grand. Her ma and da, my Nanny and Granda, live in a little cottage near Skerries and when Ma was fifteen she moved down to Dublin to work in the shop. All the shop assistants lived in a sort of lodging house that was part of the shop, so she was on the premises all the time. This doesn't sound much fun to me but she says it wasn't too bad.

When Ma worked at Whyte's, she sewed all her own clothes with the ends of the rolls of fabric they sold in the shop, which she could buy at a discount, and these clothes were so exquisitely made (that's another good word, exquisitely) that customers who came in there buying cotton or wool materials began asking her about them. She started doing a bit of dressmaking herself in her spare time and earned enough to buy a decent secondhand sewing machine.

Some of those customers were very grand people and Ma had to go to see them at home to show them the clothes and make alterations, so she's visited big houses all over the city and she knows quite a lot about how fine ladies and gentlemen live. This is why Mrs Hennessy down the road thinks Ma has notions. I suppose Ma sort of does have notions, at least in comparison to Mrs Hennessy.

And she still has the sewing machine. She always says that if you look after a sewing machine it should last you all your life. That's how she makes clothes for her grand ladies in Drumcondra and Clontarf – like Mrs Lawlor. Mrs Lawlor lives on the Howth Road in Clontarf, in a massive house with coloured glass in the door, and I'm sure she has never gone behind the counter of the shop her husband founded twenty years ago.

I've met her, though. In fact, I first met her a few months ago and I suppose that day changed my life, because without it I might not be going to work in Lawlor's tearoom tomorrow. It was back in March when I went over to her house one day with Ma to fit some frocks for her daughter, Lavinia Lawlor. They were part of Lavinia's birthday present and Ma needed her to try them on in case any final alterations were needed. At least she knew they weren't too long – she'd realised when she took the first measurements that me and Lavinia Lawlor are exactly the same height, even though she is about three years older than me, so she'd got me to try them on when she was doing the hems.

Afterwards I almost wished I hadn't gone to the Lawlors' house – not that I had a choice in the matter. My assistance was required because Mrs Lawlor had ordered so many frocks that Ma couldn't have carried them and her sewing bag all the way to the Howth Road on her own. Or at least not without getting them all crumpled up. But I felt peculiar about going. That wasn't just because the frocks started to feel pretty heavy after about half a mile, but because Lavinia Lawlor goes to school with the Dominican nuns in Eccles Street.

One of my teachers in William Street went to school there before she trained to become a teacher, and she told me that the girls in Eccles Street learn French and German and music, and play tennis and put on plays and get taken to the theatre. And then when they're finished school, some of them go on to college. Ever since she first told me about this, I've dreamed of going to that school. It's only a mile or so away – I could walk there easily. I used to dream of going there and learning how to speak French and German and read Shakespeare. That was before I had to accept that there was no chance of it ever happening in real life.

But I'm pretty sure – in fact, I know – that all of those advantages have been completely wasted on Lavinia Lawlor. When we arrived at the house in Clontarf on that day back in March, we knocked on the kitchen door underneath the front steps (of course we didn't go up the steps to the front door). A tall thin woman with a red friendly face answered the door.

'Ah, Mrs Rafferty,' she said, with a cheery smile. She had a country accent though I couldn't tell you where exactly she was from. 'Good to see you again! It's been a while, so it has.'

'I told you, Jessie, call me Margaret,' said Ma with a smile. 'Mrs Lawlor asked us to make a few things for Miss Lavinia's birthday, so I'm here to do the final fitting.'

I didn't like hearing Ma call Lavinia Lawlor 'Miss Lavinia'. She doesn't call Samira Miss Casey, and Lavinia Lawlor is no better than any of my friends. But of course I didn't say anything about this to Ma.

'I'd better show you up there myself,' said Jessie. 'The other girls are sorting out something for Mrs Lawlor in the attic.' It took me a while to realise that the 'other girls' were other servants, not daughters of the house. We followed Jessie through the lovely warm kitchen (which was about the same size as our entire house, and had big hams hanging from the ceiling. Whole hams, just for one family! I've only ever seen a ham in the window of the butcher's shop) and up the stairs to the hall.

I had never been in a house like this before, and even though I was trying to act as if I were invited to places like this all the time, I couldn't help looking around me and staring at everything. Because there was so much to stare at. The first thing I noticed was a beautiful little hall table with a gong on it. It was suspended in a wooden frame and resting on the frame was a little mallet. I suppose Jessie (or one of the other servants) hits the gong with the mallet when it's time for dinner, like they do in books.

At the foot of the stairs was a grandfather clock and the face of it was covered in stars and moons. I wish I had a clock covered in stars and moons. There were paintings on the wall – actual paintings, not just holy pictures or pages cut out of magazines, which is all we have at home. You could see where the brush had left marks on the canvas. The sun shone in through the coloured glass in the door and made a pattern on the tiled floor We don't have tiles in our house, just lino and some rag rugs.

Jessie opened a door and ushered us into the drawing room, and that was even more beautiful than the hall. It was exactly the way I imagine Pemberly, Mr Darcy's big house in one of my favourite books, *Pride and Prejudice*. The walls were papered in yellow and there was a picture rail around the top with lots of beautiful paintings in gold frames hanging off it. There was a carpet on the floor so thick and soft you practically lost your feet in it. A massive piano stood in one corner and on the piano were photographs in silver and leather frames.

On each side of the fireplace was a big sofa, with fluffy cushions, and armchairs that were about the size of the sofa in our front room. Hanging from the ceiling was a chandelier, like they have in the entrance to the picture house. I've never seen one in a house before. It sparkled in the sunlight coming in through the massive windows. This was when I stopped trying to look all casual and just openly stared at everything in amazement.

'I'll tell Mrs Lawlor you're here,' said the friendly Jessie. 'Miss Lavinia isn't home from school yet but she'll be in any minute.' She bustled out of the room.

Ma smiled at me. 'Now isn't this a treat?' she said. 'It's not often you get to visit a house like this, is it?'

'Can we sit down?' I said, looking longingly at the big sofa. I wanted to know what it would feel like to lie back in all those cushions. But Ma looked as if I'd asked if I could rip up the cushions with a knife.

'You certainly can *not*,' she said. 'And you won't say a thing unless you're spoken to.'

I thought, well, if visiting a grand house means I have to act like a dummy in a shop window and I can't even sit down for a rest after walking in the heat, I'd rather stay in the North Strand. And just as I was thinking this, the door of the drawing room opened again and a woman came in who was so tall and elegant I was instantly sure that me and Ma looked like a pair of drab little mice in comparison, even though I was wearing a cotton frock covered in tiny flowers which is one of my favourites, and Ma always looks lovely and neat and trim.

Mrs Lawlor was wearing a fawn-coloured linen skirt and a cream lace blouse with a beautiful brooch at the neck. On her feet, peeking out from under the linen skirt, were the most elegant fawn kid shoes. I suddenly felt very aware of the scuffs on my nice clean black leather button boots. Ma always tells me I'm lucky to have shoes at all because most of the children in the tenements in town certainly don't, and I know she's right, but my boots looked so old and big and clumsy in comparison to Mrs Lawlor's dainty slippers. I crossed one foot behind the other.

'Mrs Rafferty,' she said, and even though her appearance was grand her manner was warm and friendly. 'How kind of you to come.'

You *told* her to, I thought, but then I felt bad because Mrs Lawlor was being nice. She spoke as if she really were happy to see Ma. Now she was smiling at me. 'And who is this?'

'This is Betty, Mrs Lawlor,' said Ma. 'My youngest girl.'

'How do you do, Betty?' said Mrs Lawlor, and as I'd actually been spoken to I presumed it was all right to say, 'Very well, thank you.'

'Betty helped me carry over the clothes for Miss Lavinia,' said Ma. 'And she helped me with the alterations at home.'

'Well, I'm very glad you did,' said Mrs Lawlor. 'Lavinia never seems to have time for things like dress fittings. It's always the tennis club or some other romp.'

She glanced at the mantelpiece, where there was a lovely little wooden clock with roses painted around it. 'She should be home by now.'

There was a slightly awkward moment and then Mrs Lawlor said, 'Goodness, what am I doing, making you stand after you've walked here with those heavy bags? Sit down, please, do.'

And so we sat down on Mrs Lawlor's drawing-room sofa, while she sat in one of the armchairs. I wished I could roll back on the cushions but of course I couldn't. Ma was barely sitting on the sofa at all; she just perched on the very edge.

'And are you going to school, Betty?' Mrs Lawlor asked politely.

'Yes, Mrs Lawlor,' I said. 'Until the end of the summer term. I'll be leaving then.'

Mrs Lawlor smiled. 'I'm sure you'll be glad to leave. Lavinia's got a whole year of school left – we told her she had to stay and do her Intermediate Certificate but she'd rather be off playing tennis.'

And without thinking I said, 'Well, I don't want to leave. I *wish* I could do the Intermediate Certificate.'

As soon as I said it, I worried it sounded as if I was suggesting that Lavinia was ungrateful, which was of course exactly what I was thinking. Ma gave me one of her looks, a look that said I'd better remember where I was, and that I'd better not even think of telling Mrs Lawlor exactly what I thought about girls who didn't appreciate getting to go to school, and who thought leaving it meant playing tennis instead of having to go out and get a job. My Ma can say a lot with a look.

I wished I hadn't said anything, but actually Mrs Lawlor didn't seem particularly bothered by what I'd said. In fact, she laughed as if I'd made a joke.

'Do you really?' she said. 'Well, I wish my daughter had your academic enthusiasm.' The doorbell rang. 'That should be her now.'

She didn't get up to answer the door, and I realised that of course Jessie or maybe another maid would be answering it for her, even though all the servants must have been upstairs or down in the kitchen and we were in the room right next to the front door.

A moment later I heard the door open and a girl about the same size as me with shiny golden-brown hair came into the drawing room, yawning.

'There you are, Lavinia,' said Mrs Lawlor. 'Mrs Rafferty and her daughter are here with your birthday clothes.'

'Do we have to do this now, Mother?' Lavinia's voice was petulant. (That's another good word, isn't it? It means sulky, more or less.) 'I'm awfully tired.'

'Of course we do.' Mrs Lawlor's voice became stern. 'They've come all this way to do a fitting. If you want to have new frocks to wear for your party next week, you've got to make sure they fit.'

Lavinia sighed, as if she were being forced to undergo some terrible trial.

'Oh all right then,' she said. 'I'll get ready.' And she walked out of the room.

Mrs Lawlor's smile was almost apologetic.

'We'd better do this up in her bedroom,' she said, rising from her armchair. Ma stood up too. I wasn't sure if I should go with them – after all, I'd just been brought along to carry the clothes, not fit them. But Ma gave me another one of her meaningful looks so I got up and followed them up to Lavinia's bedroom, where she had already taken her frock off and was standing there in the nicest undergarments I've ever seen, in what must have been the most beautiful bedroom in the world.

Of course, I know from books that there are girls who have rooms like this, but knowing something from books is very different from actually seeing it with your own two eyes. The walls were papered in pale blue with little rosebuds, and there was a silk eiderdown on the bed in the same colours. The bed itself was a high wooden affair, painted white with a little bouquet of flowers on the headboard. I thought of my bockety brass bed, with the knob that falls off if you drop onto the bed too hard, and for the first time having that bed all to myself didn't seem so amazingly wonderful.

All the bits of furniture – the dressing table with the hinged mirror over it, the wardrobe and even the bookshelf – were white and decorated with little painted bouquets of flowers. I looked longingly at the bookshelf, which just had a couple of books on it; the rest of the shelves were occupied by little glass ornaments. There was a picture of the Blessed Virgin above the bed and lots of lovely prints in golden frames of girls frolicking in a garden with dogs. And there was a fire lit, in the bedroom, in the middle of the afternoon. I couldn't help it. I gawped. And Lavinia noticed. I could see her looking over at me with a sort of amused look on her face, and I quickly looked down at my boots, which looked clumpier and scruffier than ever.

'Right then, Miss Lavinia,' said Ma briskly, taking her tape measure and pins out of her bag, and I remembered that she was used to dealing with people like this, both as a dressmaker and also from her days in the shop. Once she was at work she no longer looked awkward or uncomfortable, though I'm fairly sure I did, standing behind her like a big eejit with nothing to do. I wished I could have just gone down to the kitchen to Jessie and had a cup of tea. Ma handed Lavinia a frock and the girl pulled it over her head and did up the buttons. Ma helped do the hooks at the back and then stood back. She looked critically at her creation and then looked at Mrs Lawlor.

'What do you think of the length there, Mrs Lawlor? A smidgen too long, do you think?'

'I think you might be right, Mrs Rafferty,' said Mrs Lawlor. 'Maybe you could pin it up half an inch, just to see.'

'Right you are,' said Ma. She turned to me. 'The pins please, Betty.'

And that's what we did for what felt like the next five years (though I suppose it was only about three quarters of an hour really). Lavinia tried on frocks, Ma and Mrs Lawlor stared at her, and every so often I handed Ma pins so she could adjust the fit. Sometimes I held the hem or pinched the waistline so she could pin it in place, but that was about it. There weren't even that many adjustments to make, but every single thing had to be tried on and examined by Ma and Mrs Lawlor, and of course Lavinia had plenty of things to say too. In fact, she kept on talking and talking in her drawling, discontented voice. She spent the entire time we were there whining to her mother about the special cake she wanted for her birthday party the following week, and how dreadfully dull school was, and how awful the teachers were because they actually try to make her read books when she'd rather be out on the tennis court.

She went on and on and on, and of course I didn't say anything in response because she didn't care what me or Ma thought. As far as she was concerned we were just things, moving around her, doing what we had been built to do. The only vaguely interesting part of her monologue (that's another word I've learned from reading, it's when someone talks on their own for ages) was when she told us some of the girls at school had started wearing little Votes for Irish Women buttons on their blouses.

Not that I care too much about votes for women. After all, my da can't vote either because he doesn't own property, and the rent on our house isn't high enough to put him on the voting register. But still, Lavinia talking about suffragettes was more interesting than listening to her go on about her birthday tea or how she was going to make her brother take her out to some tennis tournament in Howth during the summer holidays.

Eventually, however, the last frock had been tried on and Lavinia changed back into her day dress while Ma and I packed the new frocks back in their paper wrappings to take home.

'I'll have them back to you by Saturday,' Ma said to Mrs Lawlor as we walked back onto the landing (which was bigger than my bedroom), leaving Lavinia to the privacy of her beautiful boudoir.

'Thank you so much, Mrs Rafferty,' said Mrs Lawlor. She smiled at me. 'And thank you, Betty. You've been a very able assistant.'

'Thank you, Mrs Lawlor,' I said, even though I hadn't done much besides hand Ma a few pins and hold up Lavinia's hems. And it wasn't as if I was being paid for it.

'Well,' said Ma, after Jessie had given us a cup of tea in the kitchen and we were walking home. 'Isn't she a very nice lady? And isn't it a fine house?'

'She's very friendly,' I said. Mrs Lawlor was indeed nice, and the house was very fine, but something about being there made me feel peculiar inside. It wasn't until I was lying in bed (aware for the first time of how worn out the sheets and blankets were, and how the bed wobbled when I got into it) that I really figured out why I felt so odd. Part of it was plain old anger and jealousy that someone as snobbish and downright stupid as Lavinia (and yes I know that sounds harsh, but remember I had to crawl around at her feet listening to her blather on about tea parties all afternoon so I can safely say that she is not a brilliant genius) gets to go to Eccles Street and do her Inter Cert, while girls like me and Samira have to go out and get jobs. It's just, I don't know, such a *waste*. How could I not be angry about it?

But that wasn't the only thing that was bothering me. It was hard to put into words, but I tried my best to do so the next day when me and Samira were walking to school. Samira is my best friend in the whole world and she has been for as long as I can remember. We're exactly the same age – she's just two weeks older than me – but she's a whole inch taller. I know this because we measured ourselves with Ma's tape measure at the end of the school term. And when I told her about my encounter with the Lawlors, she knew just what I meant.

'I always knew there were rich people,' I said, as we trudged down the strand.

'It'd be strange if you didn't,' said Samira. She nodded towards a motorcar driving past us into town with a well-dressed, bearded gentleman at the wheel. 'They're only up the road in Clontarf.'

'Exactly, you can't miss them,' I said. 'But until I was in the Lawlors' house, none of it seemed real. You know, you can *imagine* what those rich people's houses are like but they might as well be in fairyland. Or the Enchanted Castle in that E. Nesbit book.'

'I know what you mean,' said Samira. 'It's like the people that live in houses like that are Psammeads, or something. They really only live in books but you'll never actually meet one.'

The Psammead, in case you don't know, dear reader of my memoirs, is a magic creature in another book by E. Nesbit who can grant wishes. Samira and I never have to explain these things to each other. That's one of the best things about being friends with Samira. If you met her you might think she was a bit vague – our teachers in school were always telling her to stop daydreaming – but she's not vague at all when we're talking about things she really cares about. The pair of us have read our way through half the shelves in Charleville Mall Library (and Samira has read all the Shakespeare plays as well, because she wants to go on the stage like her Auntie Maisie – but I'll write more about that later).

This means if one of us refers to something from a book, the other one always gets exactly what we mean, which is more than any of my family do. None of them ever read anything apart from newspapers and the illustrated magazines Ma's clients give her.

'That's just it,' I said. 'But now I've been in one of those houses. And it's made them real. And it's ... it's different.'

I suppose until I sat down on the Lawlors' sofa I had never really understood, not really, that there were some people – real people – who lived surrounded by painted furniture and clocks with stars on them. People who had a gigantic bedroom each, when our Eddie has to sleep on a sofa and the twelve O'Hanlons are squashed into a cottage the size of the Lawlors' kitchen.

I said this to Samira just as we reached the entrance to the school, but before she could answer, Sister Benin came out ringing the bell so we had to hurry inside. But even thought it was a few months ago now, I haven't forgotten how that visit to the Lawlors' made me feel. I know that's just the way the world is, and it's not like it's Mrs Lawlor's fault (or even Lavinia's fault, awful as she is), but there's something terrible unfair about it.

Not that I said anything about this to my family. If I said it to Ma, she would say I was being ungrateful and that I should hold my tongue and count my blessings, and it's true that we're a lot better off than some people in this city, the people crammed in houses where whole families live in one dirty room and the kids have to sleep on the floor and never wear shoes even in winter.

If I said it to Da, he'd say that he has enough to be doing, fighting for a fair wage for the working man, to be thinking about other people's fancy cushions. Eddie would just laugh at me and tell me he knew all that reading would make my brain soft. Lily would ask me to describe the cushions. I can't even imagine what Robert Hessian would say. And Little Robbie would probably just get sick on me.

Anyway, I suppose I shouldn't say or even *think* anything bad about the Lawlor family from now on, because I'm going to be working for them tomorrow, and in a way it's all because of that visit back in March. It was Mrs Lawlor who suggested to Ma that I work behind the counter in the cake shop and tearoom on Henry Street – she remembered me from that day – and of course Ma said I'd love to. It's very kind of her, I suppose, and it saves me having to go around all the shops and factories looking for work, but I don't want any job, not yet. I want to stay at school like Lavinia and learn German. Or French, I don't care which.

But I don't have any choice in the matter, so I'd better just get on with it. Tomorrow I have to report to someone called Miss Warby, who apparently is the manager of the cake shop and tea-room. I keep thinking of David Copperfield in the factory and feeling a bit sick. Though maybe some day I can write a book about it, just like Dickens did.

Janey mack, I've spent so long writing this that I think my hand is actually going to seize up and stop working and then the rest of me will do the same and maybe I'll be enfeebled, like Mrs Hennessy's Old Mother who lives with them and hasn't got out of bed for five years. So I'd better stop writing before I do myself some damage. Actually, I don't have any choice about stopping, because this pencil is practically worn down to a stub. I'll have to use the tuppence I was going to use to get a new hair ribbon to buy a new pencil tomorrow on my way to work. I certainly won't find a spare one around here.

# Chapter Three

I am so, so tired. I just got home from work and I feel like my legs are going to fall off. I've been standing so much I started to worry I'd get varicose veins, like Ma complains about. You get them from staying on your feet too long without walking. I said something about this to Rosie, my new friend from work, and she just laughed.

'You don't get varicose veins when you're fourteen, you big eejit,' she said.

'You might if you spend all day standing up,' I said, but she just elbowed me in the ribs and told me to stop acting the tin elephant which is one of her favourite phrases. She got it off her sister Josie who works in Jacob's biscuit factory. I'm lucky I get to work with Rosie because she really is the best thing about my job.

It's been nearly a week now since I started at Lawlor's, and I suppose I'm getting used to it, though I'm not sure I'd have lasted a single day without crying if it weren't for Rosie. When I arrived on my first morning, I made the mistake of going up to the front door of the shop. In fact, I was just about to push it open when someone grabbed my arm. It gave me such a shock that I yelped.

'Sorry!' said a friendly voice. The voice belonged to a small girl with curly black hair bursting out of a long plait. 'Are you the new girl?'

'How did you know?' I said.

'Old Wobbly told us there was going to be a new girl on the counter today. And only a new girl would try to go in through the front door.'

'But how did you know I worked here at all?' I felt quite over-whelmed by all this.

'First of all because the shop won't be open for another half hour,' said the girl. 'And second of all because – and don't take this the wrong way – you don't look like one of our customers.'

She said it all in such a friendly way that I couldn't be offended. Besides, it was obviously true. I was wearing a plain black uniform dress that Ma had collected from the tearoom the previous week and altered to fit me. My boots were clean but not exactly dainty. And I was wearing an old straw hat of Ma's that had seen better days and wasn't redeemed by the red ribbon I'd tied around it. I was clean and tidy, but I definitely didn't look like the sort of person who bought cakes in a fancy shop like this.

'Don't worry,' said the girl. 'I'll show you where to go. I'm Rosie, by the way. Who are you?'

'Betty,' I said, and I shook her outstretched hand.

Rosie led me down a lane and around a corner to another lane that ran behind all the shops. She pushed open a battered black door that couldn't have been more different from the glass and mahogany of the front of the shop. It led into a narrow corridor and from there we went into a little room with benches running around the walls and hooks hanging above the benches. Half of one wall was taken up by a large set of shelves divided up into different sections. In one of them I saw a pile of freshly washed white aprons and another pile of white mob caps.

'This room is what we call the cubby hole,' said Rosie. 'You hang your coat on a hook and at the end of the day you leave your apron and cap on one of the shelves.'

The white aprons and caps are part of our work uniforms and

it's strange the difference they make. Without them we're just ordinary girls in plain black dresses. With them we are Lawlor's girls.

'So you're working at the counter then, are you?' said Rosie, as we put on our caps and aprons. 'Not in the sink room?'

'That's right,' I said, trying to make sure the bow at the back of my apron was straight.

Rosie raised her eyebrows. 'Are you pals with the Lawlors or something?' Rosie sounded genuinely surprised that I was working at the counter in the cake shop, and I wasn't sure why.

'What do you mean?' I asked her.

That was when Rosie told me that by rights I shouldn't be working on the shop floor at all yet. Most girls who start work at Lawlor's have to spend a whole year washing dishes in what they call the sink room before they're allowed to work in the shop or the tearoom. She didn't even tell me this in a nasty way; she was just surprised that I'd managed to skip the sink room.

'My ma makes dresses for Mrs Lawlor,' I said. 'But I swear, I didn't know she was doing me any favours. I didn't ask for it or anything. I didn't even know.' To my horror, I felt tears come to my eyes. It was bad enough leaving school and having to go out to work. I couldn't bear the thought of everyone here hating me because I'd cheated my way up the Lawlor's ladder.

Rosie just grinned at me, which shows what a nice nature she has, because if I'd just spent a year washing dishes in a boiling hot steamy room with my fingers going all red and the skin practically falling off because of being stuck in hot water all day, I'm not sure I'd be feeling so generous towards someone who had just swanned in and got a job selling cakes straight away.

'I believe you, thousands wouldn't,' she said. 'Janey, you're not going to start crying, are you?'

'No!' I said. Clearly starting my first ever job was making me sentimental. 'I just … I didn't want to cheat.'

I threw my shoulders back and looked at Rosie as bravely as I could.

'I'll go and tell Miss … Warby. Is that the manager's name?' I said. 'I'll tell her I want to work in the washing-up room.'

'Are you mad?' Rosie stared at me. 'You wouldn't get me back in that room for a hundred pounds. Solidarity's one thing, but there's no point being a martyr. Just work at the counter and count your blessings. And share your closing cakes with the washing-up girls.'

'What do you mean, closing cakes?'

'At the end of the day, the shop girls usually each get some buns or cakes, depending on what's left over,' said Rosie. 'I always take one home to my little brother. You can share some of yours with the sink room.'

No sooner had Rosie given me this good advice than there was the sound of firm footsteps in the corridor, and a small woman with a face that looked as if it had been carved out of a granite slab appeared in the doorway. Rosie had been sitting on the bench, but at the sight of this woman she jumped to her feet.

'Unusually early, Miss Delaney.' The woman sniffed and turned to me. 'You must be Betty Rafferty. Mrs Lawlor told me about you.' From the woman's expression, she looked as if she hadn't been told anything good. Though I soon realised that she was just annoyed that Mrs Lawlor had interfered in what she clearly thought was her own personal domain: the management of the staff. Anyway, I didn't know what to say to this statement, so I just nodded and said, 'Yes, miss.'

'My name is Miss Warby,' she said, as if I hadn't guessed. 'I expect you to use my full name when you address me. I'll also expect you to arrive at eight o'clock in future. If you are so much as five minutes late, you will be fined. Now, come with me.' And without looking to see if I was following her (which I was, of course), she swept out of the cubby hole, down a passage and through a glass door into Lawlor's Cake Shop and Tearoom.

It was beautiful. When you walk into Lawlor's from the street, the first thing you see is the long curving counter, with rows of cakes displayed beneath gleaming glass and us counter girls standing behind it in our uniforms. To the right of the counter, there's the tearoom, with its potted plants and elegant tables with damask tablecloths and china with gold trim that looks fierce fancy, even though Rosie says it's not real gold, only paint.

'Miss Rafferty, this is Kitty Dunne,' said Miss Warby, introducing me to a tall and imposing red-haired girl who was standing by the till. 'Miss Dunne is the senior counter girl, and I trust you will do what she says when I'm not here to keep an eye on you all.'

Miss Warby didn't sound particularly pleased about this state of affairs, which made me feel hopeful about Kitty. If Miss Warby didn't like her, she couldn't be too bad. She did look quite serious, though, which I suppose you have to be when you're a senior counter girl.

'Miss Dunne, this is Betty Rafferty. The new girl.'

Kitty raised her eyebrows, just a teeny tiny bit. 'She's starting at the counter?'

Miss Warby sniffed. 'Mrs Lawlor's orders. Now I must attend to the kitchens.' And without a word of farewell, she spun around and marched back through the glass door. As soon as she was gone all our shoulders relaxed, even Kitty's.

'I didn't know about starting in the sink room,' I said to Kitty. 'I didn't ask for any favours.'

'I'm sure you didn't.' Kitty's tone was brisk. 'Now come on, I'd better show you how this counter works before the shop opens. We've only got fifteen minutes.' She pointed to an enormous shining metal yoke with a tap sticking out of it, standing on its own platform against the wall. 'That's the tea urn. I'll show you how to refill it later. I'm usually in charge of it, but if we're busy you might have to step in.' The tea urn let off a spurt of steam from beneath its gleaming lid. 'It's been acting the jinnet recently but it's straightforward enough. Now, as for the cakes …'

And so it began. By the time Kitty slid back the bolt of the front door and officially opened the shop and tearoom for the day, my brain was in a whirl. I wasn't sure I could remember what all the different cakes and buns were called, let alone how much they cost. My confusion must have been showing on my face, because Rosie squeezed my arm and said, 'Don't worry, you'll be grand. Just keep an eye on me and Kitty.'

And even though my stomach started churning as soon as the jangling bell over the door announced the arrival of the first customer, I *was* grand – well, most of the time. The cake counter wasn't too busy for the first few hours, and it turned out I didn't have to remember the exact names of most of the cakes because the customers didn't know them either, they just pointed at the ones they wanted and said things like, 'I'll have two of them and four of them and three of those ones with the jam, please.' Luckily each cake had a little card next to it with the price on it. I had to do a fair amount of mental arithmetic to figure out the costs of the bigger orders, but I was always good at maths at school.

At eleven o'clock, the tearoom started filling up ('Them rich ladies need a break from all their hard work buying hats and clothes down in Arnotts,' muttered Rosie with a grin) and the counter got busier too. We were joined there by another girl called Annie, who looked surprised to see a newcomer behind the counter but was friendly enough. Kitty looked after the till while the rest of us served the customers, and all in all we were so busy that I didn't have time to think about whether I liked the job or not. But at around one o'clock, perhaps because of being around all those cakes and buns, my stomach started to rumble with hunger.

'Do we get a dinner break?' I whispered to Rosie.

'Don't let Auld Wobbly hear you calling it dinner,' said Rosie. She put on a refined voice that sounded amazingly like Miss Warby's pinched tones. 'It's luncheon, if you please. Or just lunch.' Then she had to serve a customer a Mary Cake and two scones, and I had to give another one three bread rolls from the other end of the counter.

'So we *do* get a break?' I said, when we finally found ourselves side by side again. 'Yes, but we don't all take it together,' said Rosie. She put a scone in a paper bag and handed it to a dark young woman wearing a hat that looked as if it had a velvet cabbage on it and a little badge on her lapel that said VOTES FOR IRISH WOMEN. 'There you go, miss!' She turned back to me. 'We go in twos. And we have to wait 'til after the lunchtime rush dies down. I'll ask Kitty if we can take ours together, if you like.'

'Oh would you?' I felt very grateful, though by the time Kitty finally nodded at us and said, 'You can take your break now,' I felt more hungry than anything else. It was half past two. Rosie led me into the kitchen, which was very busy and bustling and smelled beautifully of bread and cakes, and a harassed-looking girl handed each of us a plate with a bread roll and some cheese. Rosie got us some water from a small sink near the door and we headed back to the cubby hole.

'So,' she said, grinning at me. 'How do you like Lawlor's?'

'My feet are killing me,' I said.

'Ah, you'll get used to that,' she said. 'Now come on, you'd better get that bread down you quickly. And use the jacks if you need them. We've only got ten minutes, and I don't know how she does it but Old Wobbly *always* finds out if you take any longer.'

I was so exhausted by the end of the day that I could only mutter a goodbye and thank you to Rosie and Kitty, and by the time I got home I could barely stand. I just slumped into the big chair by the fireplace that's usually reserved for Da. Earnshaw curled up on my feet, which I don't usually let him do because he's awful heavy for a dog that size. On that first night, however, I was too tired to push him off. I had never realised how tiring it could be, just standing all day. I know Rosie said I'll get used to it but it's been almost a week now and I haven't got used to it yet.

It doesn't help that the weather is so nice. At least, I suppose I'd think it was nice if I could sit out in it and enjoy it. But when you're stuck behind a counter next to that blazing hot tea urn, sunny weather doesn't seem nice at all.

'It could be worse,' Rosie pointed out when we were eating our bread and cheese in the cubby hole this afternoon. 'We could be in the sink room.'

And I know she's right, but when I think of girls like Lavinia Lawlor getting to spend the whole summer doing whatever they want – and not even having to help their mothers with cleaning the house and mending the clothes and doing the laundry like I always had to do in school holidays – well, when I think of that I don't even feel angry. I just feel sad.

But if I *have* to have a job – and I do – I know Rosie is right when she says it could be worse. If I have to work anywhere it might as well be at Lawlor's. Yes, the days are very long. And Miss Warby is just as much of a tartar as she seemed on the first day. She really does fine people for lateness. Annie got fined this morning because she arrived at five past eight. I'm scared of the tea urn as well. Every so often it suddenly lets off steam in a very frightening way, and I think there's something wrong with the tap. Then there are my poor aching legs and feet.

But I have a laugh with the other girls (apart from Kitty – she's nice enough but she's sort of reserved, if you know what I mean). And sometimes we get so many extra cakes at the end of the day that I can give some to the washing-up girls *and* still take one for myself.

Besides, as Ma keeps reminding me, it really is a very elegant establishment. We all look very smart in our black uniforms and the little aprons and mob caps that you have to fasten on with hair pins. Lawlor's provides the uniform dress – that's why Ma collected it before I started – but you have to pay for it yourself. They take a bit out of your wages every week until you've paid it all off.

They seem to like taking things out of your wages. But all employers seem to do that. Rosie's been telling me about the fines her sister has to pay at the biscuit factory – and the work there is much harder. And at least when I get home I can write some of my memoirs. My hands are still working all right, even if my legs are giving way.

# Chapter Four

Today was a strange sort of day. By that I mean it was actually quite interesting, for once. It started in what is now the usual way – Eddie banging on the bedroom door to wake me up and to get his smelly old boots which he'd left under my bed; me getting dressed in my work uniform dress; Ma telling me to eat up my toast and drink my tea or I'd be late for the shop (I don't know why she always says this, it's not like I don't know when I have to leave), and finally me popping into McGrath's shop to say hello to Samira.

I suppose I should tell my future readers a bit more about Samira, otherwise they'll just keep wondering 'who is this girl she keeps talking about?' Samira, as I have said, is my very best friend in the world. She lives just across the road from us with her Auntie Maisie and her da and her brother Ali. Auntie Maisie used to be an actress and Samira wants to be one too.

And I bet she could do it, because she's very good at singing and dancing and acting as well. She had hoped to start auditioning for shows straight away when we left school, but her da said there was time enough for acting when she was older. So now she has a job in McGrath's shop, just round the corner from Strandville Avenue. Her da, Mr Casey, works down the docks same as my da, but he used to work on the ships. That's how he met Samira's ma, when he sailed to London.

Samira's ma wasn't from London, even though she was living there at the time. She was from what Mr Casey calls Bonny

Bombay. Bombay is in India and she met Mr Casey because she was working as a nursemaid for this English family that had lived in India before they came back to London. The father of the family was a merchant who had dealings with the shipping company Mr Casey was working for, and sometimes Samira's ma used to take his children to the docks to see the crates come off the boats. That was when she met Mr Casey. And that's where they fell in love at first sight, like something out of a book.

Mr Casey managed to get the shipping company to keep him working for them in London instead of going off on another journey, and according to Samira's Auntie Maisie, he and Samira's ma used to have secret meetings like Romeo and Juliet until (like Romeo and Juliet) they found a priest who would marry them. It was very difficult because Samira's ma followed the Muslim religion and she didn't want to become a Catholic and Mr Casey wouldn't make her convert. And he didn't want to become a Muslim either. But most priests wouldn't marry them unless Samira's ma converted.

I say 'was' when I talk about Samira's ma because she died when Samira was being born, just after they arrived back in Dublin. Samira's brother Ali was born over in London, but he doesn't remember it or even their ma, because he wasn't much older than Little Robbie when she died. When he was little he used to say he could remember going on the ship, but I'm not sure about that, because he wasn't even two years old during the voyage, and I know I can't remember being that age.

It's sad for Samira and Ali not having a ma, especially a ma they don't even remember. At least they have one photograph of her, a picture of her and Mr Casey that was taken in a studio in London just after they got married. If my ma or da died, I wouldn't have a photo of them. In fact, if anything happened to me or Eddie or Lily there wouldn't be any pictures of us either. None of us have ever had our photograph taken. Maybe I should save up to get one done to commemorate my beauty (hem hem).

Actually, now I come to think of it, I should probably describe myself before I go any further, just in case the photograph idea doesn't come off. So! I am about five feet one inch tall, or I was the last time Ma measured me with her measuring tape against the kitchen door. I'm pretty sure I haven't grown much since then. I'm already the same height as Ma so I don't know if I'll grow much more. My hair is like a brown mop but Da says all Rafferty women have hair like that and I've seen my Auntie Rita and my Auntie Eileen with their hair down so I know this is true.

I'm very pale (Auntie Rita always says I look sickly and I need a bit of colour in my cheeks). Unlike Lily, I don't have any freckles except in summer, but also unlike Lily, I have quite bushy eyebrows. They don't meet in the middle but I'm worried if they get any more bushy they might start taking over the bit at the top of my nose. I once asked Lily if I should pull some of the hairs out so my eyebrows look like the actresses you see in the pictures, and she reminded me that her friend Maggie did that and she pulled out too many hairs until her eyebrows were practically all gone and she looked like an egg that someone had drawn a face on. I'm not sure I should risk that.

So I'm stuck with my beetling brows for now, unfortunately. Samira says my eyebrows are striking but I think that is a nice way of saying peculiar. People sometimes tell me that Earnshaw is a 'striking animal' when I take him for a walk and I don't think they mean it as a compliment. Anyway, my actual eyes are all right I suppose, being quite big and a sort of blue-grey colour, and the rest of my face is just ordinary. I realise that makes me sound as boring as Robert Hessian but it's true. Ordinary nose, ordinary mouth, ordinary chin. I wish I really did have a photograph of myself and then when this memoir is published they could put it inside the cover as a frontispiece.

But I should get back to Samira's parents. The photograph of the two of them is up on the mantelpiece in the Caseys' kitchen. They're making the very serious faces everyone seems to make when they get their photograph taken, but they're looking at each other in a way that makes you think they might burst out laughing any second. You can tell they like each other. Mrs Casey was tall and pretty, almost as tall as Mr Casey. She looks a bit like Samira, but Ali looks more like their da, with his strong jaw and a smile that goes up on one side more than the other. He has his ma's dark eyes though.

After Samira's ma died, her poor da was left with a tiny new baby and another child who wasn't much better than a baby, and so his sister Auntie Maisie came to stay to help look after the kids. She's been living in their house ever since. Back in those days, Auntie Maisie used to sing and dance and act in the music halls and she loves telling us stories of what it was like to tread the boards.

Even I call Auntie Maisie 'Auntie Maisie' instead of Miss Casey, which is what Ma says I should call her. It was Auntie Maisie who told me about the day the priest called round to the house when Samira was a tiny baby. 'He'd heard about poor Zainab,' she said (that was Samira's ma's name). 'And he went round to tell Peter' (that's Mr Casey) 'that he should give those heathen babbies — that's what he called my darling niece and nephew, he wouldn't even say their names — those heathen babbies to the nuns to look after. A man can't look after them on his own, he says, and it'd be better for them to go into an institution. "I'm not on my own," says Peter, "I've got my sister here to help. And even if I didn't, I wouldn't give the skin off my cocoa to those nuns." The skin off his cocoa! Those were his very words. And the priest went off in a huff.'

After that day Mr Casey stopped going to Mass and he still doesn't go, which shocks a lot of people around here because everyone on our road goes to Mass, apart from the Marshalls, who are the only Protestants in Strandville Avenue. And even they go to their own church at the corner of Waterloo Avenue. But Mr Casey didn't care what other people thought. He said he wasn't going to say any prayers with the men who tried to take his children away.

In fact, he almost didn't even have Samira christened, but his ma, Samira's grandma, insisted on it. She lives across the river in Ringsend and she organised it all in her local church so Mr Casey didn't have to do a thing. But even with old Mrs Casey sorting it all out, her parish priest refused to christen the baby Samira — which was the name her ma had chosen before she died — because it's not a saint's name. I think Samira is a lovely name and I'd much prefer to be the only person around here with my name, which certainly isn't the case with Betty. There were two other Bettys in our year at school and four more Elizabeths. There's even another Betty at Lawlor's but she works in the sink room so I don't have much to do with her.

Anyway, even though Auntie Maisie argued with the priest

about it, he wouldn't give in, so in the end Samira ended up being christened Sarah, which is in the Bible and which I suppose sounds a *little* bit like Samira. But although Sarah is on her baptismal certificate, everyone around here has always called her Samira, apart from some of the teachers and nuns at school who insisted on calling her Sarah. And as for Ali? All the Christian Brothers in Joey's, the boys' school where he went until he left and got a job two years ago, called him Alan.

Ali's not bad as far as big brothers go. He's quite serious a lot of the time, but he has a sense of fun too, and he's certainly less annoying than our Eddie. Ali and Samira get on well most of the time. They tease each other a lot, but it's never nasty. Maybe it's because of not having a ma and the two of them being the only kids in our area who weren't as pale as skimmed milk. As their friends we stuck up for them when anyone said something horrible, but we couldn't really understand what it was like to have those things said to us.

Because Ali and Samira get on so well, the three of us sometimes sit around the fireplace in the Caseys' front room (which turns into Ali's room at night), talking away. Sometimes Ali's pal Tom McGowan calls over too. Auntie Maisie comes in every so often to keep an eye on us and make sure we're not actually lighting the fire. (There's never enough coal to have a fire in the front room *and* the kitchen, so the front room fireplace is only lit when the whole family are in there.) Ali always has funny stories about work, but he doesn't just hold forth and expect us to sit there in silence listening to him like some boys I could mention (Eddie). He actually listens to what me and Samira have to say.

So now you know all about Samira and her family, I can continue my tale of today's events. Like I said, I called into McGrath's to say hello to Samira on my way to work, and when I walked into the shop she was leaning on the counter, gazing dreamily into the distance.

'Morning!' I said, and she jumped up with a guilty air, until she realised it was just me, and not a paying customer who might tell Mrs McGrath she was daydreaming instead of doing some productive work.

'You looked like you were away with the fairies,' I said. 'Where's Mrs McGrath?'

'She's got one of her heads,' said Samira. 'And I was just being Lady Macbeth.'

From some people that might have sounded a bit worrying, but I knew Samira was just acting out a Shakespeare play in her head. That's another good thing about me and Samira being friends. We're never ashamed to tell the other about the things we imagine, even though we know loads of people would think we were daft.

'Isn't she the one who persuades her husband to kill people?' I said.

Samira nodded. 'The very same. What do you think the odds are of a famous Shakespeare producer's car breaking down on his way to Clontarf or somewhere, and coming in and asking me to be in his new show?'

'Fairly low, I should think,' I said. 'But if one does, ask him to give me a job too. One that doesn't mean standing up all day.'

'What would you do in a theatre?' said Samira.

'Prompter,' I said. 'Whenever you forgot your lines I'd remind you.'

'I'd never need reminding,' said Samira indignantly.

'Howiya, girls?' Ali was standing in the doorway. 'Quarter pound of bullseyes please, Sam.'

'Look at you, Mr Money-bags,' I said, as Samira scooped out some sweets and put them on the scales.

'It's for Tom,' said Ali, handing over a few pennies to his sister. 'He's leaving today so we promised him we'd have a goodbye party in the storeroom.'

'He didn't get the sack, did he?' I hoped he hadn't. We all like Tom, who lives in East Wall and works with Ali in a big newspaper delivery room, sorting out the papers before they go to the shops and the street sellers. Jobs are hard to find these days, so if he got sacked from the delivery room he might find it hard to get another decent job.

'Saint Tom? Not he,' said Ali. 'He got a better job on the trams.' He grinned at Samira. 'Poor Samira's brokenhearted. He won't be coming back to our house after work so often.'

'Be quiet, you,' said Samira crossly. She does actually like Ali's friend Tom — like I said, we all do — but she hates me and Ali joking about the pair of them. Which I'm afraid to say I often do, ever since the Sunday a few weeks ago when Tom's cap fell out of his back pocket as he was leaving their house and Samira ran up the road after him shouting 'Tom! Tom!' in a sort of *Romeo and Juliet* voice. At least, that's how I described it to her, but she got very annoyed and said it was just her usual voice.

But while I don't mind teasing Samira when it's just the two of us, I'm not going to side with Ali against her, even in jest, so I looked at him as disapprovingly as I could and said, 'Leave your sister alone.'

My disapproving look must have been quite successful, because Ali laughed and said, 'All right, Queen Victoria. Sorry, Sammy. Pax?'

'Hmmph!' Samira tossed her head in a very dramatic and haughty fashion but she can never stay angry at Ali for long. 'Oh, all right, pax.'

'I'll give Tom your love,' said Ali, and before Samira could throw a jar of Bovril at him he dodged out of the shop.

'I'd better go too,' I said. 'Don't mind him.'

'I never do,' said Samira, raising her eyes to heaven, and then Mrs Hennessy came in looking for Mr Hennessy's tobacco so Samira had to serve her. To my surprise, when I came out Ali was leaning against the railings of the house next to the shop, waiting for me.

'I thought you'd have gone on,' I said.

'Eh, we might as well walk in together,' said Ali. 'If your majesty doesn't mind, of course.'

''Course not,' I said, because I didn't. We strolled towards town in a companionable silence. That's another thing I like about Ali. I never feel awkward around him, not like when Eddie's friends call around to our house. Maybe that's because unlike Eddie and his pals, Ali never makes me feel like a freak of nature for reading books and caring about things. As we crossed Newcomen Bridge, I found myself glancing down the canal towards the library and, beyond it, my old school. It seemed like forever since Samira and I were going there every day.

'Missing the old school?' It was like Ali could read my mind.

'Sort of,' I said. I gestured back the way we'd come, towards Joey's. 'Do you miss yours?'

'I can't say I miss being walloped with a belt.' His voice was light but when I looked at him he didn't look like he was joking.

'They never used a belt in our school,' I said. 'Just the cane.'

'Oh, that's all right then.' Ali couldn't hide the sarcasm.

'But I suppose it's just what they do in schools, isn't it? It's not like you can change it.' I shrugged my shoulders, even though I've always thought that it was wrong that teachers are allowed to hit children whenever they feel like it. Luckily we had Miss Hackett for the last few years, and she didn't seem to like beating anyone. There was only the odd rap on the hand with a ruler for children who were really acting the jinnet.

But I knew we were very lucky to have her as our teacher. There were other teachers in the school who didn't mind giving you a proper wallop when they felt like it. And I remembered that when Ali had been there in the junior school, some of the teachers had been fierce hard on him.

'I don't see why it can't be changed,' said Ali. His face was more serious than I'd ever seen it before. 'If I'd been able to train as a teacher, I'd reef the belt out of the hands of any Brother I saw belting a kid.'

I looked at Ali in surprise. 'Did you ever want to be a teacher?'

Now it was Ali's turn to shrug his shoulders. 'I dunno. I thought about it.'

We had passed the canal now, and were almost at the Five Lamps. 'You kept that very quiet,' I said.

'What's the point of mentioning it?' He let out a laugh that didn't have much humour in it. 'It's not like it was ever going to happen.'

'Well, I don't know if Samira's ever going to play Lady Macbeth in front of the kings and queens of Europe,' I said. 'But that doesn't stop her going on about it all the time.'

Ali laughed – a proper laugh this time, I was relieved to note.

'True enough,' he said.

'And you never know,' I said, warming to my theme, 'maybe Samira really will become a famous actress and she'll be so rich she'll be able to pay for you to go back to school and become the best teacher Dublin has ever seen.'

'I'll believe that when I see it,' said Ali with a grin. And things were fine again. But I don't think I'd ever seen Ali look as grim as he did when he was talking about being beaten by those nasty old Brothers.

After that we mostly just talked about ordinary things, like how much we want to go to the new picture palace in Capel Street, and how many midnight union meetings our das have been going to recently. I know the union is important, because all the workers are trying to stick together, but I don't know how they manage to go to all those meetings. I've never been able to stay up until midnight. I start falling asleep at around half past nine, and it's even worse now I'm working all day. I'm practically sleepwalking home from Lawlor's.

Anyway, when we reached the crossroads just before the railway bridge at Amiens Street Station, Ali veered right to go down Foley Street.

'Where are you going?' I said, stopping short.

'It's the short cut,' said Ali. 'You can skip the corner and get halfway down Talbot Street.'

'I know, but …' I looked at the ground. 'Ma doesn't let me go that way.'

Foley Street and the streets around it have a bad reputation for being what Ma calls 'very rough'. They call the area Monto, because Foley Street used to be called Montgomery Street until a few years ago.

Ali shrugged his shoulders. 'Well, if you don't want to walk that way, then I won't make you.'

I drew myself up to my full height (which still isn't very tall). I didn't want to look like a baby in front of Ali. 'No, it's all right. You're right, it would be a lot quicker.'

'Only if you're sure,' said Ali.

'Come on,' I said. And I marched down the street ahead of him.

I don't know exactly what I expected Foley Street to look like. I thought there'd be, you know, people lying around drunk in the street or fighting and that sort of thing. But it was pretty quiet that morning. There were the usual shabby old houses that had seen better days, with young women sitting outside their open doors watching us with wary eyes. There were children playing in the street too. None of them had shoes on and some of them had the tell-tale close-cropped heads that showed they'd had nits and had to have their hair shaved off.

'They're out early,' I said.

'Sure there wouldn't be enough room for them at home once the whole family was up.' Ali's tone was dry. Sometimes I forget how lucky we are. Around Foley Street whole large families are crammed into single rooms in the tenement houses, with seventy people sharing a single toilet outside. I suppose to them our house, with its very own jacks and four whole rooms, would seem like a mansion.

As we walked down Foley Street I saw a skinny kid with closely cut red hair trotting towards the door of one of the tenements carrying a battered old saucepan full of burned-out cinders. You see boys and girls doing this a lot near the tenements. I knew he must have gathered them from the ash bins of rich families across the river, and he was taking them home so his ma could use them to make a fire to cook whatever food they had. I shivered despite the warmth of the day. The kid was wearing what looked like the contents of a rag bag – a lady's coat that was much too big for him, a ragged man's shirt and a pair of shorts that looked like they were about to fall to pieces. His grubby feet were bare. There was something familiar about him.

'Poor little thing,' I said to Ali, nodding towards the boy with the cinders, who had spilled some of his load and was scrabbling at the foot of the steps to gather up fragments of coal. As he threw the last piece back into his pot, a red-haired girl in a faded blouse and skirt stuck her head out of the front door of the house. She said something to the boy and started to take the pot off him, but then she saw me and Ali. And she froze.

That was when I recognised her, and with a wave of shock I realised why the boy was familiar. The girl's name was Margaret Maguire and the boy was her little brother Tony. They used to live on our road – their da used to get casual work on the docks. Da works full time for the Dublin Port and Docks Board, and so does Samira's da, so they've got a steady wage coming in every week, but other men just go to a pub every day and hope the stevedore chooses them to work on the docks that day. If he doesn't choose them, they have no work. And no pay.

But Margaret's da got work regularly enough, and they were doing alright for a long time. They lived in a house the same size as ours. It must have been a squeeze because Margaret was the second oldest of five kids, but that's just the way it often is on our road. Me and Samira always liked Margaret. She was a year older than us but she didn't look down on us and treat us like kids, like some of the older girls (including Lily).

But then one day a crate fell on Mr Maguire's arm when he was loading it onto a lorry. All the bones in his arm were crushed, and after that he couldn't work anymore. Margaret and her older brother went out to work and their ma pawned her wedding ring, but that wasn't enough to feed the family and pay the rent for very long. It must be about six months ago when the rent man came to collect that week's payment and discovered the whole family had done a moonlight flit in the night. They'd run away under cover of darkness. No one had seen them go and no one knew where they went – or at least if they did, they weren't telling. And as far as I knew, no one from Strandville Avenue had seen any of the Maguires again – until now.

'Haven't seen you in a while, Margaret,' said Ali easily. If he was as shocked as I was to see that Margaret was living in one of the roughest streets in Dublin, with her brother spending his mornings going through other people's ash bins for fuel, he didn't show it. 'How are things?'

'Ah, you know, Ali,' said Margaret. She swallowed, as if her throat was dry. 'Not bad. How are you, Betty?'

'Grand,' I said. 'It's good to see you. Are you …' I suddenly felt as if I shouldn't even ask. 'Um, are you living here now?'

Margaret looked down at the ground. Her hands were red and cracked from hard work. The blouse that must have been white once was now a sort of grey. Her boots were battered and far too big for her. I realised they were men's boots. They must have been all she was able to find at one of the second-hand clothes markets.

'We are.' She glanced back at the house she'd come out of. I followed her gaze and noticed lots of the windows had broken panes. Bits of tatty cardboard had been used to patch the holes. I can't imagine they were much good when it rained.

'How's that big brother of yours?' said Ali, his tone still cheerful. 'Still at that night watchman job at the warehouse?'

Margaret flushed. 'He's not working at the moment. He got let go.'

Ali's voice was sympathetic. 'It's happening a lot these days,' he said.

'What are you up to yourself?' I asked. Suddenly I was very conscious of my neat Lawlor's frock. My boots, which had seemed so large and clumsy in the Lawlors' house, looked like dainty slippers in comparison to Margaret's. 'I mean, where are you working?'

'I'm charring for a family on the North Circular,' said Margaret. 'Just doing the rough work in the house, you know.' She laughed, but it sounded more like a cough. 'All the things their maid won't do.'

'Well, I hope they're paying you enough for it,' said Ali. 'And speaking of work, we'd better make haste, Betty.'

'Don't let me keep you,' said Margaret. She didn't say it rudely. She just sounded sad.

'See ya, Margaret,' I said. It felt strangely inadequate.

'See ya,' said Margaret. There was a dullness about her that hadn't been there before her da's accident. She went back into the house, and Ali and I kept going.

'Janey,' I said. 'So that's where they went.'

'It doesn't take much to end up there,' said Ali. 'One broken arm, that's all it took the Maguires.'

I have to admit that the idea shook me, how close we all could be to living squashed into one tiny room. I know Ma's always tried to protect us from that world. She's always wanted to be respectable. 'We may not have much money,' she'll say, 'but we'll never go hungry and we'll always go shod.' And she'd rather we didn't have anything to do with the people who *were* hungry and didn't have shoes.

But it wasn't Margaret and Tony's fault that they didn't have proper clothes or enough fuel. Maybe looking away from them wasn't a good thing. Maybe we all had to face up to how hard life was for lots of people in the city. How hard it could be for all of us, if we had just a bit of bad luck.

I tried to push that frightening thought out of my head as Ali and I headed up Talbot Street. Ali asked me about the cakes in Lawlor's, and I said if he wanted to know what they were like, he'd have to come in and buy one, and he laughed and said I was a good saleswoman. In fact, we were engrossed in conversation (that's another good phrase, isn't it?) until we said goodbye in O'Connell Street, at the corner of the GPO. Officially O'Connell Street is called Sackville Street, but we all call it O'Connell Street after the great politician whose statue stands at the Liffey end.

It was a hasty goodbye, because just as we were crossing the street I looked over at the clock outside Eason's and realised it was five minutes later than I thought it was.

'I'd better run,' I said. 'They dock our pay if we're even a minute late.'

'Good luck!' called Ali, as I rushed down Henry Street. I nearly slipped on some horse dung as I turned down the lane that leads to the back entrance of the shop. Rosie was in the cubby hole, tying her apron on, when I rushed in.

'You're cutting it fine,' she said.

'Is Wobbly in yet?' I whispered. I've got used to calling Miss Warby Wobbly. But only when I'm quite sure she's not around.

'She's not coming in this morning,' said Rosie with a grin. 'It's your lucky day. Well, it's all of our lucky day, I suppose.'

'Where is she?' I said in surprise. Everyone knows that Miss Warby never misses work. Jenny Byrne, who's been here since 1910, says Wobbly has never been out sick once. Jenny thinks all the diseases are scared of her. I don't blame them.

'She's got some meeting with Mr Lawlor about a new flour supplier or something,' said Rosie. 'I don't know exactly, it sounded very boring. Now come on, get that apron on. Them cakes won't sell themselves!'

Any hopes that a day without Wobbly would be a day of rest were soon dashed. I don't know why everyone in Dublin was so mad for cakes all of a sudden, but they clearly were, because we were run off our feet all day, both in the shop and the tearoom.

I had my break with Rosie, and I was still discreetly chewing a cheese scone left over from yesterday's café offerings as I walked as quickly as I could without running down the corridor to the glass door. ('No running on the shop floor!' as Wobbly is always bellowing at us.) Kitty slipped out for her break just as I reached the counter. I swallowed the last of my scone and looked up to see a tall boy who looked about Ali's age, gazing at the cakes with a dreamy expression on his face.

'May I help you?' I said in my talking-to-the-customers manner, hoping I didn't have any scone crumbs stuck in my teeth.

'Oh!' said the boy. He had yellow hair and a nice but grand voice. Of course, most of our customers are quite grand. You couldn't afford the food here if you weren't. 'Sorry, I was miles away. Um, may I have four of those buns, please?' He was holding a book under one arm, and with the other he pointed at the pink iced buns which are Da's favourites. I've taken a few leftovers home to him on the days we get extra. Not that I told the strange boy that. We're not allowed to chat with customers at all; I'd probably get the sack if I started telling one of them about my da's favourite buns.

'Of course, sir,' I said politely, and began putting the buns into a paper bag. The boy didn't stare at me while I was doing it, in the unnerving way that some customers do, like they think you're going to cheat them by not giving them everything they've paid for. He just started reading his book.

'Here you go, sir,' I said, putting the bag of buns on the counter. 'That'll be one and six, please.'

'Thanks,' he said, with a friendly smile. He put his book down on the counter and started to rummage around in his jacket pockets. I saw that the book was *The Adventures of Sherlock Holmes*, which Samira and I both read and loved over the last Christmas holidays. 'Oh lord,' he said. 'I was sure I had half a crown here somewhere … Ah, here it is!'

He triumphantly held up a coin and handed it over. As he did so, his hand knocked the book, sending it sliding off the counter and towards the tray of cakes beneath – in fact, it would have landed right in the middle of them, if I hadn't caught it in my right hand just as I took his payment in my left.

'Your book, sir,' I said, handing it over. 'I'll get your change now.'

'Well saved.' The boy sounded quite impressed. 'My friend Keyes would have killed me if his book had got covered in icing.'

'Miss Warby would kill me if a cake got covered in book,' I said, without thinking. As soon as I said it, I knew I'd done something stupid. If Old Wobbly had heard me talk to a customer like that, she'd probably have dismissed me on the spot. And what if the boy complained about me being forward!

But the boy just laughed. He had a nice laugh.

'It's a jolly good book,' he said.

'I know,' I said. 'I've read it.'

The boy looked delighted.

'Have you? I think some Holmes and Watson might have improved those cakes. They're a bit too goopy for my liking. Though don't let the owner hear you say that.'

'No chance of me letting that happen,' I said, and then I realised that I was definitely chatting with a customer now – and a male customer at that, which would have made things ten times worse in Wobbly's eyes - and pulled myself together. It really was a good thing she hadn't come in this morning. 'Will that be all, sir?'

He smiled at me. 'Yes, thank you. Goodbye.'

I nodded politely at him and he went off. (I didn't dare even say goodbye in case I found myself doing any more chatting.) The shop suddenly seemed very empty – the rush had died down, which gave Rosie the opportunity to nudge me in the ribs.

'What was that all about?' she said.

'What was what about?' I said.

'You and your man,' said Rosie. 'Looked like you were having a nice little talk.'

'I just stopped his book going into the cakes,' I said, pretending I didn't know what she was getting at. Rosie has a joke about being madly in love with the boy who delivers the flour every week – I don't think she is really in love with him, even though he really is pretty good-looking, with his curly brown hair and big green eyes – and she's always trying to find someone she can mock me about. I keep telling her we're far too young to be interested in boys and she says her oldest sister got married when she was sixteen – which is true. But I have a feeling the only reason her sister got married at sixteen was because she had a baby the week she turned seventeen.

Obviously I can tell if boys are good-looking or not, I'm not blind. But Ma's always drummed it into us that there's time enough to be thinking of boys and romance when we're older. There's no use saying that to Rosie, though.

'I bet the next time he comes in he'll be throwing his book at the buns just so you can save it again,' she said. 'His knight in a shining apron!'

I wasn't in the mood for her jokes today.

'I doubt we'll ever see him again,' I said. And I meant it. After all, we'd never seen him in here before, so why should he come back? And if he did come back, he'd probably end up being served by Rosie or Annie or one of the other girls in the shop. So there's no point in talking or thinking about him and his book.

I don't even know why I'm writing so much about him, because that wasn't the only interesting thing that happened in the shop today. Wobbly didn't get back from her trip out to Lucan to meet the new supplier until the day was practically over, and she was too tired to think of things to give out to us about, so there was no trouble on that front. When our shift was finally over, and Rosie and I were taking off our aprons and caps in the cloakroom and getting into our outdoor clothes, I noticed a familiar little red button on the lapel of her coat.

'Is that a union button?' I said. Because of course my dad is in the union – the Irish Transport and General Workers' Union, the ITGWU for short, though everyone around our way just calls it the union. He has a badge like that on his coat too – a little red hand.

Rosie nodded. 'It is.'

I was confused.

'Was it your da's?' I asked, putting on my own coat. I knew Rosie's da died a few years ago. She lives down near Smithfield with her ma and her sister and her little brother. But Rosie shook her head with a grin.

'It's mine,' she said. 'I went down to Liberty Hall yesterday and joined the union.'

'I thought the union was just for men,' I said, though as soon as I said that I realised I didn't actually know whether it was true or not. I'd never really thought about the union. If I had, I'd have taken it for granted that it was just for men and boys. Most things are, after all.

'There's a women workers' union too,' said Rosie, as we headed out the door and down the lane which led back onto Henry Street. 'It's connected to the men's one.'

'Just for women?' I was amazed. I couldn't believe I hadn't heard of this before. But then, the only people I heard talking about unions were my da and Eddie and Ali. And sure why would they mention a women's union?

'That's right,' said Rosie. 'Started about two years ago – Josie's been a member of it from the beginning. I've been meaning to join up for ages.' Josie is Rosie's older sister. I don't know why their parents gave them names that (sort of) rhyme. Josie's full name is Josephine and Rosie's full name is Rosaleen, so they always rhyme whether you use their nicknames or not. Josie works in the Jacob's factory across the river.

'I remember hearing about strikes in her factory,' I said.

'They've had a few strikes now,' said Rosie. She sounded proud of her sister. 'And they're right to walk out, the way the bosses treat them. You know, a few years ago some of the girls were sacked just for getting up a collection at work for another girl who was getting married. Sacked! For trying to give their friend a present! And then a few weeks later all the workers were expected to give money for a wedding present for the Jacobs' daughter!'

'They weren't!' I couldn't believe such unfairness.

'They certainly were,' said Rosie. 'That sort of thing is why Josie joined the union.' We were out in Henry Street now, where we usually parted ways – I go up towards O'Connell Street and Rosie walks down to Capel Street.

'So they let shop-girls and waitresses join this union too?' I said.

Rosie pointed to the badge on her lapel. ''Course they do. We're workers too, aren't we?'

'I suppose we are,' I said. I realised that even though I've been working at Lawlor's for nearly two weeks now, a part of me must still think that I'm somehow going to be heading back to school in September. I never thought of myself as a worker because I didn't want to be one. But maybe I'd better start. It's not like I have a choice.

''Course we are,' said Rosie. 'Kitty's in the union too. And a good few girls in the kitchen and the sink room.'

'Kitty?' I couldn't believe it. 'But she's our supervisor!'

'She's the senior counter girl,' said Rosie. 'And that doesn't make any difference. She's got a sense of fair play.'

'I suppose she has,' I said.

Kitty made sure everything behind the counter ran as smoothly as possible, but she was never harsh or unreasonable. And, I realised, she never went to Miss Warby when anyone was just a few minutes late.

'Anyway,' said Rosie, 'I'd better get home. Ma's not feeling too well again and someone's got to keep an eye on Francis.' Francis is her little brother. He's not much older than Little Robbie but he sounds like a much nicer child (not that that would be very hard).

I let Rosie rush home to her ma and Francis and walked slowly up to O'Connell Street. Most of the cafes and some of the shops were closing up now and I found myself noticing the girls and women who were leaving the premises after a long day's work. They all looked tired and hot and sort of wrung out, as well they might after standing at counters, and climbing ladders to get down boxes, and running around carrying plates and teapots for hours and hours on a stuffy summer's day, with hardly any breaks, all for just a few shillings a week. I got seven shillings at Lawlor's, but there are some girls working in big shops for just four or five because their bed and board is included. Girls like Margaret were earning even less. No wonder everyone in the street looked so exhausted.

I probably look just as tired and pale to them, I thought as I reached O'Connell Street. And then a delivery van driver yelled at me to watch where I was going and I realised I had been so caught up in my (very profound, if you ask me) thoughts that I'd stepped onto the road without looking, and had nearly been run over. So after that I stopped thinking about the state of working women. Thinking profound thoughts isn't very practical when you're in the middle of a busy city.

# Chapter Five

My poor legs are getting a rest today. Rosie says she'll start slapping me every time I talk about my legs in the future because she thinks I'm just malingering, but she's not reading this memoir, and she probably never will because she says she never has time for reading, so I can say whatever I like about my legs here. And the reason they're getting a rest is because it's Sunday so the shop is closed and I don't have to go to work. Hurrah! Of course I've been using my legs to walk around, but that's not half as tiring as standing behind a counter all day. Sometimes I lean on the counter and lift one leg up to give it a rest for a while, but Wobbly doesn't like us leaning on things because she says it looks slovenly.

When I started writing these memoirs I meant to document my daily life but I've just looked back at all the pages I've written and I see that I have a tendency to get distracted by things that happened ages ago and then I keep writing about them, instead of concentrating on what is happening right now. So now I will definitely focus properly on what happened today.

We went to the half past nine o'clock Mass, because Little Robbie spilled a whole pound of flour all over the kitchen floor when he and Lily called over to walk to the church with us for the eight o'clock one. (How did he get the flour? I don't even think my ma was going to do any baking today.) Then Earnshaw got into the flour and rolled around, and then he ran all over the house scattering flour everywhere, and Ma said that it wasn't too late to drown that dog in a bucket. By the time all the flour was cleared up it was so late we had to wait until the next Mass.

I was starving hungry when we got to the church because we can't have breakfast until after Mass, and as the sound of Latin droned on, the only thing that stopped me falling asleep with boredom was my grumbling tummy. (I really don't see why the Mass is in Latin; it's not like anyone around here can understand it.) As soon as we got home, we had our Sunday breakfast treat of fried eggs and a bit of bacon each, and I ate mine as fast as I could, partly because I was so hungry but mostly so I could get out to see Samira as soon as possible. Their da may not go to Mass, but she and Ali and their Auntie Maisie go to the eight o'clock one every week, and they don't have a Little Robbie or an Earnshaw making a mess to delay them, so I knew she'd be free now.

Besides, I didn't want to stay in my own home any longer than I had to. Lily, Robert Hessian and Little Robbie had come back after Mass and were going to stay until after dinner. (Eddie had gone off to meet Mary Lennon, this girl from Bayview Avenue who he's courting even though he says he isn't.) So I needed to escape being cried at and puked on by that terrible child. But most of all, I just wanted to see Samira.

One of the worst things about not going to school anymore is that we don't get to see each other every day. At least, not properly. I call into the shop on my way to work, but you can't talk properly when you've got Mrs Hennessy standing behind you demanding to buy a tin of condensed milk and half a pound of tea, or Mrs McGrath telling Samira to stop mooning about and serve some customers. In fact, these days the only time we get to have a proper conversation is on Sundays, which luckily is both of our days off. And we'd already made arrangements for this afternoon.

My plan was to sneak out while my parents and Lily and Robert Hessian were sitting around the kitchen table admiring Little Robbie's new tooth (all the better to bite me with), but unfortunately I had to go out to the jacks first, and when I was coming back into the house Lily noticed me and had an idea.

'Where are you off to?'

I paused just outside the door of the kitchen, one foot on the stairs up to the hall.

'Samira's,' I said. 'We're going for a walk down to the seafront.'

'Can you take Little Robbie?' said Lily. 'He's due a nap and you know he won't sleep unless he's in his pram.'

'No!' I couldn't believe she was asking me to spend my precious free day looking after that monster. But Ma and Da seemed to think this was a perfectly reasonable thing to ask. (I suppose Robert Hessian did too, but I can't remember if he said anything or not.)

'Sure, he'll be asleep,' said Ma. 'What difference will it make to you and Samira?'

'You're only going to be gabbing anyway,' said Da with a grin. 'You might as well do it pushing a pram.'

'We want to go to Dollymount!' I cried. 'He's not going to stay asleep all that time.'

'You don't have time to go all the way out there anyway,' said Ma. 'You've got to be back for your dinner by two.'

Then Lily piped up with a maddening suggestion. 'Why don't you go out there after dinner so he can have a little paddle? It's gorgeous weather today.' She looked fondly at Little Robbie, who was crawling around the kitchen floor with a big red face on him. He's got loads of teeth coming in at the moment so he's even redder and more angry than usual. Those pointy teeth poking through your gums must be pretty sore; I suppose I'd feel sorry for him if he wasn't so awful. But he is.

'I'm not taking him for a paddle!' I couldn't believe they were all wrecking my day off like this. Then a thought struck me. 'It's supposed to be the day of rest,' I said, in what I hoped was a holy sort of voice.

'Go away out of that, you!' said Da with a grin. 'Babies have to be looked after, even on Sundays.'

'Not by me they don't,' I said, but I knew I'd lost the battle with all of them ganged up against me. I hope in the future, when I am a famous author, people will appreciate the terrible hardships I had to go through. This is another reason why I'm writing this memoir, to document my woes for posterity.

Samira wasn't as horrified as I thought she'd be when I turned up at her door with Little Robbie in his pram. (It's massive, but Ma got it in a pawn shop on Capel Street for a very decent price.) This is because Little Robbie actually *likes* her. As soon as he saw her, his angry red face broke into a beaming smile. A smile which looks just as horrible as his scowl, if you ask me, but no one else seems to think so.

'Samma!' he said and he reached out his chubby little arms towards her.

'Aww, hello there, Little Robbie!' Samira beamed back at him. 'Thou wast the prettiest babe that e'er I nursed.'

'He isn't pretty at all,' I said. 'And you never actually nursed him.'

'Don't argue with Shakespeare,' said Samira. 'That's from *Romeo and Juliet*.' She picked up Little Robbie to give him a hug, like the traitor she apparently is. 'Aren't you a happy boy today?'

Little Robbie chuckled.

'He wasn't happy two minutes ago,' I said grumpily. 'I tried to put his gansey on and he went all stiff like he was made of wood and wouldn't bend his arms.'

'Don't mind your nasty Auntie Betty,' said Samira, still smiling at Little Robbie and bouncing him about in her arms. 'Is that a new little toothy? Yes it is!' And she tickled him under his chin and made him laugh and laugh.

'He never does that for me,' I said.

'Didn't your auntie say that making babies cry runs in the family?' said Samira, as Little Robbie gleefully grabbed her finger and started chewing it.

'It does,' I said. 'But in this case I think Little Robbie just knows what I think of him.' When I was giving out about Little Robbie over the Christmas, Auntie Eileen said that some Rafferty women seem to have a terrible effect on other people's babies. 'I couldn't walk past a baby without it bursting into tears,' she said.

'But what about Frankie and Joe?' I said. They're her kids, which of course makes them my cousins.

'Ah, they liked me well enough,' she said.

Anyway, I don't care why Little Robbie hates me, I just care that I had to take him out when we went on our nice Sunday walk. Strangely enough, Samira didn't seem to mind.

'Sure, we can't stay out too long anyway,' she said. 'We'll have to get back for dinner. He'll be asleep for most of it.'

And so we walked up our road with Little Robbie hooting away. Actually, before my memoirs go any further, I suppose I should describe the road where we all live. It's called Strandville

Avenue and it's in the North Strand, which is a very good place to live because town is a mile away in one direction and the sea is less than a mile away in the other direction.

There are not one, not two, but three railway lines along our avenue. Two of them go right over the road on big railway bridges. Then at the very bottom of the road there's the high railway embankment, and trains go along that line all the time, all the trains for Malahide and Howth and Skerries and even Belfast.

Ma hates living near so many trains, she says the smoke from the engines makes her washing all dirty when it's out on the line, but I love having all the train lines here, even though I know she's right about the smoke. When I'm asleep I can hear the freight trains passing in the night, and sometimes I imagine they're those fancy trains you read about in books, with sleeping compartments and everything, and I imagine that instead of being tucked up in bed (with Lil, in the old days, which gave me a good reason to imagine being somewhere different), I'm all cosy and warm in a sleeping train, travelling somewhere exciting and glamorous like Paris or Vienna or even Istanbul.

I said this to Lily one night, back when I still had to try to go to sleep with her horrible hooves in my face, and she said, 'What are you talking about? The furthest you've ever been from the North Strand is Skerries.' She has no imagination at all.

As we turned towards the coast road I told Samira that if she was so happy with Little Robbie coming along she could push his giant heavy pram.

'That's grand,' she said. She looked almost as cheerful as Little Robbie himself, who kept saying 'Samma, Samma!' and laughing and expecting Samira to sing songs to him. Which she did, the fool. But I suppose she thinks it's all practice for when she goes on the stage. She's a very dramatic singer. Once she flung her arm out when singing 'I Dwelt I Dreamt In Marble Halls' and knocked Auntie Maisie's favourite vase off the front room mantelpiece.

Anyway, today she wasn't too dramatic but she sounded very happy when she sang, much more cheerful than I'd be if I was pushing Little Robbie around.

'What are you so jolly about?' I said, laughing.

'I have news,' she said, giving a little skip. 'Auntie Maisie says she's going to take me to see *Romeo and Juliet* at the Majestic next week. Do you think you'll be able to come too?'

'I doubt it,' I said. 'But I'll see.'

'You can tell your ma and da it's educational,' said Samira. 'And Auntie Maisie will be with us. It's not like we're running off to see some dancing girls.'

'It's not that.' I sighed as I helped Samira get Little Robbie's pram up the kerb. 'We can't spare the money at the moment.'

'Even Auntie Maisie-rates?' said Samira.

Auntie Maisie gets in free to all the theatres because of her old pals. She doesn't perform on the stage anymore, but she knows everyone in all the theatres and music halls in Dublin. They let her and Samira in for free to all the shows and give them the cheap seats up in the gods.

These doormen are doing Maisie a big favour, and they can't really give her more than two free tickets at a time, but sometimes, if she asks well in advance, they'll give her an extra half-price seat. That's how I've been to the theatre with them. I've gone a fair few times. We went to see a very good play called *The Colleen Bawn* last year which was very exciting and which we all liked a lot. There was a bit where a girl fell off a cliff into a lake and you'd think it was real water, it was so dramatic. But much as I'd like to go to the theatre now, it didn't seem affordable.

'You know some of the bosses are coming down hard on strikers at the moment,' I said. 'I heard Ma tell Da that if he doesn't watch out he won't have a job.'

'But our das aren't day labourers,' said Samira. Everyone round here wants to be permanent like Da and Mr Casey, because at least you know that you're definitely going to earn a steady wage every week. But as my ma and da keep reminding me, no job is safe these days. And if Samira hadn't been so distracted this afternoon by her dreams of a trip to the theatre, she'd have remembered that.

'It doesn't matter,' I said. 'I heard him and Ma talking. Things are getting very hot down there. They could sack everyone.'

'Maybe just ask your parents anyway,' said Samira hopefully. 'You never know, Maisie might be able to get a ticket for nothing at all. Tommy Garland's doing the door at the Majestic these days and I swear he's sweet on her. At her age!' She looked horrified at the thought of anyone fancying her aunt. 'She's almost forty.'

'She looks younger than that, though,' I said, and it's true, she does. Back in the days before she gave up her life on the music halls to look after Ali and Samira she must have been a raving beauty, and she's still the best-looking woman on our road now, however old she is. Ma says Auntie Maisie wears too many feathers in her hats, but I know she likes her really. It's impossible not to. And whenever Maisie decides to have a new frock (which isn't often – no one on our road can afford new frocks, but Maisie sometimes gets old costumes from the theatres that can be turned into something new), she gets Ma to do it for her.

'No one can turn out a skirt as well as you, Mrs Rafferty,' she'll say. 'You're a genius!' And I swear Ma simpers at the flattery. Maisie's such a charmer, as I said to Samira.

'There you go,' said Samira. 'Maybe she'll charm Mr Garland into getting a free ticket for you. Oh, I hope you can come too. It won't be the same going to see the play without you, not after us practising it together.'

'I know,' I said. 'Janey, it feels like ages since we were acting out those scenes.'

It was last year that Samira discovered Shakespeare and decided she was going to be a serious actress. Before that she'd always talked about going on the halls like Maisie – doing a few songs and comic turns, you know, little sketches and dances, and that sort of thing. Maisie was never a big star but she did well enough in the music halls and in pantomimes.

'And I never had to rely on some aul' fella to keep me either,' she said one day when we were looking through some of her old theatre programmes. I wasn't sure what she meant by that, and she didn't get a chance to tell me because Mrs Casey, Samira's granny, sat up straight in her chair by the fire where we all thought she was fast asleep and said, 'We'll have none of that sort of talk in front of the childer!' So Maisie didn't tell us anything else about aul' fellas.

Anyway, like I said, Samira always wanted to follow in Auntie Maisie's footsteps, and I bet she still could if she wanted to. But last year, in English class, our teacher Miss Hackett read a bit of this speech from a Shakespeare play called *The Merchant of Venice*. Some girl called Portia is pretending to be a lawyer and she gives this big speech in court. (At least I think it was in a courtroom – I never read the entire play so I was never very sure of the details.) The rest of the class didn't care much about it, but I had to admit there was something kind of magical about the words, even though I couldn't understand most of it.

And if I was mildly interested in the speech, Samira was completely entranced. After school that day she insisted we go straight across to the library to find a copy of the play.

'They'll have to have it there,' she said, and she was right, they did. It was a little red book and it was in the grown-up section, but the librarian, Miss Hamilton, lets us get out books for grown-ups because we've read everything in the children's room by now. Samira took it home and read it and by the following week she'd learned that whole speech off by heart.

And believe it or believe it not, she was actually pretty good when she recited it. No offence meant to Miss Hackett, who wasn't bad at reading the speech, but Samira was much better. She made it sound like something a real person would say, not just a sort of poem. After that, she went Shakespeare-mad. She got all the plays out of the library, even the really confusing ones, and she learned loads of the speeches of the girls' parts.

But of course, there's only so much acting you can do on your own, and it wasn't long before Samira started nagging me into playing some of the other characters. That's how we ended up doing *Romeo and Juliet* together. She stood at my bedroom window and cried, 'Romeo, Romeo, wherefore art thou Romeo?' while I stood in the back garden below and pretended to climb up the drain pipe to get to her, which was good fun until Eddie came home and saw us and laughed so much I thought he was going to be sick.

I really would like to see *Romeo and Juliet* performed by proper actors (and without fools like Eddie standing around sniggering), but I was almost sure that Ma and Da would think it's too much money at the moment. Or at least Ma would. She thinks striking all the time is making the employers even more angry. But Da is sure that if all the workers hold their nerve and refuse to give in, they won't have to fear the bosses for much longer. I think he's right. It's not as if they're stopping work just for fun. They're doing it to make things fair.

Oh no, I've done it again. I've got distracted from what actually happened today and started going on about Auntie Maisie and our Shakespearean readings and strikes. So I will return to this afternoon.

We kept walking towards the sea. When we set off I had a horrible feeling that Little Robbie was going to spend the entire walk wide awake, demanding Samira's adoration and devotion, and I was even more afraid that she was going to give it to him, but to my great relief (and surprise, if I'm being honest) his eyes started to close soon after we left our house. I suppose Lily was right. He really was due his afternoon nap.

We paused for a moment after we crossed the bridge into Fairview and looked at the Tolka river spilling out towards Dublin Bay. You can see all the cranes from the docks where both our das work. As you look north towards Howth everything seems to stretch out, and soon you feel as if the city is falling away behind you and all that's ahead of you is wild waves all the way to Wales. Sometimes it smells terrible, especially when the tide is out and all you can see is mud and bits of old rubbish that people have chucked into the water, but I still love living near the sea. Rosie's ma comes from Athlone or some such place and Rosie says she'd never seen the sea until she came up to Dublin to go into service in a house in Sutton. I can't imagine what that must be like. It's like never having seen the sky.

I said that to Samira as we walked past the vitriol works (I'm glad Da and Eddie don't work there, they'd come home stinking) and she agreed.

'Especially in the summer, when everything is blue,' she said, gazing out across the bay. 'It's like you're right out there in the sky and the water. "Perilous seas, in faery lands forlorn!"'

'Is that more Shakespeare?' I said.

'Keats,' said Samira. 'Anyway, perilous or not, it's very good for calming the nerves.'

'I suppose it's not very calming in winter,' I said, thinking of the days when the wind blows straight across the sea and you have to lean forward to be able to walk at all. 'It's hard to imagine winter now, isn't it?' I looked out at the blue sky and the barely moving waves as I kicked a stone along the dusty pavement.

We continued walking along Fairview, and as we passed the turn for Philipsburgh Avenue I said, 'Has your da heard anything new about the union recreation ground they're talking of setting up down there in Croydon House? You know, the big old house with the huge gardens? Da says they're going to have all sorts of activities for the workers and their families.'

Samira knew all about it.

'They're going to have a big garden party for the workers soon,' said Samira. 'There'll be games and teas and all that sort of thing.'

'That union house reminds me,' I said. 'You know Rosie at work?'

'Well, I know who she is,' said Samira, and I don't think I was imagining that she said it a bit cagily. It felt a bit strange, talking about Rosie to Samira. Samira spends her work days with old Mrs McGrath, which is grand because she's a nice enough old bird, but they're not exactly pals. Not least because Mrs McGrath is about a hundred years old. (Oh all right, she's about sixty.) And she talks about nothing but her lumbago and how she can't reach the tobacco shelf anymore, and she has no interest in *Jane Eyre* or singing or acting or all the other things Samira is interested in.

Whereas, even though it's only been a few weeks since I started at Lawlor's, me and Rosie have become proper friends, and I suppose I do talk about her to Samira a bit. Which might be quite annoying if you were stuck with an old lady all day. Sometimes I remember how jealous I was when Samira and Lizzie French became friends when we were ten. (Lizzie moved to Ringsend after that summer and we haven't seen her since.) Then I feel guilty about going on about Rosie.

'She's joined the union,' I said.

'Has she?' said Samira carelessly. She really is a good actor, but this time the carelessness was slightly overdone.

'I didn't think girls could join it at all,' I said. 'But they can.'

Samira looked right at me (luckily the pavement was empty so there was no danger of her pushing Little Robbie's pram into anyone).

'Are you going to join?' she said.

'I might,' I said. 'And you could join too.'

Samira snorted.

'Why not?' I said.

'I work in a shop, in case you've forgotten!' said Samira. 'And you're in a teashop. We're not exactly hauling sacks down the docks.'

'But you're still a worker!' I said. 'We both are!'

'I suppose,' said Samira, but she didn't sound convinced. I'm not entirely convinced myself, to be honest. I can't really imagine ordinary girls ever going on strike like the men. But I do like the idea of us all joining together, and I said so to Samira.

'We might be able to change things,' I said. 'Do you think things are fair right now?'

'Of course not,' said Samira. 'But what can a lot of girls do to change that?'

And I didn't have an answer to that.

Little Robbie was still asleep when we reached the crescent at the end of the Malahide Road. Although it's a terrace like our road, the houses are about five times the size of ours. And there's a lovely little moon-shaped park in front of it that belongs to the owners. We wheeled the pram to the railings and peered into the park, where we could see some children running across the grass playing a game of chasing. An older woman, who was dressed so plainly I knew she must be a servant, was sitting on a tree nearby, watching them. The grass looked so fresh and cool after our walk along the dusty hot streets.

'Janey, imagine having all that grass just to play on,' breathed Samira. '"One touch of nature makes the whole world kin."'

I looked at her with my eyebrows raised. Samira laughed. 'It's from *Troilus and Cressida*,' she said.

How many plays did Shakespeare write, anyway? I hadn't even heard of that one.

'They've got massive gardens of their own, as well as the little park,' I said, turning around to look at the tall houses of the crescent.

'Well, my garden has a train running right next to it,' said Samira loftily. 'And we've got our very own jacks in the back garden.'

Somehow that seemed very funny and we both broke up laughing, which unfortunately woke up Little Robbie, who clearly wasn't sleeping as deeply as we thought. He immediately started howling and roaring (why does he *do* that? Imagine if I started shrieking every time I woke up. Ma would clatter me), and the noise attracted the attention of the children in the crescent park and their nurse.

A boy of about seven in a spotless white sailor suit ran closer to us.

'Look at that horrid gypsy girl!' he cried. He threw an apple core towards Samira. 'Go on there, gypsy, get away from our garden!'

'Ssssh, Thomas, don't be horrible,' said an older girl, who looked about eleven. She glanced at us apologetically.

'We don't want to go near your rotten garden,' I said.

'No, we don't,' said Samira in a commanding and steely voice. All her usual dreaminess had fallen away. If she ever played a Shakespearean queen, I bet she would sound just like that. 'Come on, Little Robbie. Sssh, baby. '

And we clumsily turned around his massive pram and wheeled it back to the Strand Road.

'Are you all right?' I said to Samira, who was still leaning over Little Robbie's pram and saying silly things to make him laugh (which was working, he'd stopped crying already).

'I'm used to it,' said Samira, a little grimly.

'Sorry,' I said, which I know wasn't much help. 'He was a horrible boy.'

And then Little Robbie said, 'Singing, Sam Sam!' in an extremely demanding voice, which I personally would have ignored. But like I said earlier, Samira likes him for some mysterious reason, so she gave in to his dreadful demands and started singing. It was one of the songs Auntie Maisie used to sing, all about taking a walk down the strand with a young swell. (That means a fancy young man, in case you didn't know.) Little Robbie laughed and pulled his hat off and threw it on the ground.

'How's that for ingratitude!' I said, bending down to pick it up. 'Oh look, it's all dusty.'

'He's only playing,' said Samira affectionately, jiggling the pram. 'Aren't you, Little Robbie?' And she carried on singing. Little Robbie started trying to sing along too, and then he threw his hat in the dust again. He was having a wonderful time, hooting away and chucking things all over the place. And here was I, on my precious day off, grubbing around after him. I was still trying to get the hat, which had got tangled up in the spokes of the pram wheels, when I realised someone was singing along with Samira.

'As I was walking down the strand with Henr-eee!' went a familiar, melodious voice, and I scrambled to my feet to see Auntie Maisie coming towards us, dressed in her Sunday best and waving at us. She was accompanied by a middle-aged man with a friendly moustachioed face. I knew I'd seen him before, but I wasn't sure where until Samira said, 'Hello, Mr Garland.'

'Me and Tommy decided to go for a seaside stroll,' said Auntie Maisie, with a smile. 'Tommy, you remember my niece and her friend Betty? They came to the pantomime with me last year.'

'Of course,' said Mr Garland, who I now recognised as the doorman at the Majestic Theatre. He nodded at me and raised his hat politely. 'How are you young ladies today?'

It makes a nice change being called a lady. Old Wobbly certainly never calls us that in the shop.

'Very well, thanks, Mr Garland,' said Samira.

'And who's this little lad?' Mr Garland bent over the pram to get a closer look at Little Robbie. I don't know why he wanted to do that. You can tell exactly what he's like from a safe distance.

'My nephew,' I said, as Little Robbie beamed up at Mr Garland. He prefers every single person in Dublin to his own auntie, including total strangers. 'Little Robbie.'

'He's a happy little chappie, isn't he?' Mr Garland was now making faces at Little Robbie, who was laughing fit to burst.

'Some of the time,' I said, trying not to let my true feelings about Little Robbie show.

Mr Garland made a very impressive cross-eyed face, which caused Little Robbie to shriek with glee. Auntie Maisie was looking at the pair of them very fondly. I know Samira jokes that Mr Garland likes Auntie Maisie, but when I noticed the look she gave him this afternoon, I had a feeling she might like him back. Anyway, Samira wasn't thinking about their potential romance at that moment. She had a plan.

'So what are you two up to this afternoon?' said Auntie Maisie.

'I was just telling Betty about the production of *Romeo and Juliet*,' said the cunning Samira.

'Are you going to be joining us, then, young Betty?' Auntie Maisie turned to me with a smile. I felt a bit awkward, even though I knew this line of questioning must be part of Samira's ingenious scheme to get me into the theatre with her.

'I don't think I can afford it,' I said.

'Don't you worry about that!' Mr Garland stopped making faces at Little Robbie (who looked quite annoyed at suddenly not being the centre of his attention) and stood up straight. 'I can get yiz all in.'

'You won't get into trouble or anything?' I do want to see the play, but I wouldn't want Mr Garland to, I don't know, lose his job or anything over it. And I didn't want him or Auntie Maisie to think I'd been dropping hints.

''Course I won't.' Mr Garland adjusted his hat and grinned. 'Three more little ladies squashed into the gods won't make a clatter of difference.'

'Ah, Tommy, you're very good.' Auntie Maisie seemed genuinely delighted. 'That's all arranged, then. We're going to the theatre.'

A thought struck me, one that should have hit me as soon as Mr Garland made his kindly offer. 'I can only go on Monday or Saturdays, though,' I said. 'Or Sundays if the play is on then. Otherwise I can't get there in time after work.'

Mr Garland smiled. 'Don't worry about that, Miss Betty. Whenever suits the three of you is fine with me.'

'That's all fixed then.' Maisie beamed. 'Now, we'd better get a move on if we want to get to Clontarf and back before my old ma has the dinner poured out.'

And with a jaunty wave from Maisie, and another tip of the hat and a cheeky wink from Mr Garland, they sauntered on towards the seafront. As soon as they were out of earshot Samira grabbed me.

'We're going to the theatre!' she cried, in her most dramatic voice, and her excitement was so infectious I couldn't help squealing back, and an old lady in a rusty black dress who was passing by gave us a real disapproving look and muttered something about young girls today acting like hooligans. But we were too happy to care.

'Your parents can't say no now,' said Samira as we wheeled Little Robbie across the bridge.

'You're right about that,' I said. 'It won't cost us a penny. Oh stop that, Little Robbie, there's nothing wrong with you.' Because Little Robbie, enraged that we weren't giving him any attention ever since we'd left Maisie, had decided to start shrieking at the top of his lungs. And even though Samira sang and cooed at him for the rest of the walk home, he was clearly determined to punish her and kept roaring until he was purple in the face and looked more like a plum than a tomato.

By the time we reached my house even Samira was beaten.

'He's very loud, isn't he?' she said. 'Is there something wrong with him?' She looked a bit frightened. It had taken a whole year, but she'd finally seen Little Robbie's true nature.

'This is what he's like most of the time,' I said.

Then I had to go inside and hand him over to Lily, who gave him some bread and milk which finally shut him up. But I didn't get a break from his dreadful ways because they all stayed for dinner and he managed to tip my cup of tea right into my lap, and Lily said it was an accident and he's a baby who couldn't help it, but of course I knew he had done it on purpose.

# Chapter Six

I did it. I've joined the union! It's all thanks to Rosie, really. If it weren't for her telling me about the Irish Women Workers' Union last week, I would have still thought unions were just something men joined, and I'd never have gone down to Liberty Hall today and asked for the mysterious 'D.L.' In fact, if Miss Warby hadn't behaved the way she has done over the last few days ... but I'm getting ahead of myself.

It all started on Monday. I arrived at eight as usual and hung up my coat in the cubby hole. Before I put my apron on I checked my uniform dress for stains. I check it every day, but I still feel nervous before I step out on the shop floor. You get docked a whole sixpence if your dress is dirty, which I certainly can't afford. And it's not like I have a spare work dress to wear when this one is being washed – I won't have paid off the cost of it until Christmas, so I certainly can't afford to buy another one.

Thanks to the apron, I've managed to keep my frock clean so far – we wear detachable white collars and cuffs that can be taken off and washed and dried at home, and Ma has sewed in little patches underneath the arms of my frock that I can unpick and wash to make sure I don't get sweat stains on my dress under my arms. Ma would kill me if she ever heard me say sweat, she thinks it's common and rude. I'm not sure what to say instead. In books when characters are working hard in the heat they say things like 'I wiped the perspiration from my brow' but they never say anything about sweaty armpits.

Anyway, there are no sweat stains anywhere on my dress at the moment, so I hurried into the shop, where Kitty was getting ready to open the front door.

'You're just in time, Betty,' she said. I walked as fast as I could – no running on the shop floor! – to my position behind the counter.

'Where's Miss Warby?' I whispered to Annie. Rosie was nowhere to be seen.

'In the kitchen,' Annie whispered back. 'There's some problem with the oven and they're behind on today's cakes. I could hear her roaring from the cubby hole.'

That didn't bode well. If Old Wobbly starts the morning with a temper on her, everyone in Lawlor's suffers for it all day.

'What about Rosie?' I said. Annie just shrugged. By now Kitty had opened the shop door and returned to her place by the large and frightening tea urn.

I was starting to get worried about Rosie being late. I really didn't want her to get into trouble with Old Wobbly. She's one of the most generous people I've ever met – sometimes I feel like a selfish little madam in comparison, because I'd never have even thought of giving my cakes to the washing-up girls if she hadn't mentioned it, and she takes all hers home to her ma. And she has a sense of fun. She's always teasing me, but not in a nasty way. She's very hard working, and even though she's often looking after her little brother, she's hardly ever late for work.

In fact, she's usually there before I am. Which is why it was strange not to see her waiting for me behind the counter. The first customer of the day, a woman in a purple hat laden down with feathers, was walking in through the door, and there was still no sign of Rosie. The purple-feather lady made her way towards the tearoom, just as Rosie, looking a bit red in the face, appeared in the door that leads to the corridor.

'There you are!' I hissed.

Rosie opened her mouth to speak, but before she could utter a word a bony hand grasped her shoulder.

'Miss Delaney!' said Miss Warby in a terrible voice. 'A word, if you please.' And she pushed a white-faced Rosie back through the door and along the corridor, presumably into the cubby hole.

More customers were arriving and I had to serve them, but I found it hard to concentrate, worrying what Miss Warby was saying to Rosie. As I said earlier, we get fined for being late, as much as half a day's wages. Someone told me that a waitress got the sack last year for lateness, but she had been late dozens of times. In the six weeks I've been working here I've never seen Rosie be late even once. Luckily that morning's customers didn't want anything too complicated. Some days they all want five of one sort of bun and three of another little cake and two of the scones and some manner of fancy bread too, and even at the best of times it's hard to keep hold of it all in your head.

That morning I was so worried about Rosie that just selling single crumpets and Mary Cakes was almost beyond me until Rosie, looking very subdued and with slightly red eyes, joined me and Annie behind the counter.

'Are you all right?' I whispered, as I put a customer's sixpence in the cash register.

'Fined,' muttered Rosie. 'Tell you at break.'

And that was all I could get out of her because every so often for the rest of the morning Old Wobbly would stick her head in the door, like a dragon glowering from its lair, so we didn't dare exchange another word.

Then something happened that briefly put all thoughts of Rosie and Miss Warby out of my head.

Kitty was manning the tea urn, as usual. I'm scared of that urn at the best of times, what with its steam and its malfunctioning tap. And as it turned out, both of those things caused the disaster. The urn had just been refilled, and Kitty had just finished filling a pot of tea, when a massive spurt of steam came bursting out of the tap. In her shock, Kitty dropped the pot, and boiling tea went splashing all over her foot. She let out a little scream of pain before quickly turning to the wall and biting down on her knuckles. But it was too late. Wobbly had heard her cry and rushed into the tearoom.

'What on earth is all that racket about?' She looked at the broken pot and the pool of tea, which Annie was ineffectually trying to clean up. 'Who is responsible for this?'

'It was the urn.' Kitty's breathing was shallow. She must have been in agony. 'It ... The pot fell on my foot.'

It was obvious that Kitty was in enormous pain, and seeing as how Old Wobbly holds her in high enough esteem to make her the supervisor, I thought she'd send her home or even just tell her to have a rest in the cubby hole. But she didn't.

'You should be more careful, Miss Dunne,' she said coldly. 'Per-haps if you weren't so concerned with that union of yours, you might pay more attention to the tasks at hand. Now go back to work.'

'Yes, Miss Warby,' said Kitty stiffly.

As soon as Wobbly stormed out of the room Rosie and I rushed to Kitty's side, but she didn't want our help.

'I'm fine,' she said. 'Most of it went on the floor, not me. Come on, the lunchtime rush is starting.'

At two o'clock, the rush had calmed down and I was almost dying with hunger. (Just imagine having to sell people lots of cakes and buns and having to look at people eating finger sandwiches in a tearoom and not being able to eat so much as a crumb yourself.) Kitty, who was still looking very pale and wasn't putting her weight on the foot that had been splashed, nodded at me and Rosie.

'You can take your break now,' she said, before quickly turning to greet a regular important customer who Miss Warby had told us should be given extra attention. 'Hello, Mrs Sheffield, how are you today? Where's your little dog?'

Rosie and I quickly slipped out the door and down the corridor. We made our way to the kitchen, where one of the girls handed each of us a plate containing one of yesterday's big bread rolls and a little sliver of butter. We nodded our thanks, grabbed a butter knife and a mug of tea each, and headed to the cubby hole, where we sank down on the benches. I couldn't help groaning with relief.

'My poor legs! I'll never get used to this.' I stretched my legs out in front of me and pointed my toes, then looked at Rosie, who was taking a massive bite out of her bread roll without even buttering it. 'Do you think Kitty's all right?'

Rosie shrugged her shoulders. 'She's tougher than she looks.'

She took another bite of her roll.

'What about you? What happened this morning?'

With an effort, Rosie swallowed down her bread.

'Ma's sick again,' she said, and took a swig of water. 'She's had to take to her bed. And then Francis puked up his breakfast just as I was going out the door and Josie had already gone to the factory, so I had to clean him up.'

'So Wobbly docked you?' I said. It was more of a statement than a question. Wobbly never lets anyone away without a fine.

Rosie had taken another bite of bread so she just nodded. Eventually she said, 'Yeah, course she did. A whole shilling.'

A shilling is practically a day's pay. None of us can afford to lose that. But especially Rosie. Her whole family lives in just one room. Her Ma used to work as a charwoman, doing heavy cleaning work in people's big houses up on the North Circular Road near the Phoenix Park, but Rosie says she hasn't been well over the last year. Some of the things she's said about her ma make me wonder if she drinks, like Mrs Hennessy's brother who used to stay with them and always woke up at about lunchtime and talked all strange if you met him after about three in the afternoon. He smelled like the air outside the door of Cusack's pub. I've never liked to ask too many questions about Rosie's ma, though. If she wants to talk about it she'll tell me.

Anyway, it's clear that Rosie and Josie have to look after her little brother Francis whenever they're at home, and even if he's a much nicer baby than Little Robbie (which wouldn't be hard), looking after a little kid like that is an awful lot of work. Just washing the nappies is woeful, even if you can afford to heat enough water, and I'm not sure they can. Because her ma isn't working very often, the family has to rely on what Rosie and Josie bring home as wages. And that certainly can't be enough for all four of them. Lawlor's are proud that they don't pay us girls enough to live on. Before I started at Lawlor's Mrs Lawlor told Ma that they only employ 'nice girls who live with their parents', who just need to earn a few shillings a week for pocket money and to add to the general housekeeping, which Rosie says is their excuse for not paying us a decent living wage.

It's true that most of us Lawlor's girls do live at home, and while none of our families have much money, there's usually enough food on our tables. But there are a few girls here who came up from the country, or who are from Dublin but couldn't live at home for some reason or another, and they have to cram together into tiny boxrooms in grubby boarding houses. And there are girls like Rosie who still live at home but who have to earn enough to keep the rest of the family. If Rosie loses a shilling, that means the whole family go hungry. Really hungry. I couldn't understand why Wobbly had done it, especially because we're only meant to be fined sixpence for lateness, which is bad enough. A shilling is twelve whole pence. Twice as much. Maybe there was some mistake. I said that to Rosie.

'You were only five minutes late,' I pointed out. 'It's not as though you missed the whole morning. That should only be sixpence.'

Rosie took a swig of tea. 'It should be,' she said.

'So why ...?'

We were sitting near the clothes hooks and Rosie reached up and pulled down her coat. She pointed to the little red badge.

'That's why. Someone told her I'm in the union. Or maybe she just noticed the button.'

'But she can't give you a double fine just for being in the union!' As I said the words, I remembered the way Miss Warby had just spoken to Kitty.

Rosie laughed. It was like the laugh I'd heard from Ali last week. It wasn't the way you laughed because something was actually funny.

'Wobbly can do whatever she likes,' she said. 'If she wants to punish me for joining the union, she can do it.'

'Are we not allowed join the union?' I said. 'Did she say that's why she was giving you the double fine?'

'No, not exactly,' said Rosie. 'But she grabbed my coat off the hook so I could see the badge, and then she said I was turning into a real troublemaker. She said I needed to be taught a good lesson. Like an example to the rest of you.'

'But that's not fair!' I said. I don't know why I felt so shocked. I already knew the world wasn't fair.

'No,' said Rosie. 'It's not fair. But what can I do about it? It's not like everyone's going to go out on strike to support me.'

I looked at her miserable face and a thought struck me.

'They might,' I said. If ever there was a reason to go on strike, this was it. 'They really might, Rosie. She can't do this. It's against the rules.'

I thought Rosie would cheer up at this, but right now, it felt as if all the fire had gone out of her.

'Even if the others were in the union,' said Rosie, 'and only a few of them are, Wobbly isn't actually breaking the rules.'

'She isn't?'

Rosie nodded. 'I remember when Eileen French got the sack for being late all the time. And do you know why Eileen was always late?'

I shook my head – I knew a waitress had been sacked for lateness before I started at Lawlor's, but that was all I knew about her.

'Her little sister was dying. Consumption or something, I'm not sure. Her other brothers and sisters and her ma had all died from their lungs.'

Almost all her family. What could you say to that? I just stared at Rosie in horror.

'Yeah.' Rosie sighed. 'It was just Eileen, her da and the sister, and then her da picked up a month's work in a bakery on Capel Street, so he had to leave the house at about five in the morning. And that meant the sister was left on her own all day, but sometimes she'd be coughing so badly in the mornings, coughing up blood and all, that Eileen didn't want to leave her until she had calmed down. That's why she kept being late. Not very late, you understand. Just a few minutes, most days.'

I thought of Eileen, this girl I'd never met, sitting by her sister's bed, watching her shaking with coughs. Jessie Harney's ma died of consumption last summer and before she died you could hear the sound of her coughing whenever you walked past the house. It was an awful, awful noise, like something alive was trying to get out of her.

'What happened?'

'The first few times she was late Wobbly fined her sixpence,' said Rosie. 'And then one day Wobbly fined her a whole shilling, even though she was there just two minutes after eight, and when she said that wasn't fair, it was only meant to be sixpence, Wobbly said that the fines could be changed ...' Rosie searched for the exact words. 'At the discretion of the management.'

'What does that mean?' I said.

'It means,' said Rosie bitterly, 'that they can do whatever they bleeding well like.'

There's no swearing allowed in our house so I was quite shocked to hear Rosie say 'bleeding'. Then Annie popped her head into the cubby hole and said, 'You'd better get back out there. A big gang of girls just came in and they're going mad for the Mary Cakes.'

She hurried back to the shop, and Rosie and I had no choice but to go down to the kitchen as fast as we could, without actually running, to drop in our mugs and plates. Soon we were back behind the counter. Annie hadn't exaggerated; it felt as though the entire shop was full of excited girls. And not just any girls. I recognised the school crest brooch some of them were wearing proudly on their hats, even though it was the summer holidays. These girls went to the Dominicans in Eccles Street, the same school Lavinia Lawlor went to, and from the tennis rackets most of them were carrying I assumed they were on their way to or from a tennis match.

I was sure Lavinia must be somewhere in the crowd, given that it was her ma and da's shop, but I didn't have a chance to look more closely, because me, Rosie, Annie and Kitty were kept busy selling buns and little cakes to a stream of girls who kept accidentally poking each other with tennis rackets and who changed their minds every two seconds.

'I'll have that little iced bun – no, sorry, I'll have the chocolate biscuit. No, actually, I'll have the slice of apple tart,' said a tall, fair-haired girl wearing the most beautiful soft fawn coat.

'And I'll have those two iced buns, pleased.' A shorter girl leaned over the counter to point at the plumpest buns. 'You'll pay for me, won't you Sarah? I forgot my purse.'

The tall girl rolled her eyes and smiled at me. 'I suppose I'll have to or we'll be arrested for theft. And we're not going to win the tennis match if we're in jail.'

'That'll be one and tuppence please,' I said. I was so tired and I felt so awful about Rosie losing that shilling I couldn't force myself to smile back at her. They were quite nice girls, really. We get much worse customers. But I couldn't help thinking that if fate had been different, I could have been one of them, spending my days happily buying cakes with my dear old 'chums' in a grand teashop, instead of being run off my feet for practically twelve hours, trying to remember who wanted which bun. I gave the red-haired girl the cakes she'd ordered in a little paper bag and she said, 'Thanks awfully,' and made way for the next girl in the throng.

Who turned out to be Lavinia.

'Hello, Miss Lawlor,' I said in my most polite and friendly voice. I had to be especially nice because I didn't want to have to worry about her telling her ma that Mrs Rafferty's daughter had been rude to her. But it was clear from the confused look she gave me that she didn't recognise me at all and wasn't sure how I knew her name, even though I'd spent a whole hour at her feet just a few months ago, pinning up her frocks.

'Give me two Mary Cakes,' she said. Unlike her classmates, she didn't bother saying please. I put two of the little iced cakes in a bag and was about to say, 'That'll be sixpence, please,' when it struck me that Lavinia probably never paid for anything in Lawlor's, and I was proved right when Kitty suddenly appeared at my elbow, took the bag and handed it over to Lavinia with a winning smile.

'Enjoy your cakes, Miss Lawlor,' she said brightly.

Lavinia barely looked at her. She just took the cakes and moved away from the counter.

Eventually, like a chattering flock of birds, all the Eccles Street girls left, clutching their cakes and their rackets.

'Thanks be to God they've gone,' Kitty said. Her words sounded like a heartfelt prayer. Then she rested her weight on the counter, a look of total exhaustion on her face.

That's how I knew something was very, very wrong. Kitty never breaks the rules, and leaning on the counter is Wobbly's favourite rule of all. Kitty didn't lean on it for longer than a few seconds, but that was enough. She's so reserved that I don't usually dare speak to her about personal things, but I couldn't help it. I said, 'Kitty, is your foot all right?'

She turned to me, her pale face tightening. 'It's fine.'

'But you're limping ...' I said, my voice trailing off as Kitty's expression grew more stern.

'I said it's fine,' she said.

I didn't dare ask any more questions. I knew the accident was worse than she had claimed. Kitty looked strained and pale for the rest of the working day, and when Annie asked her where she should put a cake knife that had fallen on the floor, Kitty nearly bit her head off.

What with Kitty being snappish, and the worry over Rosie losing so much of her wages, it was the most miserable day I'd spent in Lawlor's so far. I think we all felt that there was something wrong in the air. When the shop finally closed and Miss Warby, who was still in a foul mood herself, had come in and snarled at us to get out immediately so the cleaners could do their work, Annie, Rosie and I grabbed our closing buns and left as quickly as we could. (I ran down to the sink room – I knew Miss Warby wouldn't see me running, she was ordering the cleaners about in the tearoom – and handed my bun to the first girl I saw.) By the time I got back to the cubby hole, the other two were putting away their aprons and caps, and we barely said a word until we were out of the building and standing in the lane behind the shop. Rosie let out a massive sigh and leaned against the wall.

'What did she say to you earlier?' Annie asked, and Rosie told her about being fined a whole shilling.

Annie whistled.

'Janey,' she said. 'No wonder Kitty was playing down that accident. I bet she was worried she'd get the sack if she asked for a rest, the mood Wobbly's in.'

'She said it didn't get her whole foot ...' I said.

'It did,' said Annie. 'I saw. And my sister knew someone who dropped a kettle on her lap. They had to cut her stockings off. Glued to her legs, they were. By the hot water. If they'd left it a minute longer ...'

I felt sick at the thought. Poor Kitty hadn't even had a chance to do anything to her stockings. She had to keep on working, standing the whole time. No wonder she'd had to lean on the counter. I hoped her poor foot was all right.

'This is why we all need to join the union,' said Rosie. 'If enough of us were in it, maybe we could make them treat us fairly.'

'I thought you said Wobbly wasn't breaking the rules,' I said.

'She wasn't. But you were right earlier.'

The shock of losing that shilling might have beaten down her spirit earlier, but now Rosie's old fire was coming back.

'We could go on strike and *make* them change the rules,' she said. 'Stop them fining us practically a whole day's pay just for being late. Or expecting us to keep working even when we can barely walk.'

'I dunno.' Annie looked awkward. 'My da says the union are a load of troublemakers. He says they just rile up the bosses and make them angry.'

'We can't let the bosses walk all over us,' said Rosie. 'If we all stood together ...'

Annie looked away from her intense gaze.

'I'd better go home. My ma'll need my help with the tea. See yiz tomorrow.' And she trotted off down the lane without a backward glance.

Me and Rosie looked at each other.

'Do you really think we could make a difference?' I said. 'You didn't seem to think so earlier.'

'I was letting Wobbly get to me then,' Rosie said. 'I've been thinking about it all afternoon. It's true, she was keeping to the rules. But I bet your da's bosses were sticking to their rules too, and the union still came out on strike to get fair pay. Because *who makes the rules?*'

I'd never really thought about this before. I'd always presumed rules were just ... rules. They just existed. But, I now realised, that didn't mean they didn't suit some people better than others.

'The employers make the rules,' I said.

'Exactly. And they're not doing it for our benefit. It's so they can squeeze everything they can out of us for the lowest cost. They make it so they can fine us for practically nothing – that's one less shilling in my pocket and one more shilling in that Mrs Lawlor's purse.'

'I don't think Mrs Lawlor would fine you a shilling,' I said, thinking of the nice lady in the beautiful fawn skirt. 'Not personally, I mean. Maybe she doesn't even know we get fined.'

Rosie didn't look so sure of that. 'Anyway, she's turning a blind eye to Old Wobbly doing it.' She pushed a lock of curly hair away from her face. Suddenly she looked very tired.

'Are you … will you be alright?' I asked, a little awkwardly. 'For, like, food and the rent and all? Because if you're not …'

I know we're meant to be counting every penny, but surely Ma and Da wouldn't grudge me giving Rosie something out of my wages if it stopped her whole family starving or being thrown out on the street. After all, I was one of the type of girls Lawlor's boasted about employing. I was contributing to the household, but the rest of the family weren't depending on me to eat.

Rosie grinned at me.

'Would you listen to Lady Bountiful! We'll manage. Kitty might slip me a few extra closing buns.' She must have noticed my sceptical expression – Kitty might be in the union, but she's not what you'd call pally. 'She's a decent auld skin. She gave me a few buns when Ma started dri— when Ma got sick last year. And speaking of my ma, I'd better get back to Francis. Josie's working late this week.'

My head was in a muddle all the way home. I was thinking about Kitty's fear and generosity, Annie's distrust and Rosie's bravery. Luckily, by the time I reached our end of the North Strand, McGrath's shop was closing for the day. I was just passing the pub on the corner when I saw Samira leave the shop and call goodbye to old Mrs McGrath.

'Samira!' I cried. And even though I was exhausted after the long and dreadful day, I found myself running towards her as fast as I could. Samira laughed as I practically fell into her arms.

'You're not usually this happy to see me,' she said.

'Amn't I? Well, I am today,' I said.

'"Welcome ever smiles, and farewell goes out sighing,"' said Samira. 'That's *Troilus and Cressida* again.'

'I don't even think Troilus and whatshername is a real play,' I said. 'I think you made it up.' And Samira laughed and pretended to give me a dig in the ribs and the pair of us started walking home.

'Auntie Maisie called into the shop a few hours ago,' said Samira. 'Mr Garland got us tickets for the play on Saturday.' She twirled around on the path with her arms stretched out. 'Actual *Romeo and Juliet*! I can't wait. Just a few days to go!'

'Me neither,' I said, but I didn't sound quite as excited as I felt.

'You do want to go, don't you?' Samira sounded worried.

''Course I do,' I said. 'Don't mind me. Something happened in work, that's all.' And I told her all about Rosie being fined, and about Kitty having to keep on working even though she'd scalded her foot.

'I think I'm going to have to join the union,' I concluded. 'Maybe if we all stuck together, aul' Wobbly would treat us better.'

And then, to my surprise, Samira said, 'How much does it cost?'

'How much does what cost?' I said.

'Joining the union,' said Samira. 'You always have to pay a bit every month, I know that from Da and Ali. But it can't be that much or no one would be able to afford it.'

I hadn't even thought of the cost, and I told Samira so.

'Well, we'd better find out, then,' said Samira. 'There'd be something about it in the *Worker*, wouldn't there?'

The *Irish Worker* is the union newspaper.

'Probably,' I said. 'I've never really looked at the *Worker* before.'

And I'm ashamed to say that this was true. It never seemed like it had anything to do with me. But it did now.

'Well then,' said Samira. 'We'd better have a look.'

'Are you saying you're going to join it too?' I felt my spirits rise.

'I might,' said Samira.

'What's brought this on?' I asked.

Samira shrugged her shoulders.

'I dunno,' she said. 'I was just thinking behind the counter today …'

'Don't let Mrs McGrath here you say that,' I joked. 'She'd say she doesn't be paying you to do any thinking.'

Samira slapped me but she was only messing.

'Shut up, you, I'm trying to tell you something.' Her voice became more serious. 'I've been thinking about what you said the other day. About us being workers too. And you're right. I work just as hard as Ali. Maybe not as hard as Da,' she added honestly, 'but definitely as hard as Ali, with all the tins I have to take down from the high shelves. So I have just as much of a right to join the union as they do.'

'You do,' I said, grinning at her.

'And besides,' Samira said, grinning back, 'Mrs McGrath only sells goods from union suppliers. She can't object to her own workers being in the union too.'

And so when we got to my house, I went into the kitchen and found the latest issue of the *Irish Worker* on Da's chair by the fire, with Earnshaw sitting on it looking so comfortable that I felt quite bad pulling it out from under him. While Ma told me not to be messing around with that dog, me and Samira escaped to the front room and sat down on the ground before the empty grate to look through the paper.

'Look!' said Samira, pointing at a column of the paper. And there it was. A whole column and a half on the Women Workers' Union, and at the end of it there was a little advertisement that read

IRISH WOMEN WORKERS' UNION
(Head Office – Liberty Hall)
Entrance fee – 6d. and 3d.
Contributions – 1d. & 2d. per week.
Join now. Call in at the above office any day between 10 a.m. and 10 p.m.
All classes of workers are eligible to join this Union.
Irish Dancing Wednesday and Friday evenings.
Don't forget the Sunday evening socials commencing at 7 p.m.
Small charge for admission.
All communications for this column to be addressed to
"D.L." 18 Beresford Place

Samira and I looked at each other.

'All classes of workers!' I said. 'That means us.'

'So it does,' said Samira. 'Do you have sixpence?'

I nodded. 'And it says you can join for thruppence too. Maybe they don't charge young girls the full whack.'

'There you go,' said Samira. 'Call in tomorrow after work. By the time we go to the theatre on Saturday we might both be trade unionists.'

I don't know what I was expecting when I walked down Abbey Street towards Beresford Place the next day, clutching my torn out page of the *Irish Worker*. Of course, I knew about Liberty Hall – if your da or your brother is in the union, you'll have heard them talking about Liberty Hall before. It's been the headquarters of the union for about a year now. The building used to be a hotel, and it still has the look of a hotel, despite the sign that declares it to be the home of the Irish Transport and General Workers' Union.

When I approached the steps there were a number of serious-looking men walking in and out, and a few not too serious-looking men hanging around outside, laughing and smoking cigarettes. Da and especially Ma think cigarettes are an awful waste of money, but I know Eddie smokes sometimes. I've seen him with his friends down by the canal, passing one little damp smoky yoke to each other and coughing like they have consumption every time they take a drag off of it. It doesn't look like much fun to me.

As I walked past the men and up the steps I could hear one of the group mutter something to the rest of them, and then they all laughed in a kind of sniggering way. I just held my head up high and pushed open the door. I heard one of the men say, 'She must be one of your one Delia's little recruits.' The door swung shut behind me before I could hear any more.

Inside the lobby there were more men coming and going, all of them looking as if they were intent on some important business. I didn't know where I could find the mysterious D.L., but luckily one of the serious-faced men noticed me and took pity on me and said, 'Hello there, miss. What are you here for?'

All of a sudden I was struck dumb. I just held up my sheet of the *Irish Worker* and said, 'D.L.'

The man smiled. He had a worn suit and a kind face. He reminded me a bit of Da.

'You're looking for Miss Larkin,' he said. 'I think she's upstairs. Room 10.' He told me where to go and then winked at me.

'Good luck, young one,' he said, and headed off down a corridor.

I took a deep breath and headed upstairs. I nearly tripped over a big pile of last week's *Irish Worker* on my way down the upstairs corridor, but eventually I found the right room. It was large and the walls were lined with filing cabinets covered in piles of paper. In the middle of them was a desk, behind which sat a small woman with a smudge of ink on her nose and masses of dark hair, looking at what looked like a ledger. There was another chair in front of the desk but it was empty. I knocked hesitantly on the open door, and the woman looked up.

'Yes?' She sounded irritated.

'Miss Larkin?' I said. I almost wished I hadn't come; she looked so fierce.

'That's right,' she said. She didn't sound like she was from around here, and I found out later that she was originally from Liverpool over in England. 'What do you want?'

I approached the desk.

'I want to join the union.'

'Good to hear.' She looked slightly more friendly. 'What's your line of work?'

'Teashops,' I said, then realised how silly that sounded. 'I mean, I work in a teashop. And a bakery. It's called Lawlor's, it's on ...'

'I know it,' said Miss Larkin, before I could finish the sentence. 'Do you have your thruppence?' I nodded and gave it to her. 'Good. Can you read and write well enough to fill out a form?'

''Course I can,' I said, quite insulted she felt she had to ask. But her face became stern once more.

'Don't look so outraged, miss. Plenty of decent workers can't do either.'

I felt ashamed of myself. She rummaged around in her desk drawer and pulled out a form.

'Sit down and fill this in.' She handed it to me along with a pencil.

I sat down and did what she told me.

'Is your dad in the union?' she asked me, her voice still very serious.

'Yes, miss,' I said, handing over the completed form. 'Edward Rafferty. He works in the docks.'

'Good,' said Miss Larkin, glancing at the form and taking something out of the box that sat on her desk. Suddenly she smiled at me and handed me a small badge in the shape of a little red hand, the badge I'd seen on Rosie's jacket and on my dad's coat too. 'Welcome to the Irish Women Workers' Union, Miss Rafferty. Wear the red hand with pride.'

I felt quite overwhelmed for a moment. Then I stood up tall and carefully pinned the badge to the lapel of my coat. I almost felt like I should salute her. There was something about her that made you think of a general leading an army, even if her army was just a bunch of girls working in cake shops and biscuit factories.

'So what do I need to do now?' I said. 'I mean, should I go to meetings every week or what should I do?'

'We do have meetings, yes,' said Miss Larkin. 'And socials. And we're planning an outing to Wicklow in a few weeks.'

'Wicklow?' I said. I'd never been to Wicklow. I've only ever seen the mountains there from Dublin Bay.

'But,' Miss Larkin gave me a keen look with her eagle-like eyes, 'the most important thing isn't going to meetings. It's standing by your sister and brother workers, and knowing they'll stand by you if you need them. Do you understand?'

'I do, sure,' I said, and then blushed because I hadn't sounded solemn enough. But Miss Larkin didn't seem to mind.

'Good,' she said. 'I'm sure I'll see you soon, Miss Rafferty. Will you be at the Croydon Park fête on Monday? Our new recreation grounds in Fairview?'

'I will,' I said. Miss Larkin nodded and went back to her papers. I knew I was dismissed, but I had one more question.

'My friend works in a shop,' I said. 'Just the local shop, you know. Tobacco and tins and that. Can she join the union too?'

'Of course she can.' Miss Larkin looked a little outraged at the idea that she would exclude anyone from the union. 'As my brother wrote last week, all workers have the right to be represented.'

And that was when I finally realised that D.L. was the sister of Big Jim Larkin, the union leader. You'd think it would have hit me before now, but I had been quite nervous ever since I walked into the building.

'Thanks very much, Miss Larkin,' I said, 'I'll tell her that,' but she was already focused on her papers.

I scuttled out of the room, gently closing the door behind me. Then I took a deep breath and looked down at the little red badge gleaming on my lapel. I was part of the union! And with a bit of luck, soon Samira would be part of it too. As I made my way down the big wide staircase and through the entrance hall, where the men now seemed too busy to take any notice of me at all, I felt myself holding my head a little higher.

# Chapter Seven

Last night Samira and I went to the theatre, and I wish I could be with her now to talk to her about everything that happened. But it's Sunday afternoon now and I'm in my bedroom hiding from Little Robbie. This isn't how I wanted to spend the day. As soon as I woke up this morning I wanted to hurry over to see Samira before we all went to Mass. I wouldn't get a chance in the afternoon. I knew the whole family were going over to Samira's nanny in Ringsend for dinner this afternoon.

But first thing this morning, Robert Hessian came over to our house with Little Robbie in his arms, looking even redder in the face than usual. (Little Robbie, I mean, not Robert Hessian. Robert Hessian looked as boring as he usually does.)

'Where's Lily?' says Ma. And Robert Hessian looks all embarrassed and mumbles something about her having a bilious stomach which means she's lying in bed getting sick into a po. There's something going around the area, half the Hennessys have had it and so did Lily's friend Maggie Sorohan who lives in Northbrook Avenue. Her kids had it too. Of course, this meant Lily couldn't go to Mass and Robert Hessian can't be expected to look after Little Robbie on his own, or even at all as far as I can tell, and his old mammy says she can't run around after the baby on account of her legs.

We were late setting out for the church because we had to get Little Robbie into his coat, so I couldn't walk there with Samira and Ali. And when Samira found me outside the church afterwards,

Little Robbie started roaring his head off before we could do more than say hello to each other, and then Auntie Maisie and Ali appeared and took Samira off to Ringsend. Then Eddie and Da went off to some union picnic-meeting thing, and me and Ma had to take Little Robbie home.

This is a long way of saying that I am currently lying on my bed with my pile of paper and a new pencil. I am meant to be looking after Little Robbie, but he's just crawling around the back garden looking at woodlice, so far be it from me to disturb him. I can just check on him by sticking my head out the window every so often to make sure he's still alive and hasn't eaten any woodlice or got stuck in the fence or anything. And I'm going to keep writing as long as I can, because I want to write about what happened yesterday.

I was excited all day because of the trip to the theatre. I'd called into Samira on my way to work in the morning and when I went in, there was Auntie Maisie, chatting away to Samira over a tin of Mr Casey's tobacco, which she'd just been buying for him.

'I'll have it waiting for him when he gets home,' she said. 'So he won't be able to give out too much about us leaving him and Ali to fend for themselves this evening.'

'He doesn't mind us going, does he?' Samira looked a bit worried as she fingered the red union badge that she'd pinned to her blouse. Mrs McGrath had closed the shop early the day before, and Samira had gone into town and joined the union. 'He hasn't said anything to me.'

'Ah, don't be worrying, he was only joking,' said Auntie Maisie. 'He said the pair of them were going to starve to death without my cooking, but I know for a fact that they're going over to Ma and Billy and Fanny for their tea, and she's going to spoil them rotten, which is more than she'd ever be doing for me.'

Samira's grandma is a bit of an old battle axe, it has to be said. She adores Ali and Samira, and she fusses like mad over Mr Casey and his brother Billy, who lives with her over in Ringsend, but she's fierce hard on Auntie Maisie and Billy's wife Fanny sometimes. Maisie says she's the sort of woman who thinks her sons can do no wrong but that her daughters – or daughters-in-law – are always at fault. I'm glad Ma isn't like that. Though I have to say it'd be pretty hard for her to think boys are perfect with a son like Eddie.

Anyway, having been reassured, Samira turned to me, her eyes shining.

'I was going to wait to tell you until we were at the theatre but I can't keep it to myself,' she said. 'I'm going to have an audition tonight!'

'You're what?' I couldn't believe it.

'Now, calm down, Sam.' There was a warning note in Auntie Maisie's voice. 'It's not exactly an audition. God love you, I wish I'd never told you now.'

'It's practically an audition,' said Samira. 'Mr Garland called over after I'd gone to bed last night ...'

'Don't you be looking at me like that, Mrs McGrath,' said Auntie Maisie to the older woman, who had paused while arranging some tins on the shelf behind the counter. 'It was a perfectly respectable visit. My brother was right there with me.'

'I don't know what you mean, Maisie Casey,' said Mrs McGrath with a sniff, and turned back to her tins.

'Anyway!' said Samira. 'He called over and he told Auntie Maisie that some director fella she used to know is going to be at the play this evening, and he's putting on the pantomime at the Majestic this year and he wants Maisie to be in it and he might let me do some recitations for him. And as well as pantomimes, he puts on Shakespeare plays!'

I stared at Samira, my eyes wide. 'That's marvellous!'

Auntie Maisie was starting to look worried. 'It'd be marvellous if it was as simple as that. But it isn't that simple, as I've been trying to tell your silly friend all morning. I wish I hadn't even said anything now.'

'What is it, then?' I asked, confused.

Auntie Maisie sighed. 'When Tommy told me about this director fella being there – Arthur Farrell, his name is, I knew him back in the old days – I happened to ask if I could tell him about Samira's acting skills. Tommy said that of course I could and that Mr Farrell might even let her try out for him.' She turned to Samira and sounded as severe as is possible for Maisie. 'But he didn't promise anything and we don't even know what Mr Farrell thought and you can't get your hopes up!'

'I know, I know!' said Samira, but her eyes were shining and you could tell she was already seeing herself up on the stage, playing Juliet. I couldn't blame her. Meeting a real director would be a dream come true for Samira. I was delighted for her, and I set off for town with a skip in my step.

Even though Saturdays at Lawlor's are busy, there's something about early closing day that always puts the staff in a good mood. The other thing that puts us in a good mood is that Wobbly doesn't work on Saturdays. She spends the day at home playing the piano for her widowed mammy in a little house off the South Circular Road. It was Annie who told us about Wobbly's domestic arrangements – Wobbly certainly wouldn't be telling us about them herself. Annie only knows about the widowed mammy and the piano because one time back in March Wobbly was sick and Annie was sent to her house on the orders of the mysterious Mr Lawlor himself to deliver some bread and cakes to her sickbed. Or at least to her house – she didn't get anywhere near the actual bed. Old Mrs Warby took the parcel from Annie and gave her a cup of tea in their front parlour. Annie says she really was a nice old thing, so Lord knows where her daughter gets her nastiness from.

Anyway, the day seemed to fly by – at least as fast as it can when you're on your feet selling buns all day – until there I was in the cubby hole, putting my work things on my hook and bit of a shelf. I wish I'd been able to bring in another frock to change into for the theatre, but I suppose the best thing you can say about our uniforms is that at least they're just black dresses. I mean, once you take the apron and cap off no one could tell you were wearing a uniform. And I'd brought my favourite blue ribbon, the one Lily and Robert Hessian gave me for my birthday a few months ago, to tie in my hair, so I wouldn't look like I was going to a funeral.

'Look at you, all style and Johnny Idle!' Rosie grinned as I carefully tied the bow. 'I'll see you at the union fête on Monday, right?' Monday is a bank holiday so there's no work for us, thank heaven.

'I don't have a choice,' I said. 'Da hasn't stopped talking about it.'

'Ah, it'll be great fun,' said Rosie. 'Girls like us swanning about a fancy big house! Aren't you glad you joined the union?' And she gave me a wink as she headed down towards Mary Street.

I didn't have time to go home and back again to the theatre

before the play started, so to kill time I decided to take a walk over to St Stephen's Green and eat a bread and cheese roll that I'd taken from the leftovers tray (I decided that it was all right to keep it to myself today rather than give it to the dishwashers because I wasn't going home for my tea and I needed to eat something before the play). I've only ever been to Stephen's Green twice in my life because our ma says it's too far to walk to, and even though I work just over the bridge from it now, I'm always too tired after work to go all the way there. When I was leaving I asked Rosie if she wanted to take a trip to Stephen's Green with me, but she shook her head.

'Ma's awful bad again,' she said. 'I need to make sure Francis is all right. He's getting fierce peaky. I don't know if she's feeding him properly.'

It gives me a funny sick feeling when Rosie talks about her ma. No one but Rosie and her sister seems to care that her ma is not able to look after herself, let alone look after Francis.

After Rosie had gone and I said goodbye to Annie, who said she wished she could go to the theatre too, I headed across the river and past Trinity College. Rosie, who knows everything, once told me that they let girls study there now, but if they do they certainly aren't girls like me. I crossed the road and walked up Grafton Street, which was still heaving with vehicles and people. I was getting a bit tired by then, and I was looking forward to having a nice sit down on a bench by the lake in the park, when I noticed a group of girls standing on the pavement outside what looked like a café.

They didn't look like the sort of girls who'd be patronising such a grand place. They looked like the sort of girls who'd be working in it. But if so, why weren't they in it? It was clearly open. Did their employer allow them to hang around outside the front of the café? Old Wobbly would have plenty to say if we ever tried that.

But then I noticed that one of them had a little red badge on the lapel of her jacket. And as I came closer, I saw that another girl did too. And another. In fact, they all did. Just then, a well-dressed woman swept past them and into the café. As she did so, she looked at the girls with contempt.

'You ungrateful creatures should be ashamed of yourselves!'

The girls looked at each other as the door swung shut behind her and then burst out laughing. I had to talk to them.

''Scuse me,' I said, tapping one of the girls on the shoulder. 'What are you doing?'

She grinned at me. She reminded me a bit of Rosie, though she was thinner and paler. 'What do you think? We've been locked out!'

Then she noticed the badge on my lapel and her grin became wider. 'Is that the red-hand badge I see? Then surely you know about us Savoy chocolate girls? Miss Larkin's been a great help to us.'

I felt my cheeks flush. I knew I should have read the Women Workers' column in the *Irish Worker* properly.

'Actually,' I said, 'I've only just joined the union. I haven't even gone to a meeting or anything yet.'

'Well, we're out here because them in there,' she jerked a thumb towards the café front, 'are making us work in a rat-infested factory down the road. They tried to dock our wages, and when us union girls started kicking up a fuss, they locked us out.'

'What does that mean?' I was confused. I knew about strikes, of course. Da's been on a few already. But I hadn't heard of people being locked out before. At least, I didn't think I had. As I said before, I haven't always paid much attention when Da talked about the union.

'They said we couldn't be part of the union *and* keep our jobs,' said the girl. 'We had to choose. And of course we chose the union. So then they locked us out of our jobs. Not literally,' she added, noticing how I glanced towards the front door of the café, looking for a lock and chain. 'It means we can't work unless we give up the union and join the scabs.'

'Scabs?' Now I was really confused.

'You know, blacklegs,' said the girl. She laughed, but not unkindly. 'Janey, you really are new to the union game! A scab is someone who takes a striker's job – or a locked-out girl's job.' Her cheerful face hardened. 'And there's one now.'

She glowered at a nervous-looking girl who was sidling out of the front door. The girl looked so scared I felt a bit sorry for her, even though I didn't agree with her taking a job from girls who were trying to protest. I wondered if her family were starving and she needed the money to buy food for a baby like Francis. But it turned out she wasn't doing it for a starving family, because when my new companion turned to her and said, 'Do you not feel guilty, May McDermott? Would you not get a badge like this girl here, and join us?' May McDermott said, 'You know I need the money to pay for my music lessons.'

'The state of her!' said my new friend in disgust. 'Music lessons indeed. As if music lessons are worth letting down your fellow workers.'

'I suppose there must be *some* people working there because they really need the money,' I said.

'And we don't?' said the girl. 'There's some things more important than money. And fair play is one of them. My only consolation,' she added, looking more cheerful, 'is that all them scabs will be eating chocolate that the horrible rats have been dancing around on.'

'They've been *what*?' I couldn't hide my horror.

'Oh it's true,' said the girl. She shuddered. 'I've seen the creatures getting right in the trays with their horrible little feet. And after the scabs have eaten the ratty chocolates, with a bit of luck they'll get sick and die roaring. And good enough for them.' She sounded quite fierce, but I suppose I couldn't blame her. I'd probably be that angry too, if I'd had to work with a load of rats. Whatever you can say about Lawlor's, it's always clean. Then I remembered they sold Savoy chocolates in a few shops round our way. I've bought them myself sometimes, when I had a few pennies to spend on treats.

'Did the rats really get in the chocolate?' I asked, feeling queasy at the thought. 'You're not just joking me?'

'Would I lie to a fellow union girl?' said the striker. 'Half rat droppings, some of the batches must have been.' She shuddered. 'Anyway, old McMurty would rather lock us out than get rid of those rats, and I hope he chokes on his own ratty sweets.'

'Well, thanks for letting me know,' I said. 'I'll tell people not to buy them.'

'Good on you,' said the girl.

Another girl who was standing closer to the door said, 'Maggie, come here, I need to ask you something.'

'Maybe I'll see you at Liberty Hall,' said the girl called Maggie, and hurried over to join her friend. I continued up the road towards the Green, thinking about the locked-out girls. I wondered if I could be as brave as them. If Wobbly told me I had to choose between the union and my job, would I definitely choose the union? And then I thought of Rosie, and Kitty, and the Savoy girls working surrounded by rats, and I knew that for employers to force that choice on anyone was wrong.

By the time I reached St Stephen's Green I was hot and confused and needed a rest. So I found a bench near the pavilion by the lake and leaned back. The sun was still bright and warm, and even though I could hear a faint rumble of traffic outside the Green, it was quiet and peaceful in there. There was a girl with a woman in a uniform who must have been her nanny or something, standing at the edge of the pond throwing bread to the ducks. I wonder if I'd been able to stay in school, would I have had the energy to go feeding ducks in the afternoon? But I didn't want to think about what might have been. I was comfortable and sleepy and I had a play to look forward to. And then I heard a clock ring seven and I realised I'd better go and meet Auntie Maisie and Samira at the theatre.

Samira was bouncing on the balls of her feet with excitement when I saw her outside the theatre, surrounded by bustling crowds of fellow audience members making their way into the entrance lobby. As soon as I got to her, she grabbed my arms.

'You're here! Maisie's gone round to the stage door to get our tickets from Mr Garland.'

'Where's the director fella?' I said. 'Will he be sitting with us?'

'Oh, we won't see him until afterwards. Mr Garland's going to take us all backstage to meet him!' Samira hugged herself with glee. 'I can't wait! I'm going to do that Portia speech from *The Merchant of Venice*.'

It was a good choice. I've seen her do that speech before loads of times, and she really is good at it.

'There you are, Miss Betty!' Auntie Maisie had arrived, three tickets in her hand. 'Come on, let's get our seats.'

'Do you think we'll get a seat near the front?' Samira asked, as we followed Auntie Maisie into the lobby and, after our tickets were inspected, down a red-carpeted corridor and up a flight of stairs towards the gods. The gods are a section of the theatre right up the very top, with these rows of big hard benches. It's so high up that when you edge your way along the row you feel like you might fall all the way down to the stalls, and even when you sit down you sometimes feel all giddy and sick as you look down on the stage. It's not always the best view. If the actors stand at the very front of the stage you can only really see the tops of the heads, but you can hear everything all right. Because there are no individual seats, you've got to hope you can get a decent spot on the benches.

'As a matter of fact, we're not in the gods this evening.' Auntie Maisie turned to us and grinned. 'I don't know how he did it, but good old Tommy's managed to get us into the upper circle.'

That was a real treat. Whenever Maisie's got us into the theatre before, we've always been in the gods. And even though I do appreciate getting to go to a show at all, it would be marvellous to have a proper view of the stage. To say nothing of a cushioned seat rather than a bench.

'The circle!' Samira flung her arms around her aunt. 'Thank you, Auntie Maisie!'

Maisie laughed. 'Don't thank me, thank Tommy. And we've got another few steps to climb. It's the *upper* circle, remember?'

But it still gave us a much better view than the gods ever would, and it was much more comfortable too. Soon we were ensconsed in red plush seats, and though we were sitting towards the back of the circle, we were right in the middle of the row. We peered down at the stalls as the rest of the audience settled into their seats. Next to me, Samira was almost vibrating with anticipation. She clutched my hand.

'We're here!' she said. 'We're actually going to see *Romeo and Juliet*!'

'I bet they'll have nothing on the pair of us in my back garden,' I said, and grinned at her. I don't think I've ever seen her so excited.

'Well,' said Samira, and there was real determination in her voice, 'if I get to audition for this director fella, it could be me up there next year.'

'Ssssh, the pair of yiz,' said Auntie Maisie. 'The lights are going down!'

And as the last few members of the audience squeezed apologetically into their seats, the lights of the theatre were indeed dimmed, and then the curtain rose.

What followed was even better than I could have thought possible. It was one thing reading Shakespeare's words on the page, or even acting them out in the back garden, but to see Romeo and Mercutio and Tybalt fooling around together on the stage, and then Juliet and her old nurse, and then Romeo meeting Juliet at the party … It was like magic, like seeing pictures in your head suddenly come to life. All the actors were so good, you forgot they were acting. At one stage I glanced over at Samira, but her entire attention was on the stage. She looked like she was under a spell.

When the first half ended we all clapped like mad, and that

was when I realised something. Samira really was as good as those actors on the stage. I'd always thought she was a great actress, of course I did, but I didn't actually have anything to compare her with. Most of what Auntie Maisie has taken us to have been musical shows, where there isn't much serious acting, if you know what I mean. And just from reading Shakespeare I knew it'd be tricky to act his plays properly. But these actors could speak Shakespeare's words and make them sound real, and I knew Samira could do that too. If she really did get a chance to audition for this Mr Farrell, she might actually get a part.

'So what do you think, girls?' said Auntie Maisie, as we shuffled out of our seats and went in search of the lav.

'I love it, Auntie Maisie,' said Samira. 'I really, really love it.' And for a second I thought she was going to cry with happiness.

'I always thought I'd do a good job at that nurse,' said Auntie Maisie. 'Once I got too old to play Juliet, of course.'

I hadn't expected this. 'I didn't think you went in for that sort of acting.' As far as I knew, Auntie Maisie spent all her time on the stage singing and dancing, rather than performing in the likes of *Romeo and Juliet*.

She shrugged her shoulders. 'Ah, you know. I wouldn't have minded getting a chance at it.' Then she flashed us her usual bright smile. 'But of course I wouldn't have done as much singing then, and the people of Dublin would have been deprived of my beautiful voice. Now come on, girls, let's find the ladies' convenience, and if we've time I'll get you a lemonade.'

We barely made it back to our seats before the curtain went up for the second half of the play. By the time Romeo and Juliet were both lying dead in their tomb, we were all crying. And when the curtains came down and the cast emerged to take their bows, I clapped so much my hands hurt. As for Samira, I thought she was going to burst, she looked so happy, and she clapped louder than anyone in the theatre.

Then it was all over, and the audience were streaming down the stairs, and Auntie Maisie was taking us back through a corridor we hadn't noticed before, and then down a back stairs with none of the plush and gilt of the rest of the theatre. We went down another corridor, whose grey-painted walls were scuffed and had strange objects leaning against them. Auntie Maisie kept up a stream of chatter. 'That's a light filter girls; it's how they make the stage look like it's morning or late at night … The costume department is down that way …' But Samira didn't say anything at all. Her face had slowly lost its magic glow and she looked tense instead. I reached for her hand and squeezed. Samira squeezed back.

Eventually we found ourselves in an area where ropes hung down from somewhere high above and I realised we were actually at the side of the stage. I looked through the hanging ropes and there it was, the space where the actors had talked and fought and pretended to die just a few minutes ago. It was dimly lit now, with the heavy red curtains between it and all the seats in the theatre.

'Tommy said he'd meet us here,' said Auntie Maisie. 'With Mr Farrell. Oh, there they are!' A radiant smile spread across her face as Mr Garland came striding across the empty stage, accompanied by a tall man in what even I could tell was a well-cut suit (maybe I've inherited Ma's eye for dressmaking).

'Well, Miss Casey,' said the tall man. His eyes sparkled as he took Auntie Maisie's hand and kissed it. He actually kissed it! Like someone out of a book. I glanced quickly at Mr Garland, but he didn't seem to mind. I suppose people are more casual about these things in the theatre. 'How wonderful to see you again.'

'Likewise, Mr Farrell,' said Maisie. She gestured towards me and Samira. 'May I present to you my niece, Samira Casey, and her friend Betty Rafferty.'

She was doing her special grand lady voice, the one she does to make us all laugh. But I didn't feel like laughing now. I felt nervous. I could only imagine how Samira felt. Mr Farrell turned to us and did a little bow. No one has ever bowed to me before, apart from Samira when we were acting out scenes and that doesn't count.

'How do you do, Miss Samira? Miss Rafferty?' We each mumbled 'Grand, thanks' as Mr Farrell smiled warmly at us and turned to Mr Garland. 'So, Tommy, where should we have our little chat?'

'Right this way,' said Mr Garland, and he led us around the back of the picture that hung at the rear of the stage ('That's the backdrop,' whispered Auntie Maisie), down yet another corridor and into a large room with a counter running along one wall and a big mirror above it. There was a rail in one corner with some clothes hangers on it, and a lot of wooden chairs pushed under the counter.

'We use this for overflow when a show has a big chorus,' said Mr Garland, whatever that meant. He pulled out some chairs. 'Why don't you sit down, girls?'

We sat.

'So Miss Casey,' said Mr Farrell.

'Oh, call me Maisie. You used to, back in the old days.'

I have to say, you'd never guess Auntie Maisie was forty. Not when she smiles like that.

'Maisie, then.' Mr Farrell smiled back at her. 'The Dublin stage hasn't been the same since you left. I still hear people talking about your Fairy Godmother in Cinderella back in '95. Magical. Simply magical.'

'Get away with you,' said Auntie Maisie, but I could tell she was pleased.

'I know you had good reason to leave the stage,' Mr Farrell went on. 'And it does you credit that you wanted to look after your family. But when Tommy told me that your niece and nephew had left school and were out working, just after I'd decided to do Cinderella for this year's pantomime, well, I'm not going to lie, Maisie. It felt like fate.'

'Did it now?' said Auntie Maisie.

'Is there any way I can tempt you back to the theatre?' Mr Farrell's tone was pleading. 'It's a wonderful part and the money's not bad – twice what you'd have got back then.'

'I don't know,' said Auntie Maisie, looking down at her hands in their pristine white gloves. 'My dancing's a bit rusty these days. And the Fairy Godmother has to do all that spinning …'

Mr Farrell's smile faltered. 'Ah, I wouldn't expect you to do that, Maisie,' he said. 'I was thinking of you for the wicked stepmother.'

Maisie's expression froze for a split second. 'The stepmother?' I could hear the tension in her voice. 'The *old lady*?'

'We're going in a new direction with her this year, Maisie.' Mr Farrell seemed to be in earnest. 'We're making *her* the jealous one, not the stepsisters. She's Cinderella's rival. We're going to make the audience think the prince might fall in love with her instead.'

'You'd better not be putting me on.' Auntie Maisie's smile was no longer so radiant.

'Of course not,' said Mr Farrell, and I have to say he sounded genuine. 'Why would I get Miss Maisie Casey in to play an old hag? I want someone who could realistically have two grown-up daughters, but who's young and beautiful enough to be Cinderella's rival. It'll be a new twist on the old story.'

And then Auntie Maisie laughed. 'You auld flatterer,' she said. 'Send me the script.'

Mr Farrell relaxed in his hard wooden chair and smiled with relief.

'You won't regret this, Maisie,' he said. 'I have to go to London tomorrow to see about a director, but I'll be back in September and we can talk about it then.'

'Now, mister, I haven't said I'll do it yet,' said Auntie Maisie, but she was still smiling. 'And now, Arthur, I want to talk to you about Samira.'

'Samira? Of course, your niece.' Mr Farrell gave a friendly nod in our direction.

'She's a good little actress, so she is.' There was no laughter or flirtation in Auntie Maisie's voice now. She was deadly serious. 'And she can sing like a nightingale. And dance. But the acting – I'm telling you, Arthur, she's better than I ever was.'

'I'm not surprised Maisie Casey has such a talented niece,' said Mr Farrell politely.

'So I'd like you to let her do her piece for you,' Auntie Maisie went on. 'Just see if there's anything you can give her.'

Mr Farrell's smile looked a little forced but he said, 'Well, how can I say no to my favourite Wicked Stepmother?' He turned to Samira. 'Do you really want to go on the stage, Miss Samira?'

Samira took a deep breath. Then she sat up tall in her hard

wooden chair and said, 'More than anything else in the whole world, Mr Farrell.'

Mr Farrell laughed. 'Well then. Let's see what you can do.'

Samira stood up and as she did so, she suddenly stopped looking like a girl from the North Strand who daydreamed a lot and who had to leave school and work in a newsagent's. She looked like a noblewoman who was determined to save the man she loved. She launched into Portia's 'The quality of mercy' speech from *The Merchant of Venice*, and I'd never heard her do it so well. I think we were all entranced, even Mr Farrell.

When she'd finished and sat down again there was a pause before we all clapped and Mr Farrell said, 'Well, that was very good. Very good indeed. Well done.' He smiled warmly at Samira.

'Thank you, sir,' said Samira. 'So ... do you think you could give me a part?'

Mr Farrell looked surprised. 'In the pantomime? Well, I'd have to see you dance for that, and hear you sing. But even if you were a veritable Lily Langtry – or a Maisie Casey' – here he nodded graciously at Auntie Maisie – 'I'm afraid we've already cast the chorus, and the understudies too. In fact, it's all cast, apart from the stepmother. But if you come and see me next year I'm sure we can do something ...'

'Now isn't that good news?' Auntie Maisie beamed. Samira was beaming too. But she had even bigger plans.

'Thank you, sir,' she said. 'That'd be very good of you.' She took a deep breath. 'But there's something else I wanted to ask. Auntie Maisie told me that you put on touring productions of Shakespeare in the summer as well as the panto in the winter. And, well, I was hoping you could give me a chance in your company next summer. I've read all of Shakespeare, sir, everything they had in the library.'

'She has,' I confirmed. 'Even *Troilus and Cressida*.'

'Good heavens,' said Mr Farrell.

'Of course I'm not expecting to play Juliet or Cordelia straight away,' Samira went on. 'I'm not stupid or anything. I know I'd just have to be one of the crowd on stage for years and years. But I could do it, if you'd only give me a chance in one of your Shakespeare productions.'

Mr Farrell shifted uncomfortably in his seat. 'I don't doubt your determination, Miss Samira. But I don't think you're quite right for Shakespeare.' He paused as if gathering his thoughts. 'Maybe you should … focus your ambitions on other aspects of the theatre.'

I didn't know what he meant. And I could tell that Samira, like me, was torn between the need to be polite to this powerful man and the desire to demand an explanation.

'What do you mean, sir?' she said, as nicely as she could.

'Well, there's your voice,' said Mr Farrell. He looked down at his hands and I realised he was embarrassed. 'You'd need to take elocution lessons. For quite some time.'

'I can do that,' said Samira quickly.

'Of course she can,' said Auntie Maisie, in her grandest voice which doesn't sound at all like her usual one. 'I can teach her.'

'And no better woman,' smiled Mr Farrell. 'But …' He turned to Samira again. 'I know from your surname that your father must be Maisie's brother. But where was your mother from? Italy? Greece?' There was a pause. 'Spain?' He looked up at the ceiling.

'India,' said Samira, looking him straight in the face.

'Ah,' said Mr Farrell, looking down at his hands or maybe at his feet. Anywhere but into Samira's eyes. 'Well, I'm sorry my dear, I really don't think Shakespeare will suit you. Not on the stage. Good practice, of course, learning the speeches and that. But do keep in touch about next year's pantomime. We might be doing the *Arabian Nights*. I'm sure we could find something for you in that.'

He stood up, and this was clearly the sign that the evening was at an end because Auntie Maisie and Mr Garland rose too.

'I'll send you that script tomorrow, Maisie,' Mr Farrell said. 'Tommy gave me your address.'

'You do that, Arthur,' said Maisie politely, but her eyes kept moving over to where Samira was still sitting in her wooden chair, her face stiff. 'Come on, girls.'

We all said our goodbyes and Auntie Maisie led the way out of the theatre, leaving Mr Garland and Mr Farrell behind.

'Well!' Auntie Maisie's tone was bright. Too bright. 'Next Christmas panto season it'll be you up on the stage, Miss Samira.'

But Samira didn't say anything.

'We'll get a tram home,' said Auntie Maisie. 'I'm paying.' And I couldn't even protest. We walked to the tram stop in silence and luckily the last tram pulled up just as we arrived. It wasn't until we'd got off the tram at the end of Bayview Avenue that Samira spoke.

'I *was* good at Shakespeare. I know I was.'

'Of course you were,' I said.

Auntie Maisie squeezed Samira's arm.

'You were, love. As good as anyone on that stage. But I told you not to get your hopes up. It wasn't likely at all that he'd give you a

Shakespeare part. Not straight away.'

'But he said I just wasn't *right* for Shakespeare. That I'd never be right.' For the first time I thought Samira might start to cry. 'But I was *good*.'

'Good at what? Acting the maggot?' said a familiar, cheerful voice.

We looked around and saw Ali walking towards us. 'What's wrong with you, Sam? Still crying over *Romeo and Juliet*?'

'Where have you been 'til this hour?' said Auntie Maisie, crossly.

'Union meeting,' said Ali. 'How was the play?'

'He said I wasn't right for Shakespeare,' said Samira.

'*Who* did?' Ali was bemused. 'What are you talking about?'

So Samira told him. Ali's jaw tightened, just as Samira's had earlier.

'Listen to me,' he said, gripping both of Samira's shoulders and looking straight into her eyes. 'I wouldn't say this if I didn't have to. Don't let anyone make you believe you couldn't play one of them Shakespeare parts. I've heard you do those speeches.' He gave her one of his lop-sided grins, even though his tone was serious. 'It's not like you gave me a choice!'

Did I see a hint of a smile on Samira's face? I hoped I did.

'If he doesn't think you can play Juliet or whatserface, the "quality of mercy" lawyer woman, that's his fault,' Ali went on. 'He's the one who's missing out. I bet you could do a better job than whoever he's got doing Juliet right now.'

Samira sniffed. 'She was really good.'

'Yes, well. So are you.' Ali let go of her shoulders and put his arm around her. He glanced over at me and Auntie Maisie. 'Come on, let's go home.'

They set off across the road, and as if in unspoken agreement me and Auntie Maisie stood back and let them walk on together. Sometimes Ali understands how Samira is feeling better than anyone else. Including me. Including Auntie Maisie. The pair of them waited outside my house to say goodnight to me, though.

'You're going to the fête on Monday, aren't you?' I said.

''Course we are,' said Ali. 'Aren't we, Sam? Got to show our pride in the union.' And then they went home, with Maisie walking thoughtfully behind them.

I've got my own latchkey since I started work so I let myself in. Da had gone to bed but Ma was still sitting up in the kitchen, hemming a skirt by the light of the oil lamp. I told her about the play and Auntie Maisie being offered the part of the wicked stepmother, and Ma looked a little bit disapproving and said, 'I thought Maisie Casey had given up all that stage nonsense.' I didn't say anything about Samira. I pointed at the skirt in her lap. 'What's that? Are you working?'

'I've got to get this finished for Mrs Lawlor.' She yawned and stretched her arms above her head. 'But you'd better get up to bed. It's long past your bedtime.'

It took me a long time to get to sleep, even though I sneaked Earnshaw into my room and let him sleep all curled up at the end of the bed, which I usually find very comforting. I wonder how long it took Samira.

# Chapter Eight

When I wrote my last chapter, Samira looked heartbroken, and I was feeling bad for her. And though of course she's still smarting from the awful encounter with Mr Farrell, which none of us will forget in a hurry, something happened at the Croydon Park Bank Holiday fête yesterday that gave her a bit of hope as regards her career as a serious actress. But I'm getting ahead of myself as usual.

I love bank holidays. It's like a Sunday because you don't have to go to school or go to work, but unlike a Sunday you don't have to get up early and go to Mass before eating any breakfast. This morning, however, I didn't get to sleep in, because I was woken up by Da singing.

Da doesn't sing very often. He's got a sort of growly voice and he once told me that years ago, when he was at school, one of the Brothers told him his voice was so bad that he should just mime the words when they were singing at Mass. Which I think is a terrible thing to say to anyone. It's not like God cares whether you're in tune or not. Anyway, it put Da off singing for life. He doesn't even do a song at Christmas parties when everyone gets up to do a turn (even Ma sings 'The Mountains of Mourne', and very nicely she sings it too. She particularly likes it because even though the mountains of Mourne are up in Antrim, the song is about the view from the harbour in Skerries, near where her parents live).

But anyway, this morning Da was singing away like anything. It wasn't even that loud, but once I woke up I couldn't get back to sleep again, and Earnshaw was awake too and was starting to scrabble at the bedroom door, so I wrapped an old cardigan around myself and went down to the kitchen, where Da was shaving himself in front of the little mirror he keeps on the shelf above the sink.

'Morning, pet,' he said. 'You're up early on a bank holiday.'

'Not by choice,' I said, but I wasn't giving out to him. 'What was that song you were singing?'

'Ah,' said Da. 'That was "The red hand badge".' It's by some union fella called Wilson. Not bad, isn't it?'

Well, I couldn't tell if it was or not because of Da's tuneless singing. But I didn't tell him this. It might remind him of the Brothers and how nasty they were to him.

'Are people going to be singing it later?' I asked.

'They might be,' said Da with a grin. 'Now, how's about a cup of tea? Two trade unionists together.'

'All right, then,' I said. And I sat down at the table with Earnshaw sitting on my feet. Da makes the best pot of tea in the house. Ma never puts in enough leaves and Eddie puts in too many so it's like a bitter stew. But Da's tea is just right.

'Go out to the cold press and check the milk is all right,' said Da, as the kettle boiled. 'It should be grand, but ...'

I unbolted the back door and unlocked the cold press, which is in a shady corner near the water pipe. I've never seen anyone talk about cold presses in a book, so in case they're only in Dublin and my readers live in a place that doesn't have them, a cold press is like a cupboard where you keep food that needs to be kept as cold as possible. On the very rare occasions we have meat in the house for longer than a day, that's where it goes.

Same with milk. There was a full jug of milk that Ma had got in the dairy down in East Wall on Saturday. I gave it a sniff and it smelled like it was almost on the turn, but not enough that it'd spoil the tea. By the time I carried it back inside, the teapot was on the table with the cosy on it that I had knitted Ma for her birthday two years ago. It's all striped because I knitted it out of odd bits of wool but I think it looks quite good.

'You know,' said Da, putting the cups on the table. 'I haven't had a chance to say it properly, but I'm fierce proud of you for joining the union.'

'Eddie isn't,' I said. Eddie's been making what he considers to be hilarious jokes about 'union girls' playing at politics.

'Eddie's only codding you,' said Da. 'Deep down he knows you're doing the right thing.'

'Well,' I said. 'I haven't even gone to a meeting yet.'

'It's the spirit of the thing,' said Da. 'That's more important than meetings. If you have to come out for the other girls, then you will.'

I told him about meeting the Savoy Café girls.

'I feel bad I didn't know about them before,' I said. 'I never really paid any attention.'

'Sure, why would you?' said Da. 'You were a schoolgirl two months ago.'

'I know, but still,' I said. 'You talked enough about the union. I just didn't really listen to what you were saying.'

Da laughed. 'And do you think I paid heed to what my da said when I was your age?' He poured a bit of tea into his cup to see if it was brewed yet. It wasn't so he poured it back into the pot. 'I'm glad you weren't bothering your head about that sort of thing before. You got to have a bit of a childhood, which is more than some childer around here get. But now you're out working, it's good that you're standing with your fellows. Better late than never, what?'

'Yeah, I suppose so,' I said. Suddenly I was ravenous. I looked at the dresser where there was half a loaf of bread wrapped up in brown paper. 'Why don't I make us some toast while we wait for that tea to brew?'

I hadn't realised how bad I felt about my ignorance until I had that chat with Da. But after talking to him, I felt a lot better. And I felt pretty cheerful as I washed and got dressed in my best frock, until I remembered Samira, and the look on her face when we were going home. I thought we'd walk up to Croydon Park together and have a proper chat, but Da wanted our whole family to get there as soon as the fête opened because he wanted to talk to some union fella or other.

'And it means we won't miss the tea and buns,' he said, with a wink. 'I'd say the locusts of Egypt will have nothing on the union crowd when they see the refreshments.'

'No one in this family needs to go scrabbling for tea and buns,' said Ma, a little primly. 'We're all perfectly well fed at home.'

'It'll be nice to drink of cup of tea we didn't have to make ourselves, though,' said Da. Then he winked at Ma. 'Not that anyone makes a better cup of tea than you, Margaret.'

He put his arm around Ma's waist and gave her a kiss, and although she pushed him away and said 'get away with you now!' she was smiling and the prim look vanished from her face. In fact, as we set off for Croydon Park, she looked more cheerful than I'd seen her in ages, and she didn't even object when I put Earnshaw on his lead and announced that he was coming with us, even though she usually doesn't want to be seen in public with him. I realised how hard she's been working lately, and how worried and crotchety she's been. She needed a day in the sunshine surrounded by trees and grass and fun as much as any union member did.

Happily for me, who had no desire to hear Eddie's smart remarks about 'union girls', my brother wasn't with us. He was walking up with his sweetheart Mary Lennon (Ma says they'll be married before the year is out. Though if they do get married, I'm not sure where they'll live. There certainly isn't room for two people on our front-room sofa). Unhappily for me, Little Robbie was with us instead. Though at least I didn't have to look after him – Lily had recovered from her mysterious bilious complaint so she was pushing the pram. She'd tucked an old rug into the end for us to sit on and have our picnic later.

It wasn't long before we were at the entrance to Croydon House. I'd seen the entrance before, of course, with its little lodge at the gates, and I knew there was a big house up there some-where. But I'd never gone through the gates, and after Da had paid the friendly man at the gate tuppence entrance fee for each of us and we were walking up the grand, winding tree-lined drive, I felt like I was passing into another world. How was it possible that this leafy place was just a short walk from our house? The walls of the garden cut out the noise of the street and the air was fresh and clean. Earnshaw was running around trying to sniff everything. All the plants must have been a nice novelty for him.

'You could hang your washing out here without getting any smuts on it,' said Ma wistfully. And she was right. There were three train lines within a mile of those gates, but somehow none of the soot from the train made it into this garden. Maybe all the trees around the perimeter caught it before it could blow as far as the drive.

I was so entranced by the peaceful scene I didn't even care when Ma told me to take over the pram so Lily could have a rest. I pushed Little Robbie all the way up the drive and right to the steps of a house so big it made the Lawlors' place look like a little cottage. It was a grand pale building with extra wings sticking out on each side. We were all a bit dumbstruck by the sight of this mansion. Even Little Robbie stopped grizzling for a bit.

Then a vaguely familiar figure came striding out of the front door and down the steps towards us. 'If it isn't John Rafferty!' he cried cheerfully, raising his hand in greeting. 'I saw you from the window.'

That was when I realised it was the nice man who had shown me the way to Miss Larkin's office at Liberty Hall.

'I should have known you'd be here!' said Da, returning the man's beam. The two of them shook hands. 'Margaret, girls, this is my pal Tom Daly, the finest docker in Dublin town.'

'Pleased to meet you,' said Ma in her most refined voice, accepting Mr Daly's hand.

'And this is my daughter Betty,' said Da.

'I think we've met before,' said Mr Daly. 'Are you a union woman?'

'I only joined the other week,' I admitted.

'Sure, it makes no difference when you join, as long as you do join!' said Mr Daly. 'And pay your union dues of course. Someone needs to pay for all this.' He winked at me. 'Now, who would like a cup of tea?' He glanced at Earnshaw. 'You might want to tie that magnificent beast outside.'

'Sorry, boy,' I whispered to Earnshaw. 'I'll bring you a bun.'

The rest of us followed Mr Daly up the steps and into the mansion. I'd never seen anything like it. Mr Daly noticed me gawping at the high ceilings and plaster decoration and grinned.

'Not bad, is it?' he said. 'The likes of us wouldn't have been let anywhere near this place a few years ago. But it's ours now – as long as we pay the rent.' We followed him into a large dining room, where a table was spread with doorstep sandwiches and bottles of minerals. At one end of it was a tea urn which reminded me of the one at Lawlor's. Behind the table were some cheerful women and girls, chatting to each other and to their customers. Among them, I recognised Maggie, the girl from outside the Savoy Café. She noticed me too and raised her hand in greeting before turning back to her fellow tea-servers.

'It does my heart good to see all my pals sauntering into this dining room,' Mr Daly said. 'I'll get the tea. My treat,' he added, as Da took a few shillings out of his own pocket. 'The least I can do for your family, John, after all the help you've been at meetings recently.'

I think this was the moment when it dawned on me just how well Da was thought of at the union. He looked a bit embarrassed, but he didn't contradict Mr Daly.

'You're very generous, Tom,' he said. 'We'll all have a cup of tea.' He looked at the rest of us. 'Won't we?'

We all agreed that we would. Mr Daly and Da went to the counter and the rest of us gazed around at the big fancy room.

'I never thought that the union of his would have a room like this,' said Ma, staring in wonder at the high ceiling. 'You could fit our entire house in this room.'

'See, Ma,' I grinned at her. 'This is what happens when the working men and the working women stand together!'

'Go away out of that, you,' said Ma, but she was smiling.

Five minutes later, we were all sitting out in the garden on the rug, tea cups in hand. Earnshaw was rolling around on the grass next to us.

'Well!' said Da. 'Isn't this fine?'

It was more than fine. I looked around at the rolling lawns. A band was playing merry tunes and I could see a group of men setting up a game of tug-o-war. Mothers and fathers were sitting on rugs, drinking tea and eating cakes as their children ran around, playing chasing and rolling in the grass, squealing like happy puppies. Instead of the cobbles and pavements and train tracks and lanes, we had grass and flowers and space, lots of space. I felt like someone in a book, the sort of book where people go to garden parties or play tennis and croquet on the lawn. Not that I had ever seen anyone play croquet – I only knew about it from *Alice in Wonderland*.

'And look over there!' Da nudged me and nodded towards a tall man who was striding across the lawn with a broad grin on his face. 'That's Big Jim himself!'

It was Jim Larkin, the man who'd made it his mission to raise the workers of Ireland! I knew from what Da had said that he was a tough customer, but he looked very cheerful that day, without a collar on his shirt, talking animatedly to a smaller man who ran along beside him, trying to match his long stride.

'He's a fine fellow, Big Jim,' said Da fondly. 'I wouldn't want to get on the wrong side of him, mind you.'

As Mr Larkin strode off towards the band, I saw a familiar figure coming across the lawn from the direction of the gates, a small boy toddling by her side.

'Rosie!' I cried, waving frantically.

Rosie waved back. Then she picked up the small boy and hurried up to us.

'Ma, Da, this is my friend Rosie,' I said. 'You know, the one who got me to join the union.'

'Pleased to meet you, Rosie.' Da's voice was as gruff as ever, but he was smiling.

Rosie grinned at him. 'How are you, Mr Rafferty?' She turned to Ma and gave her what was, for Rosie, a very deferential nod. 'And Mrs Rafferty.'

Ma's expression wasn't quite so warm. I had a feeling she'd have preferred it if I'd never gone near the union, and she knew it was Rosie who'd given me the idea of joining. But Ma always did have lovely manners, and she said, 'Nice to meet you, Rosie. And who's this little fella?'

'This is Francis,' said Rosie, smiling down on her brother. It was a pleasure to meet him at last. He really was a little dote. He had a lovely smiley face and curly brown hair and he looked around at all us Raffertys as if he'd known us all his life and said, 'Hallo!'

Everyone laughed, and Ma told Rosie we'd look after him if she wanted to run in and get some tea and a bun. I was worried Francis might start making strange as soon as she left, but he really is a nice friendly baby (unlike some babies I could mention). He started singing a song for us – you couldn't really tell what it was, or make out any of the words, but he was clearly having a fine old time and made us all laugh. Even Little Robbie was chuckling instead of doing his usual roaring.

By the time Rosie got back to us, Francis was like part of the family; in fact, I'd gladly have swapped him for certain members of my actual family. Ma and Da certainly liked him, and I think he made Ma warm to Rosie because she was very nice and friendly to Rosie for the rest of the afternoon. Earnshaw loved both Rosie and little Francis, and Rosie loved him right back.

'I wish we could have a dog,' she said, wrapping her arms around Earnshaw's shaggy neck and snuggling her face against him, 'but we've no room. And what would we feed him?'

After a while, Rosie took Francis off to find her sister Josie, and I went off to find Samira in the big crowd. I was passing a group of girls when one of them leaned back and bumped into me, sending me stumbling backwards. I felt my elbow connect with someone's ribs and the owner of the ribs, in a familiar voice, said, 'Hey, watch out!'

I turned around.

'Kitty?' I said.

'Oh, hello, Betty,' said Kitty, looking slightly uncomfortable. Kitty's a strange one. She's in the union so I know she believes we have to stick together, but she never wants to pal around at work. Sometimes I think she might just be shy. But I felt I should at least make an effort.

'How's your foot?' I said. She'd been limping a bit the day after the accident, but she was able to stand up so I presumed – I hoped – the scald hadn't been as bad as Annie had made me fear.

'My boot got the worst of it,' said Kitty, a little stiffly. But she must have seen that I really was concerned about her because she softened a little and said, 'I got some ointment for it. It'll get better.'

'Not a bad show, is it?' I said politely, glancing at the merry crowds thronging over the lawns.

'No,' said Kitty. She almost smiled, but not quite. 'It's just what we all need.'

I was trying to think of what to say next when I heard someone say 'Betty!'

It was Samira. She looked slightly more cheerful than last night, though that wouldn't be hard.

'Where have you been?' I said.

Samira rolled her eyes. 'Da couldn't find his union badge – he'd put it on his other cap or something. Don't ask me.' She looked at Kitty and smiled politely.

'Sorry, I'm forgetting my manners,' I said. And I made the introductions. Kitty looked puzzled at Samira's name. I knew from experience what was coming next.

'Samira?' she said. 'What sort of a name is that?'

Samira took a deep breath. 'My ma was from India.'

'Oh!' said Kitty, looking surprised. 'Where are you from?'

'The North Strand,' said Samira. 'And my da's from Ringsend.'

'Oh, right,' said Kitty.

Samira returned her gaze steadily, and Kitty's cheeks flushed.

'Sorry,' she said. 'I just haven't heard that name before.'

I know Samira's got used to hearing this sort of thing, and worse, though I wish she didn't have to. It must be very tiring to have to explain yourself all the time.

'Well, it's just like being called Kitty in some countries,' she said lightly. 'And my aunt always says it'll stand out if I go on the stage.'

'The stage?' Kitty looked intrigued – or as intrigued as she ever looks, with that reserved air of hers.

'Samira's going to be an actress,' I said proudly.

'Some day,' said Samira. 'I'm just working in a shop at the moment.'

And then Kitty said the magic words. At least, they felt magic.

'You do know about the union's dramatic company, don't you?'

Samira and I stared at each other.

'The what?' I said, stupidly.

'Some people call it the Liberty Players,' said Kitty. 'But it's really called the Irish Workers' Dramatic Company. Miss Larkin started it, I don't know, a year ago. Anyway they're all members of the women workers' and the men's union. They put on plays and concerts and things. I went to the last one and it was very good. One fella did a song that he'd won a prize for at the Feis.'

'And can anyone join?' said Samira.

'Anyone in the union can,' Kitty said. 'Are you in the union?'

Samira nodded. 'I just joined.'

'There you go, then,' said Kitty. 'You should come along to the next meeting.'

'And do they do serious plays?' said Samira, anxiously. 'Not just singing and dancing?'

'Of course they do.' Kitty's tone was indignant, for her. 'They do important Irish plays. And plays about workers. They just did a labour play called *Victims*. It was very powerful.'

'Oh!' said Samira, her eyes wide. 'Do you think I could join?'

'I suppose so,' said Kitty. 'Are you any good?'

'She's more than good,' I said.

Kitty looked at me sceptically.

'She is!' I insisted 'A big stage manager said so, and everything.'

Kitty looked at Samira. 'Is that true?'

'It's true,' said Samira, with becoming modesty.

Kitty seemed impressed, despite herself.

'Well, then she should come along to the next meeting. Wednesday night.'

'I will,' said Samira firmly.

'And now,' said Kitty, 'I need to talk to a girl I know from Scott's. You know, the flourmill out in Lucan.'

'The one Wobbly was at the other week?' Miss Warby had been talking about the new supplier ever since her visit. She was convinced their flour was vastly superior to the flour supplied by Webb's, the mill we get our flour from now.

Kitty nodded. 'Their boss is talking about locking out anyone who's in the union. We should know what's going on there if Miss Warby's going to work with them.'

As soon as she'd gone, I grabbed Samira's arm.

'Did you hear that? You can be a serious actress after all.'

'This drama company might not want me either,' said Samira, but she couldn't keep the excitement from her voice.

''Course they will,' I said, though after Mr Farrell's rejection I realised she could be right. I had to hope she was wrong, though. 'I bet they won't have anyone else as good at Shakespeare in their old company.' A thought struck me. 'I can come along with you on Wednesday if you like. Moral support and that.'

Samira pondered for a moment. 'All right,' she said. 'Thanks.'

'Sure what are friends for?' I said. 'Come on, let's go into the house and each get a bottle of minerals. They only cost a penny.'

Whatever happens at the dramatic company, Samira's mood was definitely a little brighter after our chat with Kitty. She even got on well with Rosie when they finally met face to face – I'd been a bit nervous about that. I knew that if Samira had made a wonderful new pal at Mrs McGrath's I'd have felt a bit strange about it. But when we bumped into Rosie and little Francis in the queue for the penny bottles of minerals (very good they were too), Samira smiled at Rosie and said, 'Miss Delaney, I presume!'

'In the flesh,' said Rosie with a grin. 'And you must be the famous actress Samira. Betty never stops going on about how great you are!'

'No I don't!' I protested, but I was pleased. The ice was clearly broken, and when Samira sang a silly song for Francis that made him laugh until he fell back on his bottom and rolled around in the grass, I knew Rosie was charmed. We sat on the lawn with our minerals, watching Francis try to catch a butterfly.

'Imagine if we could all live here,' said Rosie. 'And sit in this garden every single day.'

'Do you not have a garden?' said Samira.

Rosie shook her head. 'Just a yard. And you wouldn't want to be sitting out there for long. But if we could all live here, I'd sit out all the time.'

'We'd never fit in the house,' I said. 'It's big, but it's not that big.'

'We could take turns,' said Rosie. 'And one of us could live in the lodge by the gate.'

'"Make me a willow cabin at your gate,' said Samira. 'And call upon my soul within the house."'

'I like that,' said Rosie. 'Did you make it up?'

Samira shook her head. 'It's Shakespeare. From *Twelfth Night*.'

'Some day,' said Rosie, lying back on the grass and looking up at the clear blue sky, 'we'll all have gardens. Or somewhere with grass anyway. I've always wanted to have somewhere with grass.'

'That should be the new union motto,' I said. 'Gardens for all!'

And sitting there on the soft fresh grass, with the sun shining and my two best friends in the world by my side, and Francis toddling around and my own family across the way, all of us bound together by the union and the idea that everyone deserved lots of afternoons like this, I felt happier than I had since the day I left school forever.

# Chapter Nine

Something very peculiar is after happening. Actually, *several* very peculiar things are after happening, so I want to write all about them while they are still fresh in my mind. Not that I will forget this day in a hurry. When I think about the moment I saw … but I'm getting ahead of myself. I need to start from the beginning.

First of all, it was strange being back in work after the fun and excitement of the Croydon Park fête. Rosie was in a miserable mood because her ma wasn't well again, and Rosie wasn't sure she was fit to take care of little Francis. She didn't give me lots of details, but I think her mother was drinking a lot last night. I know I give out about my parents, but when I think about how hard Rosie has it with her ma, my own ma and da don't seem so bad. I don't like thinking of cheery little Francis being stuck with a ma who is too drunk to look after him properly.

Anyway, because of Rosie's worries, there was none of our usual joking around today, even at break. I did ask her if she was all right and if she wanted to talk about anything but she gave me a forced sort of smile and said, 'You're grand, Betty. I need to be quiet today if you don't mind.' So we just sat there in the cubby hole and ate our cheese scones and drank our tea in silence – or at least it was silent until Wobbly appeared. I'd already been wondering if she'd noticed the red hand on my coat but I need wonder no more because as soon as she saw us her face darkened. (That's a good dramatic phrase, isn't it? I got it out of a book but I can't remember which one.)

'I've been meaning to talk to you, Miss Rafferty,' she said. 'I hope you're not getting involved in anything that might damage your prospects at this firm.'

I tried to swallow my bite of scone. Suddenly my mouth felt very dry.

'I don't think I am, Miss Warby.' I tried to sound as humble as possible.

'I beg to differ.' Miss Warby's eyes went to my coat, which was hanging on its usual peg. The badge was on the lapel, shining bright. 'I've been making allowances for you because Mrs Lawlor was kind enough to suggest you for this position.'

I felt my face get all hot and red at the idea that Old Wobbly had ever been making allowances for me.

'But I don't want you carrying on and causing trouble like those girls out in Lucan. The troublemakers there have been told today that there's no room for any of their union nonsense at Scott's.'

Which meant that they were now locked out! Like the Savoy girls.

'I'm not causing trouble,' I said. And then in case she thought I sounded cheeky I added, 'Miss Warby.'

Miss Warby sniffed.

'You have been warned,' she said. 'And in future, I think it's best if you and Miss Delaney don't take your lunch break together.'

My stomach fell. Those few minutes that me and Rosie get to spend together in the cubby hole are the best parts of the working day. I like Annie and the other girls, of course, even Kitty though she's so serious, but it wouldn't be the same having my break without Rosie. Of course I couldn't say anything to Miss Warby about this. I just bowed my head and said, 'Yes, Miss Warby.'

'You haven't got much to say for yourself, Miss Rosie.' Old Wobbly turned her stern gaze on Rosie. 'That's not like you at all. I hope you're not going to be difficult.'

'No, Miss Warby,' said Rosie.

Miss Warby gave another sniff.

'Good,' she said and, turning on her heel, she marched off in the direction of the kitchen.

'That old she-cat,' I said, as soon as I was sure she was out of earshot. 'She's a tyrant, that's what she is. Like the emperors of ancient Rome.'

'You knew there might be trouble if you joined the union.' There was a hint of a grin in Rosie's teasing tone. 'You're not regretting it already, are you?'

''Course I'm not,' I said. And it was true. The fact that Wobbly split up me and Rosie just because she felt like it was another reminder of how unfair it was that someone so petty and cruel was able to order us around. It's not like me and Rosie were plotting the downfall of the employers in the cubby hole. We were just eating scones and bread rolls and drinking lukewarm tea.

The rest of the afternoon seemed to drag along, even though we were busy enough. Before I started working, I always thought that the busy days would be the hardest and the most boring, but for some reason the days when there are lots of customers are less tiring than the really quiet days. The only good thing was that because it was a Monday, we were finished and out of there at half past five o'clock. Rosie and I couldn't chat outside the back door because she had to hurry home to check on her ma, so I set off for home and I was back there before six.

But there was a surprise in store for me. As soon as Ma opened the door to me she said, 'Don't take your coat off, we've got to go out in two minutes.'

'But Ma, it's boiling!' It was, too. It seems ridiculous to wear a summer coat in this weather. I should be out just in my frock, but Ma says no child of hers is going out without a coat like a child from the tenements, so she always makes me wear a jacket (even though the jacket is about a hundred years old and belonged to both her and Lily before I had to start wearing it).

'I just need to get something and then we'll go.' She hurried into the front room and emerged carrying a load of big paper parcels, which she dumped into my arms. 'You're coming with me to the Lawlors' house.'

'Oh Ma, no!' I said from behind the parcels, in what even I realised was a whining sort of voice. 'I'm only after getting home. I can't walk all the way to the Howth Road now.'

'It won't take long,' she said. 'I need you to pin up the hems.'

'But Ma!'

'Betty!' Ma said, in a voice that would brook no argument. 'I told you I was going to need your help the next day you had early closing, so I don't want to hear you giving out about it now.'

I vaguely remembered her saying something about helping her out, but I thought that just meant, I don't know, cleaning the grate or sewing together worn-out bedsheets or something.

'So come on now,' Ma went on. 'You're not too old to get a clatter round the legs.'

'Oh, all right,' I said. But I couldn't resist adding, 'Rosie at the shop says that hitting kids should be illegal.'

Ma snorted.

'A slap on the legs never did you any harm,' she said.

'But imagine what I might have been like if you'd never slapped me at all,' I pointed out. 'I might have been even better.'

She just laughed at that, but if I have children when I grow up, I'm never going to slap them. If they ever start acting the jinnet, I'll just show them a picture of their cousin Little Robbie and I bet that'll scare them into shutting up.

It was clear that I didn't have much of a choice about going to the Lawlors' house, so once Ma had put on her coat and hat and gathered up her carpet bag with her sewing things in and picked up one of the brown paper parcels which had fallen out of my arms, we set off.

'I suppose these are more of Lavinia's tennis dresses, or whatever she calls them,' I said, as we set out.

'Actually, Miss Clever, they're for Mrs Lawlor,' said Ma. 'Watch out!' I'd almost stepped into a big pile of horse dung, which is the sort of thing that can easily happen when you're made to carry so many parcels you can't see your feet. I was quite relieved to hear that the clothes were only for Mrs Lawlor. With a bit of luck, Lavinia wouldn't even be home. I don't know exactly why I find her so aggravating, even more so than all the other rich girls who come into the shop. I suppose it's because some of them are quite nice, while she's always so rude and haughty despite her beautiful bedroom and good school, so she reminds me of how unfair the world is.

Ma and I didn't speak much on the way to the Howth Road, mostly because it was so hot we were soon out of breath. Eventually we reached the Lawlors' house and were let in at the kitchen door by Jessie the maid – or was she the cook? Today there was another maid in the kitchen, and Jessie told her to take us to Mrs

Lawlor. We didn't even find out what her name was. She didn't say a word as she led us up to the beautiful room where we'd waited for Mrs Lawlor the last time. Mrs Lawlor was sitting at a table in the big bay window. Those giant glass panes let in so much sunshine and light, it makes our nice little house seem all dark and poky in comparison.

'Mrs Rafferty!' Mrs Lawlor sounded delighted to see us. 'And Betty too, how lovely.' As she crossed the room towards us – there were so many little tables and things she had to sort of weave her way around them – I looked longingly at the lovely fat sofa with its big soft cushions. I was so tired I'd have given anything to loll back on that sofa and put my feet up on the little embroidered footstool yoke that was placed invitingly next to it. Instead, I stood to attention like a soldier in the army.

'Hello, Mrs Lawlor,' said Ma. 'I've brought your linen blouses and the lace frock.'

'Wonderful,' said Mrs Lawlor. 'Let's go upstairs, shall we?' She smiled at me. 'I'm sure you can't wait to put down those parcels, Betty.'

'Yes, Mrs Lawlor,' I said, and then as soon as I said it I worried I'd said the wrong thing. Should I have pretended I didn't mind carrying the parcels? But surely she'd have known that wasn't true. If only it was always safe to be honest with other people.

We followed her up the lushly carpeted stairs, down the landing (which was carpeted too, in a lovely soft green with loops of pink flowers on it) and into a bedroom that was, I'm not joking you, bigger than our house. It had two big windows looking out onto the road and a giant great bed that you must need a ladder to get into, it was so high. There was a richly carved wardrobe the size of a bread van, and next to that there was a dressing table with a marble top and pretty tiles running underneath its three-part mirror. On the other side of the room was a big full-length mirror in a frame made from the same dark wood as the wardrobe.

'Unwrap those parcels there, Betty,' said Ma, gesturing towards the bed.

I wouldn't have dared go near the bed without being told to, but of course Ma has been in here before with Mrs Lawlor so she knows what's what. She helped Mrs Lawlor out of her old blouse (I didn't know where to look) and then helped her into one of the new ones.

There was the usual pinning and adjusting and very boring it was too. Mrs Lawlor chatted away to Ma about various garden parties she was going to, and how she was looking forward to the Horse Show at the end of the month. Ma said, 'That's nice,' and 'how lovely' and other meaningless things as she concentrated on making the garments fit perfectly. Eventually it was all done and Ma helped Mrs Lawlor back into her own clothes. Mrs Lawlor turned to me and smiled.

'You've been very patient, Betty,' she said. 'You're a credit to your mother.'

I could feel myself blushing. 'Thank you, Mrs Lawlor,' I said.

There was a pause and then Mrs Lawlor said, 'Could you wait here one moment?' And she went back to Lavinia's room.

I looked at Ma and whispered, 'Do you think I'm in trouble?'

Ma shook her head as Mrs Lawlor came back holding a book. It had a pale green cover with a picture of a red-haired girl on it.

'Lavinia got given this for Christmas but I know she's never going to read it. Would you like it?'

She handed me the book. It was called *Anne of Green Gables*.

'Oh, Mrs Lawlor, that's really not necessary,' said Ma, looking as appalled as if I'd taken the book off the shelf and demanded Mrs Lawlor give it to me. But Mrs Lawlor turned her smile towards her.

'Well, the last time you were here, Betty mentioned that she wanted to stay at school so I thought she must be a reader,' she said. She turned back to me. 'Are you, Betty?'

I was so stunned I could barely speak, but I managed to say, 'Yes, Mrs Lawlor.'

'There you go,' said Mrs Lawlor. 'Someone might as well enjoy this beautiful book.' She held it out to me and I took it before Ma could tell me not to.

'Thank you very much, Mrs Lawlor,' I said.

'I hope you enjoy it,' said Mrs Lawlor. 'You can read it on the tram into work tomorrow, can't you? That'll be a nice way to start the day.'

I stared at her. Was she joking? She couldn't possibly think that girls like me could afford to get the tram into work. Even if I could afford it, it was only a mile walk. The idea of anyone being so extravagant as to take a tram for that short distance left me speechless. But it was clear she wasn't joking. Mrs Lawlor assumed that of course any girl who was going into town would get a tram. What did a few pennies here and there matter to her?

Anyway, I had to answer her, so I just said, 'I walk into work, Mrs Lawlor.' Ma glared at me, I presume for contradicting Mrs Lawlor. Did she expect me to lie? Or say nothing at all?

'*Do* you? How marvellous you working girls are!' Mrs Lawlor gave a merry laugh. 'Walking all that way! And I'm sure you're never late – I know Miss Warby must keep you on your toes. A very sensible idea, to fine latecomers sixpence!'

I automatically replied, 'Yes, Mrs Lawlor.' But inside I felt sick. Any hope I might have had that Mrs Lawlor didn't know about the fining system vanished. Of course, she might not know that Old Wobbly was fining girls shillings when the whim took her. But she didn't seem to think it was wrong to take away a whole sixpence, just for being a few minutes late. Mrs Lawlor was a nice, generous woman, but Rosie was right. She didn't understand what our lives were like. And she was perfectly happy with the way things were.

'We'd better be going,' said Ma. 'We'll leave you in peace, Mrs Lawlor.' She had folded up the brown paper from the parcels and put it in her bag. As usual, she'd take it home and iron it smooth so she could use it for the next dressmaking customer.

'Thank you so much, Mrs Rafferty.' Mrs Lawlor led us across the landing and down the stairs. 'Hold on one moment, please – my purse …' And she went into the drawing room.

Ma and I waited in the hall. I was clutching the precious book against my chest and I didn't dare catch Ma's eye in case she ordered me to give it back. Instead, I looked at the pretty coloured glass in the front door. And just as I was thinking how nice it would be to have glass like that in my bedroom window to fill the room with coloured light, a shadow appeared behind the Lawlors' glass panelled door. There was the sound of a latch key, the door opened, and a fair-haired boy came into the hall.

A very familiar fair-haired boy. On whose face I could see recognition dawning.

'Hello!' said the boy who loved Sherlock Holmes, looking and sounding as surprised as I felt. 'It's you! What are you doing here?' His face relaxed into a warm grin. 'I still owe you a favour for saving that book.'

Ma looked at me in horror, clearly wondering how on earth I knew this young man and why he owed me a favour, but before I could say anything to either him or her, Mrs Lawlor was back in the hall with her purse.

'Sorry to keep you waiting, Mrs Rafferty – oh, hello Peter, what are you doing back so early?'

'Cricket match was cancelled,' said the boy. 'Which was fine by me. I only went to keep Jim company. Who are our guests?'

'This is Mrs Rafferty, my dressmaker,' said Mrs Lawlor, gesturing towards Ma. For a horrible moment I thought Ma was going to curtsey to the boy. 'And this is her daughter, Betty. Betty works in the Henry Street shop.'

Please, I thought, gazing at the boy with what I hoped was a pleading expression on my face, *please* don't tell your mother – and my mother – about our chat in the shop. And maybe it worked, because although the boy began to say, 'Why, I …' he suddenly changed his tone and said, 'I'm very pleased to make your acquaintance. How do you do, Mrs Rafferty? Miss Rafferty?'

'Very well, Master Lawlor,' said Ma. *Master* Lawlor! I didn't think people ever said that in real life, only in books. I was so stunned by all this that I just gawped at the pair of them until Ma nudged my foot with the toe of her boot.

'Yes, very well,' I said.

'Is this the right amount?' Mrs Lawlor handed my mother two pound notes and a ten shilling note. Actual pound notes! I'd hardly ever seen any before. They looked enormous.

'Perfect, Mrs Lawlor,' said Ma. 'And when you need me again, just send me a note and I'll be right over.'

'I will,' said Mrs Lawlor with a smile. She turned to her son and I realised Ma and I were dismissed. 'Now, Peter, come in here and tell me why this match was cancelled. It surely can't be because of the weather ...'

They went into the drawing room and closed the door, and I followed Ma down to the kitchen, where Jessie had a pot of tea and some scones ready for us. They were from the shop, I recognised the fluffy texture at once. I remembered Annie telling me that the family got their cakes delivered by a special van first thing every morning.

'Did I hear the front door open just there?' Jessie said, pouring some tea into her own cup.

'You did,' said Ma. 'Mrs Lawlor's son.' She looked at me suspiciously. 'What did he mean about you and a book?'

'He was in the shop,' I said. 'He nearly dropped his Sherlock Holmes book.'

'There's a lot more life in the place since young Master Peter came back from his adventures,' Jessie laughed. 'He's been in France since the start of the holidays, if you don't mind. A trip to Lourdes arranged by the school, it was, but he told me they spent most of the time just going around the countryside on their bicycles eating them strange foreign cheeses.'

This explained why I'd never seen the mysterious boy until recently. He was in France when I started working in the teashop.

'Where is he in school again?' Ma asked politely.

'That place at the top of North Great George's street,' said Jessie. 'He was at boarding school for a while, but one of the cousins persuaded Mr and Mrs Lawlor to send him to his old school. And between you and me …' She looked over her shoulder, as if to make sure none of the other servants were within earshot. 'I sometimes wish they'd sent Miss Lavinia away to school instead. We'd have a lot less extra work to do in this house if they had.' She smiled at Ma, but Ma didn't smile back.

'I'm sure Mr and Mrs Lawlor know what's best,' she said, in a prissy sort of voice. I knew she didn't want to criticise the Lawlors, not when she was in their house and Mrs Lawlor had just given her two and a half whole pounds and would doubtless give her more the next time she wanted a new skirt made, which was fair enough I suppose. But I'm sure we both knew that Jessie was right – in my experience Lavinia isn't easy to deal with even when she's just calling into the shop for five minutes, and Jessie has to pander to her every single day.

We didn't stay long after that. I could tell that both Ma and Jessie felt a bit peculiar about that awkward moment, but when Jessie walked us out to the kitchen door she said, 'I'm sorry for speaking out of turn, Margaret …' And Ma said, 'Don't bother your head about it, Jessie.' They both looked relieved that everything was all right between them again.

But Ma was still a bit quiet on the way home, which suited me very well because I couldn't stop thinking about the mysterious Sherlock Holmes-reading boy. Or Peter, as I suppose I must think of him. Never for one second did I think he might be the Lawlors' son! I wondered why Rosie hadn't recognised him, but then I realised that she was probably still in the sink room when he last visited the shop.

I was so quiet thinking about all this that Ma turned to me

when we got to Annesley Bridge and said, 'Are you all right there, Betty?'

I pulled myself together. ''Course I am. I'm just tired after being on my feet all day.'

'Sure that's nothing to your young legs,' said Ma. 'When I was in Whyte's' – that's the shop she worked in before she got married – 'we'd be standing up for twelve hours at a stretch.'

'I know, I know.' I didn't feel like getting into a big row with Ma.

Then, to my surprise, her voice softened.

'Look, Betty, I know you didn't want to come to Lawlors' this evening,' she said. 'But I've got to keep Mrs Lawlor happy. We need the money from my dressmaking.'

'I thought we were doing all right,' I said.

'We're in no danger of starving or anything, not this minute,' said Ma. 'But if the strikes go on, and if the employers don't dance to the union's tune … well, you heard the way people were talking in Croydon Park yesterday. For all their tug of war and hammocks and games, they're scared something might happen. And if things get worse and your father or Eddie lost their steady work, well, we'd be in a lot of trouble. A *lot* of trouble.'

I felt a cold feeling go down my back. My thoughts weren't on Peter any more. I've always felt, well, safe I suppose, despite all Ma and Da's recent grumblings about money. I always thought we were lucky, what with Da's steady work and us having the whole house to ourselves, no lodgers or anything. We had to watch the pennies, of course, like everyone else. And things had certainly been tighter over the last year or so.

But we'd never been really *hungry*. We'd always had sturdy shoes

*The Boldness of Betty* 159

and enough bread, and fresh milk from the dairy as well as tins of condensed milk, and a bit of meat at least once a week. I'd never been scared of the future, and I'd never thought Ma or Da were scared of it either. But Ma sounded scared now.

'So,' she continued. 'I want to make sure I can keep getting work from the Lawlors. Because I'd never ask your father to give up the union ...'

'Oh, Ma, of course you couldn't!' I cried.

'Didn't you hear me? That's what I said.' Ma sounded crotchety. 'But that means there might come a time when making a few skirts for the Lawlors is the only thing paying the rent man that month.'

I felt sick. I thought of the Maguires and their moonlight flit to that tenement. We've never had to be afraid of the rent man in our house. We always have just enough to pay him when he comes to get the money for the landlord. But there are other families round our way who don't, and every so often they have to hide and pretend there's no one in when the rent man calls to the door. They get the money to him eventually, otherwise they'd be kicked out or have to do a flit like the Maguires, but in the meantime, when the rent man comes around they just stay away from the front windows and they don't answer the front door.

I imagined me and Ma and Da and Eddie hiding down in the kitchen while a big angry man banged on our old wooden door with its flaking green paint. Earnshaw always barks his head off whenever he hears the door knocker. What if he gave us away?

'Betty?' said Ma, and I realised I was off in a day dream again.

'Sorry, Ma,' I said. 'I was just thinking.'

'I was only asking how you're getting on in the Lawlors' shop?'

'Oh!' I said. 'Grand.'

And I knew I couldn't tell her about Wobbly giving out about the union and Rosie getting into trouble. In fact, I'm going to hide this memoir in an even better place, because now there's even more reason to make sure she doesn't catch sight of what I've written. I'm going to finish up now and put my manuscript right under my mattress. It might be a bit lumpy, but sure the bed's lumpy enough already so I probably won't even notice.

# Chapter Ten

It was strange going in to work today. I kept thinking about Peter Lawlor. What if he came back in again? Should I pretend that I didn't know him? Would he be as embarrassed as I felt at the thought of seeing him again? I tried to distract myself by reminding myself I was meeting Samira at Liberty Hall after work to go to the first meeting of the dramatic company, but my mind kept drifting back to Peter Lawlor.

In fact, I was so busy thinking about him I barely noticed when Miss Warby came in to the tearoom just as we were closing up. If Rosie hadn't pinched me and hissed 'Betty!' in my ear, I wouldn't have even turned around to give Old Wobbly my full attention.

'Girls,' said Miss Warby, with no attempt at a polite greeting. 'I have some news. As of tomorrow, the shop will be closing an hour later.'

Us shop girls exchanged glances.

'May I ask why, Miss Warby?' said Kitty, politely.

Miss Warby clearly didn't appreciate the question.

'Because Mr Lawlor says so!' She sniffed. 'But if you require further explanation, I would have thought you must have noticed how busy we've been during the evenings. Mr Lawlor and I agree that the warm summer weather seems to be bringing people into town. It would be foolish not to take advantage of this rather than closing when there are still cakes and buns left in the day's stock.'

'And will we be getting any extra pay for this extra work?' Kitty's tone was still polite, but there was steel there too.

Miss Warby's cheeks flushed. 'You certainly will not!' she said. 'Hours and pay are at the discretion of the management – as you well know, Miss Dunne. Now finish up here and let the cleaners do their work.'

And before Kitty could say anything else, she swept out of the room, leaving us all staring at each other.

'An hour!' Rosie's voice cracked. 'I won't get back to Francis until after his bedtime!'

I didn't say anything. My legs were already aching. How much more would they ache after another hour standing up behind the counter? And how much more hungry would I be by the time I eventually got home?

'I'll talk to her tomorrow morning,' said Kitty. 'Maybe we can arrange something. A change in the shifts, something like that. And if we can't arrange something, well … I'll have to talk to Miss Larkin.'

My spirits rose a little at that, and Rosie looked a little more cheerful as we said goodbye.

When I arrived at Liberty Hall, Samira was waiting for me. She was wearing her best cream blouse and a nice blue skirt and she looked very pretty and smart, as I told her when she nervously asked me how she looked.

'I'm trying not to get my hopes up,' she said, as we made our way up the steps and into the spacious hall. 'They might be just as bad as Mr Farrell.'

I was going to tell her I was sure they wouldn't be, but I stopped myself. There was no guarantee that the union folk wouldn't have the same narrow-minded views as that charming theatre director. And after we'd followed the paper signs pinned to the wall saying 'DRAMATIC COMPANY' and walked into the large and crowded room that was used as a theatre, it's true that quite a few people stared at us – or rather, at Samira, as she went up to Miss Larkin, who was standing behind a table beneath the stage, and said, 'Excuse me, I'd like to join the drama company.'

'Would you now?' said Miss Larkin in her brusque manner. She looked over at me. 'What about you?'

'Oh, I'm grand,' I said quickly. 'I just came here to, um, wish her luck.'

Miss Larkin didn't look very impressed by my amateurish carry on, and for a horrible moment I thought she might turn Samira down for needing a supporter at her audition. I wanted to tell Miss Larkin that me coming along had been my idea and had nothing to do with Samira, but luckily I didn't need to because she just turned to Samira and said, 'Right now, Miss – what's your name again?'

'Miss Casey,' said Samira, and then blushed at her own formality. 'Samira Casey.'

'Well then, Miss Casey. Get up on that stage there and show us what you can do.'

Every eye in the room was on Samira then as she climbed the steps at the side of the stage. There were men and women of all ages there, and a few girls of our age. Some of them looked sceptical as they watched Samira walk to the centre of the stage, while others looked merely curious. One man whispered something to his friend and they sniggered. My stomach was churning with nerves.

And then Samira drew herself up to her full height and launched into her 'quality of mercy' speech. She didn't try to put on a grand lady's voice. She sounded like what she was, a girl from the North

Strand, but one full of passion and wisdom. Surely, I thought, *surely* they couldn't deny how good she was. But I thought of Mr Farrell and my stomach lurched again.

When she finished there was a moment of dead silence, and then some of the company members began to clap. A few more joined in. Some of them remained impassive, arms folded, but the others more than made up for it. There were even a few cheers.

'Well!' Miss Larkin's expression was inscrutable. 'That was very good, I must say. But Miss Casey, we work with modern plays here. Plays about the hardships and joys of life, and especially Irish life, in this twentieth century.'

Samira didn't flinch. 'Just show me the play,' she said. 'And I'll give it my all.'

'Really?' said Miss Larkin. 'And what about music and singing?' She gestured towards a stout man sitting by a piano in the corner of the room. 'That's an important part of what we do too.'

'I've been singing and dancing all my life,' said Samira. She turned to the man at the piano. 'Do you know "Kitty McCrea"?'

The man nodded and played the opening bars.

And taking a deep breath, Samira launched into one of the songs Auntie Maisie used to sing in her stage days, all about a Dublin flower seller. It was the perfect song to showcase her talents, because it starts out quite jolly and cheerful and there's even a little dance bit, and then the end is all sad because the flower girl dies of a broken heart and her lost love lays flowers on her grave. By the time Samira sang the final note, her voice pure and true, a few people were wiping tears from their eyes.

'That was …' Miss Larkin paused, 'very good indeed. I think you'll be a fine addition to this dramatic company.'

Samira beamed. 'Thank you, Miss Larkin.' She caught my eye and I grinned back at her.

'Now, get down off that stage.' Miss Larkin's tone was brisk. 'We're reading through a new play tonight, and there might be a part for you in it.'

She turned to me. 'And if you're not going to audition yourself, you'd better leave us to it.'

'Yes, missus,' I said. 'I mean Miss Larkin. Sorry. I'm going now.' And despite my embarrassment I had a spring in my step as I headed back through the building and out to Beresford Place. At last someone appreciated Samira's acting!

I was feeling so pleased, imagining how Samira was going to be the star of the society's next production, that I almost stepped in front of a tram.

In fact, I probably would have if a familiar voice hadn't cried 'Watch out!' and a strong hand hadn't grabbed my shoulder and pulled me back.

'Ali!' I said.

'I'm used to Samira walking out in the road without looking.' Ali's eyebrows were raised. 'But I thought you usually had your feet on the ground.'

'I was thinking of Samira, actually,' I said. 'She just got in to the dramatic company.' I told Ali what had happened. He was delighted.

'About time someone appreciated her,' he said. 'You heading home now?'

'I am,' I said. But then a thought struck me. 'But what are you doing out? Shouldn't you still be in the loading bay?'

Ali took a deep breath. 'Not anymore. I've been locked out.'

I stared at him. 'You haven't!'

'I certainly have,' said Ali. 'Mr Murphy came into the delivery room and said if we wanted to keep our jobs we had to leave the union.'

Mr Murphy is the man who owns the newspaper where Ali works, loading papers into the vans that take them to newsagents. Mr Murphy owns a lot of other things as well, hotels and shops and even the tram company, where Eddie works in the parcel delivery section.

'But you've got a right to be in the union!' I said.

'Not according to him,' said Ali calmly. 'Watch out for that van!'

I nearly got run over again. When we'd reached the other side of Amiens Street I asked Ali what he'd said when Mr Murphy made his declaration.

Ali's eyes were bright but his voice was calm. 'I said it wasn't fair to make us choose but if I had to, I'd always pick my union. And so did about fifty other fellas. So out we went.'

'Janey!' I said.

'We've been picketing the rest of the day. And when some of the newsboys found out what happened to us, they said they wouldn't sell the paper.'

You wouldn't want to be messing with those newsboys. They've been out on strike themselves before, and even though half of them don't have shoes on their feet, they take their job of selling newspapers on the streets very seriously.

'What do you do now?' I asked.

Ali shrugged his shoulders. 'Keep on picketing, I suppose. Until the bosses change their minds.'

'Everyone seems to be coming out on strike,' I said. 'Or being locked out for being in the union. Those girls in the Savoy, that mill out in Lucan …'

'We're standing up for ourselves at last,' said Ali. 'And some people don't like it.' He looked at me and smiled. 'But it's worth it, if we manage to make a difference. Isn't it?'

I glanced at his serious face and the dark curls poking out from beneath his tatty old cap and for a moment I could see him up on some platform somewhere, addressing a meeting, making everyone feel things as strongly as he did. Changing the world. Or at least changing Dublin.

'Yes,' I said, smiling back. 'It is.'

I was rolling up bits of old newspaper to make firelighters later that evening when there was a knock on the door. I answered it to find Samira on the door step, her eyes glowing.

'I got a part!' She practically bounced into the hall, she was that happy. 'A speaking part!'

'Ah, Samira, I'm delighted for you!' And relieved too, though I didn't say that. The Dramatic Company are going to be putting on a concert including some short plays. One is called *Dispute* and it's a play by some English lady, all about a man who goes out on strike. Samira's going to play the striker's daughter.

'What's the part like?' I asked.

'It's not a very big part,' said Samira, 'but I've got a few lines. And Auntie Maisie says there's no such thing as a small part, only small actors. A good actor can make any part important.'

'She's not wrong,' I said. 'What's the play like?'

'Well, it's not Shakespeare,' said Samira, 'but it's very good all the same.'

'Just think!' I beamed at her. 'You'll be up there on a stage in a costume and everything.'

'I know!' Samira hugged herself. 'And if I hadn't joined the union, it wouldn't have happened.'

'What does Auntie Maisie think?' I was sure she'd be even more thrilled than me.

'She doesn't even know. I haven't been home yet,' said Samira. 'I should go and tell her.'

After Samira had gone, I realised I still hadn't said a word to her about meeting Peter Lawlor. Ever. I hadn't told her about talking to him in the shop and now I hadn't mentioned meeting him again. I don't know why, because usually we tell each other everything. But somehow Peter Lawlor was different. And I wasn't sure why.

Anyway, I decided not to think about that now. After all, I had the whole house to myself for once, and I had to take advantage of it. Ma had gone down to Mrs Connolly for a cup of tea and Eddie and Da weren't home yet, so I got the book Mrs Lawlor had given me and took a tatty old cushion out to the back garden so I could read in comfort with Earnshaw by my side. And I'm glad I did, because not only is *Anne of Green Gables* one of the best books I've ever read in my life, it's about an ordinary girl, the sort of girl you never normally see in books.

Instead of living in a big house with servants and nurses and governesses and all that, she has to go and work for these old farmer people, and at first they don't want her, but then she makes them like her. She gets to go to school too, even though she's helping them on their farm and in the house. I made myself stop reading after an hour because I don't want to finish it too quickly, which is quite impressive self-control if I say so myself. Anne in the book is always imagining things about the place where she lives to make everything more romantic and beautiful, so I tried doing that myself. It wasn't as easy as Anne makes it look. But then, she was surrounded by sparkling waters and rolling fields, not railway arches and sooty trees. If you live around here, your imagination has to work even harder.

# Chapter Eleven

It's happened. I don't think I really thought it ever would, but it's happened. Us union girls have walked out of Lawlor's. We're on strike! And it feels like my whole life has been turned upside down.

It happened like this. Just before the shop opened this morning, Miss Warby bustled into our area behind the counter. 'I've just been telling the bakery staff,' she said, without so much as a word of greeting. 'From now on, our flour will be supplied by Scott's from Lucan. So if any deliveries arrive at the shop door, you are to send them around to the staff entrance.'

For a moment I wasn't sure why the name Scott's was so familiar. Then I remembered – they were one of the firms where the workers had been locked out for joining the union. I glanced at Rosie. She looked as nervous as I felt. Then Kitty stepped forward.

'I'm sorry, Miss Warby,' she said, her voice firm, 'but I won't sell buns made with Scott's flour.'

Miss Warby couldn't have looked more shocked if Kitty had jumped on top of the counter and danced a polka.

'What on earth do you mean, Miss Dunne?' she said.

'Most of Scott's are out on strike,' she said. 'They had no choice. They were locked out when they were made to choose between the union and their jobs. Which means this flour is being milled and delivered by the men who aren't standing by their brothers and sisters. Well, I won't handle it.'

'Neither will I,' said Rosie.

I took a deep breath. This was it. This was why I'd joined the union. To stand together with my fellow workers, hoping they'd do the same for me. Well, I couldn't expect anyone to stand by me if I wouldn't stand by them. I felt sick with fear, but I stepped forward too.

'I won't either,' I said.

There. I'd done it.

'This is outrageous!' said Miss Warby, her cheeks flushed.

'We're in the union,' said Kitty. 'And we don't do business with people who break a strike.'

'What about you, Miss Annie?' Old Wobbly's voice was shaking with rage as she turned to poor little Annie, who looked as if she was going to burst into tears. 'Are you in this union too?'

'No,' said Annie. 'But …'

'But nothing!' said Miss Warby. 'Go upstairs to my office and wait until I have dealt with these … these hooligans!'

With a tearful glance back at us, Annie fled. I didn't feel angry with her for leaving us. She wasn't a member of the union, after all. But we were, and we had to do our duty. Miss Warby turned her ferocious gaze on Kitty.

'Miss Dunne,' she said. 'I can assure you that you have no choice in this matter. Mr Scott is a personal friend of Mr Lawlor and this new arrangement was confirmed several weeks ago. I am only doing you the courtesy of telling you about it because the first delivery will arrive today and I wished to avoid any confusion with the men. Tomorrow you will be selling buns, and bread rolls, and cakes, all made with Scott's flour. You will, however, be fined half a crown this week for this appalling insolence, and you should count yourselves lucky that I'm not giving the three of you the sack. And I will have to speak to Mr Lawlor about allowing you to remain in this union of yours at all. Now open the door, Miss Dunne. This shop should have been open for business two minutes ago.'

'No,' said Kitty.

'I beg your pardon?' Miss Warby's cheeks were purple with rage.

'I won't deal with scabs,' said Kitty calmly. 'And that's what these new delivery men are – covering up the strike, pretending it's not happening. Well the strike *is* happening, and I support it, and I'm not dealing with Scott's.' She took off her apron and cap. 'I'm walking out.'

'So am I,' said Rosie, pulling out one of the hairpins that kept her white cap on her black curls.

'And me,' I said, untying my apron with trembling fingers.

'You can't do this!' cried Miss Warby, and was that a touch of panic I heard in her voice? 'You need to open the shop!'

'All right,' said Kitty and, laying her apron and cap on the shining glass counter, she walked around to the front door and drew back the bolt. 'It's open. And now we're walking out.' She looked at me and Rosie. 'Coming, girls?'

'We are,' said Rosie and walked around the corner. I followed, laying my own apron next to Kitty's.

'Come back here!' cried Old Wobbly. There was no doubting the fear in her voice now.

'We're withdrawing our labour,' said Kitty, 'in keeping with the principles of our union.' And she marched right out of the door, me and Rosie at her heels.

'But who's going to man the counter? Who …' Old Wobbly began, and then the door swung shut behind us and cut off the sound of her outraged voice. I felt all hot and dizzy.

'Well,' said Kitty, and her voice wasn't quite as firm as it had been just a few moments earlier. 'That's that, then.'

'We're out,' said Rosie.

We looked at each other, our eyes wide.

'We should have done something long ago,' said Kitty. 'I should have talked to the union when they tried to bring in longer hours. And all those fines. Making the girls work in the sink room with no ventilation. Paying us below the going rate because they tell themselves we're just earning a bit of pin money. Well, they won't take us for granted now. Especially when the other union girls in the kitchen and the washroom hear about this and come out too.'

I'd never seen Kitty so animated. But now that we'd walked out, the rush of excitement that had sent me through the gleaming front door was starting to drain away.

'Janey,' said Rosie, taking her union badge out of her pocket and pinning it on her chest. 'It's a good thing the weather's too good to need a coat. If we'd left anything in the cubby hole, we'd never get them back. Wobbly'd probably send them all to the pawn shop.'

I said a silent prayer of thanks that for once I'd ignored Ma and gone out without a coat today. My badge was in my pocket too.

Kitty snorted as she pinned on her own badge. 'Wobbly's never been inside a pawn shop in her life.'

'Um,' I said. 'What do we do now?'

'We go and tell the union what we've done,' said Kitty. A worried look passed over her features. 'Really, we shouldn't have walked out without talking to them first. You'd better go.'

My stomach churned. 'Shouldn't it be you?'

But Kitty shook her head. 'Miss Warby might want to negotiate with us,' she said. 'And if she does, I'm the one she'll talk to, so I should stay here. Besides, there are other union members in there who should be joining us as soon as they hear what we've done. I should be here to keep an eye on everything.'

I didn't want to argue with her, so I took my own badge out of my pocket, pinned it on and walked as fast as I could towards the quays. By the time I reached Liberty Hall I was very hot and dusty and was starting to feel sick about what we'd done. But I took a deep breath and trotted up the steps and into the building, which was full of men walking around having earnest and sometimes heated conversations with each other. I ignored them and hurried up the stairs to knock on the door of Miss Larkin's office.

'Come in!'

I pushed open the door nervously. Miss Larkin was behind her desk, looking through what looked like a list.

'I'm from Lawlor's cake shop,' I said. 'On Henry Street.'

'I don't need any cakes, thank you. Close the door on your way out.'

'No, that's not … We've come out. On strike.'

'Really?' Miss Larkin glanced up from her list. She didn't sound exactly friendly, but she did look interested. 'Lawlor's cake shop, you said?'

'It's just three of us,' I said. 'So far. But I'm sure more girls will join us.'

'Hmmm,' said Miss Larkin. 'Can you tell me why?'

I told her about Kitty's declaration and how me and Rosie had followed her.

'Right,' she said. 'I'll go down and talk to this Miss Warby.' She stood up and put on a hat that was hanging on a nearby stand.

'I was wondering … could we get something to make signs

with? Cardboard and that?'

Miss Larkin pushed back a curl that had escaped from her hair-pins and stood up from her desk.

'I'm impressed, Miss ... what's your name?'

'Betty Rafferty,' I said.

'Well, Miss Rafferty, you all did a good thing today, standing by your brothers and sisters. And you've got the support of the union behind you. But you can't start picketing until I've talked to this supervisor of yours. Maybe we can resolve this without a strike.'

'And if we ... if we do go on strike? What'll happen then?'

Her stern expression almost softened. 'Don't worry. We won't let you starve.'

She shook my hand, and I followed her out of the door and down the stairs. As we hurried around Beresford Place and down Abbey Street, she asked me a few questions about conditions at Lawlor's. I told her about the fines, and the extra hours, and the pretence that we were all just earning a bit of pin money, and how Miss Warby disapproved of our union badges and told us not to cause any trouble. I told her about Kitty's injury, and the washing-up room, where girls had to spend whole days with their hands being scalded by the hot water. Miss Larkin didn't say much, which was all right by me, because there was something so force-ful about her I felt rather intimidated.

And I also felt nervous, because as I was trotting along behind Miss Larkin, trying to match her long stride, it really struck me that going out on strike meant that I'd lost my full wages. I didn't regret walking out. But I did feel worried, thinking about how Ma was going to react when she heard. I didn't know how much strike pay we'd get.

When we arrived at Lawlor's, Kitty and Rosie were marching back and forth in front of the door – Kitty was marching slowly because her foot isn't entirely better yet. But they weren't alone. Jenny Byrne was there – she told me she'd just joined the union a few days earlier. There was also a girl called Joan, who I recognised from the washing-up room, and a few more from the kitchens. In fact, it was quite a crowd. Kitty stepped forward when she saw Miss Larkin. I realised for the first time that she was nervous herself.

'Which of you is Kitty Dunne?' said Miss Larkin.

Kitty raised a hand that almost, but not quite, shook with nerves.

'Right,' said Miss Larkin. 'Let's go and see this Miss Warby of yours. The rest of you, well done for coming out.' And she marched through the glass door of the shop, with Kitty at her heels.

'Janey,' said Rosie. 'She's on the warpath! What happened down at Liberty Hall?'

I told her all. 'We can't be officially on strike until the union says it's all right,' I said.

'Well,' said Rosie. 'Even if we're not striking yet, we can still let the customers know we've walked out.'

So we did. Or at least we tried too. But every time I started to say, ''Scuse me, we've walked out,' to a customer, they just ignored me and pushed their way through the door. It was very discouraging, even with all the other girls being there.

'I hadn't realised there were so many of us in the union,' I said to Rosie, looking around at my fellow strikers.

'I've told you before. You need to pay more attention,' said Rosie. But she was grinning when she said it.

It felt like hours and hours, but was only about forty minutes later, when Miss Larkin and Kitty came around the side of the building. Miss Warby must have made them leave by the staff entrance at the back.

'Well, girls,' said Miss Larkin, as we all drew around her. 'I've talked to your Miss Warby, and I've talked to Mr Lawlor on the telephone. I've made it clear that you refuse to handle Scott's flour, and Miss Dunne and I have brought up your other grievances.' She paused.

'And?' said Rosie, impatiently. 'What did they say?'

Miss Larkin turned her formidable gaze on her. 'Patience, Miss …'

'Delaney, Miss Larkin,' said Rosie, abashed.

'They assured me they have no plans to change their arrangement with Scott's, and they insist that their terms and conditions are fair and honest. Well, you girls clearly disagree. Which is why I told them we had no choice but to declare a strike.'

Even Rosie was silent at that. We all looked at each other, our eyes wide. It was official! We were out on strike. There was no turning back now.

'All of you union girls, are your dues up to date?' Everyone nodded and mumbled yes.

'Then you'll be eligible for strike pay. Come along later to Liberty Hall and we'll sort that out. For now …' Miss Larkin's stern features twitched into a smile, 'you'll have to show the fine ladies and gentlemen who frequent Lawlor's cake shop and tearoom that they're making a mistake!'

'Should we make signs and that?' asked the irrepressible Rosie.

'We don't have to,' Kitty said. 'But should we?' She looked at Miss Larkin.

'Now you mention it, it wouldn't hurt,' said Miss Larkin. She turned to me. 'Come back with me to Liberty Hall and we'll get you some old scraps of cardboard and some paint. You can make a few signs.'

'What'll I paint on them?' I wasn't sure I was ready for so much responsibility.

'ON STRIKE will do,' said Kitty.

'It might make some of the customers think before they buy a Mary Cake,' said Rosie, with a grin.

Miss Larkin seemed deep in thought as we hurried back to Liberty Hall in silence, but once we were inside she turned to me.

'You'll find some cardboard and paint in the theatre room where the dramatic company meets – you remember where that is?'

I nodded.

'Off you go, then. And Miss Rafferty?'

I paused in the hallway. 'Yes?'

'Well done. All of you.'

There was no one in the theatre, and I rooted around in a cupboard until I found some card that was clearly left over from the props for the current production. It was surprisingly heavy; I wasn't going to be able to carry many signs back to Henry Street.

There was a tub of paint on the table, so I used it to write ON STRIKE on two bits of card and FAIR PLAY FOR ALL WORKERS on another. It was just poster paint so it didn't take long to dry, but the wait was long enough for me to start worrying even more about telling Ma about the strike. I couldn't think about that now, though, or I'd risk losing my nerve. Instead, I paced up and down the stage until the paint was dry, reminding myself that we were doing the right thing.

When I got back to the shop I felt bad about not having enough signs for everyone, but there would be time enough to sort out more signs in the future, and no one seemed to mind not having one today. For now, I handed one to Rosie and one to Kitty, seeing as we were the ones who were out first, and kept one for myself.

It didn't take long before I found myself wishing I'd given my sign to one of the washing-up room girls, but it felt cowardly to admit that and besides, I had to conquer my embarrassment if we were going to keep striking. But if you've never stood in the street holding a sign, you probably don't realise how peculiar it feels, drawing attention to yourself and saying 'There's a strike on here,' to anyone who was about to go into a shop. I was sure everyone was staring at us, which is a very uncomfortable feeling. I said as much to Rosie.

'But sure that's the point,' she said, reasonably. 'We *want* them to stare at us. Otherwise they wouldn't know there was a strike on.'

'I know that,' I said. 'I just feel fierce … conspicuous, I suppose.'

'Just think of Old Wobbly,' said Rosie. 'And how angry she is. Who do you think she got to cover our places behind the counter?'

'Maybe she stepped in herself?' I said.

'How many buns would you like, madam?' said Rosie, in a perfect imitation of Wobbly's haughty tones, and we both broke up laughing.

Kitty wasn't impressed. 'A bit of dignity please, girls!' she said sternly.

'Ah come on, Kitty,' said Rosie. 'What's the point of standing up for ourselves if we can't have a bit of fun doing it?'

I couldn't argue with that. Besides, I needed cheering up as more and more people walked straight past our signs and into the shop, even though we said, 'Don't cross the picket line!' every time they approached the door. It was all very discouraging. We'd been there for about twenty minutes when a grand lady whose perfectly arranged brown hair was streaked with grey walked up to the door. I recognised her as one of our regular customers. She was holding the lead of a small white woolly dog, who looked up at me with piercing eyes that looked like black buttons and then barked like mad.

'Ignore them, Barnaby!' said his mistress in haughty tones. 'Those little troublemakers aren't worth your attention.' And she swept into the tearoom. As she pushed open the door, the little woolly dog Barnaby looked back at me and barked again.

'Janey,' said Rosie. 'I'd rather be safely out here than in the shop with that little monster.'

I laughed, but it was hard to keep my spirits up, being ignored or disparaged all the time. In fact, by the time Barnaby and his owner had marched out again, with the lady ignoring us and Barnaby glowering at us with his button eyes, I wanted to put down my sign and run home.

And then I looked at Kitty and Rosie and all the other girls. Kitty might have looked very serious – as usual – and Rosie might have looked as if she was about to burst out laughing at any minute – also as usual. But we were all out there because we believed in something bigger than ourselves. We believed in fair play, and sticking together. And if the other girls could stand there with their signs, so could I.

'One for all and all for one!' I said aloud.

'What?' Rosie said, confused – as well she might be.

'It's from a book I read,' I said. '*The Three Musketeers*.' I'd got it out of the library and read it last winter. In fact, for weeks I used to read a bit of it to Da every evening when he was resting in the big kitchen armchair after work.

'Oh right,' said Rosie,. 'Well, it's a good old motto. Especially as the three of us were the first out.' She grinned at me. 'What is it again? One for all!'

'And all for one!' I smiled back at her.

That was when a lady in a very grand hat, who was on her way into the shop, paused on the pavement at the sight of our signs.

'What's all this about?' she said. She looked like she was about Ma's age, though her clothes were finer than anything Ma could afford to wear, and her hat was pinned to her hair with a beautiful ivory pin.

'We've come out on strike,' said Kitty, in just the sort of voice she used to say 'That'll be ninepence, please' to customers.

'Really!' said the lady. 'How very impressive. Well done, girls! There'll be no Lawlor's cakes for me until this is sorted out.'

I couldn't believe my ears.

'Do you mean it?' I said, which I realised later must have sounded rather rude, and as if I was accusing her of lying. But I don't think she minded very much, because she just laughed.

'Of course I mean it,' she said. 'I haven't set foot in the Savoy on Grafton Street since the girls went on strike.' She shuddered. 'Though once I learned about the rat-infested chocolate that didn't seem like much of a loss.'

'Oh!' I said. 'Well, thanks very much.' That felt a bit overfamiliar, so I added, 'Madam.'

The lady laughed. 'Courage, girls, courage!' she said, and walked

down the street towards Arnotts. Rosie and I looked at eac_
our eyebrows raised.

'Who'd have thought it!' Rosie said just what I was feeling. 'A fine lady like that!'

And the thought of the friendly lady kept us going for the rest of the morning. In fact, she wasn't the only one to refuse to cross the picket line that day. At lunchtime a nice-looking young man in a worn but well-cut suit (you really can tell I'm my ma's daughter, I'm always noticing how clothes are made these days) took his hat off to us and said, 'I won't be coming back here until you get fair play.' A dark-haired young woman with a hat like a velvet cabbage, who I recognised as another regular customer, stopped when she saw us and said, 'Good for you, girls. Keep it up!' before walking on.

And there were plenty of working men – and a few women – who nodded at us as they passed and pointed to the red hand badge on the lapels of their jackets. It's strange what a big difference that made. It reminded us that we are part of something bigger than just Lawlor's cake shop and tearoom. By the time Kitty said, 'All right, girls, that'll do,' at the end of the working day, we were all tired but we also felt exhilarated.

'See you back here tomorrow morning,' said Kitty. 'We'll keep on picketing until Mr Lawlor sees sense.'

My exhilaration started to fade away after I'd said goodbye to the others and began the walk home. By the time I let myself in the front door, it had entirely disappeared. Earnshaw bounded up the stairs towards me and I gave him a big cuddle to calm my nerves.

'Hello, love,' said Ma cheerfully when I came down into the kitchen, Earnshaw by my side. She was cutting slices of bread for

*The Boldness of Betty* 183

nough butter for everyone today.'

...said.

...ng with you?' said Ma, looking up from her work.

...ng happened?'

...as,' I said. 'Not something bad or anything. Well, I don't think it's bad, but…'

'Out with it!' said Ma. Her tone was stern but her eyes were worried.

'I'm on strike,' I said.

Ma's breadknife fell on the table with a clatter.

'Ah, Betty!' she said.

'We had to!' I said. And I told her what had happened.

'It's not just the Scott's flour business,' I explained. 'Miss Warby's a tyrant. She really is. She fines girls a day's wages just for being a few minutes late – she did it to Rosie, Ma, and she's got a whole family to feed. And they pretend we're all just working for pocket money when half the girls need their pay to live …'

'Stop it, Betty!' Ma's cheeks were flushed with emotion. 'It's one thing your father joining a union – it's right for the working men to stick together. They can stand strong and hold those employers to account. But a girl like you, causing trouble! And for Mrs Lawlor, too!'

'It's got nothing to do with Mrs Lawlor!' I said. 'She's never in the shop.'

'And do you think she'll see it that way, do you?' said Ma. 'Do you think she'll give me any more dressmaking work when she hears my daughter has walked out of her husband's shop? Will her friends give me any?'

My stomach churned. I remembered what she had told me on

the way home from our last visit to the Lawlors', about her fear that dressmaking could be our only source of money if Da and Eddie went on strike. She hadn't even considered the idea that I might come out too. And I hadn't thought of what it would do to her dressmaking when I did it.

'Will that Miss Warby of yours be at work tomorrow?' said Ma. I nodded. 'Then you're going right back there, and then you're going to tell her you're very sorry, and then you're going to ask her – no, you're going to *beg* her – to give you your job back.'

My mouth felt very dry. 'I can't, Ma.'

'What do you mean, you can't?' I couldn't remember the last time I'd seen Ma so angry.

'I have to stick with the girls,' I said. 'We're trying to make things better for everyone.'

Ma stamped her foot. Actually stamped. Earnshaw huddled up to my legs.

'And how's it going to make it better if we can't eat?'

'I'll get strike pay,' I said. 'Kitty told me how much, two and six a week ...'

'Two and six! Not even half your weekly wage!' said Ma. She sat down at the table and put her head in her hands. 'Everything Mrs Lawlor's done for you ... giving you that book and all ...'

For the first time since I came home, I felt annoyed.

'I know it was nice of her to give me that book,' I said, 'but I'm working all the hours God sends for a few shillings a week, just so she and that daughter of hers can live like queens in that big house, never lifting a hand!'

Ma looked astonished to hear me arguing with her like that and I felt quite astonished by myself. I don't know what Ma would have said next if Da hadn't arrived home that very moment. 'Only me!' he said cheerfully as his heavy tread rang out on the stairs. He paused in the kitchen doorway and took in the tense scene. 'What's been going on here?'

'She's gone on strike,' said Ma.

'Betty?' Da turned towards me. I nodded.

'It's true,' I said. And I told him everything that had happened. His expression grew troubled as I went on.

'And we picketed until the shop closed,' I said.

Da walked over to Ma and put a hand on her shoulder.

'Margaret,' he said, giving her a squeeze. 'She had to do it. You know she did.'

'I know no such thing!' said Ma and then, to my horror, she flung herself into a chair, laid her head down on the table and burst into tears. Da looked at me, his eyes grave. 'Take Earnshaw out to the garden for a while, will you?'

I didn't say a word. I just grabbed Earnshaw's collar and led him out of the kitchen, closing the door behind me.

I got my book and when me and Earnshaw were settled on the warm grass, leaning against the back of the jacks, I tried to read. But even though *Anne of Green Gables* is now my favourite character in any book ever, I couldn't really concentrate on her adventures with her bosom friend Diana when I could hear the rumble of Da's voice and Ma's increasingly loud tones coming from the kitchen. I couldn't make out what they were saying but it clearly wasn't going very well. Ma and Da hardly ever argue, and the sound of it made me feel peculiar. And I felt a wave of panic at the thought of Ma losing all her dressmaking clients. Apart from the money, she had worked so hard to get all those jobs.

Eventually the voices stopped, and a moment later Da walked out into the garden. He crouched down next to me and Earnshaw and sighed.

'Well,' he said. 'Your ma's having a lie down.'

'Is everything all right?' I said, even though I knew that was a stupid question.

'I wouldn't say that,' said Da, 'but she's not going to make you go back and ask for your job.'

My shoulders sagged with relief. I hadn't realised I'd been so scrunched up.

'But,' Da continued, 'she still doesn't approve of you going on strike. She understands why you did it, but she's not happy about it.'

'Do you think Mrs Lawlor will really stop using her as a dress-maker?' I hoped despite all reason that he'd say no. But he nodded.

'I'd be surprised if she didn't, Betser,' he said gravely. 'But I reminded your ma that Mrs Lawlor isn't her only client.'

'Mrs Lawlor will tell all the others,' I said. My guilt was now almost overwhelming.

Da smiled gently. 'She doesn't know all of them, only her Clontarf friends. Your ma's still got the Drumcondra ladies. She can try and get more work off them.'

'Da,' I said, 'we are doing the right thing, going on strike. Aren't we?'

Da took my hand in his big warm paws. 'Yes, pet. Yiz are. It's not going to be easy. Strikes never are. But sometimes they're the only way to take a stand. You and the other girls are standing together with the other workers. That's a good thing.'

'All for one and one for all,' I said.

Da laughed. 'Except there's a lot more than three of us in the union,' he said.

'Where's my tea? I'm starving!' came a loud and boorish voice from the house – Eddie was home. So me and Da went back inside and I finished slicing the bread and spreading it with dripping. Ma came down for tea but she didn't say much and I didn't dare utter a word so it was an unusually quiet meal.

'Janey,' said Eddie. 'It's like having your tea in a morgue.'

After tea Ma went to see Mrs Connolly down the road – doubtless to give out about her terrible daughter and tell Mrs Connolly she was lucky Frances was too small to give any trouble. And I went out to the still sunny back garden to write this. I feel terrible about upsetting Ma but things won't be as bad tomorrow. Will they?

# Chapter Twelve

Well, I suppose I didn't have to worry for too long about Ma being angry with me. Because Eddie's out of a job now too, so she's too busy being angry at him to pay as much attention to me. When she's not giving out to Eddie, she's giving out about the union in general. And if the rumours are true, even more people are going to be locked out or going out on strike over the next while, so I can't see her calming down.

We certainly won't be going back to Lawlor's in a hurry. We've been picketing every day for nearly a week now, and Miss Warby refuses to consider negotiating with us. In fact, she seems to be pretending we're not there. She's going in and out by the back door, and when she does use the front door she just sails past us with her nose in the air.

Only once in the last week has she deigned to say a word, and that was the second day of the strike. She paused in front of Kitty, who was holding a nice big sign that said STAND BY THE WORKERS, and said, 'Miss Dunne, when you started working for Lawlor's, I was convinced I saw a girl I could be proud of. And yet you have chosen to throw your lot in with a gang of young hoydens. I must tell you frankly that I am ashamed of you.'

Kitty may not always be the easiest person to get on with, but there really is something sort of, I don't know, majestic about her. She's like I imagine Queen Maeve from the legends, and I can't imagine Queen Maeve was always much fun to pal around with either. Her steady gaze didn't falter as she faced Miss Warby.

'I'm sorry you feel that way,' she said. 'But we're only doing what's right.'

Miss Warby sniffed. 'I think you'll find that what you consider right today will not help you in the future.' And with that, she strode into the shop.

The thing about Old Wobbly, though, is that now she has no power over us, she's easy to ignore. What's more difficult is seeing the other Lawlor's girls cross the picket line and go in to work. I know they need the money, but so do we, and it'd be nice if we were all standing together. Some of them avoid our eyes as they hurry down the lane to the staff entrance, but others are more defiant.

The other day I was standing by the door with a pile of hand-bills that the union had printed up, when a girl I recognised from the kitchen marched up to me and Rosie, a cross expression on her face.

'What do you lot think you're doing?' she demanded.

'You all right, Lizzie?' said Rosie, laying down her picket sign.

'Now you mention it, Rosie, I'm not,' said the girl called Lizzie. 'Auld Wobbly's been in a foul mood ever since you started this stupid strike of yours. And the shop and tearoom girls are saying the takings are down 'cos you're stopping people coming in.'

Rosie and I exchanged pleased glances. The pickets were making a difference!

'We're not stopping anyone coming in, Lizzie,' said Rosie. 'They just don't want to cross a picket.'

'You and your pickets!' Lizzie scoffed. 'Some of us have to work for a living.'

'We know that!' I could tell Rosie was trying to keep her temper. 'We're not doing this for fun, Lizzie. We're doing it so the Lawlors make things better for all of us. Including you, not that you deserve it.'

'Well, I didn't ask you to,' said Lizzie, and she turned and marched down the lane to the staff door.

'Scab!' shouted Rosie.

'Rosie!' I said.

'Well, she is.' Rosie shrugged her shoulders. And I couldn't argue with her. But it was a different scene later when Annie hurried past us as she arrived for the afternoon shift. She caught my eye and looked away nervously, as though she thought we were going to yell something at her. Instead, Rosie just said, 'How's it going, Annie?'

Annie froze and turned around to face her.

'Ah, you know,' she said. She looked down at her hands. 'Not the same without the two of yiz.'

'You could always come out with us,' I said hopefully, but Annie shook her head and took a step back from us.

'I couldn't, Betty. You know I couldn't. My ma would kill me, and my da's not well …'

She looked so forlorn and scared that even Rosie didn't have the heart to give out to her.

'Well, I can't say I'm not disappointed, Annie,' she said.

'I hope yiz get what you're asking for,' said Annie quietly, and then she hurried down the lane and around the corner.

Rosie sighed. 'Well,' she said. 'I tried.' She put her picket sign up on her shoulder. 'You can lead a horse to water and all that. And speaking of people who don't like strikes, how's your ma?'

'Barely talking to me.' I held out a handbill to a woman who was on her way into the shop. 'Would you like to read about the union?'

'I would not!' The woman didn't even look at me as she pushed open the glass doors.

'Did your da not persuade her?' Rosie asked.

'He did his best,' I said. 'But she thinks there's a big difference between men being in the union and me being in the union.'

'I don't see why,' said Rosie. 'We're all workers, after all.'

Somehow I felt I had to explain Ma to Rosie. 'She doesn't see it that way. She thinks that girls should only work out for a few years and then get married and have babies.'

'Nice for some,' said Rosie, 'that can afford to do that.' And I knew she was thinking of her own ma, who sometimes leaves little Francis tied to the table while she scrubs floors up in the big North Circular Road houses. At least, she goes out and scrubs floors when she hasn't drunk too much.

'Well, that's what Ma did, apart from the dressmaking, and Lily did it as well,' I said. 'And she wants it for me too.'

'Does she have a husband picked out for you?' said Rosie with a grin. And it was at that moment something happened that pushed all thoughts of my mother and Annie and even the strike out of my head. A strangely familiar voice said, 'Miss Rafferty!'

I froze, just like Annie did when we greeted her.

'Master Lawlor!'

Because it was him, Peter Lawlor, walking towards us with a smile on his face that faded when he saw my handbills.

'I say,' he said. 'What are you up to?'

I could feel my face go hot and I hoped I wasn't too red. I

forced myself to meet his eyes.

'I'm handing out handbills,' I said. And then, in case that wasn't clear enough, 'Because I'm on strike.'

'Oh!' Peter Lawlor glanced down at his feet and looked a little flustered for a moment. But when he turned his gaze back to me, he looked as cheerful as ever. 'Mother told me there was some sort of disturbance here but …' He smiled at me. There was something so carefree about his smile. 'Well, you certainly are brave!'

'Oh!' I said. 'Well, thanks.'

There was a pause. I was suddenly very aware of Rosie standing just a few feet away, her eyes wide.

'Anyway,' said Peter Lawlor. 'I'm actually here to pick up a few cakes and things for Mother from the shop. She's having friends for tea this afternoon – you know the sort of thing. I'm sure your mother's the same.'

A part of me wanted to say that of course she wasn't, that my mother had never had friends round to tea in her life – not the sort of tea he meant, the tea you read about in books, with little cakes and scones and cream. Tea with a friend for Ma meant a cup of tea in the kitchen, in between one of them peeling potatoes and cleaning out the grate. But I didn't say that. I just said. 'Oh right, I see.'

'So …' said Peter. 'I'd better, um …'

His carefree confidence seemed to have left him as he gestured towards the door of the shop. And so did mine, apparently, because even though I knew I *should* launch into a speech about our cause and ask him not to go into his own father's shop, instead I just gave him a non-committal nod and didn't say a word as he walked through the big glass doors.

Rosie, however, said plenty of words, starting with, 'Is that that boy you were talking to in the shop a few weeks ago? Why did you call him' – she put on a grand voice – '"Master Lawlor"?'

''Cos that's who he is,' I said. 'He's Mr and Mrs Lawlor's son. He's just back from France.'

'But he said your name. How do *you* know him?' There was genuine astonishment in Rosie's voice. It was if she'd discovered I had a secret life where I was best pals with rich boys who went on French holidays. I hastened to tell her how we had met, and she looked quite disappointed. I think she was hoping there was some sort of secret love affair going on. Which is quite ridiculous, of course.

'Maybe,' she said hopefully, 'you could ask him to put in a good word for us with his da.'

'Ask him yourself!' I hissed, as the tall fair figure of Peter pushed open the door and walked out, a bag of cakes in each hand.

Rosie grabbed one of my handbills and held it out to him.

'Do you want a handbill, sir?' she said innocently.

'Oh, well, um, all right,' said Peter, rearranging his bags of cakes as he took the handbill. 'Thank you.' He nodded at me and smiled, a little awkwardly. 'Goodbye, Miss Rafferty.'

'Bye,' I said, and watched silently as he strode confidently up Henry Street to get his tram back to that big house on the Howth Road.

'Well!' said Rosie cheerfully. 'We might have made a convert there!'

'I doubt it,' I said. 'We're fighting his da, after all.'

'Plenty of people disagree with their das. And their mas,' she added, giving me a meaningful look.

'Yes, well,' I said. 'I wouldn't be relying on him to sort everything out. Besides, I don't even know him.'

'Sez you,' said Rosie. 'Ow, get out of that!' She's so sensitive. Just because I had whacked her with my bundle of handbills.

A few minutes later, two girls a little bit older than me came up to us and looked curiously at our signs. They had well-made frocks and hats, like the things Lavinia and her friends wore, only not as showy. One had thick brown hair that was falling out of its ribbons, while the other had copper-coloured curls. I noticed that the brown-haired girl had a badge saying 'Votes for Women' pinned to her collar.

'What are you striking for?' asked her red-haired friend.

I told her.

'Goodness,' said the brown-haired girl. 'That's jolly brave, walking out like that. Well done.'

'Thanks,' I said. 'We couldn't put up with being treated like that.'

'You're right,' said the brown-haired girl. 'It wasn't fair.' She paused. 'And if you *didn't* do anything, then nothing would change.'

'That's true,' I said.

'We're trying to change things as well,' said the red-haired girl.

'You're not on strike!' They couldn't be workers, surely. Not only did they not look like girls who had to go out and work, but they certainly didn't sound like them. They sounded like Lavinia and Peter Lawlor.

'Well, no,' said the red-haired girl. 'We're in school. But we're, well, we're suffragettes.'

'Sort of,' said the brown-haired girl. 'We painted something on a post box last year. And we've chalked things on the street.'

'And we've started a suffrage society in school,' said the red-haired girl. 'It's got quite popular actually.' She paused. 'Are you … do you believe in votes for women?'

'I suppose so,' I said. 'Though my da can't even vote, so I believe in getting votes for men like him too.'

The girls looked a little embarrassed. I had probably sounded a bit sharper than I meant to sound.

'We do think everyone over the age of twenty-one should have the vote,' said the brown-haired one earnestly. 'I mean, it's not fair that some people should have a say and others can't, is it?'

'I won't argue with you there,' I said. 'The world could do with being a whole lot more fair.'

'It certainly could,' said the red-haired girl.

'Well, good luck,' said the brown-haired girl. She held out her hand. I shook it.

'Thanks,' I said. 'My name's Betty, by the way.'

'I'm Mollie,' said the girl. 'And this is Nora.'

'Keep up the good work!' said Nora and, with a wave, the girls walked away. I looked after them. They seemed like nice girls, really. And they weren't wrong about it being important for women to have their say as well as men. But at the moment, the most important thing for me was getting workers treated fairly. Votes could wait until the strike was over.

I was exhausted by the time we finished picketing for the day. In fact, I was so tired by the time I got to the Five Lamps, I didn't even hear Samira calling my name until she was practically in front of me.

'What's wrong with you?' she said.

'Oh, nothing,' I said. 'It's just tiring, standing out there all day.'

'I don't know why I never thought of this before, but where do you … you know …' Samira raised her eyebrows.

'There's a newsagent's down the road that lets us use their toilet,' I said, correctly interpreting her expression. 'Are you off to the dramatic company?'

'I've been practising my lines all afternoon,' said Samira, beaming. 'Mrs McGrath says she doesn't even have to go to the play now, she already knows it by heart.' She struck a dramatic pose. '"Oh Father, listen to your only child!"'

'Very dramatic,' I said, impressed. 'Oh, howiya Eddie.'

For my brother was walking towards us. Or rather, trudging. I felt a tremor of unease. This wasn't Eddie's usual confident strut.

'All right, girls,' he said. He hadn't even bothered to make an obnoxious joke at us. Something must be wrong.

'Are *you* all right?' I said.

Eddie sighed. 'I am, yeah. But … well, I've lost my job.'

'Eddie, you haven't!' I felt my breath catch in my throat. 'Tell me you're only joking.'

'It's no joke, I can tell you that,' said Eddie. 'It was because of Mr Murphy. A gang of us in the tram company delivery room said we wouldn't handle his newspapers 'cause of what he did to the union members there. So we got the sack.'

Mr Murphy owns the tram company as well as the newspaper Ali used to work for.

'How many of you got sacked?' asked Samira.

Eddie shrugged his shoulders. 'I dunno. Couple of hundred, someone said.'

'A few *hundred*?' I stared at him.

A church bell started to ring.

'Janey, I didn't think it was that late,' said Samira. 'I'd better go. Good luck, Eddie!'

Eddie was quiet as we walked home. Eventually I said, 'What do you think Ma's going to say?'

'She'll understand,' said Eddie, sounding more confident than me.

'I don't know about that,' I said. 'She was fuming about me going out on strike. She still is.'

'That's 'cause you're a girl,' said Eddie, in a very annoying voice. 'It'll be grand.'

But it wasn't, and I can't pretend a little bit of me wasn't delighted when, after Eddie told her the news, Ma shouted, 'You big eejit! What did you go and do that for?' It wasn't that I agreed he was a big eejit, at least not when it comes to the union – I think Eddie and the other lads were right to stand up for their union brothers – but I have to admit that it was satisfying to see Ma giving out to someone else for once, after a week of her telling me to go back to work and stop my messing.

Eddie pointed out that he'd get strike pay but Ma didn't care.

'First Betty and now you!' she said. I didn't know whether she was going to stamp her feet in rage or burst into tears. I wouldn't have been surprised if she'd done either. And I felt bad, because I don't like seeing her upset, but I also don't like being given out to all the time just because I'm taking a stand.

Of course, when Da got home there were more discussions and arguments. I took my book and Earnshaw and headed down to the end of the garden, but when I got to my usual comfortable sunny seat on the far side of the jacks, Eddie was there already.

'Hiding out, are you?' I said. But I didn't mean anything bad by it.

Eddie seemed to understand because he just nodded.

'You'd think I was a bleedin' baby, the way she carries on,' he said. 'Not a working man.'

'We're all babies as far as she's concerned,' I said.

Eddie sighed and scrambled to his feet. 'I suppose I'd better go back in.'

'Well, you can't stay out here forever,' I agreed. 'But I'm staying, if you don't mind.'

'So much for solidarity between the workers,' said Eddie, but he winked at me as he said it.

I was glad it's August and the evenings are still long and bright and warm, because otherwise I would have had a cold old time waiting outside until the sounds of arguing died down. Eventually I ventured back into the kitchen and found Ma slapping dripping onto some thin slices of bread as if she was slapping an enemy soldier in the face.

'Can I give you a hand there, Ma?' I said.

Ma looked up at me and, to my horror, I realised that she'd been crying. Ma hardly ever cries and now I've seen her cry twice in less than a fortnight.

'There's nothing left to do now,' she said. 'And you'd better enjoy this bread and dripping because at the rate this family is going, we won't have any food in the press at all in a few weeks.'

I looked nervously at Da, who was sitting in his usual seat by the grate, his face grave.

'It won't come to that, now, Margaret,' he said. He walked over to her and laid a gentle hand on her arm. 'We'll be grand whatever happens.'

'And if we can't pay the rent?' said Ma. 'Will we be grand then?'

There was no answer to that. Our tea was a very gloomy meal, and not just because it was only bread and dripping and tea made with condensed milk. Ma's been economising more than ever since I went out on strike. Afterwards I scurried away and called down to Samira's house; I knew she'd be home from her practice by then. Samira herself answered the door.

'Betty, the very girl! Do you want to hear my lines?' she said, without even saying hello.

'And good evening to you too,' I said.

'Sorry,' said Samira. 'Do come in, Miss Rafferty.' She gave me a very elegant curtsey, practically sweeping down to the ground. I'd never tell her this in case it made her all self-conscious, but she really is very graceful. Auntie Maisie's the same. She looks like she's dancing even when she's just reaching up to the top shelf of the press to get a tin of sugar. I know if I tried curtseying like that I'd fall over.

Samira was on her own in the house. Ali and Mr Casey were out at some union thing, and Auntie Maisie had gone to the theatre to see Mr Farrell.

'She's taking that evil stepmother part for Mr Whatsisname,' said Samira, as we settled down in the front room.

'Janey!' I said, curling up on the stiff horsehair sofa. 'We'll get to see her on stage at last.'

'She wasn't going to take it, after what he said to me the other week.' Samira fiddled with the end of one of her plaits. 'She told me so this morning.'

'What happened to change her mind?' I asked.

'Well, it struck me that she hadn't said anything about it at all, not since the night at the theatre,' Samira said. 'So I asked her what she was going to say to him when he came back to Dublin. And that's when she told me she was going to turn him down. She said she didn't want to work with him anymore.'

Samira's expression was serious. 'She said she was sorry for how she acted when we left the theatre — being all happy about him saying I could join the panto next year. I know she was trying to cheer me up.' Samira looked down at her hands. 'But it just made me feel like she wasn't taking it seriously. She didn't understand what it was like for me.'

'So why did she decide to take the job then?' I asked.

'*I* told her she had to say yes,' said Samira.

'That was very big of you,' I said. And I meant it.

'I dunno,' said Samira. She sighed. 'If I hadn't managed to get the part in the Dramatic Company play, maybe I wouldn't have talked her into taking the part. But Auntie Maisie gave up her life on the stage for me and Ali, and I know she really wants to act again. This might be her only chance. And besides …' Samira's face broke into a grin, 'if she stays in with Mr Farrell, she can take him to my play, and then he'll see just how good I am and eat his words! Not,' she added, 'that I'd take a job from him myself, even if he got down on his knees and begged me to play Juliet.'

'Good,' I said. 'Janey, just imagine if he did.' And there was a little pause as we both pictured that satisfying scene.

'Well, I'd better keep practising, then,' said Samira. She jumped to her feet and struck a pose in front of the fireplace. 'This is the scene where Tessie — that's my character — tells her father she's changed her mind and supports the union after all.'

After Samira had performed some of her lines (I told her she might have gone too far in her big speech when she flung herself on the ground and beat the carpet with her fist until the dust flew up and made her sneeze. She reluctantly agreed.) I told her about how my ma was losing the rag over Eddie being out on strike too.

'Do you think our das will be out next?' said Samira.

'I wouldn't be surprised,' I admitted. 'It feels like something's in the air.'

And it still does. That was a few days ago and there's talk of even more men at the tram company going out if the employers don't respond to their demands. Ma isn't happy about this at all, but at least she's had a little bit of good news. She wrote to all her Drumcondra clients, telling them she was available for more work – she likes to call them clients, as if she was one of those French dressmakers that have big studios and little velvet sitting rooms where the ladies go and try clothes on. I've read about them in some of the magazines Ma's customers give her when they're finished with them.

Anyway, one of those Drumcondra ladies wrote back to her and asked her to make some clothes for her daughter's wedding that's coming up in a few months. And another one asked her to call over today to alter a dress for some big party she's going to on Saturday. So even if Mrs Lawlor and all her Clontarf friends abandon her, Ma will still have a bit of work. Which is more than you can say for me and Eddie – at least for now.

# Chapter Thirteen

Today was a hot and sunny day. I'm writing that down so that, when someone reads this memoir in fifty years, they'll know what the weather was like on the day that the union brought the city to a halt.

Not that I knew anything unusual was going to happen when I left the house this morning with my picketing sign – which I have to say is getting a bit grubby around the edges. Maybe I should go to Liberty Hall and get some more cardboard? Although they're probably going to be short on cardboard for signs soon, given what's going on.

When I was leaving the house this morning Ma clamped her old straw hat down on my head and fixed it to my hair with a pin.

'If you're going to spend the whole day making a show of yourself outside that shop, I don't want you getting sunstroke,' she said. Which is the most encouraging thing she's said to me since the strike started. I thanked her and headed into town, and I have to admit that I was grateful for that hat because it kept the sun out of my eyes, even though it's a bit too small for me thanks to all my hair. It sort of perches on top of my head and if it wasn't for the pin it'd just fall right off.

I got to O'Connell Street shortly after nine and pushed my way through busy crowds that had gathered around the pillar. I was wondering why there were so many people in summer suits and nice hats, but then I remembered that the Dublin Horse Show was starting today, out in Ballsbridge. I've never been to the Horse

Show, of course, but you can't help knowing about it. Ma's made her clients plenty of special frocks for it over the years.

After pushing through all the crowds, I was quite hot and bothered when I got to Lawlor's and joined the few girls who had already arrived.

Kitty was there before me, of course. She's always the first to arrive and the last to leave. And it's a good thing she's there the whole time, because on days like this, when everyone is hot and sticky and dusty and the last thing we want to do is march up and down in front of a cake shop holding a sign, Kitty's like a general on a battlefield, making sure we're well organised. In fact, today she quickly decided that her troops needed to be fed. A few of the girls hadn't shown up yet, and those that had didn't look very enthusiastic. By a quarter to ten everyone was drooping a bit.

'We need to get a few buns or something,' Kitty decided. 'Betty, you go and get them.'

It feels like Kitty's always asking me to do errands. I can't decide if I'm her servant or her second in command. But I couldn't deny it was a good idea to hand out some buns.

The girls like Joan from the washing-up room, who don't live at home with their families, have begun skipping breakfast to save a few bob and it's starting to show. Joan's been looking very peaky over the last few days. And the enticing smell of delicious bread and cakes wafting towards us every time someone opens the door of Lawlor's doesn't help.

Kitty handed me sixpence and told me to get a bag of buns from Yeates's bakery over on North Earl Street. They're a good union establishment – they stopped using Scott's flour as soon as the dispute broke out. I looked at the sixpence and then back at Kitty.

'Are you sure you can afford this?' I said hesitantly. Every penny counts when you're out on strike. The strike pay is good but it's not quite as much as we used to get paid.

'I can't do it every day,' said Kitty. 'But keeping up morale is important. Go on, off you go.'

She can be very bossy, but she was right about keeping up morale, so I hurried up Henry Street and scampered across the road, which was full of trams and delivery vans and even a few motor cars. The young woman behind the counter in Yeates's bakery smiled when she saw my red hand union badge.

'A sixpenny bag of buns, please,' I said, handing over the coin Kitty had given me.

'Good to see another union girl,' said the bakery girl, putting a bun into a paper bag.

'I'm on strike at the moment,' I said. 'Lawlor's, over on Henry Street.'

'Are you now?' said the bakery girl. 'Picketing?'

I nodded. 'That's why I'm buying buns. To keep the girls going.'

'That's a good idea,' said the girl. She filled the bag of buns and to my alarm started loading more into another bag.

'Sorry, miss, I just wanted one sixpenny bag,' I said. I didn't want to be charged for too many buns.

'I know,' said the girl. She handed me both bags and winked. 'That should keep you going 'til dinnertime.'

'Thanks … thanks very much,' I stammered. 'That's very …'

'I hope you enjoy them,' said the girl. 'Now get back to that picket line!'

I was still thinking about that bakery girl and how kind she was and how pleased the girls would be to see all those buns when I reached O'Connell Street. And then, just as I was about to cross the road, something extraordinary happened.

All the trams stopped.

They weren't stopping at junctions, or to let another vehicle turn a corner. They just stopped dead in their tracks, wherever they happened to be on the road. The Number Sixteen stopped right in front of me, and the driver and conductor calmly got out of their tram. I looked up and down O'Connell Street and saw other tram drivers and conductors doing the same. There were at least a dozen trams stopped on the tracks to my right, going up to Rutland Square, and as many if not more to my left, down towards the bridge, going in both directions. All the traffic on the street had ground to a halt, because the stopped trams were blocking the roads. I'd never seen anything like this before.

For a moment I thought that there must be some problem with the electrical wires that power the trams, but then a man in an elegant fawn suit stuck his head out of the Number Sixteen.

'Hie there, driver!' he said. 'What's going on?'

The driver took something out of his pocket and attached it to the buttonhole of his jacket.

'What's going on,' he said, 'is a strike.'

And with a rising feeling of excitement, I realised that what he had attached to his jacket was the red hand badge of the union. Next to him, the conductor was doing the same thing. I looked at the next tram down and saw its driver and conductor were pinning on their own badges. And so were the men from other trams. It was as if the street was suddenly illuminated by lots of tiny red lights.

'But I have to get to Rathfarnham!' the suited man cried.

'Well,' said the conductor, thoughtfully, adjusting his red hand badge. 'You could always walk.'

'This is outrageous!' said the man.

Another man appeared next to him in the tram entrance, a tall man with a magnificent moustache. 'Is the Dalkey tram running?' he said.

'That depends who's driving it,' said the conductor. 'But if it's my friend Puddiner's day on that route, and I think it is, then no, it's not.'

'But why?' demanded the moustachioed man.

'Because Puddiner's in the union too,' said the conductor cheerfully. He turned to the driver. 'Got your badge on, Davy?'

'But this is outrageous!' said the moustachioed man. 'It's Horse Show Week!'

'I know,' said the conductor regretfully. 'And there was I hoping for my usual place in the Royal Box. Still, no rest for the wicked.' And he and his driver pal turned to go. Which is when he noticed me staring at them, my eyes wide and my red hand badge shining from my jacket lapel. He raised his hat.

'Howiya, miss,' he said. 'What do you think of all this?'

'It's …' I couldn't find the right words to describe what I thought of it. Everywhere I looked I could see drivers and conductors standing calmly beside their trams. The air was full of the sound of angry hooting – other vehicles were trying to make their way around the trams that had stopped at junctions, and passengers were yelling at the departing drivers. It was incredible. Us girls had caused a bit of annoyance to Miss Warby and some of the customers. But these tram workers had brought the biggest street in the biggest city in Ireland to a halt!

'I'm out on strike too' was the only thing I could say.

'Are you now?' The driver and conductor exchanged amused glances. But there was nothing sneering about it. It was a friendly sort of amusement. They reminded me of Da.

'The bosses won't forget this in a hurry, will they?' said the driver.

'No, mister,' I said. 'I don't think they will.'

'I demand you take me to Rathfarnham!' yelled the fawn-suited man, and he looked so angry I thought I should get back to Lawlor's and tell the others what was going on before a fight broke out.

'Good luck!' I said to the striking tram men. The conductor gave me a cheery wink as the pair of them tipped their hats in farewell.

I made my way through the parked trams and other vehicles to Nelson's Pillar, and as I gazed all around me and took in the scene, a giddy feeling bubbled up inside of me at the sight of all those stopped trams and the crowds of passengers and curious onlookers that were gathering around them. Maybe we really could make a difference. Maybe our strike and the girls in the Savoy Café and the tram drivers all added up to something, something big and important that would change the whole world – or at least Dublin.

I was almost skipping with excitement as I passed another stopped tram on the other side of the street, but then I nearly stepped out in front of a bread van that was squeezing around the side of it, and the driver shouted, 'Watch where you're going, you little eejit!' After that I stopped dreaming about the brave new world where workers ruled, and hurried down to Lawlor's, where the group of striking girls had grown since I headed off on my bun mission.

'What's going on up there?' demanded Kitty. From where the strikers stood, you could see the gathering crowds on O'Connell Street.

I paused for dramatic effect and held one of the bags of buns aloft. Samira would have been proud of me. 'The tram drivers are on strike!' I announced. There was a very gratifying gasp of amazement and excitement. 'Oh, and the conductors too,' I added, which didn't sound quite as dramatic. 'All the trams on O'Connell Street have stopped!'

The entire group of strikers broke out in excited chatter.

'I don't believe it!' said Rosie.

'You can go up and see for yourself,' I said. I looked at Kitty. 'Can't she? I mean, it *is* union business.'

'I want to go too!' said Joan from the washing-up room.

Kitty looked thoughtful. 'I suppose you can go. Just for a minute, mind you. The rest of us will keep the picket going.'

I handed her the bag of buns.

'The girl in the shop gave me a free bag because we're on strike,' I said. 'This should keep everyone fed.'

'Come on!' said Rosie, grabbing my hand.

I looked apologetically at Kitty and then hurried up the street with Rosie and Joan.

By the time we reached O'Connell Street the mood was changing. Large numbers of policemen were making their way through the crowds of onlookers, and we could see a scuffle taking place across the road, where some Dublin Metropolitan Police officers were trying to arrest a group of strikers. Some of the watching crowd cheered their support, while others erupted in boos. The DMP men started to push back the encroaching crowd, and further down the street I could see a few trams were starting to move again. My excitement began to curdle into nervousness.

'What's going on?' I asked a barefoot newsboy, who was leaning on a lamp-post and taking in the scene.

'They've brought in some company scabs to drive the trams,' he said. He pointed in the direction of a tram that was jerking along its track in stops and starts. 'But half of them are ticket inspectors and they don't know how to drive the bleedin' things!' He laughed raucously and then started coughing.

'We might have known that Mr Murphy would fight dirty,' said Rosie grimly.

'He's not the only one,' I said nervously, looking at the policemen pushing back the crowds. They were anything but gentle. 'Maybe we should get back to Lawlor's.'

'I could do with my bun now,' admitted Joan. Just then we heard people yelling somewhere down the street in the direction of the bridge. A tram, clearly driven by a scab driver, was trying to make its way up O'Connell Street, but strikers were surrounding it and pounding on the sides, stopping it from moving. The joyful atmosphere was turning dark.

'Come on,' said Rosie. 'Let's go back to our nice cosy picket.'

It took us twice as long to get back to Lawlor's as it had taken to get from there to O'Connell Street just a short time earlier. The crowds were continuing to grow and the policemen kept pushing people back from the trams, adding to the crush of bodies. But the good thing about being quite small is that sometimes you can just wriggle through a crowd, and that's what we did. When we told the others that things were rowdy on O'Connell Street, some girls looked worried, some looked excited, and Kitty's face hardened with resolve.

'We knew this would be a tough fight, girls,' she said stoutly. 'We can't give in!'

There was a strange sort of nervousness and excitement in the air for the rest of the day. Lawlor's had fewer customers than usual, probably because people couldn't get into town with no trams. But some of the customers that did turn up were very cross with us. At about three o'clock I held out a handbill to a middle-aged lady in a pale blue coat.

'Would you like a handbill?' I said.

She turned to me, her eyes blazing.

'I certainly would not!' she said. If she hadn't been a lady, I might have said she snarled. 'Have you seen what's been happening up on Sackville Street? Chaos, that's what it is! Lawless chaos!'

'They're just withdrawing their labour,' I said, as politely as I could.

The lady snorted. 'They're a gang of rowdies,' she said. 'And I hope the police put some manners on them.'

And with that, she swept into the shop. Rosie and I exchanged glances.

'Well,' said Rosie, 'at least it shows that striking makes a difference.'

'True,' I said.

By the time we finished our picket for the day, things had calmed down in O'Connell Street, although there were still crowds of men standing around. I was disappointed to see trams were moving up and down the road. As I passed the GPO, I caught sight of the newsboy from earlier, and I asked him what the story was with the vehicles.

'More scabs and blacklegs,' he said, spitting on the ground. 'But the tram company are calling a curfew.'

'What does that mean?' I asked him.

'The trams are going to stop running at seven instead of twelve tonight,' said the newsboy. 'To stop gangs of strikers attacking the drivers – that's what they say.'

'*Has* anyone been attacking them?' I said. I didn't particularly like the idea of attacks.

The boy shrugged his shoulders. 'A few have. I dunno.' And with that vague answer, he strolled off in the direction of Rutland Square.

As I walked down Amiens Street and onto the North Strand, I tried to work out if there were fewer trams than usual. It felt as if there were, and most seemed to be heading away from town and towards the depot in Clontarf. The strike really was having an effect!

When I got home, I met Eddie just coming out of the front door.

'Where are you off to?' I said. 'I hope you weren't thinking of taking a tram.'

'Ha ha, very funny I don't think,' said Eddie, tousling my hair in his irritating way. 'I'm going to a union meeting. Mr Larkin's going to speak to us.'

'Do you think …' I hate asking Eddie a serious question. It just gives him notions of his own importance, but I actually did want to know what he thought. 'Do you think you'll win? The tram company strikers I mean.'

And for once Eddie didn't answer me with a patronising smirk or a joke.

'I dunno,' he said. 'But things couldn't go on like the way they were.'

I couldn't argue with that. And even though Ma grumbled about Eddie getting himself mixed up in trouble and even though Da sadly pointed out that not all the tram men had walked out today, for the rest of my life I don't think I'll ever forget how it felt on that glorious, magical moment, when the tram drivers just said no, we're not going to put up with this anymore and, for a little while, made everything stop.

# Chapter Fourteen

It's three days since the tram men walked out, and Dublin feels very peculiar right now. I said this to Samira this morning, when I walked into McGrath's shop on my way to the picket line.

'It's peculiar in here, anyway,' said Samira, as she rubbed at the worn shop counter with an old rag and the remains of a battered tin of lavender polish. 'We barely sold a thing yesterday, only tobacco and a few tins of condensed milk. All the women are trying to save their pennies in case more strikes are on the way.' She scrubbed at a particularly greasy spot on the counter. 'Mrs McGrath is talking about closing the shop in the afternoons. Most of our sales are in the mornings.'

'What'll you do then?' I said. 'Will you still have a job?'

'Maybe.' Samira looked absently at the cloth in her hand and then back at the counter. 'Have I cleaned this bit before?'

'Samira!' I snatched the cloth out of her hand. 'You're away with the fairies again.'

'I'll be grand,' Samira assured me. 'Sure, I can work only mornings for a few days. And it'll give me time to practise my lines. It won't be forever.'

'I dunno,' I said. 'It doesn't feel like Mr Murphy and his pals are going to give in any time soon.'

It really doesn't. The tram workers are still out on strike – or at least a good lot of them are. They went on a big parade through the centre of the city on Wednesday. It was a grand sight, all of them marching past our picket line and around O'Connell Street like a veritable army, with their union badges in their buttonholes, singing new words to the tune of 'A Long Way To Tipperary':

It's the wrong thing to crush the workers
It's the wrong thing to do
It's the right thing to wipe out tyrants
Murphy and his crew!

More employers around the city have been locking out their workers for joining the union. Most dramatically of all, Mr Larkin was arrested yesterday, though he was let out on bail. I'm not sure exactly what he was arrested for – Da said it was just for causing trouble to the bosses. He was meant to be speaking at a big meeting in town on Sunday, but everyone's saying the police are going to try and stop it taking place. I wasn't planning to be at the meeting anyway – the Women Worker's Union are going on a picnic that day, so I'll be there instead. In the meantime, everyone is tense and worried.

'At least our play will keep the workers' spirits up,' said Samira, and I couldn't tell if she was joking or not. She really does take her acting very seriously.

'How did the Wednesday rehearsal go?' I asked. 'Are you getting on with all the other actors?' I hadn't seen much of Samira this week. I'm trying to help Ma more in the house in the evenings, to give her fewer reasons to grumble and grouse at me. She's been like a bear with a sore head since Eddie stopped working.

'Grand,' said Samira. There was a pause. 'A few of them are a bit off with me but most of them are nice.'

'Off with you?' I didn't like the sound of that.

'It's just two of them, this aul fella called George and a girl called Josephine,' said Samira. 'Passing remarks about my name and that. Nothing I haven't heard before.'

'I hope someone stuck up for you,' I said. 'I mean,' I added hastily, 'I know you can fight your own battles, but you shouldn't have to.'

'Well, actually.' And to my surprise, I noticed that Samira's cheeks were flushed. 'Tom gave out to them for having no manners. They didn't say anything after that.'

'Tom!' I stared at her. 'Ali's friend Tom? I didn't know he was in the Dramatic Company!'

Samira started polishing the counter very hard and didn't meet my eye. 'I didn't know either until I saw him there that first night I went. He turned up late – you must have just missed him.'

'And why didn't you tell me all this before now?' I demanded.

Samira stopped polishing and looked up at me. 'Because I knew you'd start teasing me about it!'

Now it was my turn to look away. 'Ah, you know I don't mean anything by it.'

'I do know,' said Samira. 'But it's *not* funny. You wouldn't like it if I said something about you and Ali, would you?'

'Ali!' I stared at her. 'Why would you even mention him?'

Before Samira could reply, there was a loud bark and Earnshaw bounded into the shop, his tail wagging so hard he knocked a packet of soap powder off the shelf near the door.

'Earnshaw!' I exclaimed. 'What are you doing here?'

Eddie appeared in the doorway. 'He followed me out and I couldn't get him to go back.'

'Well, he can't stay here,' I said. 'You'd better take him home.'

'Can't do it, Betser. I'm meeting the tramway lads and we're going to picket the tram company offices – I should have been at the Five Lamps ten minutes ago.'

'I have to go to *my* picket!' I cried, but it was no use. Eddie ran – actually ran – away from me. By the time I'd squeezed past Earnshaw's bulk and got out to the street, Eddie was already practically at the railway bridge. I returned to the shop, where Samira was trying to stop Earnshaw jumping up on her nice polished counter.

'I'd better take him home before he wrecks the shop,' I said. 'If he does that, you really will be out of a job.'

But when I got back to our house, the door was shut and there was no answer when I knocked. I remembered Ma had said she was going to one of her Drumcondra dressmaking ladies this morning to do a fitting for some grand party she was going to tomorrow, something about the end of the Horse Show. She must have left the house after me and before Eddie. And I didn't have my latch key.

'You big eejit of a dog,' I said, taking hold of Earnshaw's collar. 'Let's see if Lily can take you until Ma gets home.'

But Lily, when I called at the Hessians' house, said she couldn't, because of looking after Little Robbie.

'I would have thought looking after Earnshaw would be easier than Little Robbie,' I said. 'Earnshaw bites less, anyway.' Which didn't go down very well. But Lily *did* give me a bit of old rope to use as a lead. I tied it to Earnshaw's collar.

'I suppose you're just going to have to join the union,' I told him, and we headed back up the road and around to the North Strand. As we passed McGrath's shop I was relieved, when I glanced in the open door, to see Samira serving a few customers. At least they were getting *some* business.

Earnshaw was so excited about being out with me during the day that he fairly pulled me along the street at top speed. I had to haul on his rope when we reached O'Connell Street to stop him dashing out into the road and heading for all the flower stalls by the pillar. There were some striking tram men there too, and I was afraid he'd knock one over and cause more commotion. There's been talk that there have been more attacks on the tram men who refused to go on strike and are still manning the trams.

Our arrival at Lawlor's caused a sensation.

'What,' said Kitty, sounding more like a warrior queen than she has all week, 'is *that*?'

'Earnshaw, my old pal!' said Rosie, dropping her picket sign and flinging her arms around him.

'Does he bite?' said Joan nervously.

''Course he doesn't,' I said, truthfully.

Hesitantly, Joan crouched down next to Rosie and rubbed behind Earnshaw's ears. He wagged his tail in pleasure.

'What's he doing here?' Kitty demanded, and I told her about Earnshaw's escape.

'I couldn't leave him roaming the streets,' I said. 'He might have got hit by a motorcar. Or someone might steal him.'

Kitty sighed and rolled her eyes to heaven. 'I don't think there's much chance of that. Oh well, he'll have to stay, I suppose. But keep him under control!'

'Consider him protection,' said Rosie, 'if the police come down and start making trouble.'

'I think they've got enough to be doing with the tram men,' said Kitty.

'You'd think the tram men were asking for hundreds of pounds a week each, and days off every Saturday and Sunday,' said Rosie, taking up her picket sign again. 'They just want two bob extra a week, and to get their day off every eight days instead of every fortnight.'

I suppose we had been lucky in Lawlor's in that sense – the shop is closed on Sundays so we had to get a whole day off every week.

As I could have told Kitty he would, if she'd given me a chance, Earnshaw behaved very well. In fact, I think he did us a favour, because his impressive appearance attracted the attention of passers by who might otherwise have grown accustomed to seeing our picket there and ignored it accordingly. By the afternoon, even Kitty had to admit he was a draw. One young man actually came up to us and asked, 'What sort of a dog is that?' I wasn't able to answer him, because of course Earnshaw's origins are lost in the mists of time (or the mists of the Dublin docks), but it did give me an excuse to give him one of my handbills.

'You should take Earnshaw in every day,' said Rosie as the young man walked away. Unlike some people, he actually seemed to be reading his handbill, and hadn't just stuffed it in his pocket or, as in the worst cases, ripped it up and thrown it away. There are few things more annoying when you're out campaigning than seeing someone waste a perfectly good handbill.

'I think I will,' I said. 'Ma'll be happy to have him out of the house during the day, he's always trying to get into the front room when she's got her pattern pieces laid out.'

Just then, a tall young man, whose straw boater was pulled low over his eyes against the afternoon sun, approached the shop.

'Don't cross the picket line!' cried Rosie, jumping up and down and waving her sign around. Kitty gave her a cross look. She thinks we should be dignified at all times. But as Rosie says, dignity isn't everything.

The young man pushed his hat back, and I realised to my general confusion that it was none other than Peter Lawlor. Who I suppose is not technically a man at all, but a boy.

Rosie didn't miss a beat. 'Hello there,' she said brightly. 'Have you come to join us after all?' She looked at me and winked. 'I knew that handbill you gave him the other week would work.'

'Um, I haven't, actually,' said Peter Lawlor. 'I'm helping out.'

'Helping out what?' I said.

'In the shop.' Peter Lawlor shifted from one foot to another. 'They've had to, well, move staff around from one section to another and they're short behind the counter. Father was complaining about it last night, so I said I could help out.'

'Your father wants you working behind the counter? Doing our jobs?' I could barely believe my ears.

Peter Lawlor looked embarrassed. 'He thinks it'll be good publicity. For Lawlor's, you know. The family pitching in, and all that, to save the shop during the strike.'

'I don't suppose your sister is coming along too,' I said.

'Um, no,' said Peter. 'It's not really Lavinia's sort of thing. But I, well, I felt I had to.'

'And what,' said Rosie, smiling at him in a way that only those who knew her could tell was dangerous, 'do you know about serving people buns?'

Peter Lawlor laughed awkwardly. 'Not much, I suppose. But you know, I spent all term translating Virgil and learning about higher mathematics, so selling cakes can't be that hard, can it? I mean, you girls can all do it …' His voice trailed away as he real-ised just what he was saying.

'Well, isn't it very good of you to lower yourself to our level,' said Rosie sweetly. Peter Lawlor took a sideways step towards the door.

'I'm sorry, Miss …?'

'Delaney,' said Rosie. 'Rosie Delaney.'

'Miss Delaney.' He looked imploringly at me. I thought I saw real regret in those wide eyes. 'And Miss Rafferty. I didn't mean to insult you.'

'That's quite all right, Master Lawlor,' I said, in my best Ma voice.

For a second I thought Peter Lawlor was going to say something else, but then Earnshaw gave a decisive bark and Peter Lawlor touched the brim of his boater and headed into the shop.

'Well!' Rosie turned to me, fire in her eyes. 'The cheek of him!'

I didn't say anything. I just fiddled with Earnshaw's makeshift lead. I had a strange sort of feeling in my belly. It wasn't until we were finishing up for the day that I realised the feeling was disappointment. Although why I should be disappointed in my employer's son, a boy I hardly knew at all, I don't know.

I had said goodbye to the others and was walking slowly up Henry Street with Earnshaw when I heard a voice calling me. Or rather, I heard a voice calling 'Miss Rafferty!' which no one has ever called me in my life besides Miss Warby – and one other person. And when I turned around, just at the O'Connell Street junction, I saw that person running towards me.

'Are you and your dog getting the tram home?' said Peter

Lawlor, struggling a little to catch his breath. 'Would you think it terribly forward of me if I accompanied you?' He smiled hopefully at me. I have to admit he has a nice smile. But just like dignity, nice smiles aren't everything.

I drew myself up to my full height, which isn't very tall, but still.

'Girls like me can't afford to get the tram,' I said.

Peter Lawlor's smile faded, replaced by an embarrassed look.

'Oh, sorry, I didn't mean …'

'And even if I could, I wouldn't,' I went on, as severely as I could. 'The tram men are on strike.'

'But the trams are still running until seven,' said Peter Lawlor. 'Not everyone is striking.'

I sighed. He really didn't understand.

'That doesn't matter,' I said. 'I can't deal with any business where some people are on strike. Like Savoy chocolates. I used to buy them as a special treat sometimes. But not anymore.'

'I got a box of them for my mother this week,' said Peter Lawlor.

'Well, I hope you didn't eat any,' I said. 'They're full of rat droppings, from what I've heard.'

Peter Lawlor went pale beneath his golden tan. 'Are they really?' I nodded.

'The factory's riddled with rats,' I said. 'That's why the girls are out on strike. Well, it's just one of the reasons why.'

'Good Lord,' said Peter Lawlor.

'Anyway.' I was tired. It was a long day and Earnshaw was getting restless. 'I'd better be off.'

I started to cross the road but Peter Lawlor said, 'Wait! Please.'

I turned around.

'Would you … may I walk with you?' He really did look sincere.

Maybe he wanted to know more about strikes. And even though Ma and Da wouldn't approve of me associating with boys they don't know, I didn't think Ma would object to Mrs Lawlor's son. Maybe he'd put in a good word for her with his Ma.

'It's a free country,' I said, marching across the road. 'Well, sort of. I can't stop you anyway.'

'Jolly good,' said Peter Lawlor, hurrying after me. But when we'd crossed the road and reached the top of Talbot Street neither of us seemed to be able to think of anything to say. We walked along in a slightly awkward silence for a while, and then Peter Lawlor swallowed and said, 'Have you read a lot of Sherlock Holmes stories?'

It was a strange thing to ask out of nowhere, but I knew he was just making conversation.

'All the books they have in the library,' I said. 'I don't know if that's all the stories Mr Conan Doyle ever wrote.'

'What's your favourite?' asked Peter Lawlor, sounding as if he really wanted to know.

'*Hound of the Baskervilles*,' I said, without hesitation. If I'd read that story when we got Earnshaw, I might have called him Baskerville instead. Though I can't really imagine him being called anything but Earnshaw. It really does suit him, somehow.

'Come, Watson, the game's afoot!' said Peter Lawlor in a very dramatic way. I looked at him in delighted surprise, and he grinned back at me. I'd never known anyone beside Samira who quoted stories like that before.

'"They were the footprints of a gigantic hound!"' I replied, as dramatically as I could. I love that line in the book.

Peter Lawlor laughed. 'It's jolly exciting, isn't it? It's one of my favourites too. Though *The Final Problem* is marvellous as well ...'

And some of the awkwardness that had been between us seemed to fall away, just a bit. We talked about books all the way to the Five Lamps. Peter Lawlor didn't really share my and Samira's love of Shakespeare ('I have to read too much of him at school') but he was intrigued to hear about her dreams of acting fame.

'We've got a theatre at school,' he said. 'We do concerts and plays there every year.'

'A theatre?' I thought he was joking. 'An actual theatre? With curtains and, like, sets and everything?'

'Yes, all of that,' said Peter. 'We did *King Lear* last term. I played Gloucester. I don't know if I was any good, but I got to stagger around the stage screaming in that bit where his terrible wife goes for him and gets his eye. So that was rather jolly. And we were allowed to skip Greek for a few weeks.'

I already knew that Peter's school must have been very grand, but its own theatre! I've never heard the like.

And yet despite the fact that he went to a school that sounds like something out of a story, Peter Lawlor was easy to talk to once you got started. He may not love Shakespeare, but he does share my and Samira's love of Dickens, and we agreed that *Great Expectations* was the best.

'Though I'm partial to *A Tale of Two Cities*,' I said, as we crossed the road at the Portland Place. 'I don't blame those Frenchmen for starting a revolution.'

'You can't agree with chopping people's heads off, surely.' Peter Lawlor sounded shocked.

'Of course I don't,' I said. 'But you know, they were treated terribly, and that nobleman fella told them to eat grass if they were hungry ... Things had to change. Like they have to change here.'

'I hope *you* don't want to chop my head off,' said Peter lightly.

'Some people around here might,' I said, trying to keep my own voice playful. 'They don't take kindly to scabs.'

'I can't be a scab – what a horrible expression, by the way!' laughed Peter. 'I'm just helping out my father. It was rather fun, you know.'

'Working behind the counter?' I said.

'Yes,' said Peter cheerfully. 'I mean, it was quite jolly talking to the customers and picking out the buns they wanted and all that. I enjoyed it. Much more fun than doing Latin and Maths. I might stay on and help for a while instead of going back to school next week.'

'And you didn't get tired?' I said.

'Well, not really,' said Peter. 'I mean, I suppose I did feel like a sit down after about two hours, but then I had my break in Mrs Warby's room so I could rest for half an hour or so …'

'Half a what?' I interrupted. 'You got a half hour break? After working just two hours?'

'Don't you?' Peter Lawlor looked surprised.

'Of course I don't!' I thought I'd said this in a calm and pleasant tone, but Peter Lawlor's shocked expression suggested I hadn't. 'I don't get a break until I've been working for at least five hours – six, sometimes. Even then I only get five minutes, and it's in the little cubby hole not Miss Warby's room. And I've got to work for another four hours afterwards.'

'Goodness, really?' Peter Lawlor said. 'Have you girls talked to Miss Warby about it?'

I took a deep breath, but my voice still trembled with irritation when I answered him. 'Of course we have! She was trying to make us work even longer hours!'

Peter Lawlor looked uncomfortable, as well he might.

'Oh,' he said. 'I see.'

I wasn't sure he did, not really. Especially when he said, 'But are you sure *striking* is the way to solve these things? I mean, look at the tram men – I don't think the strike has made my father any more inclined to support them. He keeps saying what a nuisance it is, all the pickets and the curfew. He had to get a cab home from a meeting yesterday evening.'

'That's part of the point,' I said. 'It reminds people like your father how much they need the tram men.'

'But all this fuss! People breaking tram windows, fighting in the streets. Wouldn't things be better if everyone just, I don't know, took things a bit less seriously?'

A part of me wished he was right. Quite a big part of me. I imagined living a life where I didn't have to take anything seriously. Where I had long summer holidays that I could spend reading Sherlock Holmes stories, where I didn't have to worry about pickets or whether Ma would have enough money to buy food without my and Eddie's full wages – and maybe Da going out on strike soon as well. A life where I didn't have to worry about anything but what book I'd read next or what play my school would put on in its theatre next term. Suddenly I felt very sad.

'This is my road,' I said. I pointed towards the junction of Strandville Avenue.

'Gosh, is it?' Peter Lawlor looked rather surprised, though I'm not sure why. 'I say, what nice little cottages.'

'Well, goodbye,' I said. And I stuck out my hand. He shook it.

'Goodbye,' he said. 'And no hard feelings about me helping out my old Pa, eh? I mean, it's just a bit of fun.' He ruffled Earnshaw's fur as he spoke.

I didn't trust myself to answer that. It may have been a bit of fun for him, but not for us. I just said, 'Bye so.' And then I ran across the road without looking back, Earnshaw bounding along beside me. For some reason I felt that if I stayed with Peter Lawlor for a second more I might start to cry.

# Chapter Fifteen

I wrote that last sentence just three days ago, but so much has happened since then it seems more like three years. Then the city was just striking. Now it feels like it's at war. And I don't think anything will ever be the same again.

Saturday started out like any other day – at least for me. I've got used to the new routine of going in to the picket. Those of us who can spare food from home have started taking in a bit of bread and cheese wrapped in newspaper, so we have something to eat in the middle of the day. One thing about working in Lawlor's, you quickly got used to having your dinner given to you, even if it was only a bit of bread and butter. We share our food around now so the girls who aren't living at home always have a bit to eat. I was just wrapping up my bread and cheese when Ma said, 'I forgot to tell you last night, Betty, Mrs Dickson sent a telegram.'

'A telegram!' Mrs Dickson is one of Ma's Drumcondra clients. That woman must be made of money.

'She wants me to go and fit her frock this evening,' Ma said. 'She says it's urgent.'

'Oh, Ma!' I said. 'She's practically in Phibsboro!' I didn't fancy that walk.

'She's not there this evening,' said Ma. 'She's staying over in her sister's house in Ballsbridge for some sort of Horse Show party.'

'Ballsbridge!' My heart sank even further. 'Ma, we can't walk all the way home from there.'

'She says she'll pay for a cab home,' said Ma impressively. That silenced me. It might be worth going all the way over to Balls-bridge to fit some lady with notions if I got to go in a cab. I've never been in a cab in my life.

'You'd think she'd pay you a bit more,' said Da, 'if she can afford telegrams and cabs.'

'Well, if I do a good job this time, maybe she will,' said Ma.

I had been going to take Earnshaw into town with me again, but I couldn't because Ma said I had to go over to Ballsbridge straight from the picket.

'And you can leave that picket carry-on of yours early, too.' She would accept no argument. 'I'll meet you outside the GPO at five o'clock.'

Town was peaceful enough that day, though that odd, electric feeling was still in the air, as if the city was waiting for something to happen. The big O'Connell Street meeting that Mr Larkin had planned for the next day had been officially banned. There were posters up all over the place, warning that anyone who tried to gather on O'Connell Street would be moved away or even arrested. Another meeting was planned for that day up in Croy-don Park; Kitty said she was going to it. Our picket was peaceful enough all day – no one hurled abuse, and quite a few people took our handbills. In fact, the worst thing that happened was Rosie making arch remarks about Peter Lawlor.

'Just keep working on him, Betty,' she said with a wink. 'You'll have him supporting a worker's republic by Christmas.'

I know she's my friend but she can be fierce aggravating some-times. I was quite relieved when the time came to meet Ma. Kitty didn't mind me leaving a bit earlier than usual – town was fairly quiet anyway, and everybody was all fidgety and excited because we were looking forward to the Women Workers' picnic the next day.

When I got to the GPO, Ma was there holding the suitcase that she found in the pawn shop and then cleaned and lined with brown paper. Normally Ma wouldn't set foot in the pawn shop, in case anyone she knew saw her and thought she was from one of those families that have to pawn their good clothes every week and only get them back for Sundays. But she saw this case in the window the other week and realised that if she was going as far afield as Drumcondra to see her clients, she'd better have something better to carry their clothes in than a lot of paper parcels.

'There you are,' she said, as I trotted up to her. 'How was your whatdoyoucallit?'

She knows perfectly well it's a picket, but I didn't feel like arguing with her about this.

'It was grand,' I said. I pointed in the direction of Ballsbridge. 'Lead on, Macduff!'

That's Shakespeare. Samira must be rubbing off on me.

'You talk a fine lot of a nonsense,' said Ma, but she was smiling. 'Come on.'

It took us quite a long time to get to Ballsbridge. I took the case from Ma after a while, and by the time we knocked on the kitchen door of the house where Mrs Dickson's sister lived, I was very hot and (sorry, Ma) sweaty. The servant who answered the door looked at me with what I could only describe as repulsion, which was a bit harsh. I couldn't possibly have looked *that* bad.

'No hawkers,' she said, and started to close the door. But Ma stepped out from behind me and, in her grandest voice, said, 'We're not selling anything. I am Mrs Dickson's private dressmaker, and I have an appointment.'

'Oh!' said the servant. 'Well, I beg your pardon, Miss …'

'Mrs Rafferty,' said Ma. I swear she was standing on her tip toes, all the better to give this woman her most imperious look.

A few minutes later we were being led up a back stairs to a huge bedroom where Mrs Dickson was waiting for us, sitting in a velvet armchair reading a novel and wearing a beautiful evening frock that had taken Ma days to make. What looked like diamonds gleamed from her hair. She barely gave us a glance as we came in.

'Oh, Mrs Rafferty, there you are. I've decided I want that fastening to hold up the train after all. That won't take you long, will it?'

'Of course not, Mrs Dickson,' said Ma, smiling politely, even though I bet she was thinking, as I was, that Mrs Dickson could easily have worked out where she wanted the fastening and sewn on a few buttons and bows herself instead of dragging us all the way across town to do it. 'Where would you like the train to fall?'

By the time Mrs Dickson had decided on the arrangement of her train, which took a ridiculously long time, and I had crawled around on the floor helping Ma to pin it in place, and Mrs Dickson had been helped out of the dress so Ma could make the changes, and I had held up the dress for her so the ends didn't fall on the floor and finally helped Mrs Dickson back into it, it was after seven o'clock.

'You really have saved my evening, Mrs Rafferty,' said Mrs Dickson, in her lazy way, as I buttoned up the back of the dress and arranged the fixed train. 'I just hope all my sister's guests can get here.'

'Is there any reason they shouldn't, Mrs Dickson?' said Ma politely, tidying away her measuring tape and needle case.

'There's been some sort of disturbance over in Ringsend,' said Mrs Dickson, looking at herself in the enormous mirror on the door of her wardrobe. 'Something to do with those awful tram strikers. Rioting in the streets, I hear – that's what my sister's cook said. I just hope it doesn't spread down the coast road. My cousins are coming from Blackrock.'

Ma and I exchanged worried glances.

'Really,' said Mrs Dickson, adjusting the diamond comb in her hair, 'the police need to show those strikers what's what. It's outrageous, all this fuss just because they want a few extra shillings for doing less work!'

Ma shot me a warning look, but there was no need. Of course I wouldn't say anything to Mrs Dickson. I *thought*, however, plenty of things as we got our things ready and left the house.

There was a cab station at the end of the road, and the jarvey in the driving seat looked amused when we asked if he could take us to the North Strand.

'Janey,' he said, as we climbed awkwardly into the cab. 'You ladies are a long way from home.'

'Don't worry, you'll be paid,' said Ma, in her most crushing voice, and the jarvey said, 'Sorry, missus, I didn't think I wouldn't be. I'll get you there soon enough.' And off we went.

I have to admit, I did enjoy riding in that cab. As we sped over the Grand Canal and along a wide road full of elegant old houses, I couldn't help imagining I was a character in a book travelling somewhere exciting in a carriage – Catherine Morland in *Northanger Abbey*, going to stay in a mysterious old house, or even Sherlock Holmes in a London cab, pursuing some dangerous criminal. Ma seemed to be enjoying it too, looking out the window with interest.

'We could be anyone as far as they know,' she said suddenly, gesturing towards some elegantly dressed ladies and gentlemen who were entering a house in Merrion Square. 'They just see a cab going by. The people inside the cab could be grand people like them, as far as they're concerned.' I'd never heard Ma say anything like that before. Then she shook her head and gave a little laugh. 'Don't mind me.' She sat back in the slightly grubby cushioned seat. 'Goodness me, this is a lot easier on my back than walking, that's for sure!'

The cab went past the end of Grafton Street – I looked up the street and saw that the Savoy Café girls had finished their picket for the day – and then around in front of Trinity College. But when we were on Westmoreland Street, the cab began to slow down. As we arrived at O'Connell Bridge, I could hear a faint rumbling sound and the cab stopped altogether.

'I'm sorry, ladies,' said the jarvey. 'I'm not going any further.'

Ma was outraged. 'But you said you'd take us to the North Strand!'

'I know, and I'm very sorry,' said the jarvey, and to be fair to him, he sounded as if he really was. 'But there's something kicking off across the river, and I'm not taking my horse into a riot.'

'A riot!' I stuck as much of myself as I could out of the right-hand side window of the cab. Across the river, on Eden Quay – down near Liberty Hall, in fact – I could see a mass of people gathered in the late evening light. I realised that the rumble I'd heard was actually the sound of shouting.

'We'd better walk home by Talbot Street, Ma,' I said, trying to sound calmer than I felt.

The jarvey was very apologetic, and wouldn't even take the full fare from Ballsbridge into town, but Ma was still grumbling as we headed towards the bridge.

'It'll just be another one of them union meetings,' she said, as we reached the statue of Daniel O'Connell and crossed to the corner of Eden Quay. 'I don't know why the jarvey wouldn't take us.'

'I don't think the meetings are usually that large,' I said nervously, looking down the quay. 'Or that rowdy. And I think ... I think I can see policemen.'

In the distance, I could see men in the uniforms of the Dublin Metropolitan Police, all in a line, confronting the crowd.

'What are they doing?' said Ma.

'I don't know,' I said.

And then, suddenly, I heard someone cry 'Give it to them, boys!' and the line of policemen charged at the crowd. Their batons were raised and the crowd, mostly men, but I could see a couple of women and girls and boys too, began fleeing down the quay towards us. I saw a man trip and fall sprawling on the road. He struggled to get up but people streamed over him. Somewhere in the crowd, someone screamed.

'Ma, run!' I cried, and took her hand. Behind us, the sound of the crowd and the policemen who had charged them rose up like a massive wave as we fled down O'Connell Street.

We ran past Clery's, pushing past curious onlookers who were making their way towards the source of the commotion.

'I can't run anymore,' panted Ma, staggering to a halt. Her hat was askew and her cheeks were flushed – I had never seen her look so dishevelled. I could barely breathe myself. I was never very good at running. I was always being caught when we played tip-the-lamp on the Avenue. I looked back and saw the crowd had moved onto the bridge.

'They seem to be going over the river,' I said. I glanced towards the corner of Earl Street. 'If we go down that way it'll be grand.'

But I was wrong.

The crowd hadn't been moved across the river. Or at least, not all of them had. We were halfway down Earl Street when a wave of people broke out in front of us. They flooded out of Marlborough Street, pursued by the police, who had their batons in their hands and were thumping anyone they could get near. A rock flew through the air, followed by a bottle, and then the sky was full of flying missiles as the people fought back. Ma grabbed my hand and pulled me into a doorway. Everywhere we looked, people were shoving, pushing, falling, trying to avoid the policemen's clubs and the bottles and stones that were being hurled at the constables.

'Oh God, Betty, we need to get back to O'Connell Street!' said Ma. But when we looked back the way we had come, we saw that a line of policemen were blocking the top of the road.

'Stay back!' roared a tall, sturdy DMP man, as a pale man approached the line, dressed in what would have been a decent suit if it hadn't been freshly covered with dust from the road.

'I'm just trying to get home!' cried the man, but the policeman shoved him backwards, sending him sprawling in the gutter.

'I said stay back, you bowsie!' the policeman bellowed.

The pale man managed to scramble out of the way as the policeman aimed a kick at him, but he was nearly knocked down again as the angry, desperate crowd surged towards O'Connell Street. Ma and I pressed ourselves back into the doorway.

'Someone's going to get killed,' said Ma, her voice trembling, and that was when the policeman shouted, 'Come on, lads!' and he and his comrades charged again. I heard a girl's voice call 'Father!' and looked up to see a girl of around my age with bright golden hair trying desperately to make her way through the panicking crowd.

'Get back, you!' roared another policeman and to my horror, he lifted his baton and landed a savage blow on the fair girl's head. She fell to her knees, blood spilling from the wound on her temple.

'Jesus, Mary and Joseph,' said Ma. 'We need to help that poor child.' She was stepping out of the doorway, but I pulled her back when we saw two other women help the shaking girl to her feet and half drag her to the other side of the road, where they took shelter in a doorway. I realised that the fair girl was dressed like Lavinia Lawlor or one of her friends. She definitely wasn't a union girl.

I don't know what happened to her or if she was all right, because it was clear we couldn't stay in our doorway for much longer. The police were still trying to beat back the crowd, and as the officers moved towards us we had no choice but to move with it.

'Keep hold of my hand, Betty,' said Ma, and we plunged into the chaos.

It felt as if we were diving into a strange and terrifying sea, buffeted along in a roaring, fighting throng, swimming against the tide as we attempted to push through the masses of people, trying to get to the road just a few hundred yards away that would take us home to the North Strand. But getting there was impossible. The crowd was moving – or being moved – in that same direction, pursued by the police. There was no way out of it. It was safer to let it carry us along than to attempt to break out of the jostling throng.

There was one moment when I thought we might actually die there. It was when Ma stumbled over a loose paving stone. Her hand slipped from my grasp, and in a second she was on her knees.

'Ma!' I cried, reaching out to help her up, but I was pushed forward by the crowd and in a second I couldn't see Ma anymore.

'Ma!' I screamed. 'My ma's fallen!' But no one noticed me. They were all trying to get away from the police batons. I screamed again. 'Ma!'

But then I remembered being shorter than the men around me could actually be useful. I managed to wriggle under their elbows and around their legs and somehow I pushed my way back to Ma, who had staggered to her feet and was looking around desperately, trying to find me.

'I'm here, Ma!' I grabbed her hand as the people around us started to chant, 'Down with the bloody police!' (I'm sorry about using bad language in my memoirs, but it really is what they said. I heard them say plenty of worse things too, which I won't write here.) Soon the cry was taken up by what must have been hundreds of others.

'Bless us and save us,' said Ma. 'The world's going mad.' And although her voice was shaking, she clung tightly to my hand. 'We're going to have to push through them. We'll never get away if we don't try.'

But the police were blocking our way out to the main road, batons raised, and we had no choice but to go with the mass of people as they moved, still chanting, towards Foley Street, the street Ma had warned me never to go down.

'This way!' Ma said. Somehow we managed to push our way to the side of the crowd, just as the police made what surely must have been one last push, clubbing their way through the crowd and sending most of it towards the flats of Corporation Buildings.

If we hadn't managed to shelter in another doorway, I don't know what might have happened to us. Because as the police advanced towards the flats, I heard the sound of smashing glass.

'What's happening now?' Ma stared upwards with wide eyes. The women in the flats were flinging bottles from the balconies and stairwells to stop the police getting any further. And they didn't stop at bottles. I saw clinkers and plates, and then a policeman cried out as a chamber pot flew through the air and caught his shoulder.

'Mother of God!' I said, and it shows how shaken Ma was that she didn't slap me for taking the Blessed Virgin's name in vain.

'Come on!' she said, and pulled me down a blessedly clear laneway towards Amiens Street. We half ran, half staggered, the sounds of smashing glass, screams and shouts ringing in our ears. And even though we were exhausted and terrified, we didn't stop moving, not for one second, until we reached the Five Lamps. That was where we paused, doubling over, trying desperately to get our breath back.

When I could breathe normally again, I glanced at Ma. She didn't look at all like her usual neat self. Her hat was askew, her carefully pinned hair falling beneath it. A button had gone from her coat, and the cuff was torn. Her skirt and jacket were grubby, and when I looked down at myself I saw that I was much the same.

'Ma?' I said. 'Are you all right?' And then suddenly, to my own surprise, I burst into tears. Ma flung her arms around me.

'I'm grand, love, and so are you,' she said. 'Don't be crying, now.'

'I'm sorry,' I said, wiping my eyes. 'I thought …'

'I know, love,' she said. She sighed, a juddering sound with a hint of tears in it. 'Come on. Let's go home.'

Earnshaw bounded up the stairs to greet us when he heard the lock in the door, and Da rushed out of the kitchen. He still had his coat and cap on.

'Oh thank God,' he said. 'Thank God.' And then he hugged both of us so tightly I thought he would never let go. 'I was just about to go out looking for yiz. When I came home and I couldn't find you …'

Da had been outside Liberty Hall earlier when the trouble kicked off but had been behind the line of policemen so hadn't been caught up in the charge. He had managed to get away then, and had arrived home not long before us. He'd called to the neighbours looking for us but of course they had no idea where we were.

'Where's Eddie?' said Ma.

Da's face was grim. 'I don't know. He was going over to Ring-send with some of the lads, to protest at the depot.'

'Ringsend!' Ma and I stared at each other. 'That's where the trouble started.'

'He'll be grand,' said Da, but his cheerfulness sounded forced. 'But I might go out and have a look for him all the same.'

If Eddie hadn't been missing, I think Ma would have locked the door and refused to let him go anywhere near town. But as it was, she just embraced him tightly and said, 'Be careful.' Then she turned to me and said, 'You're not going to that women workers' picnic tomorrow. I'm not letting you out of my sight.' And I was so tired and scared I couldn't argue with her. I didn't much feel like leaving the house ever again, anyway.

We were huddled in the kitchen drinking tea with extra sugar (Ma said if ever there was a time to not worry about wasting sugar, this was it) when we heard the front door open an hour later.

'Eddie!' Ma jumped to her feet. But a moment later Da came down the stairs, his face grave and his suit dusty.

'I couldn't find him,' he said. 'I couldn't even get into town.'

It turned out that the fighting had spread all the way out to Amiens Street, and Da found it impossible to get through it. After he narrowly avoided both a hurled bottle and several policemen's batons, he had no choice but to turn back.

'It'll calm down in a few hours,' he told Ma. 'And when it does, Eddie will come home.'

But Eddie didn't come home in a few hours. Da stayed up so long waiting for him he fell asleep in the kitchen armchair, and when I came down the next morning, Eddie's whereabouts were still unknown.

'He'll show up at Mass,' said Ma. There was a sort of forced optimism in her voice that was somehow more upsetting than if she'd been crying. 'He wouldn't dare miss Mass. Not Eddie.' But when we got to the church there was no sign of him. All the way through Mass, Ma kept looking behind her, as if hoping Eddie would sneak in late. But he didn't.

As I came back from communion I saw Samira and Auntie Maisie sitting on the opposite side of the church. There was no sign of Ali. As soon as Mass was over I practically raced down the aisle – Ma was still so worried she didn't even try to stop me running in church – to make sure I didn't miss the Caseys. They sometimes go over to Samira's granny straight after Mass on Sundays.

I caught up with them just outside the church, where Auntie Maisie was talking intently to Mrs Ward who lives on Leinster Avenue.

'And that was the last you saw of him?' she was saying as I approached.

Samira caught sight of me and rushed to my side. 'Have you seen Ali anywhere?'

'No!' I clutched her arm. 'You haven't seen Eddie?'

'No.' Samira wrung her hands together. 'Ali never came home last night. No one's seen him. And people are saying someone from the North Strand was half killed in town last night. But no one knows who.'

For a moment there was a rushing sound in my ears, almost like the roar of the crowd last night.

'Eddie didn't come home either,' I said, and my voice sounded as if it were coming from somewhere very far away.

'You don't think … it can't have been that bad …' Samira's voice trailed off.

I thought of the policeman clubbing that fair-haired girl, of the blood in her golden hair. 'I was there,' I said. 'It *was* that bad.' And I told her what had happened.

'We've got to go and look for them,' said Samira. 'They might still be in town somewhere. Waiting for that meeting of Mr Larkin's.' She swallowed nervously. 'Or … or they might be injured.'

'We can't go into town,' I said. 'That meeting was banned, there'll be trouble – it won't be safe to go there.'

'Betty.' Samira's voice was as intense as it was when she gave

Portia's speech. But this time all the emotion was real. 'He's my *brother*. I have to.'

Well, I couldn't say no to that, could I?

I didn't tell Ma where we were going, of course. She'd have dragged me back to Strandville Avenue by my hair if she'd known I was planning to be anywhere near O'Connell Street. But Samira did whisper to Auntie Maisie to tell Ma that we were going to look for Ali, and then we ran off through the gossiping after-Mass crowds before a stunned Maisie could say another word.

'Is she following us?' Samira asked as we hurried past the Five Lamps.

I looked around. 'No, we're grand.'

'You don't think anything bad will happen today, do you?' Samira tried to sound hopeful. 'I mean, the police won't be going around hitting anyone. They must have realised how mad that was, yesterday.'

'I don't know,' I said truthfully. 'I wouldn't have thought they'd ever be hitting girls and kicking men when they were down. But they did.' And, I thought, their tempers wouldn't have been improved by being pelted with bottles and chamber pots. Though I couldn't honestly blame the women in the flats, not after what I'd seen a few minutes before. Those policemen wouldn't have thought twice about smashing their skulls. Really, though, I didn't want anyone to be hurt at all.

Despite the proclamation banning the meeting, there was a small crowd gathered in the middle of O'Connell Street when we got there. People were just standing around, chatting in groups of four or five, and when we passed through the crowd hoping for a glimpse of Ali or Eddie, we heard snippets of their conversations.

'Do you think Big Jim will show?'

'I wouldn't put it past him!'

'Did you hear? He's been hiding out somewhere.'

Most of the people on O'Connell Street didn't seem to be there for the meeting, though. They were just having a Sunday stroll, and some had clearly walked round the corner from Mass at the Pro-Cathedral. There were, however, more policemen on the street than usual. I glanced at them nervously. I didn't think I'd ever trust a policeman again.

'It's no use,' said Samira. 'They're not here.'

I looked around me one last time. 'They might be ... hey! Ali!'

And there he was, about ten yards away, talking intently to someone who turned around at the sound of my voice and revealed himself to be Eddie – Eddie with a black eye, but otherwise looking perfectly well. I felt a wave of relief break over me.

'Thanks be to God,' breathed Samira.

But then, just as Ali and Eddie started to make their ways towards us, someone shouted, 'Larkin! It's Larkin! He's in the Imperial!' The crowd turned almost as one to face the window of the grand hotel, where a tall bearded man was starting to speak.

'I am here today in accordance with my promise ...' he declared, but I couldn't hear what he said next because so many people started shouting and cheering and pushing their way forward. I lost sight of Eddie and Ali.

'He didn't have that beard a few days ago!' said a man standing behind me.

'He's in disguise!' said someone else. He chuckled. 'And in William Murphy's hotel too.'

'He'll be shopping in Clery's next,' joked the other man. Clery's is part of the same building as the hotel, and Murphy owns it as well.

'Where's Ali? And Eddie?' said Samira. But the crowd had now swelled so much, as more and more people ran over to see Mr Larkin, that we couldn't see them at all.

'At least we know they're all right,' I said. I looked back up at the balcony. 'Janey, where's Mr Larkin gone?'

The police must have been on his tail because the union leader had disappeared from the window. A tall, elegant woman in a green coat stood up in a nearby motorcar and said, in a very grand voice, 'Three cheers for Mr Larkin!'

But even as people were cheering, some of the policemen who had been positioned opposite the hotel rushed over and tried to get the woman and her companions to move their vehicle. It looked like they were trying to force it off the road.

'Leave them alone!' someone shouted, and that was when I heard the sound of smashing glass and realised someone had thrown a rock through one of the plate glass windows of Clery's department store.

After that, everything was chaos.

'Get them!' bellowed an angry voice, and the policemen charged the crowd. As I grabbed Samira's hand, I caught a glimpse of Mr Larkin being taken away by policemen. The green-coated woman tried to say something to him, but another policeman punched her in the face. I couldn't believe what I was seeing.

'Come on!' I cried. 'We'll find the lads later! We need to get away!'

But we couldn't. The policemen pushed the crowd back across the road towards the GPO, and we couldn't break out of it. A few feet away, I saw a policeman strike an old woman with his baton as she tried to run away from the madness.

'Where can we go?' Samira cried.

That was when I had an idea that turned out to be a very bad one.

'Prince's Street!' It's a little road at the side of the GPO – it's a dead end but there's a little lane running from it to Abbey Street. 'We can get away down the lane.'

On a normal day, it would have taken less than a minute's gentle stroll to reach Prince's Street. But this wasn't a normal day. As we were shoved along by the panicking throng, a sharp elbow dug into my side, and a heavy boot trod on my heel. And when we finally made it to Prince's Street, we realised that there was no escape that way. A line of policemen, batons drawn, were ranged across the bottom of it, blocking our access to the lane.

'This way!' Samira tried to pull me back to O'Connell Street, but we were trapped. To get to safety we would have to make our way through what looked like a forest of whirling batons. And the police seemed to be using those weapons on anyone who was unlucky to get near them. I saw a policeman dive towards one terrified man, who cried, 'Have you no mercy?' before being beaten to the ground.

'Help!' someone howled. 'Help me!'

I turned to see a policeman shoving a woman to her knees and beating her on the head. I gasped in horror as he began kicking her in the ribs.

'They're going to kill her!' said Samira, staggering back as a desperate man shoved past her.

'Betty, look out!' yelled a familiar voice. I whirled around to see a raised baton descending towards my face, and then someone shoved me out of the way.

'Eddie!' I cried. He had saved me from the policeman's blow, but he'd taken the weight of the weapon himself. The policeman whacked him again with the club and I heard something crack, a horrible sound. Eddie screamed.

I grabbed his jacket and pulled him away as hard as I could, and he staggered out of the policeman's reach. Luckily the crowd was so chaotic, his attacker was engaged with another victim and didn't pursue us.

'Where's Ali?' Samira was desperate. But Eddie could barely speak. He was clutching his left arm with his right hand.

'My arm …' he said. 'I think it's …'

'Oh Janey, Eddie, don't faint!' If he did, we'd never get away.

'Ali!' Samira screamed. He was over by the wall of the GPO, but at first glance he might as well have been on the other side of a wild river. Between him and us a pair of policemen were beating a pair of working men who were howling in pain. Ali saw us and started to move towards us, but then something caught his eye and he froze.

'Ali, come on!' shouted Samira, as a wave of panicking people rose up between us. For a moment I thought Ali was crushed beneath their feet, but then he appeared before us, clutching the hand of a small girl.

'She was in that doorway,' he gasped. 'I couldn't leave her.'

'We need to get out,' I said. 'Eddie …'

Ali tried to hide his horror at the sight of Eddie, his face white, his arm at an unnatural angle.

'That way looks clear,' he said. 'Let me help Eddie.' He put

Eddie's good arm around his shoulders, and we put our heads down and tried to wriggle our way out of the crush.

I don't know how we got across O'Connell Street, but somehow we did. The whole thing felt like a terrible dream – the screams, the violence, the sense of being trapped, the panic of people running in every direction, trying desperately to get out of the way of the batons and boots. When we reached a miraculously quiet side street we all sat on the ground. That was when I noticed that my hands were shaking.

'Are you all right?' Ali asked the child. She nodded, her terrified eyes wide.

'Where do you live?'

'Railway Street,' said the child.

'It's on our way home,' said Ali. 'You can walk with us.'

I turned to Eddie. He was still holding his left arm. 'Are you all right?'

Eddie shook his head. He had another black eye to match the first shiner and blood was trickling down his face from a cut on his forehead.

'My arm's broken,' he said. He bit his lip.

'Can you walk?' Samira asked.

'Just about,' said Eddie.

'Here,' I said, taking the sash off my Sunday frock. 'Let's tie your arm up in that.' None of us really knew how to make a sling, but we managed to get Eddie's arm held up. When he finally felt able for it, he put his uninjured arm around Ali's shoulders again and, keeping to the backways, we staggered down towards Amiens Street.

No one said anything. Eddie was in too much pain, and the rest of us were too shocked. When we left the little girl at the end of her road, which was just where Ma and I had been trapped the previous night, crowds were beginning to gather there too. Clearly people knew about what had been happening in O'Connell Street. There was tension in the air, but things were quiet enough – until we reached the Five Lamps.

'What's that crowd coming up over the canal bridge?' said Samira.

'It must be everyone who was at the other meeting up in Croydon Park,' said Ali.

'But why are they running?' I said.

'Is that … Mr Carroll from the Phelans'?' said Ali.

'It is!' said Samira. 'And whatsisname, Mr Ward.'

The two policemen who lodge at the Phelans' house at the top of our road were racing towards us, and as soon as we saw their terrified faces we realised that they were being chased. Behind them a huge crowd was advancing, and at the front of it was a group of men who were clearly in hot pursuit of the policemen.

'Jaysus,' said Ali. 'They're going to tear them apart.'

'Good enough for them,' muttered Eddie. 'Bleeding policemen!' I couldn't blame him for not feeling sympathetic. If I'd seen someone fight back at the policemen who were beating the crowd in Prince's Street, it wouldn't be the policemen I'd be feeling sorry for. But there was something horrible about seeing anybody hunted. And besides, Mr Carroll and Mr Ward hadn't been belting anyone. They must have been on their day off, because they weren't in uniform.

In fact, judging by the state of their clothes, Mr Carroll and Mr Ward had already received a few blows. But just as the hunters reached their prey, the door of a house opened and a man ran out and grabbed Mr Carroll's hand.

'Get in here, yous!' he shouted, pulling them towards his house.

The policemen flung themselves through the doorway and the man slammed the door. The policemen's pursuers weren't giving up that easily, though.

'Gregory!' someone bellowed. 'Give us them police b——s!' And he used a word that I can't even write down in full, though I have heard it a few times. A stone smashed through one of the house's windows.

'Come on,' said Ali. 'We need to get home.'

And, by keeping to the other side of the road, we managed to get past the crowd besieging the home of the man called Mr Gregory and crossed the canal bridge. By the time we reached our road, people were standing on their front steps talking to their neighbours with grave expressions on their faces. They had clearly heard that the city was in a terrible state of chaos.

We said goodbye to Samira and Ali, and our front door opened before I could even knock at it; Ma must have been in the front room looking for us out the window.

'Oh thank God!' she said, and flung her arms around Eddie. He cried out in pain. 'Oh Eddie, love, what happened to you?'

'Policeman broke my arm,' said Eddie through gritted teeth and for a moment I thought he might go all faint again. 'I'm grand.'

'I thought you were dead,' she said. She pressed her lips together and dashed a tear away from one eye. Ma hardly ever cries and now here she's been in tears twice in one week.

'Ah, you don't need to worry about me, Ma,' said Eddie. His voice was surprisingly gentle. 'I'm made of steel.'

'And you!' Ma turned to me and gave me a smack on the legs. 'Running into town like that! What were you thinking?'

'I wanted to find Eddie!' I said. 'And I did.'

'What happened?' demanded Ma.

We told her about Mr Larkin and the police charging the crowd again. I opened my mouth to tell her about Eddie saving me from the policeman's baton, but then I thought it might upset her even more to hear what danger I'd been in, so I kept my mouth shut. She had a look at Eddie's arm and shook her head.

'You need a doctor,' she said. 'I'd try and set it myself but I don't know how. It might go wrong.'

'I need it to go right,' said Eddie in alarm. I knew we were all thinking of what happened to Mr Maguire when he couldn't work anymore. His injury was far more serious than a broken arm but still, an arm that didn't set right wouldn't be much use in Eddie's line of work.

Ma sighed. 'At least I still have the money Mrs Dickson gave us for a cab. That'll cover a bit of it. Betty, run round to Doctor Clarke.'

I was so tired I could barely stand but I couldn't expect Ma to go and get the doctor from Fairview herself. We never get doctors usually, even Doctor Clarke, who people call the doctor of the poor because he doesn't charge working people his usual rates. The only reason I even knew where he lived was because I had to go and get him when Mrs Phelan got very sick after she had her last baby. There was blood everywhere and I was very frightened but Doctor Clarke saved her. He didn't look too happy about being disturbed on a Sunday afternoon, but he came and splinted up Eddie's arm anyway.

'You need to be careful, young man,' he said as he left. 'Keep yourself out of trouble.'

'He will,' said Ma, handing the doctor some money. He looked at the pile of coins, looked at Ma's pale, drawn face and then handed some of them back without saying a word.

'Doctor!' said Ma, as Doctor Clarke turned to go. But he shook his head.

'Just tell that son of yours not to get mixed up in any more riots,' he said, and left.

I was so tired at that stage I just went to bed. I didn't even hear Da come back (safe and sound) from his search for the both of us. This morning I had a huge bruise all down my side from when Eddie slammed in to me, and Ma said I had to stay home from the picket. For once, I didn't object. I've spent the whole day in bed writing this. Ma isn't too happy about me going back tomorrow – in fact, I think she'd be happy if I never went anywhere near town again. But of course I'll be going back. And after everything that happened over the last few days, things will have to calm down. Won't they?

# Chapter Sixteen

Something terrible has happened. Something really, really terrible. Worse than anything I have written about before. Worse than the riots. Worse than Eddie breaking his arm. Worse than everything. I don't even know how I'm going to write it all down but I must, I must. I have to make sure there's a record of it. I should be asleep now because Ma sent me there straight after my bread and dripping this evening, but I can't go to sleep until I write about it.

I don't know where best to start, but I suppose this morning will do. I felt much better after my day of rest, and Ma was so busy fussing over Eddie she didn't bother giving out to me about the dangers of picketing. So even though there was only a tiny scraping of marge on my one thin slice of bread at breakfast this morning, I'd had two cups of tea (with condensed milk, not fresh) and I was feeling quite cheerful as I strolled down Henry Street in the sun with Earnshaw at my side. Ma was pleased when I suggested taking him in with me. I think she thinks he might scare away any baton-wielding policemen.

From a distance I could see the clump of strikers outside the tearoom – you can see Kitty a mile away, she's so tall and her hair is so bright. But the girls weren't marching around or holding signs today. It was clear something was wrong. They were all huddled together, and when I came closer I could see that Annie was with them and she looked as though she'd been crying. As I joined the group I noticed there was no sign of Rosie, but that wasn't unusual. She was often late for things, on account of her ma.

'What's going on?' I said, trying to sound cheerful to cover the sick feeling that was already building inside me. 'Don't tell me the union have called off the strike.'

'It's Rosie,' said Kitty. Her face was very white.

My stomach churned. I thought about what I'd seen over the last few days. 'What happened?' A horrible thought struck me. 'Was it the police? Did she get hit?'

'No.' I had never seen Kitty look like this before. 'Her house fell down.'

For a moment I thought I hadn't heard her properly.

'What do you mean her house fell down?' Was she trying to make some strange sort of joke? That wasn't like Kitty. 'Houses don't just fall down!'

I'd never been to Rosie's house, but I knew where it was because she'd told me it was right by the Father Matthew Hall, where our school entered a singing competition in the big Feis every year. It was on Church Street, past the vegetable market – I could picture the row now. They were just ordinary brick houses with shops on the ground floor and two floors of rooms above that. I knew from what Rosie has said that there are families in every single room of her house, so it's very crowded, but so are most houses around there. It was a normal house. It couldn't fall down. That just didn't happen.

'It did,' said Kitty. 'And so did the one next to it.'

I felt as if I was going to be sick. 'Were … were there people in it?' I said.

Kitty nodded. 'Most of them got out …'

'Oh God Almighty,' I said. This time I wasn't taking the Lord's name in vain. This time it was a real prayer. 'Oh Kitty, not Rosie.

Oh please God, Kitty, she's not dead ...'

'Rosie's grand,' said Kitty, and I almost collapsed with relief. 'But …'

'But what?' That little word made the sick feeling return.

'Her ma,' said Kitty. 'And her little brother. They didn't get out.'

Suddenly everything seemed to go very quiet. The sounds of the horses and lorries and crowds on Henry Street faded away.

'What?' I said.

'They're dead,' said Kitty. 'Both of them.'

It was as if she had told me it was snowing in July. 'But they *can't* be.'

'It's true,' said Annie, sniffing. 'Loads of people died.'

'Rosie's ma was one of them.' Kitty's voice was dull. 'I heard it all from one of the neighbours on my way in here this morning. Rosie's ma was in a friend's room on the middle floor when it happened – she'd left little Francis back in the Delaneys' room. She and her friend ran out to the landing when they heard the cracking sounds, and the friend ran down the stairs, but of course Mrs Delaney went back to her room to get Francis and then the ceiling of the whole floor fell down and Mrs Delaney and Francis were both …' She broke off and swallowed. If Kitty were the sort of person who ever cried, she'd be crying now.

'But Francis … he can't be … He's not *dead* …'

Kitty nodded, and I felt a ringing in my ears. I thought of the laughing little boy at the union fête, how cheerful and jolly he was even though his mother was a drunk who sometimes tied him to a table leg so she could go to the pub and get a mug of porter. I remembered him singing his song and playing games and even making Little Robbie laugh, which is something I can never do. I remembered how he charmed Samira. And now he's gone forever. Crushed under – oh I couldn't think about it. I still can't.

'Where was Rosie? When it … when it happened?'

'She was outside the house talking to one of the neighbours,' said Kitty. 'And her sister was out picketing. They're both all right. I mean,' she added, 'they weren't injured.'

'Where is she now?' I said.

'I think they're at the house,' Kitty said. 'Or what's left of it.' When I write down her words they look cold, but there was nothing cold about the way she said them. Or the way her face looked.

'I have to see her,' I said. 'I have to … come on, Earnshaw.'

And then, without really knowing why, I was running, running down Henry Street and Mary Street, Earnshaw bounding along beside me. A part of me noticed that people were looking at me crossly, jumping out of my way with outraged cries of 'Well really!' from the most grand ones and 'Watch where you're bleeding going!' from the less grand. Me and Earnshaw darted across Capel Street (we got another 'watch where you're going!' from a coal van driver) and down Little Mary Street, but after that I couldn't run anymore. I was so out of breath I had to stop and bend over until the air came back into my lungs. When I could breathe again I kept going, just walking quickly this time. I hurried past the market and down towards Rosie's house.

Or where Rosie's house had been.

Church Street was unrecognisable from the street I remembered on my outings to the Feis. Most of the shops were closed and there were people standing in almost every doorway, soberly watching the workmen who were lifting piles of rubble from what had been Rosie's house and the house next door. Other groups of people stood in the road, their faces pale and drawn. I couldn't see Rosie anywhere.

''Scuse me.' I approached a red-eyed man, his hands and face dusty and his clothes grubby and torn, who was standing with his arms around a small girl. 'Do you know Rosie Delaney? Have you seen her?'

For a moment I thought the man wasn't going to answer me. Then he seemed to pull himself together and said, 'Bridget Delaney's Rosie?'

'That's it,' I said. He shook his head. 'Terrible, it was. You heard about her mother? And the kiddie?'

I nodded.

'I was the one who found him in the ruins. Under what was left of the table. Perfect, he was. Not even a cut on him.' For a second I thought he was about to cry and that scared me. I'd never seen a man cry before. 'Poor little fella. When his sisters saw him ...' His voice trailed off and he pressed a dusty fist against his eyes, as if to ward off his tears. It seemed cruel to trouble him any more, but I had to ask if he knew where Rosie was now, so I did.

'I think she's at the Murrays,' he said. 'The house with the black door.'

I thanked him and hurried down the dusty street, slowing down when I reached the rubble where Rosie's house and the house next door had been. The whole front of both houses was totally gone. Where once there had been rooms full of people and furniture, there was just a pile of stone and soil and scraps of broken furniture and bits of rotten wood that looked as if they had once been floor beams. Part of the walls of the house was still there, with a few floorboards still sticking out. The fireplaces were still in the walls, their grates full of rubble. There were holy pictures hanging on the wall of a room that didn't have a floor.

I tried to understand how the building could have collapsed. In the middle of the pile of rubble I could see what looked like half of a massive marble fireplace. What state had the building been in? What did it take to crack a huge marble fireplace in half? For a long moment I stood and stared at it. I thought of Mrs Delaney, crushed by the falling house. And little Francis – I pushed the heavy, horrible thought as forcibly out of my mind as if I was physically pushing a coal van out of the road.

The black door of the house where the Murrays lived was open, but there was no one in the hall when I walked in.

'Hello?' There was no answer. I looked around but there was no sign of life on the ground floor so I raised my voice. 'Rosie? Rosie Delaney?'

I heard a door open upstairs and a tired-looking woman appeared at the top of the stairs.

'She's up here. But she's not in a fit state to see anyone. Who are you?'

'Betty Rafferty,' I said. 'I'm a friend from work. Can I see her?'

'You can't take that dog up here,' said the woman, pointing at Earnshaw.

'Betty?'

It was Rosie. She was standing next to the woman at the top of the stairs. Her hair was a tangled mess, and even from where I stood I could see that it was full of dust. Her face was grey with dirt, and she had a nasty cut on her right temple. She was wearing her black Lawlor's work dress, but it was covered in dust too, and there was a massive rip in the skirt. The cuffs were gone. But what was more shocking, and upsetting, than her bedraggled and battered clothes and hair was the expression on her face. Or rather the lack of it. There was no light in her eyes. No life, even. No sign of the girl who made me laugh and think and do things. She looked like the ghost of Rosie.

'Oh Rosie.' It was all I could say. I could feel tears prickle my eyes, but I clenched my fist and dug my nails into the palm of my hand to make the tears go away. I could cry later when I was on my own. Right now, I had to be brave, for Rosie's sake. I just wished I knew what to say.

'Is that Earnshaw?' said Rosie.

'Um, it is,' I said. 'He was with me when I heard about … about the house.'

'I tried to dig him out,' said Rosie, her voice as lifeless as her eyes. 'I was talking to Kathleen Murray on the steps and I heard the noise and then the whole house fell and I tried … I tried …'

Earnshaw looked up at Rosie, trotted to the foot of the stairs and put his front paws on the bottom step. He gave his usual friendly bark. And that was when Rosie rushed down the stairs and flung her arms around him, burying her face in his shaggy fur, sobbing her heart out. The woman who I presumed must be Mrs Murray looked down at us, fiddling with her apron.

'Well,' she said, her tone uncertain. 'I suppose he can stay for a short while.' She paused. 'That's the first time she's cried since it happened,' she said. Then she went back to her room.

I didn't say anything for a while. I just sat down on the stairs next to Rosie and let her cry into Earnshaw's fur. Finally, when her shoulders had stopped shaking, I said, as gently as I could, 'I'm very sorry, Rosie. Very, very sorry.' I couldn't think of anything better to say. Rosie looked up at me, the grime on her cheeks now streaked with patches of white and pink where her tears had washed it away.

'He was in our room,' she said. 'She'd tied him to the table so he wouldn't get into … into trouble when she went to Mrs Salmon's to borrow some tea. She was just looking for tea. Only tea. She wasn't even drinking …'

Her voice trailed off into a wail and she started crying again as though her heart would break. I flung my arms around her and tried my hardest not to cry too, but in the end I couldn't help it. We cried together, clinging on to each other as if each of us were the only thing that could stop the other being carried away into a lonely sea. Earnshaw squashed himself in between us so we were clinging to him too. He may look like nothing on earth, as Da is fond of saying, but he's a very comforting dog.

After a long time Rosie's tears died down into hiccupping gulps and I felt I could ask her what had been troubling me since I'd seen the ruin of what had been her home.

'Where are you going to stay? And Josie? Are you going to Margaret's?'

Margaret is her older sister, the one who got married when she was only sixteen.

Rosie shook her head. 'We can't go there. She and Paddy and the baby are sharing with his family out near the Black Church and they've only got two little rooms between nine of them.'

'So what are you going to do?'

Rosie shrugged her shoulders. 'Mrs Murray says we can stay here tonight. But we can't stay for too long. It's not fair to take advantage.'

If I took her home, I thought, Ma couldn't object. I mean, she couldn't throw out a poor homeless orphan who'd just lost her little brother too. No one could do that. But then I remembered how worried Ma has been about the striking, and how snappy she'd been. I didn't really know how she'd react if I presented her with Rosie and announced that I'd asked her to move in to our house. Another mouth to feed is no small thing at the best of times, let alone when we're all on strike.

Then I looked at Rosie, at the bleak expression on her face – or rather the lack of any expression at all – and I knew I at least had to try. So when Mrs Murray came out and called in Rosie for a bit of dinner, I told them I'd be back tomorrow, and Earnshaw and I hurried home as fast as we could. Which wasn't very fast because I was exhausted. I looked longingly at the trams speeding down Amiens Street as I trudged towards Strandville Avenue. By the time I pushed the front door open I could barely stand.

'Betty!' Ma's voice was a horrified gasp. 'What happened to you?'

I looked down and realised I was all covered in dust and dirt from hugging Rosie.

'Oh, Ma,' I said, and then my voice cracked and I had to wipe away a tear. 'It's Rosie.'

And I told her everything that had happened. When she heard about Francis her hands flew up to her face and I knew she was thinking of the fête and how he'd made us all laugh.

'The poor little mite,' she said, in a shaky voice.

I felt very nervous about asking her if Rosie could stay, but it turns out there was no need to ask at all. Because when I reached the bit about Rosie not being able to stay with the Murrays for long, Ma immediately said, 'Bring her here.'

I stared at her. 'What?'

'She can stay here. Until she and her sister find somewhere else.' Ma's face was still very serious. 'I'm sorry there's no room for her sister, but I'm sure she can stay with a friend.'

'Oh, Ma!' I flung my arms around her and hugged her as hard as I could, forgetting all about how grubby my blouse was. Ma hugged me back with all her might.

'I wouldn't want to think of you being without a home, if something happened to us,' she said. Then she looked down at her own blouse. 'Look at the state of me! I'd better sponge this off. And you, get changed and have a rest. At least the weather's decent. If I rinse your clothes out they'll be dry by tomorrow morning.'

So I got changed into my oldest dress that still fits me (only just about, it's so short I think I might be arrested for making a spectacle of myself if I went outside in it) and then I lay down on my bed with Earnshaw at my feet and stared up at the ceiling and thought about Rosie and her sad, drunk ma and her happy little brother for a very, very long time.

# Chapter Seventeen

It's been nearly a month since I last wrote my memoirs. I haven't had the energy to write anything until now. Actually, I'm not sure I have the energy now, but I'm writing all this down for posterity, as I told Samira this afternoon when I called into her at McGrath's and found her perched on the shop counter swinging her legs and gazing dreamily into space.

'I don't want to be rude, or anything,' said Samira, tearing herself away from her dreams of the stage and looking down on me from the counter, 'but who do you think is going to be reading these memoirs in the future?'

'People who want to know what it was like in Dublin in 1913,' I said.

Samira made a noise with her nose that in anyone else I'd have called a snort. 'I don't know if anyone will care much about that.' She grinned. 'Especially with you writing it all down.'

'Well, you never know,' I said. And then I pushed her off the counter. Mrs McGrath has taken to her bed again with her rheumatics, and even when it's open the shop is not what you'd call busy at the moment, because so many of the people who live around here are on strike and don't have any money to spend. The good side of this is that Samira has time to sit on the edge of the counter and practise her lines and, when I call in, chat to me (or rather insult me).

I feel very guilty even writing these words, but it's been a relief to joke with Samira again after the horror of what happened to Rosie. I have to say that Ma's been marvellous since the first moment I told her about it. She went round to Lily's house that very evening and dug out some old frocks from the rag bag, and then, with some help from me, she started cutting things down and sewing them back up until she'd made Rosie a brand new dress that looked as good as new. Because of course Rosie had lost what little clothes she had when the house collapsed. She'd lost everything.

The next morning, while Ma was still busy with her sewing machine, I went to the Murrays to collect Rosie and bring her home from Church Street. On the way there I stopped at Lawlor's so I could tell Kitty and the others what was happening. I said I might be away from the picket line for a day or two so I could look after Rosie, depending on what she needed.

'I'm sorry,' I said. 'You know I want to be here.'

'Don't you worry about that,' said Kitty, her voice unusually gruff. 'You're looking after your friend. *Our* friend.'

I nodded because I was so full of feelings I knew that if I said anything I might start crying again. And I knew I had to pull myself together before I saw Rosie. She needed me now. I couldn't start bawling and crying in front of her.

She was sitting on the front step of the Murrays' house when I got to Church Street. Across the road, men were still digging through the ruins, trying to salvage what they could.

'They've been there all morning,' said Rosie, her voice still dull. 'But there's nothing left to save. They said it could have happened at any time, the building was in such bad condition.' I saw that Mrs Murray must have brushed and sponge-cleaned her frock. It was as clean as it could be, given the circumstances, though there were still large rips in the skirt and elbows where she'd torn the fabric on the rubble.

'You don't have to stay here looking at it, Rosie,' I said. And I told her about Ma's invitation to stay, just for a few days.

Her eyes brightened, just a little bit. 'It was really her idea?' she said. 'You didn't ask her to do something?'

'I wouldn't lie about this,' I said. 'Not now. So … do you want to come?'

''Course I do,' said Rosie, and for a second she sounded like her old self. She paused. 'Thanks, Betty. I won't forget this.' Then she went into the house to tell Mrs Murray, and to leave a note for Josie, telling her where she was going.

Neither of us were very talkative on the way home. I tried to keep up some normal chatter, but everything I said seemed stupid, so after a while I just trailed off. The silence that followed wasn't awkward, though. It was like we both knew there was nothing to say, not right now. Just as we reached Eden Quay, I felt Rosie's warm little hand slip into mine. I squeezed it as tight as I could. We held hands all the way home.

Ma had left the front door on the latch, and when I pushed the door open I could hear the sound of the sewing machine coming from the front room.

'Ma?' I said.

The machine stopped, and Ma appeared in the doorway, holding a scissors.

'Hello, pet,' she said, tucking the scissors into the belt of her dress and taking Rosie's hand. 'I'm sorry about your mother and your brother. Young Francis was a fine little fella.'

'Thanks, Mrs Rafferty.' There was a hint of a wobble in Rosie's voice. Ma noticed it too, and said, in a cheerful, brisk tone, 'Now, why don't you come in here and try on this frock I'm after making for you? I was just cutting the thread on the last hem.'

After Rosie had tried on the dress and Ma had made a few adjustments, Ma said, 'So, Miss Delaney, I hope you'll recommend this dressmaking establishment to all your friends.' And Rosie actually laughed, just for a moment, but then she stopped and her face fell as she said, 'I shouldn't be laughing.'

'Yes,' said Ma, gently. 'You should. Don't you feel bad about getting a laugh wherever you can find it. Now, the pair of you can help me peel some spuds. Mr Rafferty and my Eddie are out at a meeting this evening, but the three of us will need some tea.'

The spuds were pretty feeble – more roots than actual potato – but Ma said there'd been a run on potatoes because people were getting worried about being able to afford to buy more if the strike pay ran out. She'd managed to get the last ones in the grocer's shop that morning. What with peeling potatoes and chopping cabbages, Ma kept us both busy for the rest of the afternoon. Josie called over at about five o'clock to tell Rosie about the funeral arrangements – the family had always paid into a funeral fund so there was money for the coffins and the grave. Ma and I made them a pot of tea and then left the two sisters in the front room. Earnshaw wanted to go in with them and Ma grabbed his collar, but as she was pulling him back Rosie said, 'Can he stay with me? There's something fierce comforting about him.'

''Course he can stay, pet,' said Ma. As she closed the door, I saw that Earnshaw had rested his big shaggy head very gently on Rosie's lap.

Later that evening, after Josie had left and Rosie was in bed wearing one of Lily's old shifts, me and Ma did the washing up and I asked Ma how she knew just what to say to distract Rosie from her troubles. 'You did a better job cheering her up than I did,' I said to Ma, as she passed me a wet plate. Somehow Ma had shown Rosie that she cared about her and was going to look after her but she definitely wasn't going to fuss over her, which I knew would have driven Rosie demented.

'Ah, you know,' said Ma. Her gaze didn't move from the basin of soapy water. 'I remembered what it was like when Tessie died.'

To my shame, I had forgotten about Ma's sister Tessie. I'd never met her – she died when she was eighteen and Ma was sixteen. She got pneumonia one winter and was gone in just a few weeks. I thought about her and my own dead brother and sister who I couldn't even remember and realised that Ma had known plenty of grief in her time. But then, who hasn't at her age?

'Thanks, Ma,' I said. 'For everything.'

The whole family looked after Rosie for the next few days. Ma kept her busy, and also gave her peace and quiet when she sensed Rosie needed it. Da was his usual self, like a warm and friendly bear. He was the only person who could make Rosie laugh. Even Eddie behaved himself, coming home from the picket line with a little bag of sweets that he casually left next to Rosie's plate of teatime bread and dripping without saying a word. And Earnshaw seemed to be able to tell when Rosie was feeling really upset. Then he'd come over to her and just sit by her side and she'd stroke his furry ears until she felt better. He'd have slept on her feet at night if that hadn't meant sleeping on my head, seeing as me and Rosie were top to tail in my bed.

Rosie wanted to take him to the funeral, but Ma told her the priest wouldn't let him in the church.

The funeral would have broken your heart. I know it broke mine. They buried Mrs Delaney and Francis together in the one coffin. I couldn't think about what was inside the coffin, it made me too sad. The church was packed full of people, including all the girls from work. Some of the scabs were there too, including Annie, but no one said anything about the strike to them. It wasn't the time or the place. Besides, they cared about Rosie too, in their own way.

That night Rosie sobbed and sobbed. I crept down to her end of the bed and held her tightly without saying anything. I didn't bother telling her not to cry. She needed to cry that night. Over the next few nights she sometimes woke up with a start, which would always wake me up too. She was having bad dreams. She didn't say much about them, apart from the fact that they always involved falling buildings and trying to find Francis.

The day after the funeral, she told me she wanted to go back to the picket line.

'Are you sure?' I said. 'I can represent you if you like.' An idea struck me. 'I could even wear your badge as well as my own. One on each lapel.' Rosie's union badge was one of her few possessions that hadn't been destroyed. She'd been wearing it when the house fell.

'You're all right,' said Rosie. 'I want to go back. I want to feel like I'm doing something to ... I dunno. Make everything better.'

'We *will* make things better,' I said, and then I ran down to the kitchen to tell Ma we were both going to the picket. She was so pleased that Rosie was going out and about that she didn't even bother to say something about us needing to work things out with Lawlor's.

When we got to Lawlor's, there was a surprise in store. Kitty and the other girls who'd been there just a few days before were on the picket line, but so was …

'Annie!' I cried.

Annie smiled weakly at us.

'Hiya, Betty. Howiya, Rosie. I'm sorry about your ma. And your brother.'

'I saw you at the funeral,' said Rosie. 'Thanks for that.'

'Least I could do,' said Annie, looking down at her hands.

'But what are you doing out here on the picket line?' I couldn't understand it. 'Have you joined the union at last?'

Annie flushed. 'No,' she said. 'Well, I don't think I have. But I couldn't sign this.' And she took a piece of paper from her pocket and handed it to me.

I read it aloud to Rosie.

'"I hereby undertake to carry out all instructions given me by or on behalf of my employers, and further, I agree to immediately resign my membership of the Irish Transport and General Workers' Union (if a member) and I further undertake that I will not join or in any way support this union."'

I stared at Annie. 'What's this?'

'Miss Warby handed these papers out to all of us this morning,' said Annie. 'She said we had to sign them or we'd be sacked.'

'What?' I couldn't believe my ears. What was Old Wobbly playing at? It was bad enough threatening people who were in the union. But forcing people who weren't even in it to denounce their friends!

'It's not just her,' said Annie, as if she could read my mind. 'It's loads of businesses. She said all these different employers got together and came up with it. They want to destroy the union.'

'But you're not in the union,' pointed out Rosie. 'Why are you out here? What difference does it make to you?'

'I know I'm not,' said Annie. 'But, you know, yiz all had the right to join it. And it's not fair to tell people they can't support their friends. So I told her I wouldn't sign it.'

'You did what?' I tried to imagine Annie standing up to Miss Warby and failed. Annie looked faint just remembering what she'd done.

'I told her it wasn't right,' she said. 'And she said something like, "But *you* didn't go out on strike with the rest of the brats" – sorry, girls, that's what she called you – and she said "I'm sure they've made their feelings about your decision very clear." And I said yiz had, but that making everyone sign that bit of paper was wrong, and I couldn't do it. And then … then she gave me the sack.' Annie blew her nose on the employers' pledge and then burst into tears.

When we'd comforted her and she'd calmed down a bit, she told us that several other girls had refused to sign the pledge. Even though I felt very sorry for Annie, it warmed my heart to hear all this. It showed that we weren't alone in our struggle.

And it really is a struggle now. I don't mean just for Rosie (though how she's able to put one foot in front of the other I don't know; she really is fierce brave). I mean it's a struggle for everyone. It's a few weeks now since workers were asked to sign that pledge and lost their jobs as a result, and it's reached the stage where people are going hungry – and I mean really hungry, not just missing breakfast. The strike pay is all right, but the funds won't last forever, and there are people like Annie who were locked out of their job without even being in the union, so they don't get any strike pay at all. Annie's been looking for work in a union-friendly shop, but she's been doing that for ages now, and so many other people are out looking for work too that jobs are very scarce. She hasn't had any luck so far.

In fact, it's fair to say that people are getting pretty desperate. Da isn't striking yet, but that's because his bit of the docks haven't been asked to handle any products from striking companies. He says it's only a matter of time before his lot go out – or are locked out by the bosses. Until then, we have enough money to spend on food. But I can't remember when I last saw some real butter – it's been margarine and dripping on our bread for weeks. Same with fresh milk (though to be honest, I do like the condensed). And Ma's cutting the slices of bread much thinner, so the loaf lasts for longer.

Other people are in much more dire straits, though. Like Rosie. She and Josie found a room in another house near Church Street – they moved in about ten days ago. It's a tiny little place, the sort of thing people in books who live in grand houses would call a box room, with nothing in it only a rickety old bed and an old packing box to serve as a table. Not even a chair. There are some nails in the wall for them to hang their clothes up, but that's it.

Me and Ma took her over there, and when Ma saw the state of the room she sort of froze in the doorway and said, 'You know, you can stay with us for a while longer, Rosie.'

But Rosie shook her head. 'Thanks, Mrs Rafferty,' she said. 'But me and Josie have to stick together.'

Ma said of course she understood, and before we went home

she took Rosie in her arms and held her there for a long time. When she stood back her eyes were shining.

'You take care of yourself, now,' she said. She took Rosie's hand and put something in it. I caught the flash of a coin. It looked like half a crown. 'I wish I could give you more, pet. And if you need anything just come to us.'

Rosie nodded.

'I'll see you on the picket tomorrow,' I said. And then I threw my arms around her too. She held on to me very tightly.

'I'll be grand,' she said into my shoulder. 'Don't you worry about me.'

But I do worry about her, even though she's been insisting that she's all right, and I know Ma has been worrying too. She and Josie are both on the strike pay, and with the rent on their little room to pay, that doesn't go far. And they had to buy new – or rather second-hand – things after everything they owned was lost. But Rosie still makes jokes.

The other day on the picket, Joan was saying that her ma has pawned a clock her old employer gave them as a wedding present. Joan's da and brothers are all locked out and they don't have a penny coming in only the strike pay.

'Ma was saying she'll have to pawn the chairs next,' said Joan gloomily. 'And she was asking how much she'd get for our boots too. We'll be sitting on the floor in our bare feet by Christmas.'

'I'm sitting on the floor anyway,' said Rosie. 'And I didn't even get any money when we lost our chairs.' She laughed. 'Not very fair, is it?'

There was a moment of shocked silence then Annie said, 'Rosie … you can't joke about that.'

But Rosie shrugged her shoulders. 'Why not? If you don't laugh, you'll cry.'

I suppose she's not wrong. And even if she jokes about what happened to her, it doesn't mean she's not still destroyed by it. Some days she comes in to the picket with red eyes and an expression on her face that makes it clear you shouldn't dare ask if she's been crying.

I worry about her getting enough to eat, and Ma does too because she keeps telling me to bring Rosie home for tea, and when I do she always makes sure Rosie gets a nice big slice of bread and dripping. But I know Rosie goes to bed properly hungry most nights, and she's not the only one.

'If you could have anything you wanted for dinner,' said Joan the other day, 'what would you eat?'

'Fish and chips,' said Rosie promptly. 'We used to go to the chipper one Friday a month before my da died.'

'I'd have a rasher of bacon all to myself,' said Joan. 'Lovely and crispy.'

And we all sighed.

'What would you have, Betty?' Rosie asked.

'Toast,' I said. 'With real butter. And maybe an egg.' I imagined biting into a perfectly browned slice of toast, with the butter all melted into it, and for a moment I could almost taste it.

'That's enough dreaming, girls,' said Kitty, but not unkindly. 'We're none of us starving to death.'

We might not be, but I have a horrible fear that some people aren't far off it. When I passed the end of Foley Street on my way home the other day, I glanced down the road and saw Margaret Maguire sitting on the front step of her house, leaning against the door frame. She used to be a fine plump girl, and now she looked as thin as a ghost. Her feet were bare and her legs looked like sticks. I shuddered to think how little she must be getting to eat.

You might think that with people starving, and after what happened in town with the police, and then the employers trying to force people to renounce the union, that people would think it wasn't worth fighting anymore. I mean, if the police are going to start whacking people on the head just because they've come into town for a union meeting – or even if they happen to be in town when the union are doing something – it would be easy to say, 'Let's give up and do what they want. We can't win this one.'

But the opposite thing seems to have happened. It's like everyone's more fired up than ever, like the police and then the anti-union pledge reminded us that the other side aren't playing fair, and that means we'd better stand up for ourselves. I can't speak for everyone, but us Lawlor's girls are not going to be bullied.

Besides, there is hope on the horizon – literally on the horizon, if you're looking out over the river. The unions over in England have been collecting money for the Irish strikers, and they've organised for a ship full of food to be delivered to Dublin this week. The British government might not do much for Ireland, but its workers are standing by us!

Miss Larkin told us union girls that some members of the Drapers' Assistants' Association (which is a fancy way of saying the union of people who work in drapers' shops – they have notions, those fellows) were going to come along to the quays and hand out special food parcels.

'And there's a plan to set up a kitchen at Liberty Hall,' she said.

'So I hope you girls are experienced at peeling potatoes.'

I am, but not by choice, the way Ma orders me around. Anyway, of course I'm going to help in the kitchen, and so are Rosie and Samira.

'At least that way I'll definitely get a proper dinner,' said Rosie. It was hard to tell if she was joking or not. It sometimes is, these days.

# Chapter Eighteen

I'm writing this on Saturday night, and after the long walk home from the South Wall quays I feel too tired to drag myself up the stairs and go to bed, so I'm going to stay here at the kitchen table and document what happened when the *Hare* arrived in Dublin.

The *Hare* isn't an animal, like the rabbit yokes that live on Bull Island. It's a boat from England, and it arrived in Dublin today, full of wonderful, magical food. At least, it felt magical when Samira, Rosie and I stood on the South Wall in Dublin Port and watched it move through the mist into the harbour. Even though the drapers' assistants were going to be giving out the parcels, we wanted to have a look and also see if we could do something to help.

'Do you think there'll be biscuits?' said Rosie, as the boat, festooned with flags, came into sight.

'Bound to be,' said Samira. 'They wouldn't have us all go without something sweet. Janey, I haven't had a biscuit for weeks.'

There was a moment of silence while we all thought about biscuits. Then Samira sniffed the air.

'Am I imagining things,' she said, 'or can you smell bread?'

'I can,' said Rosie. 'I thought I was imagining things myself. I'm going mad with hunger.'

'I can smell it too.' I turned away from the river and towards the shed where the food was going to be distributed. 'It's coming from over there.'

It turned out that lots of fresh loaves had been ordered for the food parcels from Irish bakeries, and they had been delivered the night before.

'Don't let me near those loaves,' said Rosie. 'I'll have them all ate before they've started handing out the food.'

'"Unquiet meals make ill digestions",' said Samira. 'That's Shakespeare,' she added, when Rosie gave her a quizzical look.

'How's your playacting going?' Rosie asked. I liked seeing them get on so well. They'd met a few times since Rosie's ma died, and unlike some people, including me most of the time, Samira always seemed to know exactly what to say to Rosie. I think she's made her feel a little less alone.

Of course, Samira never needs any excuse to talk about the dramatic society.

'It's going very well,' she said. 'Did you hear we're going to be doing a big show soon to raise money for the strikers? The play's going to be part of it.'

'You can give my share of the profits directly to me, thanks very much,' said Rosie with a grin.

'I don't think so,' said Samira, smiling back. 'But you *will* get some of it. It'll go towards the strike pay.'

'And how's Tom getting on at the drama company?' I said archly.

'Fine,' said Samira, a little sharply. 'He's singing in the chorus. There's going to be songs and things, not just the short plays.'

'Who's Tom?' Rosie was understandably curious.

Samira gave me a furious look.

'He's my brother's friend,' she told Rosie firmly.

'Speaking of boy friends,' said Rosie, the mischief maker, 'we haven't seen Master Peter Lawlor back at his da's shop recently.'

'Master Peter Lawlor?' Samira was confused. 'Who's he?'

I could have killed Rosie.

'He's Lavinia's brother,' I said. 'I met him when I was in the Lawlors' house with my ma. And he's been in to Lawlor's a few times.'

'He has?' said Samira.

'Betty's been having great chats with him,' said Rosie.

'Just because he nearly dropped his Sherlock Holmes book on some cakes,' I said, trying to sound casual. 'And he came back one day while we were picketing.'

'Scabbing for his da,' said Rosie helpfully.

'Shut up, you,' I said crossly.

'You didn't tell me anything about this!' Samira looked hurt, and I felt guilty for making her feel left out.

'There's nothing to tell!' I insisted, which isn't entirely true. Walking home from town with a boy – who happens to be my employer's son, no less – is definitely *something*, but I hadn't said a word about it to anyone. I had meant to tell Samira, honestly I had, but the first time I saw her after it happened was when we went into town to look for Eddie and Ali, and after that Rosie lost her ma and Francis, and, to be honest, walking home with Peter went quite out of my head. Not least because we haven't seen him since then – he hasn't been back to Lawlor's since, presumably because he's been busy doing lessons in that grand school of his. I haven't even thought of him once. Well, not very often.

'Honest, Samira,' I said. 'I had more important things to be thinking about than Peter Lawlor. I've only talked to him three times in my life, once in his house and twice on the picket line.'

'Four times,' said the irrepressible and extremely irritating Rosie. 'You forgot when he dropped his book on those cakes.'

'He didn't drop it, I caught it,' I said crossly. 'And I wouldn't even have remembered it if you didn't keep going on about it.'

'Sorry, Betty.' Rosie sometimes realises she's gone too far. 'I was only teasing you.'

'It's grand,' I said, eager to change the subject. 'Hey, look – the ship's almost in!'

It was around one o'clock when the ship arrived, but the queue of strikers and their families had begun hours earlier. One of the union men told us some of them had been there since six in the morning, clutching the food tickets they had collected from the union. So as the ship drew in to the river wall, there was already quite a big crowd, mostly women and kids, waiting patiently in front of the shed. I saw a thin woman wrapped in a shawl over a ragged dress, holding a tiny baby tightly to her chest. The baby looked pale and sickly, not chubby and red-faced like Little Robbie looked when he was that age.

Most of the women were wearing shawls, not coats, but one woman near the front of the queue reminded me a bit of Ma. She was wearing a straw hat with a ribbon on it and a neat, clean coat and skirt, and she didn't look at anyone, not in the face anyway. She just stared down at her feet as if she was ashamed to be queuing up for food. You'd think everyone would be talking to each other and even joking, the way people do when they have no choice but to wait for something, but for most of the time we were there, there was a strange silence.

Still, tired, quiet and hungry they might have been, but the crowd erupted into cheers when the boat eventually made it to the dock. A man who turned out to be one of the English union men climbed on top of a packing case to address the crowd.

'Rest assured, this first ship will not be the last!' he cried. 'Your fight is our fight, and we are going to stand by you until it is won!'

The crowd cheered some more. But once the speeches were over and the long task of unloading the ship continued, the queuing women returned to their former silence.

'Janey, it's like a funeral,' said Rosie after a while.

'There must be something we can do,' I said.

'Let's go and see if we can help,' said Samira. '"Once more unto the breach!"'

But the drapers' assistants looked quite affronted when we asked if we could hand out some of the food parcels. They're quite stuck up, in general, and they think they're much better than us ordinary union members.

'We've got this well in hand, thank you!' said one pale young gentleman, taking a ticket and handing over a large sack of food to a girl around Lily's age.

'I hope that Miss Larkin didn't send you,' said another young man sternly. 'It was arranged that we should give out the parcels.'

We reassured him that we were here in a private capacity.

'We just wanted to see if we could help,' I said, as meekly as I could. 'We'll go now.'

'Actually,' said another drapers' assistant, looking at his pals with a hint of apology in his voice. 'I could do with a bit of help for a few minutes.'

He whispered in the pale young gentleman's ear. The pale young gentleman looked at him disapprovingly. 'I must say I think you should have gone before you came in here!'

'I'm really not feeling very well, Jim,' said his colleague.

The pale young gentleman sighed, looked at the long queue

and looked back at me, Samira and Rosie. 'All right, you can shift these parcels to the table so they're ready for him when he comes back.'

'Aye aye, Captain!' said Rosie, which earned her another disapproving look from the pale young gentleman.

The parcels, as it turned out, were very heavy.

'What's in these yokes, anyway?' Rosie asked, bending her knees as she lifted up a bulging package.

'Ten pounds of potatoes,' said one of the drapers' assistants promptly. 'And then there's the sugar and tea ...'

'And jam,' said one of his mates. 'And butter.'

'Real butter!' I said.

'I think so,' said the first drapers' assistant. 'Though it could be marge. I haven't checked. And a loaf of bread.'

'There's some tinned fish too,' said his friend. 'And a few biscuits, I think.'

Samira, Rosie and I looked at each other. I felt my mouth water. And Rosie's stomach rumbled loudly.

'Janey,' she said, laying the package on the table, ready to be handed out. 'That's a fine feast.'

'Suppose so,' said the drapers' assistant. 'It's for a whole family, though. Meant to feed five people. So it won't last that long.'

By the time we'd transferred over the sacks the missing assistant hadn't returned yet so the pale young gentleman looked at the three of us and sighed. 'One of you had better take his spot until he comes back,' he said.

'I'll do it,' said Rosie quickly. 'I want to help them.'

'Grand,' said the pale young gentleman. He looked up at the patient procession of people that now snaked its way right out the door of the shed. 'Next! Have your ticket ready!'

There was an old packing case sitting near the distribution table but out of the way of the queue, so Samira and I sat on it and watched Rosie and the assistants hand over the parcels. I thought she might ask me some more questions about Peter Lawlor, but we were both pretty subdued as we watched the sad, silent queue. There was no sign of the drapers' assistant whose place Rosie had taken, so we were there for ages and ages, and we witnessed a few sorrowful scenes. Some women had heard that food was being given out but hadn't realised that you needed a ticket from the union to get it, and I'll never forget the expressions on their faces when they realised they and their children would be going home hungry.

One woman, holding the hand of a little girl in one hand and an empty basket lined with newspaper in the other, looked so forlorn when she walked away empty handed I thought she was going to faint. Then another woman, who had just collected a parcel, put her hand on her shoulder.

'Maureen, love,' she said. 'I don't need all this tea and sugar. Why don't you take some of mine?'

The forlorn woman looked at her with wide eyes. 'Ah, May, I couldn't,' she said.

'Don't be stupid,' said the woman called May. She rummaged around in her parcel. 'Here, give us that newspaper, I'll make a few little packages for you.' And she kneeled down on the floor of the shed, folded a bit of newspaper and poured some of her tea into it and made a small parcel, before doing the same with the sugar.

'Bless you, May Fegan,' said Maureen. Her voice was shaking. 'I won't forget this, so I won't.'

'Come on, pet,' said May. 'I'm taking you home.'

I glanced across at Rosie, who was still handing out parcels. I hadn't seen her look so serious since – well, you know when. Like that woman Maureen, she knew what it was like to be hungry – really hungry, not just hungry the way me and Samira are feeling, missing our toast and bacon and real butter. Even before the strike, there were days when Rosie didn't get any tea when she got home. And now ...

'Does Rosie have a food ticket?' I said suddenly. Neither Samira nor I had taken one. Our das are still working and it didn't seem fair to take food when there are some families that don't have more than a shilling a week to spend on meals.

'I think so,' said Samira. 'But will they give her a parcel just for her and Josie? Maybe they're only for big families.'

The thought that Rosie could be denied food, after everything that's happened to her, and after her coming here to try and help other people, was unbearable. Just then, I saw the drapers' assistant who Rosie had replaced finally return from the jacks. I ran over to him. He was looking a bit green around the gills. I hoped whatever was wrong with him wasn't catching.

'Are you all right?' I said.

He nodded. 'Better than I was. My mam said that pie was on the turn but I didn't believe her.' Then he remembered that he was meant to be a dignified drapers' assistant and adopted a more lofty manner. 'Anyway, I'll get back to work now.'

'Our friend who's helping,' I said. 'She has a food ticket. Can you make sure she gets a parcel?'

'She can't skip the queue,' said the assistant. 'There's people who've been waiting since six in the morning.'

'Of course not,' I said. 'But can you make sure she gets a parcel all the same?'

'I'll do my best,' he said, and he went over to the table and resumed his position. Rosie joined us a moment later.

'All right, girls,' she said, but her breezy manner seemed a bit forced. 'Our work here is done.'

'Aren't you going to wait and get a parcel?' Samira said. 'There's not that many left now. It won't be long.'

Rosie shrugged her shoulders. 'Me and Josie are grand. There's some over there who have ten mouths to feed.'

'But Rosie!' I began. Rosie interrupted me.

'It's grand. I swear it is,' she said. 'Come on. We might as well go.'

But as we were leaving the shed, someone called, 'Girls! You girls!' and we looked around to see the pale young gentleman waving imperiously at us.

'You must have left something there, Rosie,' said Samira as we made our way back to him.

'I don't think I did,' said Rosie. 'It's not like I had anything to leave.'

But the young man had got up from his seat, letting one of his mates take over his place, and was walking towards us carrying a food parcel, which he thrust into Rosie's arms.

'You've got a ticket, haven't you?' he said. 'There's only ten people left, you might as well just take this now.'

'Uh, I do have one,' said Rosie. 'But you don't need to …'

And then, to my immense surprise, the pale young gentleman said, 'You remind me of my sister. She'd have wanted to help out too.' And before Rosie could say another word, he ran back to his table.

'Don't look a gift horse in the mouth,' said Samira. 'They've got enough parcels left for the people who are waiting. You don't have to worry about letting someone else go hungry.'

'All right,' said Rosie. She looked down at the heavy parcel in her arms. 'Me and Josie will have a feast tonight.' And she burst into tears.

'Come on,' said Samira, putting an arm around her shoulders. 'Don't cry all over that nice English butter. You don't want it to be too salty.'

That made Rosie laugh a little bit. She wiped her eyes on the parcel.

'Don't mind me. I'm grand,' she said. 'Would you look, it's practically dark outside.'

We had been in the shed for much longer than I thought. We walked along the quay with women and children carrying parcels, all going home to a decent meal, maybe for the first time in weeks. But although I didn't want to say it then, I couldn't help wondering what they would do when that food ran out.

# Chapter Nineteen

I've been home for an hour sitting in front of the kitchen fire, and my feet still feel wet. Picketing wasn't so bad when it was sunny, but it's a lot worse now that autumn's really here and the weather's turned.

'Well,' said Ma, drying my hair roughly with a towel that's so worn out you can practically see through it, 'if you hadn't walked out of the job, you'd have been nice and dry behind a counter full of cakes, instead of standing out in the rain all day.'

I sneezed. Then I sneezed again.

'How's the new dress for Mrs Dickson going?' I asked, sticking my bare feet as close to the fire as they could get without getting burned.

'Almost there,' said Ma, hanging the towel on the back of a chair to dry. Mrs Dickson has given Ma a few jobs since our visit to her sister's house. I think she might feel guilty about sending Ma into the middle of a riot. And that's a good thing too, because my and Eddie's strike pay doesn't go that far.

And now we've got Robert Hessian and Lily to worry about too. Yesterday his bit of the docks was asked to handle goods from an anti-union company, so they went out. He's got his strike pay, of course, but Lily isn't earning anything and Robert Hessian's da doesn't earn much at the printers where he works – not enough to make up for Robert Hessian's lost wage, anyway. Lily was almost in tears when she called over last night, talking about Little Robbie going hungry. I didn't like hearing that. I know he's a terrible child but I don't want him to starve or anything.

I said this to Da and he just ruffled my hair and said I wasn't to worry, Little Robbie would be grand, but I'm not a little kid anymore and I could tell he was worried too. After all, he's admitted that he'll probably be out himself sooner or later, the way things are going at the moment.

Then Ma will be the only one of us earning a penny outside of strike pay (however long that lasts). And a few frocks for Mrs Dickson don't make up for all the clients Ma lost when Mrs Lawlor and her pals stopped employing her. Even when she did have those clients, it wasn't like her dressmaking was ever a full-time job – it was just to earn a few bob extra. She never thought she'd have to keep her entire family – and Robert Hessian and Little Robbie too, if you count them as family, which I suppose you have to – on a few bits of dressmaking. I keep waking up in the night and worrying about it, but then I remind myself that Da is still working as usual and that nothing bad is happening right now.

The Caseys aren't doing too badly, because while Samira may be working half hours and Ali's locked out, her da's still working, and Maisie has started rehearsals for her role in the panto. I didn't realise she'd get paid before the play starts its run, but apparently she does. When I was in Samira's last night Maisie told us all about the show.

'It's not exactly Shakespeare,' she said, leaning against the Caseys' sitting-room door as Ali, Samira and I sat on the floor, 'but it's a very grand production. So grand,' she added, producing her handbag from behind her back, 'that there was a box of these backstage.' And reaching into the bag, she drew out three wrapped chocolates and threw one of them to each of us.

'Chocolate!' exclaimed Samira.

'Thanks, Auntie Maisie.' Ali tried to be dignified but his eyes were bright with excitement.

'Don't worry,' said Auntie Maisie. 'They're not Savoy. I'm not breaking a strike AND eating rat droppings.'

'Don't talk about rat droppings.' Samira quickly unwrapped her chocolate and popped the whole thing into her mouth. Her eyes closed in bliss.

I bit into my chocolate and led the sweetness melt on my tongue. I couldn't remember the last time I'd had a treat like that.

'And how are you, young Betty?' said Auntie Maisie, sitting on the edge of the sofa. 'I haven't seen you for a while, I've been so busy at the theatre.'

'She's been busy with her new fancy man,' said Samira. 'Ow! Stop pinching! What was that for?'

'You're acting like Rosie,' I said crossly. 'And she's bad enough.'

'What's this about a fancy man?' There was something strangely forced about the lightness in Ali's voice. I hope he wasn't shocked by Samira's nonsense.

'It's nothing,' I said, glowering at Samira, who had the decency to look a little embarrassed. 'I met the Lawlors' son when I was in their house and then he turned up at the shop.' I still hadn't told Samira about walking home with him. I felt guilty about keeping something from her – even though of course it wasn't anything important, not really – but I was glad I hadn't told her anything, now that she was blabbing about it in front of Ali. And Auntie Maisie too of course.

'And what's he like, this Lawlors' son?' said Ali, still in that slightly forced tone.

I shrugged my shoulders and looked down at my hands. I fiddled with the chocolate wrapper. Somehow I couldn't meet Ali's gaze. 'I don't know. Friendly. Couldn't understand why we were striking. He was scabbing for his da.'

'Right,' said Ali. He scrambled to his feet. 'I have to see Tom about something.'

'What sort of something?' said Samira. 'It's eight o'clock!'

'Don't go. You're great gas,' said Auntie Maisie, but Ali just kissed her cheek and said, 'It's union business. Thanks for the sweets, Auntie M.' And then he was off.

Auntie Maisie raised an eyebrow. 'I think someone might be feeling a bit put out.'

'I don't know what's wrong with him,' grumbled Samira.

But I think I did. He was horrified that I was all pally with one of the employers – or at least one of their children. The fun of the evening was gone after that, and I couldn't even enjoy hearing Auntie Maisie's stories about her costume fittings, even when she told us that she gets to wear a ball dress so covered in tiny glittering beads that 'it feels like it weighs as much as I do. I can barely walk in it!' In fact, I felt so distracted and odd that I went home earlier than I had intended. Samira walked me to the door.

'Are you all right?' she said.

'I'm grand,' I said, more cheerfully than I felt. 'Just tired, that's all. Are you still up for working in the Liberty Hall kitchen on Wednesday?'

A lot of us union girls have volunteered to help make meals for poor children.

''Course I am!' said Samira. 'Do you think the other girls will mind if I practise my lines while we're peeling carrots, or what have you?'

I tried to think of a polite way to tell her that they might find it a bit irritating after a while. Inspiration struck.

'You probably shouldn't,' I said. 'Sure, it'll spoil the play for them! You don't want them knowing what's going to happen before they see it on stage.'

'I never thought of that,' said Samira. Her face brightened. 'Maybe I could sing for them!'

'Let's see what it's like first,' I advised. 'It mightn't be a singing sort of place.'

Whatever sort of place the kitchen is, it'll be warm and dry, so I'm quite looking forward to it. It'll be better than standing outside Lawlor's in the freezing wet rain all day. Somehow the cold and damp makes the hunger even worse. We're still buying a few buns off the Yeates's bakery, and they slip in the odd free one, but you need more than buns to keep you going when you're out in the rain all day marching up and down outside a cake shop. I saw an umbrella in the pawn shop window on my way to the picket this morning, and I was sorely tempted to buy one. But an umbrella seems like a luxury at the moment. And if there's one thing we Dublin workers can't afford right now, it's luxury.

# Chapter Twenty

I know that I keep writing about how tired I am, but really, I can't help it. Sometimes I remember the time, just a few months ago, when I was able to sit down all day in school looking at books, and then just did a bit of housework for Ma in the afternoons, and I can't understand how I ever thought I was even a tiny bit tired back in those happy golden days. Ever since I left school I've either been standing up all day working *inside* the shop or standing up all day picketing *outside* the shop. And now I've started working in the food kitchen, I'm spending most of my days either sitting down hacking away at potatoes with a knife or standing up all day chopping things. Both of which are hard work.

But at least, as Rosie pointed out, it's warm and dry. And when you see some of the people who come in there, you know you have to count your blessings. Besides, Rosie would clatter me if I did any complaining about sore legs, and rightly so, I suppose.

We started working in the kitchen a few days ago, though we weren't chopping any vegetables that day. Someone had realised that, because the Liberty Hall building used to be a hotel, it had to have a proper kitchen, even if that kitchen hadn't been used for years. And that someone was right on both counts, as we discovered when us union girls were asked by Miss Larkin to help clean it up.

Quite a big crowd had answered her call for helpers, including me, Rosie, Joan and Kitty and some of the Savoy girls, as well as Rosie's sister Josie and lots of her friends from the biscuit factory.

One of the biscuit factory girls is called Rosie too; she's only a little thing but you could imagine her leading an army some day. And it was a good thing there were so many of us, given the hideous sight that greeted us in the large but neglected kitchen.

'Janey,' said Rosie, looking doubtfully at a pile of pots that looked as if they hadn't seen a dishcloth in twenty years, 'I don't fancy eating anything cooked in here.'

'Ah,' said a very grand voice from just behind us, 'that's where you girls will prove your mettle.'

We turned around to see a tall, elegant lady looking down on us with bright eyes. I realised with a jolt she was the woman in the green coat who had cheered on Mr Larkin in O'Connell Street and got punched by a policeman for her pains.

'We've all got to roll up our sleeves and get stuck in, girls,' said the lady, taking off her coat (it was a soft brown, today) and suiting the action to the word. I couldn't help thinking that her graceful arms and elegant pale hands didn't look as if she'd done much kitchen work before. Playing the piano and painting pictures, maybe, but not cleaning out a grate.

I glanced at Rosie, whose expression as she looked at the mysterious lady suggested that she was thinking the same thing. In fact, there were a few other well-dressed ladies present who didn't look like they knew much about scrubbing pots. I wondered where all these strangers had come from. It was quite a relief to see the familiar figure of Miss Larkin (even if she can be a bit frightening), guiding latecomers into the gloomy kitchen.

'Girls,' she said, gesturing towards the mysterious lady. 'For those of you who don't know her already, this is Madame Markievicz. She's going to be working in the kitchen with you.'

'Once we've cleaned it up, of course,' said Madame Markievicz. That's how her name is spelled, by the way. She is married to a Polish count – like someone in a book – so I suppose it must be a name from Poland. But she is not from Poland herself. Someone said she was from Sligo, but she doesn't talk like Mrs Hennessy on our road, who was born and reared in Sligo before she came to Dublin. Madame is a lot more imposing and dramatic than Mrs Hennessy too.

And I have to hand it to her, she did get stuck in with the rest of us that day, as we scrubbed and cleaned and mopped and wiped. Horrible work it was too – I'm well used to doing housework, but our house has never been in such a state as this. Everything was absolutely covered in filth. I don't know how things could have possibly got so dirty. It was as though whoever was running the hotel just closed up the kitchen on the last day, without even rinsing out the pots. The whole place was massive, too, so just cleaning the floor took ages – you could have fit four of our kitchen into that big room. The range was about the size of my bed and there was a big copper thing that one of the Jacob's factory girls said was called a cow boiler, which is a horrible name. Her da is in the army and told her about them – they're used to make stews for lots and lots of people at once.

No one had made stew in this one for a long time. It took hours and hours – and lots of hot water – to get it looking halfway decent, and by that stage my hands were red and raw from the water and the carbolic soap.

'Lucky Samira,' I said to Rosie. Samira had to work in the shop that day and couldn't join us. 'She's probably sitting on that counter reciting her lines right now.'

Rosie wiped her forehead with a damp hand. 'She'll be in here peeling potatoes and chopping carrots soon enough.'

I leaned back on the big table that, thanks to the Savoy girls, was now scrubbed to a state of shining cleanliness. 'Chopping carrots is going to seem like a holiday after scrubbing out all them pots. What were they cooking in them, wall plaster?'

'Well,' said Rosie, looking proudly around at the gleaming kitchen. 'It's all done now.'

And it was. Madame Markievicz and Miss Larkin gathered us around the table and thanked us for all our work.

'Tomorrow,' said Miss Larkin, 'we start feeding the hungry women and children of this city. And we wouldn't be able to do it without you girls.'

Somehow I didn't feel as annoyed about cleaning out the dirty kitchen when I heard that.

When I came home, Ma was horrified when she saw my bedraggled appearance and heard what we'd been up to.

'I sent you to Lawlor's so you wouldn't have to do that sort of rough work all day!' she said. 'And look at the state of you.'

I explained that we had to get the kitchen in order and it wouldn't be so bad after that – we're going to take turns to clean up after the day's cooking, so it's not as if we'll all be washing pots *every* day. But Ma was still annoyed by the whole thing. She softened a bit when I reminded her why we were doing all that scrubbing, but not much.

I had to remind *myself* why we were doing it, to be honest, when I got up at the crack of dawn the next day. We had to be there early to start getting things ready because the word had spread fast among the hungry families of Dublin, and we all knew there would be a lot of meals to prepare. I had just enough time to get a slice of bread and marge into me before there was a knock on the door and I answered it to see Samira, looking as tired as I felt.

'Ready for your first day of union action?' I said, as we headed up the road.

'It's not my first day of action!' Samira was indignant. 'The dramatic company is union action too. I'm telling you, I think I've learned more about workers' rights doing that labour play than I ever learned hearing Da go on about wage disputes.'

I suppose she has a point there. You can learn a lot from a story.

'And even if we were doing a comedy,' Samira went on, 'plays are important too. Haven't you heard that song "Bread and Roses"?'

'I don't think so,' I said.

'Miss Larkin printed the words in the *Irish Worker* women's column last year,' said Samira. 'We sang it at one of the dramatic company practices.' And as we headed towards the canal bridge, she raised her voice in song.

*Our lives shall not be sweated*
*From birth until life closes.*
*Hearts starve as well as bodies*
*Bread and roses, bread and roses!*

People turned to look at us as we strode past, but to my surprise I realised I didn't really mind. That's another thing picketing does for you; you really stop caring about people gawping at you. And Samira clearly wasn't bothered either because she didn't stop singing as we marched over the bridge.

*As we come marching, marching*

*Unnumbered women dead*
*Go crying through our singing*
*Their ancient cry for bread.*
*Small art and love and beauty*
*Their drudging spirits knew*
*Yes, it is bread we fight for*
*But we fight for roses too!*

I don't know why, but when I heard Samira sing those last few lines, I thought I might start to cry. Because whoever wrote that song was right. We're fighting for bread, for food, and everything you need to buy it – a fair wage, and fair treatment at work. But there's more to life than work. There are books, and music – and concerts, like the show Samira and the rest of the drama society are putting on. Those things are roses of life. And sometimes it's worth reminding people of that, including yourself. Songs are a very good way of getting all riled up for a cause, I think.

'I like that,' I said, when Samira had finished the song with a rousing 'Bread and roses, bread and roses!'

'I'll teach it to you if you like,' said Samira. 'We can sing it while we peel potatoes.'

'I don't think anyone wants to hear me sing,' I said, because while I'm always in time when I clap out a beat to someone else's song, Eddie once told me that my own voice sounded like a cow getting stuck in a drain. And even though I gave him a clatter for it, I couldn't deny that he was right. But Samira said that didn't matter.

'I mean,' she said honestly, 'it *would* matter if you wanted to sing in the concert. But it's different just singing with your pals.'

Maybe she's right. Though we didn't get a chance to try out her idea because when we got to the kitchen at Liberty Hall we soon found ourselves working so hard we could barely draw a breath, let alone start a sing-song.

We arrived just as some of the locked-out men were carrying in loads of vegetables in big crates and putting them in piles on the big table. Water was being boiled in the big cow boiler (I know it's a horrible name, but we've all started using it), and some of the men were stoking the fire beneath it. Miss Larkin and Madame Markievicz were deep in discussion when we entered, so we joined Rosie and Joan, who were standing near the massive sink.

'Welcome to the Liberty Hotel,' said Rosie, bowing so dramatically that we couldn't help but laugh. I introduced Samira to Joan, whose face puckered in a frown when she heard Samira's name.

'Samira? That's a very funny …' Then she suddenly broke off and rubbed her arm. 'Ow! What did you do that for, Rosie?'

'To remind you not to make personal remarks,' said Rosie sweetly. 'Howiya, Samira?'

Just then, Miss Larkin clapped her hands and said 'Girls!' in a voice that demanded our attention. We all whirled round to face her.

'You're all here because you want to feed the hungry people of Dublin,' she said. 'Well, here's your chance to do it.' She turned to two of the Jacob's girls. 'Miss Hackett and Miss Toolan, come over here …'

And she divided us into groups, all with different tasks to do. I was glad me and Rosie and Samira were in the same group. We were each given a knife and an apron and directed to a bench near the big cow boiler. There was a sack of potatoes at the end of it and we distributed the potatoes among ourselves. Then we sat on the bench, filled our aprons with potatoes, and started peeling. Whenever we finished with a potato, we threw it into a big clean bucket. Kitty and some of the Jacob's girls were cutting up bits of meat on the big table, and other girls were chopping carrots and onions at the other end. Out of the corner of my eye I could see some lads carry in trays full of freshly baked bread.

Even though Ma makes me do it regularly, I've never been very good at peeling potatoes. I'm always scared I'll peel a bit off my thumbs. I said this to Rosie and she said, 'Sure if you do it'll be another bit of meat in the stew', and me and Samira both elbowed her and told her not to be so disgusting. Anyway, I managed to do my first potato without injuring myself, and after a while I got quite quick at it. I wasn't as good as the others, though. We started having a competition to see who could peel the fastest, and Samira won three times and Rosie won four times and I didn't win even once.

Eventually the big old cow boiler was full of some meat and lots of vegetables, all bubbling away. The smell of meat was delicious. I haven't had any meat for ages now.

'Do you think we'll get some stew?' whispered Samira.

I'd been hoping the same thing. But before I could answer her, the doors of the kitchen were flung open and the first of a long queue of waiting women and children began to stream into the kitchen, holding tickets in one hand and jugs, bowls and pots in the other. It was time for us to feed the city.

The rest of the day was a blur of faces and steam and voices and the sound of knives chopping and spoons scraping. Everyone had to present their ticket, same as at the shed, and whatever vessel they'd brought to take the stew home in. They also got a loaf of bread each. Some people didn't realise they had to take their own containers, and when one woman was asked for her jug and said she didn't have one, I thought she was going to start crying. But the man who was on duty at the time said, 'Well now, don't worry about that.' Then he produced a washed-out tin can and filled it full of stew for her.

After the first rush of people, we had a bit of a break and got to eat some of the stew ourselves. We fairly dived into it, and if I hadn't been aware of Madame Markievicz standing nearby I'd have stuck my face right into the bowl and licked up the last drop. As it was, I was able to use a nice chunk of fresh bread to mop it up, and delicious it was too. But soon we were back at work again, because we're giving out food three times a day, and there's not much time to rest when you've got to cook that many meals.

During the third shift a little girl who only looked about four years old came in clutching a jug. She looked very serious as she walked right up to one of the well-dressed women who were helping Madame Markievicz at the cow boiler, held out her ticket and said, very seriously, 'Are you the right lady?'

The woman smiled at her and said, 'I am. Would you like to give me your ticket?'

'Are you sure you're the right lady?' The small girl looked suspicious. 'Will I get my jug back again? I can't take home no one else's.'

'Don't worry.' The lady's voice was gentle. 'You'll get it back. Just wait over there for a minute.'

Looking suspiciously back at the lady, as if she expected her to run off with both the ticket and the jug, the little girl went over to the wall where a few other hungry citizens were resting as they waited for their food to be served. She still looked a bit wary when the lady beckoned her back a few minutes later, but her face brightened when she got her precious jug back, filled with stew, and she trotted off looking happy enough. Though I wondered what her home must be like, where they had to send out a baby like her to get the dinner.

It was almost dark by the time the giant cauldron of a boiler was scraped empty, and then we had to clean everything again. It wasn't half as bad as the previous day's work had been – we didn't have to scrub off what felt like a hundred years' worth of grime this time – but it was still hard work. Eventually all the plates and spoons and knives and tables were clean once more, and Miss Larkin addressed us all.

'Well done, everyone,' she said. 'Go home and get some sleep. We'll be busy again tomorrow.'

And that was the end of our first proper day in the kitchens. We were all so exhausted by the end of it that we barely said good-bye to Rosie and the others. Samira and I staggered off towards Amiens Street.

'My hair smells of stew,' said Samira, sniffing one of her thick dark plaits.

I pulled out one of my own brown mop-like waves. 'Mine too,' I said. I flexed my fingers. 'I've had my hands curled around that knife for so long I thought they were going to stay like that forever.'

'I'll be dreaming about potatoes tonight,' said Samira. She looked at me, her face suddenly worried. 'You don't suppose it'll damage my hands for acting, do you?'

'What do you mean?' She does get notions sometimes. I

suppose all actors do.

'I've got to show all my emotions on stage!' she said. 'I can't do that if my hands are horrible little potato-peeling claws.'

I told her I was sure peeling potatoes for a few days wouldn't spoil her acting career. But now I'm worried that she was right about the effects on your hands. Maybe all that peeling will spoil my writing. If I wasn't so concerned with recording everything for posterity, I wouldn't have picked up my pencil this evening. But still, as I told Samira just before I wearily pushed open my front door, it's all for a good cause.

# Chapter Twenty-One

Samira had no reason to worry about working in the kitchen being bad for her acting (she says the next dramatic company rehearsal went perfectly well, and she was able to wave her hands around as much as she wanted), but it turns out that she was right to worry about dreaming about potatoes. Every time I fall asleep, I find myself seeing potato peelings falling in front of my eyes. And even though I haven't sliced anything off my fingers, I have cut myself a few times. My hands are a state, to Ma's dismay.

'If you'd just stayed behind the counter at Lawlor's, you'd have lovely soft hands!' she said when I came home last night. 'They didn't even make you work in the washing-up room there.'

I think Ma might have been getting a bit carried away. To hear her talk, you'd think that before the strike I was a young lady of leisure like Lavinia Lawlor, a girl who'd never lifted a hand in her life. But I've scrubbed enough pots in our own sink, and so has she. I reminded her of this and she told me she'd have less of my cheek, thanks very much.

'And if you're that keen on housework,' she added, 'you can bring Eddie his tea.'

Poor Eddie (I never thought I'd write those words)! His arm is still in a sling and it'll stay there for another week. The good thing is that it seems to be healing well so he should be right as rain eventually. But eventually can feel like a long time. Although he's been back out picketing for a few weeks, he's not really able to hold a heavy sign for long (not that he'd ever admit it). Da told me that he gets worried about someone accidentally bashing into him on the picket line because any time he bumps his bad arm it's agony.

I feel particularly bad about Eddie because he wouldn't have been injured at all if he hadn't been saving me from a policeman's baton. That could have been my head instead of his arm. I actually said this to him a while ago and I thought he'd enjoy rubbing it in – he usually doesn't miss an opportunity to make fun of me – but he just looked at his splint and said gruffly, 'I wasn't going to let a peeler bash my sister.' He's not that bad, really. Not that I'd ever tell him that. I just said, 'Well, thanks very much.' And he said 'Ah, go away out of that.'

Anyway, I didn't mind making him some toast and margarine. It barely even counted as work after a day's chopping and peeling. I was on carrots today, which meant standing up at the table for hours. The kitchens are busier than ever at the moment, and we've been getting more grand ladies coming in – including suffragettes. There's a lady called Mrs Sheehy-Skeffington who went to prison last year for smashing windows. She came along to the kitchen with some of her fellow suffragettes, who all seemed to know Madame Markievicz quite well. They were bustling about the place, and I was just getting started on my pile of carrots when a young-sounding voice said, in a loud whisper, 'I say, can we help out here?'

I turned to see two girls about my own age wearing simple, slightly worn blouses and skirts that nevertheless looked much more expensive than anything the rest of us were wearing. I couldn't figure out why they were familiar until one of them, a girl with red hair, said, 'Oh hello!'

I realised they were the two suffragette girls I'd met outside Lawlor's back when we first went on strike. They went to Eccles Street, I remembered, the same as Lavinia Lawlor.

'Can we help?' whispered the brown-haired girl.

I remembered her name was Mary or Maggie or something else beginning with M.

We were actually a bit short of workers that day – Samira had to work in the shop, Rosie had been put on pot-washing duty and Kitty had been out for two days with a bad cold – so I budged over and handed them each a knife.

'Do you know how to peel and chop carrots?' I asked.

The two girls looked at each other.

'Well, sort of,' said the dark-haired one. 'I mean, I've helped.'

I sighed. I had a feeling these sorts of girls might be more trouble than they were worth.

'Just look at what I'm doing,' I said, as I topped and tailed a carrot. 'What are your names again?'

'I'm Nora,' said the red-haired girl, closely observing my hands. 'And this is Mollie.'

'And I'm Betty.' I finished chopping my carrot and put it in the pile for the pot. 'Why are you here, anyway? Shouldn't you be in school?'

'We've got a half day,' said the girl called Nora, hesitantly chopping the end of her carrot.

'And we heard that Mrs Sheehy-Skeffington and her friends were helping here,' said Mollie. 'So we knew it wasn't just for union girls.'

'Did she bring you along?' I was surprised that the suffragettes were recruiting schoolgirls to our cause.

'Oh heavens, no,' said Mollie. 'She doesn't even know who we are. I mean, we're just ordinary supporters of the suffrage campaign. But we read about the kitchen in the *Citizen* yesterday.'

'The *Citizen*?' I said. 'No, peel the carrot away from you. That's right.'

'It's the Irish suffrage newspaper,' said Nora. 'It said there were girls helping in the kitchen, so we thought we'd come along and do our bit.'

'Oh right,' I said.

'We're here because of you, really,' said the dark-haired Mollie, who seemed to be getting the hang of carrot chopping. 'We've been thinking about your strike, ever since we saw you that day. And I talked to Maggie about it – her sister Jenny's in the union, she works in Jacob's …'

'Who's Maggie?' I asked.

'Oh, she's …' Mollie hesitated before saying, 'she's our general servant.'

She looked embarrassed, but I wasn't surprised to hear they had servants. Most girls like that do.

'Anyway,' Mollie went on, 'when we heard what happened in town with the police at the end of the summer, well, we felt we had to do something.'

'I was there,' I said, not without a bit of pride. 'That day when the police charged.'

'Heavens, were you really?' Mollie's voice was full of awe. I wasn't used to anyone sounded so impressed by me. Especially someone who went to a fancy school.

'I was. The police broke my brother's arm,' I said.

'They did *what*?' said Nora.

'How did it happen?' asked Mollie, her eyes wide.

And as the three of us continued to work on our carrots, I told them everything that happened over that terrible Saturday and Sunday. The two Eccles Street girls listened with rapt attention.

'Goodness, how awful,' breathed Mollie. 'Were you awfully scared?'

For a second I considered lying but I felt that wouldn't be right. So I said, truthfully, 'I was terrified.'

'We were caught up in a sort of riot last year,' said Nora. 'After the English suffragette threw a hatchet at Mr Asquith.'

I vaguely remembered that. 'What happened?' I asked. And they told me how the suffragettes had been trying to give speeches 'just across the road from here' when they were attacked by a mob.

'But the policemen saved the speakers,' said Mollie. 'And they saved my sister Frances too. Some men tried to throw her into the river but the policemen stopped them.'

Turns out even Eccles Street girls can get caught up in street fights. Though in their cases, the police come to the rescue.

'Janey,' I said. 'Was she all right?'

'She was all shaken up, but she wasn't badly hurt,' said Mollie. She finished chopping one carrot and took another out of the pile. 'She's in college now. Doing modern languages.'

'What's that?' I said. It didn't sound like a real subject to me.

'French and German,' said Mollie. 'I think I'd rather like to do it myself.'

'You *have* got much better at French lately,' said Nora. 'I say, Betty, where should I put these peelings?'

A pang went through me as I showed Nora what to do. She and Mollie seemed like decent, friendly girls, and it was good of them to try and do their bit for our cause. I liked them a lot already. But the idea that some girls could not only go to a school like Eccles Street, but could plan to go to college afterwards ... it was almost unbearable. It was like they were living in another world, one that me and Samira were forbidden to enter. I didn't say this out loud, though. I knew I wouldn't be able to get the words out without sounding bitter. Mostly it all just makes me feel sad.

'So do your ma and da know you're here?' I said, taking a new carrot from the pile.

'Oh goodness, no,' said Mollie, putting her peelings into the slop bucket. 'They think I'm in Nora's house practising Latin verbs.'

'And mine think I'm at Mollie's,' said Nora. 'We're lucky our mothers don't really know each other. We'd never get to do anything at all if they ever compared notes.' She leaned towards me. 'By the way, where's the lav?'

I told her where the jacks was and returned to my chopping. I was going to ask Mollie about their mothers and what they thought of their suffragette activities when a delicious smell wafted towards me and I looked up to see none other than Ali, striding in with a tray full of fresh bread on his shoulder. I glanced away. I hadn't seen much of him since that evening in the Caseys' house when he left in a hurry.

'Today's loaves, courtesy of the Locked-out Workers' Delivery Association!' he said cheerfully as he passed the table, followed by Tom and some other locked-out boys, all laden with bread trays. And as soon as he'd handed over his tray of loaves, he was back at our table.

'So my sister's abandoned you again, has she?' he said with a smile.

'I don't think it counts as abandoning,' I said. 'She's working in the shop, remember?'

Ali scoffed. 'She's sitting on the counter practising her lines, if I know Samira. Hey, watch out!'

For Mollie had grabbed a carrot from the bottom of the pile, and the ones above it had started to tumble down and roll across the table. Ali grabbed them before they could roll onto the floor.

'Here you go,' he said, handing them over to Mollie.

'Thanks awfully,' she said. 'That was very stupid of me.'

'Are you locked out too?' Ali tried and failed to keep the surprise out of his voice at the sound of Mollie's ladylike tones.

Mollie looked away, flustered. 'Well, no,' she said. And she explained how she and Nora had come to Liberty Hall.

'I hope you don't think we're being all Marie Antoinetteish,' she said, looking at both me and Ali. 'You know, the way she used to pretend to be a shepherdess for fun even though she was the Queen of France. We're not just playing. We really do care.'

'I think it's pretty decent of yiz.' Ali's gaze was warm. 'If more girls like you were on our side, we'd be doing well. I'm Ali Casey, by the way. I'm locked out and I'd usually be picketing but they needed more lads to take in the grub today.'

He held out a hand and Mollie took it and shook it firmly. 'I'm Mollie Carberry.'

They smiled at each other. And for some reason I felt my stomach churn. Suddenly I wished Ali had stayed on his picket today and had never come into the kitchen.

'Well,' I said, more brightly than I felt, 'the carrots won't chop themselves.' I thought Ali might collect Tom and head off when we got back to work, but he stayed standing by the table.

'So you're a suffragette?' said Ali, as Mollie took a carrot – from the top of the pile this time – and cut the top off.

'Well, sort of,' said Mollie. And she told him about how she and Nora went to lots of meetings and started a society at school, and how they had painted slogans on a post box last year.

'Hey now, that's pretty good going!' Ali looked impressed. 'You could have been arrested!'

'Well,' said Mollie, 'we were jolly scared the whole time. And,' she added honestly, 'we haven't done anything so daring since.'

'Still, it was brave of you,' said Ali. He looked at me. 'Wasn't it, Betty?'

'Very brave,' I muttered, focusing my gaze on my carrots. 'But we really need to concentrate on these carrots, so if you don't mind ...'

'Sorry Betty, I didn't mean ...' Ali gave me an odd look. 'I'd better get back to the picket line. Tom's gone already.' He touched the edge of his cap. 'See you later, Betty. Nice meeting you, Mollie.'

And with a friendly wave, Ali was gone.

'What a nice boy!' said Mollie.

'He's my friend's brother,' I said, without looking up from my carrots.

'He's a lot nicer than my brother,' said Mollie, sweeping her peelings into the bin. 'At least he supports your cause.'

'And yours doesn't support yours?' I said. 'My own brother's fierce annoying but we're both in the union. So's my da.'

'Oh, Harry's not as bad as he used to be,' said Mollie, taking another carrot. 'But that's mostly thanks to his friend Frank. Well, he's my friend Frank as well, I suppose ...'

Her voice trailed off, and when I glanced at her I realised she was blushing. If Rosie was there she'd have made some joke about Frank being Mollie's young man, but I didn't feel like teasing my new friend.

'Anyway, Frank's jolly decent about these things,' said Mollie. 'He was arguing with Harry – that's my brother – about the strike the other day. He's on your side too.'

'Oh goodness, you're not talking about Frank again, are you?' Nora had returned from the lavatory.

'What do you mean, again? I never talk about him!'

Nora snorted. 'Oh *no*, of course you don't.'

'Oh shut up, Nora.' Mollie slammed her knife down into a carrot with such vigour that a slice flew off the table and landed in the potato bin.

'Heavens, Moll, I'm sorry!' exclaimed Nora. 'You don't need to start firing carrots everywhere! Pax?'

'As long as you don't make any more fatuous jokes,' said Mollie. 'All right then, pax.'

They grumbled at each other for a bit longer, but it was in a good humoured fashion, the way me and Samira and Rosie tease each other. Oddly I hadn't felt like laughing at Nora's jest about Mollie and her friendship with this Frank boy. In fact, I felt something a bit like … could it be relief? But why?

By the time the first batch of stew and bread was being handed out (the word had clearly spread about bringing your own receptacle, because practically everyone had a jug or a bowl or an old tin today), Mollie and Nora were fit to drop.

'Gosh, my poor legs,' said Mollie, rubbing her stockinged calves. 'Is it all right if I sit down now?'

I told her it was. 'But we'll have to start on the afternoon meal in a few minutes,' I warned her. 'We're doing three meals a day, remember?'

Mollie and Nora exchanged anguished glances, but I'll give them this, they didn't utter one word of complaint about it, at least not while they were at Liberty Hall. In fact, as the afternoon wore on, they got quite good at chopping up those carrots. We started a competition to see who could peel and chop the fastest, and unlike my potato peeling battles with Rosie and Samira, I won all of them. But I must admit it was pretty close.

And while we were laughing over our chopping race, I forgot that they were Eccles Street girls with servants, girls who would be in university in a few years while I was … well, what would I be doing when they were in their fancy college learning German and French? Probably not back at Lawlor's, anyway – I can't imagine they'll ever take me back at this stage. But I didn't think about my future when I was with them. For a while, in that hot, noisy kitchen, we were all just girls, doing whatever we could to make sure hungry people had one hot meal a day and trying not to drop too many carrot chunks on the floor.

When the cow boiler had been scraped of its last drop, we all filed out of the kitchen, too tired to speak. Mollie and Nora looked like they were going to fall over at any minute. We stumbled down the front steps and paused on the pavement.

'Which way are you going?' said Mollie.

I pointed in the direction of Amiens Street. 'That way. Towards the coast road.'

'We'll walk around the corner with you,' said Nora. She paused. 'If you don't mind.'

''Course I don't,' I said. It was funny to think of some girls from

Lavinia Lawlor's school wanting to walk with me. Though I suppose Lavinia's brother had done the same – not that there was any point in thinking about that. I haven't seen Peter Lawlor since that day. I wonder if he's been in to do any more strike-breaking over the last few weeks? He could easily have gone into the shop by the back lane without me seeing him from the picket line.

I shook thoughts of Peter out of my head as we walked around the side of Beresford Place. Mollie and Nora were going to walk home by way of Gardiner Street.

'Do we look like we've been in a kitchen instead of practising Latin verbs?' Nora asked. 'I mean, we didn't spill any stew or anything on ourselves, did we?'

I assured them they had not.

'Neither do you,' Mollie assured me. 'Though I suppose your mother doesn't mind you being there, does she? I mean, if all your family are in the union …'

'I think she'd rather I wasn't,' I said, and I explained about Ma and her dressmaking and losing the work from Mrs Lawlor. Mollie and Nora were very sympathetic.

'I'll never complain about my family not understanding things again,' said Nora. 'Gosh, how awful.'

'Do let us know how you get on,' said Mollie.

I realised I'd like to see them again. 'Thanks for coming today,' I said. 'It's been nice.'

Mollie's face brightened. 'We can write to you and arrange to meet some time. If you don't mind giving me your address,' she added.

''Course I don't,' I said.

There was confusion as we realised we didn't have any paper, but then Nora drew a tattered handbill for a suffrage rally out of her pocket and Mollie found a nub of pencil in her jacket pocket and, leaning against a wall at the end of Gardiner Street, I carefully wrote my name and address. Mollie put the leaflet in her pocket and offered me her hand.

'Goodbye, Betty,' she said. 'It was nice meeting you.'

I shook her hand, and Nora's too. 'Maybe we'll see you back in the kitchen.'

'We'll be at school during the day until Christmas,' said Nora sadly. 'So I shouldn't think so, I'm afraid. You don't think the strike will still be going on then, do you?'

'By Christmas? Ah no, they'll have sorted something out by then,' I said. But after I had bid the girls farewell and set off home in the drizzle, I didn't feel quite so sure about that.

# Chapter Twenty-Two

I haven't written for a few days, because I didn't want to waste my precious pencil, but I'm writing now, because things are not good and somehow I feel that writing about it all will make me feel better. I wish I could hide away up in my bedroom, but we can't afford to spare a candle for just one person at the moment. (I've got used to getting undressed and into my nightie in the dark.) So I'm writing this in a corner of the kitchen.

Ma and Da are sitting at the table talking in low voices and drinking some very weak tea – Ma's been reusing the tea leaves all day, so it's practically just water at this stage. And Eddie's over in Bayview Avenue visiting his sweetheart Mary (she's been fussing all over him recently because of his arm, the big eejit). Earnshaw's sitting on my feet which, even though he weighs as much as a small pony, is good because I need the extra warmth. Actually, it's not just about the warmth. Earnshaw is a very comforting sort of animal, and we all need comforting right now.

And this is why: Da's finally out on strike. I feel very, very scared. I suppose I always knew he was going to go out eventually, but for the last few months the fact that he was still working gave me a strange sense of safety. Me and Eddie are on strike pay. (For as long as it lasts – and that's another issue that I don't want to think about, because it's almost two months since we went out, and now there are so many people striking the union must be low on funds.) Ma has lost half her clients. But as long as Da was still working for his usual wage, we were all right.

But now Da's on strike pay too, more than me but the same amount as Eddie, because everyone gets the same if they've been in the union for over a year. And although it's better than nothing, and more than some people earn at the best of times, we're in trouble. Now there's only half a slice of bread and dripping for my tea. I told Ma she should come in and get some stew from the kitchens but she flushed bright red and said we weren't there yet.

'There's no shame in it,' I said. 'You should see some of the people who call in with their jugs.'

But Ma insisted we didn't need any union stew. I think I do, though, especially as it's getting colder and colder and the nights are starting to draw in. It's a good thing I'm still working in the Liberty Hall kitchen a few days every week, because at least that means I get some dinner there.

And it's not just me who could do with hot meals. Little Robbie's looking fierce peaky and has a bad cough, which is why Lily went to the kitchen for the first time yesterday. I was standing at the big table chopping carrots as the first batch of soup was being given out when I heard a familiar terrible shriek. When I looked up, there was Lily at the top of the queue, holding Little Robbie with one arm and holding out a jug with the other.

'Back in a moment,' I said to Kitty, who was chopping onions by my side. 'I have to help my sister.'

Kitty took one look at Little Robbie, who was bright red in the face and wriggling like a salmon, and said, 'Take your time. There's no hurry.' Which was pretty decent of her, I have to say, because we were busy enough.

Then I hurried over to Lily, who was trying to stop Little Robbie flinging himself out of her grasp and onto the flagged stone floor. I grabbed the little wretch before he could make good his escape.

'Thanks, Betser,' said Lily. She looked so tired that I didn't even give out to her for calling me Betser. I held onto Little Robbie as he wriggled and writhed.

'Mama!' he howled, reaching out towards her, but Lily barely looked capable of holding onto him with two arms let alone one, so I held him fast.

One of the men was on duty at the cow boiler that day. 'There you go, missus,' he said, pouring a ladle full of stew into Lily's jug.

'Thanks very much, mister,' said Lily. She moved to let the next woman in the queue have her turn. 'I'll take him back, Bets.'

'You can't carry him and that full jug,' I protested. 'Where's his pram, anyway?' A horrible thought struck me and I leaned in to whisper, 'You didn't pawn it, did you?' That pram is Lily's pride and joy. It's second-hand, of course, but it's in pretty good nick.

'Of course I didn't,' said Lily. 'We're not doing that badly yet. It's up in the hall, but I couldn't leave him there, not when he's in one of these moods.'

He's always in one of those moods as far as I can see, but I didn't say that to Lily.

'Well, at least let me carry him up the stairs,' I said. And she was too tired to argue. As we went up to the hall I couldn't help noticing that Little Robbie felt less heavy than he used to, and once his tantrum subsided he seemed all listless and feeble. There was something very wrong about a baby losing any of his chubbiness – even if he'd always used those fat little paws to hit me with. Despite that brief fit of rage in the kitchen, it was clear he really wasn't behaving like himself. As we reached the top of the stairs, he started to cough, a horrible hacking sound.

'How long's he been coughing?' I said.

'All week,' said Lily flatly. 'It's going to his lungs.'

I didn't even bother mentioning going to Doctor Clarke. There was no money to pay him and although he hadn't charged us the full payment for Eddie's arm that day, even a quarter of his fee would be too expensive for any of us now. I felt sick with worry as I waved Robbie and Lily goodbye and headed back to Kitty and the chopping table.

I know Lily didn't tell Ma about her visit to the kitchen, but I think she should have. Ma really should conquer this ridiculous prejudice against taking food she's entitled to. I know it's all because she doesn't want to think of our family as being the same as the women who live in the tenements and wear shawls instead of hats and whose children run around barefoot, but I've met enough of those women now to know that there's nothing wrong with them. We *are* the same as them, when it comes down to it. We're all locked out together – or our husbands and fathers and brothers are. Samira's da is out too, and now the only one bringing in a full wage in her house is Auntie Maisie.

'I never thought I'd be the breadwinner in this family,' said Auntie Maisie when I called round to Samira's last night. She tried to sound like she was joking but you could tell it was a little bit forced.

'Maybe I'll get a paying role after my concert,' said Samira hopefully and Maisie smiled proudly at her and said she wouldn't be at all surprised. But even if Samira does get offered a part after her stage debut, the concert's not until the beginning of December and that feels like a long way away now.

And it doesn't look like the dispute is going to end any time soon. There have been loads of meetings and conferences, with union leaders coming and going between here and England. The Lord Mayor even got involved, but the situation is still the same. The employers won't budge. An MP set up a special committee to try and make peace, but the employers rejected his ideas, and told him and his pals that they won't work with the union under any circumstances. And of course the union is still holding out against the employers' demands. So as Da said the other day, when he came home and told Ma that he was out on strike, it's a stalemate. No one wants to give in.

It's not as if we're never tempted, though. I was picketing with Rosie today in the lashing rain, and every time a customer went in or out of the big glass doors, we got a little blast of warm air that just served to remind us how cold and wet we were. By late afternoon, when the gloom of the evening was starting to descend, I found myself looking longingly at the glowing lights of the tea-room. I'd only ever worked there in summer, where it often got too hot behind the counter next to the horrible old tea urn blasting steam all day.

But now, as the rain soaked through my boots, I couldn't help thinking that it looked pretty cosy in there, among all those cakes. The tea urn mightn't seem so menacing when you needed its warmth. Rosie must have guessed from the look on my face what I was thinking, because she nudged me in the ribs and said, 'Just think of Auld Wobbly. You wouldn't really want to be in there letting her walk all over you, would you?'

I sighed. 'You're right, I wouldn't. I'm just thinking I'd like to have dry feet.'

'Wouldn't we all?' said Rosie. 'If only Earnshaw was here, he could sit on our feet and keep us nice and cosy.'

'If it wasn't so wet, I'd bring him in,' I said. I know he cheers up Rosie. She always tries to put on a brave face, and she's pretty good at it most of the time, making her usual jokes and teasing me about stupid things. But the only time I see her properly smile, a big wide grin the way she used to before her ma and Francis died, is when she sees Earnshaw. I wish I could take him in every day. But it wouldn't be fair to have him out in weather like this. It's not the cold – he doesn't mind that – but he's got so much hair that once he's wet it takes him forever to get dry again.

I was thinking about how much I wish I could help Rosie when, in the crowded rainy street, I saw a glint of fair hair beneath an umbrella and my stomach tied itself in a knot. Surely he should still be in a classroom doing Latin or Greek, or whatever else he was learning? But as the owner of the umbrella moved towards us, I saw that it was indeed Peter Lawlor.

'Hello, Betty,' he said. 'How are you getting on?'

'We're getting on marvellously,' said Rosie, doing her best impersonation of a fine lady. 'Can't you tell?'

'I'm grand,' I said. 'Why aren't you in school?'

'It's five o'clock,' said Peter. I hadn't realised how late it was. 'But actually I'm on my midterm break.'

'So you're on holiday?' I tried and failed to imagine what that might be like.

'Oh, we've been given lots of work to do, I can assure you,' said Peter. 'In fact, I should be translating some Ovid right now. But I wanted to come in and …'

'Do a bit more scabbing for your da?' said Rosie. She was smiling, but there was a sharp edge on her voice. None of us like scabs, but Rosie gets really, really angry about them. Whenever she sees any of the girls who are scabbing in Lawlor's she yells something at them. She always says that if they had stood by us, the employers would have had to give in and we wouldn't be out here, cold and hungry, and I know she's right. But I realised that I don't like yelling at people, even scabs. I just turn away from them and ignore them as they walk in. Rosie says I'm too soft-hearted. She's probably right about that too.

Peter met Rosie's challenging gaze with a smile. 'I'm not helping out in the shop, if that's what you mean. I'm just here to buy a few cakes for Mother.'

'Well,' said Rosie. 'Give her our regards.'

Peter didn't say anything in return, he just winked at her and walked into the shop.

'The cheek of him!' said Rosie. She prodded me with her picket sign. 'You're very quiet.'

'What?' I said. 'I'm just tired.'

'It's not too late to put in a good word for the workers with your man.' Rosie nodded in the direction of the shop.

'He wouldn't listen to me,' I said.

'I think he would,' Rosie said.

'All right, maybe he'd listen, but he wouldn't do anything about it.' I thought of the conversation we'd had when we'd walked down the North Strand together and my fists clenched with frustration at the memory. 'He doesn't understand why it's so important.'

'You could persuade him,' Rosie insisted. 'He's sweet on you. You must have noticed.'

'No he isn't,' I said.

'I bet he thinks he can have any of the Lawlor's girls he wants,'

Rosie went on. 'You hear things, you know, about bosses and their sons …'

'Shut up, Rosie!' I snapped. She was making everything all grubby-sounding, as if Peter was one of those men in books who take advantage of innocent young maids. I didn't think he was like that at all. Rosie looked startled by my vehemence.

'I was only joking with you,' she said. 'Pax?'

I didn't say anything. She'd really gone too far this time. I just held out a handbill to a passing young woman. 'Would you like a handbill, miss?' I said.

'Betty?' There was a hint of a tremor in Rosie's voice as the woman walked on, handbill in hand. 'I'm really sorry. I didn't mean anything by it.'

And then I remembered how worried I'd been about Rosie earlier, and I knew I couldn't stay angry with her. I wasn't particularly pleased with her, but I wasn't going to stop talking to her.

'Fine,' I said gruffly. 'But I don't like you talking about Pe— about him like that. It's not funny.'

'I won't do it again,' said Rosie. And she sounded so genuinely contrite I thought she might actually be on the verge of tears. I put my arms around her and gave her a quick hug.

'You'd better not,' I said. And Rosie squeezed me right back.

It was getting properly dark now, and Lawlor's was about to close its doors. I realised I hadn't noticed Peter Lawlor leaving – he must have slipped out while I was accepting Rosie's apologies.

'I'm going to head home,' I told her.

'I'll wait for the scabs to leave,' said Rosie. There was a warlike gleam in her eye. 'I want that Lizzie from the kitchen to look me in the eye when she's walking out with her pockets full of buns.'

'Don't get into any trouble, now,' I said nervously. I wouldn't put it past her to go for Lizzie some day, and I understand how angry she is because I can't bear to look at Lizzie myself, but it wouldn't be worth getting into trouble for it. Some factory girls have been arrested for attacking scabs.

'I'll be the soul of virtue,' said Rosie.

I laughed and waved my farewell. The rain had eased off a bit as I trudged up towards O'Connell Street, sticking as close as I could to the shopfronts in the hope there'd be a bit of shelter there. Which is why I ended up walking straight into someone coming out of a newsagent's shop near the corner, and making them drop their parcels all over the grubby wet pavement.

'I beg your pardon!' I cried. 'Let me help you.' I crouched down to pick up one of the parcels, and found myself looking straight into Peter Lawlor's bright eyes. I jumped to my feet as if I'd been stung by a nettle.

Peter picked up his parcels and smiled at me.

'It's a good thing these buns don't have any icing on them, or they'd be in quite a state right now,' he said.

'I'm very sorry,' I said stiffly. 'I won't keep you any longer.' I started walking up the street but Peter Lawlor hurried after me.

'Wait a minute!' he said. 'It's raining.'

'I was aware of that,' I said, as formally as I could.

'Well,' said Peter. 'Would you like to share my umbrella?'

Pride and the desire to be less wet fought inside my heart. The desire to be less wet won.

'Yes, please,' I said. 'Um, thanks very much.'

We reached O'Connell Street in silence.

'Aren't you getting a tram?' I said.

'I'll walk you some of the way,' said Peter. 'If you don't mind.'

Thanks to his umbrella, I no longer had rain blowing right into my face.

'I don't, particularly,' I said, in my grandest voice.

The silence descended again as we crossed the street and headed down North Earl Street. Eventually Peter said, 'I'm sorry, Betty.'

'For what?' I said.

Peter sighed. 'Saying the wrong thing. Insulting you and your friend. She doesn't like me very much, and I don't blame her.'

I smiled despite myself. 'There's nothing personal about it. Scabbing just makes Rosie angry, that's all.'

'What about you?' Peter Lawlor's tone was grave. 'Does it make you angry too?'

'Of course it does.' I couldn't believe he'd even asked. 'If it wasn't for scabs, the factories and cafes and warehouses wouldn't be able to keep going. If no one was in there doing the work, employers would have to take us strikers seriously. They'd have to listen to all our demands, and do something about them.'

'But your demands …' said Peter. 'I mean, is standing out in the wind and rain really better than working in the tearoom under Miss Warby? Wouldn't you and … Rosie, isn't it? Wouldn't you rather be warm and dry, even if you get fined the odd shilling?' He laughed. 'Maybe if Rosie was warmer, she wouldn't be so angry …'

'Rosie's ma and her baby brother were killed last month when their house fell on them,' I said, and my voice was as chilly as the October wind. 'And now she and her sister are living in a room with barely a stick of furniture. I don't think standing by the Lawlor's tea urn for eight hours a day would cheer her up. '

'Oh my God, Betty.' Peter Lawlor looked truly stricken. 'I'm sorry, I …'

I didn't want to hear his apologies. 'She's got nothing to lose, now,' I said. 'And neither do lots of the girls. Except … except the idea that we're all together in this fight. We matter to each other, Master Lawlor, even if we don't matter to some people.'

'You matter to me,' said Peter Lawlor. And then as soon as the words were out of his mouth he went bright red, and I could feel my own cheeks flushing too. We trudged down the rainswept street in silence for a few moments that felt like hours. I almost felt like telling him to go and get a tram, but I couldn't encourage him to travel by scab labour. Eventually he spoke.

'What happened to Rosie … it's horrible. And it's not fair. I do see that, Betty.'

'Good,' I said gruffly.

'I wish things were different,' said Peter, not looking at me.

'So do I,' I said.

The sound of church bells rang out.

'Oh blow it, I didn't realise it was so late,' said Peter. 'I do have to get these buns home to Mother.' I followed his gaze as he glanced back up the street and saw a tram approaching. 'I'd better get this.' He looked back at me, his face stricken. 'I really am sorry for offending you.'

'It's all right,' I said, although nothing was all right, not really.

'Would you apologise to Rosie for me?' said Peter, as he jumped on the tram. And I nodded back at him as it started to move away. For some reason I don't want Rosie to hate Peter Lawlor. Even though I'm not sure exactly how I feel about him myself.

# Chapter Twenty-Three

Little Robbie might be going to England! Not just him on his own, of course. He'd be going with Lily and lots of other strikers' children too. A grand English lady has come to Dublin and she says there are lots of trade unionists in England who are ready to take in Irish children of striking and locked-out workers until all this is over. Her name is Dora Montefiore which sounds like something out of a book, and the first time I saw her was in the Liberty Hall kitchen a few days ago. I was at the big table with Rosie and Kitty and a big group of the Jacob's girls, all chopping away, when I noticed a finely dressed lady walking in with Miss Larkin. She was followed by two other younger ladies, one fair and one dark haired. The fair one was dressed in the height of style.

'My ma would love that frock,' I said to Rosie.

'What are they doing here?' said Rosie. 'They're not dressed for peeling potatoes.'

The visitors looked all over the kitchen, and seemed very interested in what was going on. The fair-haired young lady peered in at me and Rosie and our pile of carrots.

'And how long have you girls been on strike?' she asked politely. She only looked about Lily's age and she had a funny sort of voice. I'd never heard anyone talk like that before. And neither had Rosie, because she said, 'We've been out for two months' before adding, 'if you don't mind me asking, why do you talk like that?'

The young woman laughed and said she didn't mind at all. 'I'm an American,' she said. 'But I live in England. My name's Mrs Rand.'

'I'm Miss Delaney,' said Rosie, in her grandest manner.

'Well, Miss Delaney,' said Mrs Rand with a smile. 'We've been hearing all about you brave striking girls over in London, and we wanted to see you for ourselves.' She gestured towards the older lady. 'That's Mrs Montefiore. She's a very fine woman. And over there is Miss Neal.' She nodded towards the dark-haired stranger. 'She knows what it's like to work for a living, like you girls.'

'Does she?' I said, trying and failing to keep the surprise out of my voice. I didn't want to be rude, but most ladies who come to visit the kitchens and help out aren't used to getting their hands dirty.

'She certainly does, Miss …?'

'Rafferty,' I said.

'Well, Miss Rafferty, Miss Neal set up the Domestic Workers' Union of Great Britain. She used to be a parlourmaid.'

'*Really?*' I looked at the dark-haired young woman with more respect.

'Mrs Rand!' called Mrs Montefiore from the other side of the kitchen. She talked funny as well, but in a different way. She sounded a bit like Madame Markievicz. It wasn't long before Mrs Rand was manning the cow boiler and helping one of the men dole out the first round of stew of the day, and Miss Neal was sitting on a box in the corner, quietly peeling potatoes. They worked there for the rest of the day, but I didn't know the full purpose of their visit to Dublin until after I'd got home that evening.

We'd just finished our tea (what there was of it) when Lily called round to the house. It hadn't been raining that day, thank goodness, but it's getting fierce cold now, so it took ages for my hands to warm up when I got home. Da always says we have no need for one of those fancy rubber hot water bottles because we have Earnshaw, but even though I'd been curled up next to him for half an hour, my poor paws were still quite red and stiff when I answered a knock on the door to find Lily on the doorstep, her face almost glowing with excitement.

'What are you so happy about?' I said, but not in a rude way.

'I need to tell you all about something,' said Lily, and she hurried down to the kitchen, where Ma was pouring freshly boiled water into a tea pot that had contained the same leaves all afternoon.

'Lily!' said Ma. 'Are you alright?'

'I'm grand,' said Lily. 'Have you heard about the Save the Kiddies scheme?'

'The what?' Ma put the woolly cosy on the teapot, the one I knitted out of odds and ends. 'Sit yourself down, Lil, and calm yourself.'

'Maggie Sorohan told me all about it,' said Lily, taking a cup down off the shelf. 'These English ladies are organising it.'

'English ladies?' I said. 'Is one of them called Mrs Monteforry or something like that?'

'That's right,' said Lily. 'There's three of them. There's going to be a big meeting in Liberty Hall tomorrow, to let us know how it'd work. But we know they want to take strikers' kids over to England, to stay with union families there.'

'Lily!' Ma's voice was full of horror. 'You wouldn't send Little Robbie away to that heathen place.'

'I would if they'd feed him,' said Lily stoutly. 'He's lost weight, Ma, and he's not himself, you know he's not. You've heard that cough.'

'But Lily, he's just a baby,' said Ma. 'You couldn't let him go away on his own.'

'Maggie said they might take mothers too,' said Lily. 'I'd go with him.'

I thought Ma was going to burst into tears. 'Lily!'

'It wouldn't be forever,' said Lily. 'Just until all this fuss is over.'

'And when will that be?' said Ma. 'It's been months now!'

'Exactly, Ma, it *has* been months!' cried Lily. 'And every month has meant less food for all of us. I'm not letting my baby starve.' She sounded like a tigress.

'But England, Lil!' said Ma. 'It's so far away!' I thought she was being ridiculous myself – what's wrong with going to England for a few months? – but she really did look distressed, and Lily's tone softened.

'Look Ma, Maggie might have it all wrong,' she said. 'But I'm going to that meeting anyway.'

And nothing Ma could say would make her change her mind.

The next day I was on duty in Liberty Hall, and everyone in the kitchen was talking about the Save the Kiddies scheme. Some girls were a bit sceptical of it.

'The cheek of them English ladies!' said Maggie from the chocolate café. 'Coming over here swanking about the place, thinking they know what's best for us.'

'What's best for my little sisters is food,' said a girl who worked at Jacob's. 'So if Mrs Montefiore wants to make sure they're fed, she can swank all she wants.'

'Ssssh!' hissed Rosie. 'She's coming in with Miss Larkin.'

Everyone shut up and suddenly became very interested in whatever they were chopping or peeling.

'All right, girls!' Miss Larkin's voice rang out around the crowded kitchen. 'I need some volunteers to help Mrs Montefiore with some parcels.'

Rosie caught my eye. 'It'd make a change from chopping carrots,' she said.

And that was how we found ourselves in an upstairs room in Liberty Hall, opening big parcels of cardigans and pinafores and combination underwear under Miss Neal's capable supervision. She talked funny too, but in a different way to the other two. I liked her. It was good to see a working union girl who was doing so well.

'Where did all these things come from?' I asked her, folding up a soft wool jumper and putting it in a pile marked 'BOYS' CLOTHING AGED FIVE TO SEVEN'.

'Ordinary people back home,' said Miss Neal. 'Workers like yourselves, and people like Mrs Montefiore and Mrs Rand who support the workers. They want to help.'

I thought of all those people far away across the sea thinking of us and sending us jumpers and coats and pinafores and felt tears prickling at the back of my eyes. I remembered the man who had come with the *Hare* and reminded us that our fight was their fight too. It was good to know we weren't being forgotten by the rest of the world.

'We spread the word that we were looking for things for children,' Miss Neal went on. 'And, well, you can see for yourself what happened.'

There was a sort of choking sound from the other end of the table and I saw that Rosie was crying. She was trying to hide it but you could tell.

'Miss Delaney, what's wrong?' Miss Neal rushed to Rosie's side.

But I could tell what was wrong. Rosie had taken a jumper out of one of the parcels, a red woolly thing that someone somewhere had made for a little boy. A little boy around Francis's age.

'It's just reminded her of something,' I said. I reached over and squeezed Rosie's hands. 'Do you want to go back to the kitchen, Rosie?'

Rosie shook her head and rubbed her eyes.

'I'm grand,' she said, but she still sounded all choked up.

'Only if you're sure,' Miss Neal said, hovering close by.

'I'm sure,' said Rosie. She held up the jumper. 'Where should I put this?'

Miss Neal showed her where to put it and we kept on working. Miss Neal asked us a lot of questions about our work and the union and when we'd come out on strike. Rosie was subdued at first, but she livened up a bit when she was telling Miss Neal about Auld Wobbly, doing her best impersonation of Wobbly's ranting.

Miss Neal laughed. 'We've got plenty of Ol' Wobblys over in England too,' she said, in her funny but friendly voice. 'You're doing something very brave, you Dublin girls.'

No one's ever called me brave before, I don't think. I didn't know what to say. Even Rosie looked a bit flustered. Neither of us are used to getting praised. So I decided to change the subject and asked, 'How long are you here in Dublin for?'

'I don't know, to be honest,' said Miss Neal. 'As long as it takes to get the kiddies ready to go over, I suppose.'

'My sister wants my nephew Little Robbie to go,' I said. 'Her husband's out on strike. She's coming along to the meeting later.'

'Well, I hope we'll be able to help them,' said Miss Neal.

'How old is your nephew?'

I told her and she bit her lip. 'It's really for children over four,' she said. 'But the Socialist Party down in Plymouth have offered to take some mothers too. So if your sister's willing to go, her baby might have a chance.'

I thought of how light Little Robbie had felt in my arms the other day in the kitchens. I remembered the sound of his relentless cough. A chance, even a small one, was better than nothing.

After we finished I decided to stay on in Liberty Hall to go to the meeting. I didn't bother asking Rosie if she wanted to stay. She'd done well enough sorting out all those little boys' clothes. I knew it would be too much for her to see all those hopeful mothers with their kids. It wasn't as though she didn't want those children to be safe and well, of course she did. But their good fortune just reminded her of everything Francis would never get to do. On her way out the door Rosie paused and looked back at me.

'I hope Little Robbie gets to go,' she said.

I almost found myself making a joke about how I'd finally get rid of him but I stopped myself in time. Those jokes aren't so funny anymore.

I didn't have too long to wait before the mothers started arriving. Mrs Montefiore had bagged a big room in Liberty Hall and it soon started to fill up with mothers, babies, and little kids who were too young to be left at home with their older brothers and sisters. I waited outside the door until Lily and her friend Maggie arrived. Lily was holding Little Robbie and I felt my stomach knot with fear when I saw him. It had only been a few days since his tantrum in the kitchen but he looked worse. I know Lily and Robert Hessian were doing without so that he could eat as much as possible, and Ma's been passing on food too, but he really did look listless. He kept coughing, but that was the only sound he made as Lily carried him in. I never thought I'd miss all that awful roaring.

'Howiya, Betty,' whispered Maggie, who was holding her own little fella, Jimmy. She looked around the big spacious room. The last time I'd been there was for Samira's audition. 'This place is something, isn't it?'

I smiled at her. 'It's a lot less swanky down in the kitchen, I can tell you.' I glanced around the room and saw the visitors from England making their way to the far end.

'We'd better find some seats.'

It was easier said than done – the room was jammed. But we managed to squeeze into some chairs at the far side just as Mrs Montefiore took to the stage. I glanced around and saw that more and more women were cramming themselves in at the door.

It wasn't the quietest crowd I've ever seen, because there were lots of babies in it and it's hard to keep babies quiet at the best of times. But all the mothers gave Mrs Montefiore their full attention.

'We have a message from the workers of England to the wives of the strikers in Dublin!' she cried. 'There are 300 homes and 600 loving parents waiting to look after your kiddies as if they were their very own. And they are willing to do this until Mr Murphy …'

The crowd booed loudly at the name of the hated tyrant. Mrs Montefiore paused until it ceased.

'Until that … that *man* has accepted the people of Dublin's demands. I can assure you that your little ones will be met with every kindness. And for those who fear that they will lose your

Roman Catholic faith if they travel across the water, I can assure you that we have many Catholic families who are ready to share their homes.'

The audience cheered. Lily clapped as hard as she could with Little Robbie perched on her lap. He looked more cheerful, I was pleased to notice. It was probably because he likes roaring and shouting so much, and the cheering made him feel as if he was among kindred spirits. Everyone was in a good mood by the time the meeting ended, and Mrs Montefiore and Miss Neal told all interested parents to call to Liberty Hall the next day, or the day after that, to register their interest.

The visitors left to yet more hearty cheers. (Little Robbie joined in, looking quite his old terrible self.) As we left the building he was still hooting away, with only a few little coughs, but Lily looked more serious.

'I understand why they're only taking the older ones,' she said, 'but I hope we've got a chance of getting over.'

'You deserve it if anyone does,' said Maggie. 'And with a bit of luck my Joey will get to go too.' Maggie's Joey is five. She was very young when she got married, barely sixteen, and Joey came along not long after that. She and her husband and Joey and little Jimmy live with another family in a house the same size as ours. She used to be a fine big girl but her husband's been locked out since the beginning of September and she's as skinny as I am now.

'I hope they all get to go,' said Lily. And then she glanced around at the rest of the crowd as if seeing them properly for the first time. In comparison with some of the women there, Lily, in her shabby but neat hat and coat, looked like a fine lady. There were mothers there wrapped in shawls with ill-fitting shoes on their feet; at least one was barefoot. And while Little Robbie was bundled up in a little woollen outfit Ma had knitted for him out of bits of Da's old jumper, there were some babies who didn't seem to be wearing anything at all under the tattered blankets they were wrapped in. 'There's lots who might need it even more than we do.'

I told Samira about the meeting as we walked in to Liberty Hall this morning. (The shop wasn't open today so she was helping in the kitchen.)

'Imagine Little Robbie on a boat, the little dote,' she said fondly. She is still inexplicably charmed by him. 'They might give him a teeny sailor hat.'

I shuddered theatrically at the thought.

'He mightn't get to go anywhere at all,' I reminded her. 'Let alone dress up for it. Lily has to ask whether they'll take him. How's the show coming along?'

Samira's face lit up. 'Miss Larkin singled me out at the rehearsal the other night. She said I was doing very well.'

Which is high praise coming from Miss Larkin, and I told Samira so.

'I know, I could barely believe it,' she said. 'And you'll never guess. There's talk of moving the production out of Liberty Hall.'

'What do you mean?' I said. Where else could the union put on a show? 'To Croydon Park? I don't think there's the right sort of rooms.'

'No!' Samira paused impressively. 'The Gaiety Theatre!'

I stopped dead right in the middle of Amiens Street. Samira, on the stage of one of the biggest theatres in Dublin!

'The *what*?'

Samira hugged herself gleefully.

'I know!' she said. 'I couldn't believe it myself, to be honest with you. But they think we could sell enough tickets and it'd be great publicity for the strike fund. And the dramatic company too, of course.'

'Janey!' I was dazzled. 'That's one in the eye for Auntie Maisie's Mr Farrell.'

Samira grinned. 'Isn't it just? But,' she added, 'it's not definite or anything. It might not happen. So don't tell anyone yet.'

'I won't utter a single word,' I vowed. We walked along in a companionable silence for a few minutes before I said, 'How's Ali doing?'

Whenever I've called round to Samira in the evenings recently, he's been nowhere to be seen. In fact, because Auntie Maisie's been rehearsing all hours, we've had the house to ourselves.

'Ali?' Samira sounded surprised. 'He's grand. Busy. He's been at a lot of union meetings, same as Da.'

'Oh, right, I should have thought of that.' It was only as I said these words that I realised I'd been worried he'd been avoiding me. I had been snappy with him that day in the kitchen. It felt like forever since we'd last had a proper chat around the fire, like we used to have. Mind you, there isn't much fuel for any fires these days.

We turned the corner onto Beresford Place. There was a big queue of women streaming out of Liberty Hall, most of them with babies in their arms and older children hanging off their shawls.

'Janey,' said Samira. 'There must be hundreds of them.'

We had to squeeze through the crowd as we climbed the steps to the main entrance, and it wasn't much easier to get along when we reached the hall. We edged our way towards the kitchen when something – or rather someone – familiar caught my eye.

'Howiya, Margaret,' I said.

Margaret Maguire was huddled in a shawl, holding the hand of her shaven-headed little brother, the one I'd seen carrying home the clinkers of coal from rich people's fires. There was another kid holding her other hand. I thought it was a girl at first, but then I realised it was a little boy, wearing a ragged girls' frock. The poorest people in this city can't afford to be choosy about what clothes they pick up in the second-hand stalls.

I tried to hide it, but I was shocked at Margaret's appearance. She looked even thinner than the last time I saw her, and her red hair was straggly and dull. She didn't even have the heavy men's boots she'd been wearing that day. Her feet were bare and dirty, and blotchy with cold. Samira's eyes widened as she took in the piteous sight. She hadn't seen Margaret since the Maguires did their moonlight flit. I had told her about me and Ali meeting Margaret that day, and how changed she was, but hearing something isn't the same as seeing it with your own eyes. Still, Samira rose to the occasion.

'It's been a while since I've seen you, Margaret,' she said with a warm smile.

I remembered Margaret once thumping a kid from Leinster Avenue who was calling Samira and Ali horrible names.

Margaret forced a smile in return.

'Hiya, Samira,' she said. Her voice was hoarser than it used to be. 'Hiya, Betty.'

'So,' said Samira, 'are you signing up for the kiddies' scheme?'

Margaret nodded. 'I'm going to try anyway. One of the mothers in our house told me about it last night.' She squeezed the hand of the shaven-headed boy. 'You'd like to go on a boat, wouldn't you Tony?'

The boy shook his head and looked at his own grubby toes.

'Ah, you would,' said Margaret. She turned to the other little boy. 'And I bet you would too, Joe.'

There was despair in her eyes as she turned back to us. 'I won't keep you, girls. Are you working here?'

'In the kitchens,' I said. 'We'll be serving dinner in a few hours, if you're still around.'

'Thanks,' said Margaret. The mass of women and children started to move a little towards the stairs.

'Good luck,' said Samira.

We didn't say much as we went down to the kitchen. All Samira said was 'Janey, I didn't realise things were that bad for the Maguires.' And her voice was a little shaky when she said it.

We were both on potato-peeling duty that day with some of the Jacob's girls. The good thing about peeling is that you can do it sitting down, and we were chatting away, having a good laugh, when one of the union men came in and said something to Miss Larkin before walking out again. Miss Larkin came over to me.

'You were helping the visitors yesterday, weren't you?'

'Yes, Miss Larkin,' I said.

'So you know where the room is. The ladies are overwhelmed up there and they can't take a break from their work, but they need something to eat and drink. You and Miss Casey can make them some tea and sandwiches and take them up.'

My hand was stiffening up from potato peeling already so I was happy to oblige, and Samira was intrigued by the prospect of seeing the mysterious visitors. A moment later, we were trotting up the stairs to the room the ladies had taken over, each of us carefully carrying a full tray. It was pretty cramped on the stairs, because the queue of mothers and children was still trailing all the way down them and into the hall. Which is why I nearly dropped my tray over the bannisters when someone bashed into me as she rushed down the stairs.

'Hey, watch where you're going!' I cried.

The shawled figure stopped and turned around, and I saw that it was Margaret Maguire. Her face was streaked with tears.

'Margaret!' said Samira. 'What happened?'

'They can't take the lads,' said Margaret, wiping her eyes with a grubby hand.

'But why?' I asked, balancing my tray against my hip.

Margaret sniffed. 'Da's not in the union anymore. I didn't realise ….' Her voice trailed off.

'Oh, Margaret.' My heart went out to her.

'I didn't want to go to England anyway,' piped up Tony.

Margaret laughed shakily. 'Well, I didn't want to lose you,' she said. 'Come on, you little eejit, let's get yiz both home.'

She nodded a farewell at us and hurried down the stairs, her little brothers scurrying after her.

Silently, Samira and I continued up the stairs.

In the visitors' room, all was chaos.

'One at a time, ladies, please!' cried Mrs Montefiore, but the women were ignoring her. There were at least three crowded around the desk the whole time we were there. Miss Neal caught my eye and hurried around to help me and Samira set down the trays.

'Thank you, girls,' she said. She glanced over at the queue. 'We're going to have to take turns to have our dinner. We can't keep them waiting for any longer than we have to.'

'Miss Neal,' I said cautiously as I poured out some tea. 'We met a girl we know on the stairs. She said she was turned down because her da's not in the union.'

Miss Neal sighed and ran a hand over her dark hair. 'I hate doing it, but we can't take anyone whose family aren't on strike or locked out. Or anyone whose father hasn't agreed to them going.' Her eyes were bright. 'I wish we could look after all of them.'

We shouldn't need to send kids like them over to England just to get them fed, I thought that evening, as Samira and I walked out of Liberty Hall, past the mothers and children still queuing to get seen by the visitors from England. If people just had jobs where they were paid well and treated fairly, they'd be able to feed all their children right here. But as they don't, I hope the visitors help as many families as possible. And if that means Lily and Little Robbie going off to Portsmouth or Plymouth or whatever it's called, well, I'm all for them. If we can just get the children fed through this horrible wet cold winter, maybe everything will be all right.

# Chapter Twenty-Four

I last wrote here just a few days ago, and since then everything has gone wrong. And it's not because of our English visitors. No, it's because of Irish people getting a lot of stupid notions in their heads! Even Little Robbie has more sense than some of them – but I'm getting ahead of myself.

At first, things seemed to be going along smoothly enough. There were even more applicants for the scheme than the visitors had expected, but fair play to them, those ladies stayed in that room in Liberty Hall for two days from morning to night, seeing every woman who came in. Even though the queue was always out the door and they had to refuse a fair few of them, they took lots of names. And once things were organised, it all moved pretty fast. The first batch of kids and their mothers set off for some suffragette lady's house in England almost straight away.

Late on Tuesday afternoon, I was helping to clean up the kitchen, where everyone was talking about a big march that was going to take place on Thursday. It was going to be a protest because the employers rejected that MP's peace committee the other week.

'We should make a banner,' said Rosie, passing me a scrubbing brush. 'I've always wanted to hold one. What do you think we should paint on it?'

I was scrubbing at the table and trying to think of the perfect statement for a banner when I heard someone calling my name.

'Lily!' I put down my brush and hurried over to her. 'What are you doing here?'

'We're going to England!' Her eyes were bright with excitement.

'Janey!' I said. 'Is it definite?'

'Seems to be,' said Lily. 'We have to be ready tomorrow. They're only taking a few mothers over but they said we were good candidates for that group in Plymouth."

'Oh, I'm delighted for you, Lil.' I beamed at her. 'And Robbie.' And I really was, and not just because it meant getting rid of Little Robbie for a while. In fact, a strange part of me felt a bit peculiar at the thought of him and Lily heading off across the waves and staying in another country for weeks and weeks. But I knew it would do them both good.

'I'd better go and get him,' said Lily. 'He's sleeping up in the hall.'

I took off my apron. 'I'll walk home with you.' The scrubbed table had been my last chore of the day. 'See you tomorrow, Rosie!'

Rosie waved at me and turned back to the mugs she was stacking on a dresser.

On the walk home, Lily looked more cheerful than she had in ages.

'It won't be for long, of course,' she said. 'Just a month or two. But imagine! A place where we'll always be warm and have enough to eat!'

'It sounds like heaven,' I said. 'I'm mad jealous of you.' I didn't really begrudge Lily and Little Robbie getting to go. The weather has got even worse over the last few weeks, and I didn't like the thought of Little Robbie going hungry over winter, not with his cough. Mrs Hennessy says it's asthma – her Paddy used to get the same sort of odd cough as a little kid and that's what it turned out to be.

The first thing Ma said when we let ourselves into Number 48 was 'How's Little Robbie's cough?

'Not as bad today,' said Lily. 'Maybe because it's finally stopped raining.'

I knew what she meant. When it rains, the damp smoky air feels like it's settling into your lungs every time you breathe.

'Listen, Ma,' Lily went on. 'I've got some news for you. Good news.'

I didn't think Ma would be hugely pleased, after the way she'd been talking the other day, but still I wasn't prepared for what happened next.

'But Lily!' Ma looked distressed. 'Did you not see the archbishop's letter?'

Lily looked at me, but I was as ignorant as she was. 'What letter's that, then?' she said.

'Mrs Hennessy was at Mass this morning and they read it out then,' said Ma. Mrs Hennessy is fierce holy and goes to Mass every single day, not just Sundays and Holy Days of Obligation. 'It said that Catholic mothers shouldn't be sending their children off to that heathen land.' She took a deep breath. 'And that if they did, they shouldn't call themselves Catholics.' She looked as if she was about to cry.

'But I'd be going with him!' said Lily.

'But Lily …' said Ma. 'The bishop said …'

'I don't *care* what any stupid bishop said,' said Lily. Ma gasped. 'This is a good chance for Little Robbie,' Lily went on. 'And I'm going to take it. Whether you like it or not!'

She marched up into the hall, bundled Little Robbie back in his pram and left. I wouldn't say she banged the door behind her, but she didn't exactly close it quietly. I put my arms around Ma and hugged her tight.

'She's right, Ma,' I said. 'She'll be with him the whole time. And they have Catholic churches in England, you know.'

But she couldn't be comforted, until Da got home and she told him all. He held her gently and said, 'It's only for a few weeks, Margaret. And she's only going to England, not the other side of the world.'

'You read that letter from the Archbishop, didn't you?' sniffed Ma.

'I did,' said Da. 'And I wish him and his priests had as much concern for those children's bellies as he has for their souls – not that their souls are in any danger. Those church men are auld hypocrites, that's what they are.'

'John!' Ma blessed herself. 'Don't talk about the bishop like that.'

'Go and talk to Lily, Margaret,' said Da gently. 'Otherwise she'll be off on a boat tomorrow with Little Robbie and then you'll wish you'd talked to her and made peace tonight.'

Ma was silent for a long time and then she wiped her eyes with her apron and said, 'All right.'

She was gone a long time. After a while I made a pot of tea and poured out a cup for Da.

'Thanks, pet,' he said.

'You don't think Little Robbie will be in any danger, do you?' I asked Da.

Da snorted. 'He'll probably be safer than he is here,' he said. 'How many are going tomorrow?'

'I'm not sure,' I said. 'A fair few. Lil said some of the kids are being bathed in the Tara Street baths first. I suppose they mightn't have had a bath in a while. And once that lot are washed I think they'll all be going to England straight away.'

Da sighed. 'Well, I never thought I'd wish my grandson and my daughter across the sea,' he said, 'but I hope they're off as soon as possible.'

Things looked brighter the next day, and not just because the weather was clear and fine. Ma had come back late the night before, her eyes red but her head held high.

'I gave her my blessing,' she said. 'I trust her to do what's right.'

Da gave her a squeeze. 'I'm proud of you, Margaret,' he said. 'I know it's not easy for you.' And she squeezed him back.

So I felt cheerful as I headed in to Liberty Hall early that morning. I knew I'd get to see Little Robbie and Lily there before they went to get the boat, because the children and any mothers who were going with them were going to meet up with the kids who were being washed at the baths and their mothers, and then they'd all get the boat train to Kingstown together. Another group of children were leaving from the North Wall quay that night.

When I arrived at Liberty Hall I was grabbed by Miss Neal.

'Miss Rafferty!' she said. 'How good are you at sewing on labels?'

'Not bad,' I admitted. 'My ma's a dressmaker.'

'Perfect,' she said. 'Come with me.'

And so I spent the morning with a few other girls, in the room full of clothes parcels, sewing on name labels to the donated clothes, along with some other new garments that Mrs Montefiore had bought in Dublin. Little Robbie was going to be the best-dressed person in our family, I thought, decked out in all this finery. On some of the jumpers I sewed little green and red rosettes – the colour of Ireland and the colour of socialism. I'd just sewed the last label on when the door of the room burst open and Mrs Montefiore appeared.

'Miss Neal!' she said, and I noticed that her cheeks were flushed and she wasn't nearly as serene as she usually was. There was a smear of dirt on the brim of her hat. 'Something's happened!'

'Mrs Montefiore!' Miss Neal hurried over to her.

'I've just come from the baths,' Mrs Montefiore said.

'Where are the children? Are they in the corridor?' Miss Neal peered past her comrade.

'They're still at the baths!' said Mrs Montefiore. 'We couldn't get them away!'

We all stopped our work and stared at her.

'But … but why?' said Miss Neal.

'We were stopped by a group of priests!' said Mrs Montefiore. 'That letter from the archbishop seems to have sent them into a frenzy.'

'What do you mean? How did they stop you?'

'With physical force!'

We were all openly gawping at Mrs Montefiore now.

'They assaulted Mrs Rand,' she went on, 'and they stopped us collecting the children. The mothers were very upset. Indeed, Mrs. Rand and I were the only two calm persons in that yelling, wailing, hysterical multitude. And we barely escaped unscathed – some of the priests' supporters threw mud at our cab as we got away. This country, really! And this city! It's worse than everything we heard!'

That explained the dirty hat. Though I felt a twitch of irritation at the way she talked about Dublin.

'But the children?' said Miss Neal.

Mrs Montefiore's voice was full of emotion. 'Lost to us for now, I'm afraid. But there are other children here, and their mothers and we must make sure we get them safely on the boat train.'

I swallowed. 'My sister and my nephew are meant to be leaving from here,' I said. 'They're probably downstairs now.'

Mrs Montefiore looked over at me. 'Well, if they managed to get here they should be all right. We have asked some of the union men and boys to escort everyone over to the station.' She turned to Miss Neal. 'Is everything ready?'

Miss Neal looked around at her workers and we all nodded back at her.

'More or less,' she said.

'Then let us get the garments down to the children,' said Mrs Montefiore. 'There isn't a moment to lose.'

The entrance hall was full of children and their mothers when we staggered down the stairs with our parcels of clothing, but despite the inevitable noise and confusion it didn't take long before each child had been given its clean, warm garments. I found Lily sitting on a bench near the stairs, Little Robbie in her lap. He seemed to be enjoying all the chaos, but Lily's expression was grave.

'I heard about what happened in Tara Street,' she said. 'Do you think we'll get to the station all right? The boat train's going from Westland Row.'

'Of course you will,' I said, with more confidence than I actually felt. 'The station's practically around the corner. Well, it's around the corner once you cross the river.' I could hear people shouting outside and glanced towards the door. 'I'll have a look and see what's going on out there.'

When I got outside, I wasn't sure whether the crowd gathered in front of the building was friendly or not. Some were union men I recognised, but there were a few strangers shouting 'kidnappers!' and 'heathens!' I thought of Lily and Little Robbie pushing past those angry faces and felt sick.

And then a familiar figure bounded up the steps towards me.

'Howiya, Betty,' said Ali. He gestured back at the crowd. 'This is getting lively.'

'Lily and Little Robbie are inside!' I said. I forgot about things being strange between us lately. 'How are they going to get to the station?'

'That's why I'm here,' said Ali. He flexed his lean right arm like a strongman on a poster for the circus. 'I'm the bodyguard!'

'You are?' I said.

Ali laughed. 'Well, one of them. Word got out at the picket that there was help needed here.' His expression hardened and he shook his head. 'Priests stopping mothers sending their kids to safety.'

'It sounds mad,' I said, and told him what Mrs Montefiore said. 'Attacking women! And them men of the cloth and all.'

'I'm not surprised,' said Ali grimly. 'That old parish priest wanted my da to give up me and Samira, remember? Da had to fight to keep us. And now they want to stop these women protecting their babies. They don't care about kids at all.'

I was quite shocked by Ali's words, but I couldn't really blame him. It was true, the priest hadn't shown much interest in keeping the Caseys together as a family. And if the Church had done enough to look after hungry children since the strike began, maybe we wouldn't have queues going out the front door of Liberty Hall. Even thinking those things makes me feel guilty – I knew what Ma would say if I said them aloud – but I can't help it.

'Workers!' cried a familiar voice. 'Listen to me!' The faces of the crowd, union men and protestors alike, turned up to a window in the floor above us. Ali ran down the steps and followed their gaze to find out what was going on.

'It's Big Jim!' he said, bounding back up the steps. 'He'll keep them occupied for a while. Come on. Let's check how the kids are getting on.'

We went back to the lobby and found that the nervous mothers and their increasingly fractious children had been joined by more union men with the red hand on their jackets.

'What's it like out there, Betty?' Lily asked in a scared whisper. She noticed my companion. 'Morning, Ali.'

'Alright, Lily,' said Ali cheerfully. 'I'm walking over to the station with you.'

'Is it safe?' Lily held Little Robbie tightly.

'It's grand,' I said. 'Mr Larkin's talking to the crowd now. They're all distracted by him.'

'Don't worry, ladies!' called a short but powerful-looking man. 'We'll get you on that train all right. Everyone ready?' There was a murmur of assent. 'Come on, then!' He marched out of the front door, followed by the little parade of women and children.

'Let's go, Lil!' I said. 'I'll walk over there with you.'

The crowd were relatively peaceful as we made our way out. Mrs Montefiore and Mrs Rand were bundled into a cab with one of the smaller kids, and the rest of us set out across the bridge on foot, in the direction of the station.

'See?' I said brightly. 'You'll be on that train in no time.' I chucked Little Robbie's chin, which was still chubby enough, thank goodness. 'Just think, Little Robbie! You're going on a boat!'

Little Robbie bit me and laughed.

'Ow!' I said. 'Janey, he hasn't lost his fighting spirit.'

Lily laughed weakly. 'At least his asthma's not as bad as it was yesterday.'

'A few weeks in the lap of luxury,' said Ali, 'and he'll be fitter than ever.' Little Robbie beamed at Ali, showing his shining little teeth. Ali pointed at the grinning Little Robbie and then winked at me. 'All the better to bite you with.'

I laughed despite myself.

'Lucky me,' I said. We were almost at the station now. 'What's going on up there?'

The entrance to the train station is across from the railings of Trinity College, and usually you'd be able to see right inside to the ticket offices from the other side of the road. But now the doors of the station were closed, and an agitated crowd was gathering outside them. I could see some black-clad priests standing with their backs to the doors.

'Stand back, Lil,' said Ali. 'I'm going to have a look.'

'I'm coming with you,' I said.

Ali looked for a moment as if he was going to say something to stop me, then he nodded.

'Come on,' he said.

We hurried across the road and found the priests engaged in fierce argument with Mrs Montefiore and Mrs Rand.

'I demand that you let me pass!' said Mrs Montefiore, in ringing tones.

'And I *demand*,' said the priest, a tall man with a face that would have looked pleasant if he hadn't looked so angry, 'that you refrain from stealing these innocent children away from their good Catholic homes.'

'We're stealing no one!' retorted Mrs Montefiore. She was jostled by the crowd behind her but quickly regained her footing. 'The children are travelling with their mothers' blessing. Indeed, several mothers are accompanying us across the water, and the others will travel with us on the train to take their children to the boat.' She glanced across the road and saw the group of waiting women and children, protected by their union bodyguards. 'Come on, ladies! The train awaits!'

The group hurried across the road.

'I need to stay with Lily,' I said, as the women and children reached the pavement in front of the station, but before I could reach her and Little Robbie, the crowd seemed to swell, shoving me back towards the doors, and I lost sight of her.

'Betty!' cried Ali, and then he was pushed away by the increasingly angry group.

It was like I was back in the horrible crush of the police charge that day on O'Connell Street. Children were crying and screaming as we were jostled against the doors of the station. I was pushed around by the crowd, shoved this way and that. For a split second, I caught a glimpse of Lily's best blue hat.

'Lily!' I screamed, but then a red-faced man whose jacket bore the rosette of the Ancient Order of Hibernians shoved me back.

'Go home, you stupid girl!' he snapped.

'Calm yourselves, men!' roared the priest, but he had chosen to intervene too late and his flock didn't obey.

If the station workers hadn't decided to open a door at last, I don't know what would have happened. We might have been crushed against the closed doors. But luckily they did. Mrs Rand almost fell through the entrance as the door opened, and I saw Mrs Montefiore take the tickets out of her leather attaché case and hand them to her colleague. Then she turned back to the crowd.

'Come on, ladies!' she cried. 'It's time!' To my great relief I saw Lily and Little Robbie standing next to her, just a few feet away from me. Little Robbie was red in the face from roaring.

'Follow Mrs Rand!' Mrs Montefiore cried. 'Hurry, my dears.' The women and children surged forwards; I lost sight of Lily again, but I managed to get inside the station just as Mrs Montefiore ushered in the last mother.

'That's everyone accounted for!' she said breathlessly.

'We have to get them on the train now,' said the barrel-chested man.

And that, it turned out, was easier said than done. I tried to keep as close to the group of mothers and children as I could, but the priests and their Ancient Order of Hibernian supporters had entered the station too and they made it difficult. Some of them had started singing 'Faith Of Our Fathers' at the top of their lungs.

'Think of the children!' yelled a scrawny, grey-haired man, as the children wailed.

'Kidnapper Larkin!' roared another man. There were even more of them now, and the crush inside the station was almost as bad as it had been outside.

'Let us pass!' cried Mrs Montefiore, trying to force her way through the crowd. But the men kept pushing in front of the women and by the time we all reached the platform I still hadn't got close to Lily and Little Robbie. At that stage, however, I was more worried about them actually getting safely onto the train than being able to say goodbye to them.

Then Ali's blessedly familiar face emerged through the crowd.

'Can we get right up to the train without tickets?' I said breathlessly. 'I don't have one of those platform tickets.'

'I don't think they're checking for tickets today,' said Ali, as we stumbled onto the platform. A few yards away I could see Lily and Little Robbie boarding the train just behind Mrs Rand, whose elegant hat was now askew. Lily paused in the doorway, casting her eyes desperately across the crowd. I waved as hard as I could.

'Goodbye, Lily!' I shouted. And to my relief she saw me. We beamed at each other for a second and then she hurried into the train carriage. Mrs Montefiore attempted to follow, but a priest grabbed her arm and pushed her back.

'I can't let you get on this train,' he said.

But Mrs Montefiore didn't flinch. 'My good sir, this is assault,' she said, and at those words the priest let go of her arm as if it were hot coals. He was still standing between her and the door of the carriage, but it looked as if he wouldn't use force to stop her getting on board. Still, his rowdy supporters were nearby, and I wasn't so sure about them. Neither was Ali.

'I'm going to help her onto the train,' said Ali. 'The Hibernians mightn't be as easily put off as the priest.'

'Go on!' I said. But as Ali attempted to push through the crowd and hurry to Mrs Montefiore's aid, one of the Hibernians blocked his path.

'Get away, you _____!' he said, using a horrible word that I won't even write down.

'Out of my way!' Ali said brusquely and tried to move around him. In answer, the Hibernian punched him in the face.

'Ali!' I screamed.

Ali staggered backwards into my arms, blood trickling from his nose.

'You're a lot of savages, thinking you can kidnap Irish children!' snarled his attacker. Behind the brute, I could see Mrs Montefiore attempting to board the train once more. But before she could get on board, one of the priests swung the door at her, smashing it into her arm. She cried out in pain but managed to evade him and get on board. I turned back to Ali.

'Are you all right?' He was staunching the blood from his nose with his hanky.

'I'm grand.' His voice was muffled. 'Jaysus, the train should have left five minutes ago. Why won't it go?'

Just then, the shrill blast of a whistle rang over the shouts and cries of both the crowd and the children who were peering out of the carriage windows. The train began to move slowly along the platform, but I saw two of the priests jump on at the last minute.

'Well, they've got away,' said Ali. 'Even if those priests are going with them. Don't look like that, Betser! Lily and Robbie are fine.'

'I know,' I said, my voice wobbling. 'It's just …'

'Ah, Betser,' said Ali, and he put his arm around me. I don't think he'd ever done that before. I didn't really mind him calling me Betser. He smelled nice. Warm and … with a sort of boy smell. I feel strange even writing that down. He only held me for a brief moment. But it was a nice moment.

'Come on,' he said. 'Let's go home.'

Luckily the crowd dispersed quickly enough once the train left, and we crossed the river in peace.

'I think we can give ourselves the rest of the day off,' said Ali.

And even though a part of me thought I should be on the picket line or in the kitchen, I was so exhausted by what had happened at the station that I agreed.

We didn't talk about what happened in the station on the way home. In fact, we didn't really say anything for a while. Then Ali asked how the kitchens were going, and I told him and asked him what it was like living with not one but two actresses. He laughed.

'I'm starting to think I should have joined this dramatic company myself,' he said. 'At least I could make them listen to me practise lines as much as I have to listen to them. I'm even dreaming about those daft plays.'

'Samira and Auntie Maisie aren't that bad, are they?' I said.

Ali gave me a meaningful look. 'Let me ask you one question. Do *you* feel like you've already seen Samira's play about a hundred times?'

Now it was my turn to laugh. 'Just her bits of it.'

'Well, imagine *living* with her,' said Ali. 'And Tom's practically as bad with his song. I'm telling you, I'll be delighted when this concert's finally over. Though I know Samira'll be signing up for whatever show they put on next.'

'Don't suppose you ever felt like treading the boards yourself, did you?' I asked.

Ali shook his head. 'Not me,' he said. 'Maybe I take after my ma's side of the family.' He glanced away from me, and I wondered if he was thinking of all the relations he's never seen, far across the sea. I've never met my grandparents on da's side – they died before me and Eddie were born – and loads of kids on our road never see their grandparents 'cause their parents came from faraway places like Sligo or Kerry, but that's not quite the same thing as having a whole family thousands of miles across the sea, maybe speaking a language you don't even know. It wasn't fair that Samira and Ali never got to know them.

'Anyway,' said Ali. 'Did I tell you about Granny? She's convinced Auntie Maisie isn't going back on the stage after all.'

'What does she think she's doing every night?' I said.

'According to Granny she's being wined and dined by a rich gentleman who's showering her with jewels,' said Ali, and we laughed about that all the way to Strandville Avenue.

Ma's face was drawn with worry when she answered the door to my knock.

'Did they get away all right?' she said.

'They did,' I said, and I saw her shoulders sag with relief. I decided it was better not to tell her about the fuss at the station, at least not straight away.

'I'll make you a cup of tea,' she said.

'Where's Da?' I asked.

'He's gone down to the North Wall with Robert Hessian,' said Ma, putting the kettle on the fire. 'To make sure those other children get away safely.'

I curled up in Da's armchair and drank my tea and thought of Lily and Little Robbie. They might already be out at sea now, I thought, wrapping my fingers around my tea cup and letting it warm my hands. How long does it take a steamer to get over to England?

'I might go to bed early,' I said. 'I'm exhausted.'

'You look like you're coming down with something,' said Ma. She laid a cool hand against my forehead. 'You're warm.'

'I don't feel warm,' I said.

'Well you'd better get to bed then,' said Ma, a little too briskly. 'We can't afford any doctor's fees. I'll get you a hot brick.' And she shoved a brick into the fire to heat it up.

An hour later I was tucked up in bed with my library book, *Little Women,* which has been one of my very favourite books since I first got it out of the library a few years ago. At least I didn't have scarlet fever, I thought. I pressed my feet against the nice hot brick, which was wrapped in clean old rags to stop it burning me, and felt very cosy. I love this book and I love the March sisters, even though they don't squabble quite as much as me and Lily used to. Jo wants to be an author, just like me. I was just wondering if I could send any of my stories off to publishers like she did in the second book, *Good Wives,* when I heard the sound of the front door opening. I thought it must be Da, and I knew he'd come up to check on me once Ma told him I wasn't feeling too well, but then I heard a familiar sound. A wrong sound, now. The sound of Little Robbie, wailing.

I scrambled out of bed, wrapped an old shawl around me and, ignoring the cold linoleum beneath my bare toes, hurried down the stairs and into the kitchen. Da was there, and so was Lily, clutching Little Robbie to her. He had stopped wailing and was sucking his thumb.

'I found them on Amiens Street and took them home,' said Da.

'Why aren't you on a boat?' I said to Lily. For a second I wondered if I really had come down with a terrible fever and was seeing things. When Eddie had the measles years ago he thought there was a horse in the room, a giant horse with eyes of fire, but it was only Earnshaw.

'I couldn't get on the boat in Kingstown,' said Lily. Her eyes were red and I could see she'd been crying.

'What do you mean? Did someone stop you? Grab you or anything?' Da's jaw tensed.

'No, not exactly,' said Lily. She sat down in the big chair. 'But the priests were at us the whole way down in the train, and some of the other mothers started getting all upset, crying and praying and that. And then when we got to Kingstown, there were more people there making a fuss on the quay. I lost sight of Mrs Rand and all the others, and then I left my bag at the station and after I went back and got it there were so many angry fellas shouting and roaring and singing hymns I just … I couldn't fight my way through them to the boat. Not on my own. I was too frightened.'

'Oh, Lily, I should have gone with you,' I said.

But Lily shook her head. 'You couldn't have done anything,' she said. Then her face sort of wobbled and she handed Little Robbie to Ma and said, 'Can you take him out for a minute, Ma?' There was something in her face that stopped Ma saying anything. She just took Little Robbie, who was clearly too tired after all his adventures to protest, and hurried up to the front room. As soon as the door closed behind her, Lily burst into tears.

'I'm a terrible mother!' she wailed. 'I should have been braver.'

'There's nothing terrible about you, pet.' Da's voice was gruff as he crouched down by the side of the chair and took her hand. 'It's the fault of … well, I'm not going to say what I think of them.'

'But Little Robbie …' sniffed Lily.

'He'll be grand,' said Da firmly. 'I was telling Peter Daly about his chest and he said his youngest had troubles too and they tried a bit of eucalyptus oil and it made a fine difference.'

I'd never heard of this oil and neither had Lily. 'Is it cough medicine?' she asked.

'Not exactly.' Da squeezed her hand. 'Peter said if you put this oil in some hot water and breathe in the steam it's good for relieving the breath.'

It sounds a bit odd to me but it's surely worth a try. Though good luck to anyone trying to get Little Robbie to do anything at all, let alone breathe in special steam.

'It's not just the coughing and the breathing,' said Lily. 'I need to keep him well fed.'

'And you will, love,' said Da. 'We all will. We'll all do without if needs be.' He looked at me. 'Won't we, Betty?'

I didn't even have to think about it. ''Course we will.'

Lily let out a long juddering sigh.

'I'd better get down to Robert,' she said. 'You don't think he'll blame me, do you? For not taking Little Robbie to safety?'

''Course he won't,' said Da. 'He knows things were getting rowdy today. Sure, when I bumped into you on Amiens Street I was on my way down to the North Wall to meet him. So you'll be a nice surprise for him when he gets home.'

Lily stood up from the chair and Da held her close in a big hug.

'Thanks, Da,' she said. And then, to my surprise, she took my hand. I don't know if she's ever done that before. 'Thanks, Bets. You were fierce brave yourself today, you know.'

'Ah, I wasn't,' I said awkwardly. I'm not used to being praised by Lily.

She went up to collect Little Robbie and take him home, and as soon as she'd gone Da looked at me closely.

'You're as white as a sheet,' he said.

'I think I have a cold,' I said. 'That's why I was in bed when you arrived.'

'You'd better get up there right away.' He paused for a moment and then said, 'I'm proud of you, pet.'

'Thanks, Da,' I said.

I thought I'd be up all night worrying about Lily and Little Robbie, but I really was sick because I fell asleep straight away. And the next day I properly had a cold, and Ma wouldn't let me leave the house. I missed the big protest march but it sounds like it went well and there was no real trouble from police or scabs. Rosie told me about it when I came in to the picket a few days later. She was marching behind the Savoy girls.

'You should have seen their banner,' she said. She adopted a dramatic pose: '"Women workers locked out by the sweating employers of Dublin".'

I was impressed. 'That's very good,' I said.

'It was indeed,' said Rosie. 'And we were right up the front of the parade, too. You should have heard all the people cheer as we marched past!'

'Really?' I said.

'Well, some people were cheering. They were clapping and all.'

But all the marching doesn't change the fact that we're still locked out, and only a few of the kids who were meant to be going over for a rest in England managed to get there. I hoped that the other group who were meant to be sailing from North Wall Quay the same day as Little Robbie was going from Kingstown would get away safely, but apparently there was practically a riot – Robert Hessian has a few nasty bruises from trying to protect the children – and the Hibernians even stopped Mrs Montefiore taking some other kids up to Catholic families in Belfast on the train. And to make things even worse, the ladies have been charged by the police with kidnapping, even though they were taking the children with their parents' permission! The whole world seems to be against us — at least, that's how it feels at the moment.

# Chapter Twenty-Five

Mr Larkin is in jail! He has been charged with sedition, which just means causing trouble as far as I can tell, and sentenced to seven whole months! The police raided Liberty Hall and put him under arrest. I wasn't there at the time, thank heaven. I've seen enough police batons to last a lifetime. There was a big protest, of course. At least a thousand workers turned out in the lashing rain to demand his release, but it didn't do any good. He's off in prison now, and while our fight goes on, the Save the Kiddies scheme is definitely at an end. Mr Connolly, who's taken over the union while Mr Larkin is in prison, says that they're going to use the money intended for the scheme to feed children in Liberty Hall, and they're starting up a breakfast club so the children can start each day with full bellies. So that's what we're doing in the kitchen now.

I never thought I'd be back manning a tea urn after I left Lawlor's, but that's what I was doing this week in Liberty Hall. We're making tea for the mammies who take their kids to get breakfast, as I discovered the other morning after I turned up at the kitchen at the crack of dawn. Actually, it was before the crack of dawn, because it's getting light later and later now winter is really drawing in. And I can tell you that if it was bad having to get up in the dark to go to school, it's a lot worse getting up in the dark to walk all the way into town and then spending the day working on your feet. Not that I complained when I was in the kitchen, of course. But if I can't do a bit of complaining in my own memoir, where can I?

Anyway, even though Ma had to practically drag me out of my nice warm bed this morning, I was wide awake by the time I reached the kitchen, and Miss Larkin said, 'Right, girls, which of you have worked on a tea urn before?'

I didn't want to tell a lie, but I wasn't exactly dying to volunteer for tea urn duties. I know what those urns are like. For all I knew this one was even more temperamental than the one in Lawlor's, and I couldn't forget what happened to Kitty. I don't think her foot's ever really healed from that scalding. Rosie says she thinks she's scarred for life.

But, still, I know how an urn works, and I had to do my duty, so I put up my hand. And it turned out I was the only one to do so, because for some reason I was the only Lawlor's girl in the kitchen that day, and none of the other girls had ever worked behind the counter in a place that served cups of tea.

'Over here, please, Miss Rafferty,' said Miss Larkin briskly, and soon I was ensconsed next to a table that held some big jugs of milk and an enormous urn, which was letting off little blasts of steam in an alarming fashion.

'Don't look so nervous. It won't kill you,' said Miss Larkin, and disappeared upstairs.

I wasn't so sure about that, and my face must have showed my fear because, as the first breakfast eaters began to crowd around the kitchen door, one of the grand ladies who helps in the kitchen came over and said, 'Are you all right?'

'I'm grand, missus,' I said. I'd seen her from a distance in the kitchen, usually manning the cow boiler, but I wasn't sure what her name was.

'Do you want a hand with the tea?' she said. 'I just came in to deliver some eggs and it seems I'm surplus to requirements for now.'

'Yes, please,' I said.

The first children of the day were coming in for their bread and butter and boiled eggs, some of them accompanied by their mothers but quite a lot of them on their own. The noise was indescribable. It was like the schoolyard on a particularly lively day, except it was happening indoors where the sound couldn't escape.

'What's your name, dear?' said the lady. 'I'm Miss …' But whatever she said was drowned out by a shriek. A child had tripped over another child's foot and banged its knees.

I didn't want to ask her to repeat herself over the hooting and shouting. So I just said, 'I'm Betty Rafferty.' And after that we were both too busy to talk for a while, because we were filling mugs and handing them out and telling children and their mothers to go in various directions.

Eventually everyone had been served, and the lady and I leaned back on the table and smiled wearily at each other.

'Well done, Miss Rafferty,' said the lady. 'Where did you work before all this?'

'Lawlor's on Henry Street,' I said. And I told her about our strike and about the tea urn scalding Kitty.

The lady's brow furrowed. She was quite old but you could tell she'd been very pretty when she was younger. 'Oh yes, I've met your Miss Warby. Quite the … martinet.' There was a brief pause before she continued. 'I run a shop and restaurant just down the road. The Irish Farm Produce Company.'

'Is that the place that only sells vegetables?' I said. Annie had once told me about some sort of restaurant that wouldn't give you any meat but I hadn't believed her. The lady smiled.

'No, not just vegetables, we have lots of excellent eggs and honey and butter and bread, but we don't sell anything with meat in it,' she said. 'And we have very good cakes.' She glanced at the watch on her wrist. 'Heavens, I didn't realise it was so late. I must dash. Goodbye, Miss Rafferty. Well done today.'

'Goodbye, missus,' I said. I still didn't know her name but I didn't want to ask for it now, in case it looked like I hadn't been listening when she told me earlier. How strange to think of someone who owns a café supporting our cause! I suppose not all employers are like the Lawlors. That thought made me feel quite cheerful for the rest of the day. And I was able to take home a loaf of bread for Lily and Little Robbie, who is looking a bit better now, thank goodness. That eucalyptus oil seems to be working, even though Little Robbie upturned the basin and just missed Lily's lap the first time they tried it. Anyway, he certainly hasn't been coughing as much since he started his steam-baths.

But, still, everything is still terribly tiring. It's not just your body that gets exhausted from all the picketing and kitchen work, it's your mind as well. Today was Sunday, and after Mass was over and we'd gone home for breakfast (a slice of bread and a scrape of margarine each) I felt like I needed to get away from everything, just for a while.

'I'm going for a walk, Ma,' I said.

She was in the front room, laying out the pieces for a nightdress she was making for Mrs Dickson. Mrs Dickson keeps on asking her to do little jobs – I think she still feels guilty about sending us into town that night of the police charge. I hope she stays feeling guilty, if it means Ma keeps getting work.

Anyway, Ma said it was fine for me to go for a walk but to make sure I was back for my dinner.

'And take Earnshaw with you,' she said. 'He keeps trying to get in here and the scratching at the door is driving me mad.'

A few minutes later I was on my way down to Samira's house, Earnshaw straining on his lead. But there was no answer when I knocked on the door. I knocked again, and Mrs Connolly next door stuck her head out.

'They're not in, love,' she said. 'They've gone over to Ringsend. Went early and everything to get to the ten o'clock Mass for old Mr Casey.'

I'd forgotten it was Samira's grandad's anniversary this weekend. They always have a Mass for him every year. It's the only time Mr Casey sets foot inside a church.

'Thanks, Mrs Connolly,' I said. 'Come on, Earnshaw.'

I pulled my old hat firmly down over my head and stuck my hands in my pockets to keep out the worst of the wind. (I could generally manage to keep a grip on the lead while holding it in my pocket, unless Earnshaw tugged it with all his strength.) Then I turned right and headed across Annesley Bridge and out towards the sea.

I couldn't remember the last time I'd walked out along the coast road. It might even have been the summer, when the waves were blue and bouncing, and the sky was clear and bright. Now the grey clouds seemed to weigh down on top of my head, and a wicked wind blew in from across Dublin Bay. But there was something fresh and bracing about it, and other people clearly thought so too, because there were quite a few walking along beside the low wall between the road and sea. Every so often a scab-driven tram would come rattling past us on its way into town. I knew Rosie would have shaken her fist at them, but I was too tired, so I just scowled. Earnshaw barked, like the good dog he is.

I didn't really have a thought in my head as I went along, and that was very refreshing after the stresses and strains of the last few weeks. The more I walked, the calmer I felt. I wasn't thinking about those angry priests, or Little Robbie's cough, or Ali getting punched in the face. I just looked at the sea and the clouds and the sky, which was starting to clear by the time I passed the Town Hall in Clontarf.

In fact, I wished I could have walked all the way to Howth and back, but my legs clearly didn't agree, because when I reached the wooden bridge that leads out onto Bull Island and Dollymount Strand they were really starting to ache. I paused in the middle of the bridge to lean on the wooden railings and look down at the swirling grey water underneath.

'Do you think you could learn to fish, Earnshaw?' I asked him. 'You could get us a nice big trout or something for our tea.'

'He won't be catching any trout there, I'm afraid,' said a friendly and familiar voice from behind me. 'They're freshwater fish.'

'Peter!' I whirled around to see none other than Peter Lawlor standing on the wooden boards, a beautiful soft blue scarf tucked snugly into his dark brown overcoat and a brown tweed cap on his fair curls.

'I *thought* it was you walking ahead of me. Well, actually,' he said, 'I was pretty sure it was Earnshaw, and then I realised that if it was Earnshaw, then the girl next to him was probably you.'

'He does have a distinctive sort of shape, all right,' I said.

'Where are you off to?' said Peter. 'If you don't mind me asking.'

I shrugged my shoulders. 'Nowhere. Just walking.'

'Me too,' said Peter.

'I was about to …' I almost said that I was about to go home, but suddenly I didn't want to go home. 'Walk down to the beach.'

'Would you mind if I went with you?' Peter said. 'I was going there anyway,' he added hastily.

I shrugged my shoulders again. Ma would have given me a slap on the legs if she'd seen me doing that in public; she thinks it looks fierce vulgar. 'It's a free country.'

I remembered the awkwardness of our last meeting, the time he'd apologised for being thoughtless. Our footsteps sounded very loud as we walked across the wooden bridge.

'I love this bridge,' said Peter. 'It always makes me feel like I'm going to, I don't know, a Viking settlement or something.'

'When Samira and me were little we used to pretend it was a bridge from a fairy tale,' I said. 'You know, like the Andrew Lang fairy books. With some magical creatures living underneath it.'

Peter grinned. 'Don't tell anyone, but I used to imagine that too. I used to run across as fast as I could in case a troll tried to eat his way through the boards and grab me. Only Lavinia would never join in the game. She doesn't have much of an imagination,' he said thoughtfully.

'My brother Eddie didn't either,' I said. 'But Ali did. Still does, I suppose.'

'Who's Ali?' said Peter.

'Samira's brother,' I said. But somehow it seemed strange talking about Ali to Peter, so I changed the subject. 'It's funny to think of us both coming out here on Sundays.'

'We might have run past each other,' said Peter.

'I suppose we could,' I said. 'The beach belongs to everyone.'

I realised that was true. Not everyone could afford to take picnics in big hampers or fly kites on the sand. But the sound of the waves, and the feel of the sand under your feet – that really did belong to everyone. Suddenly I was very glad I'd walked all the way out to Bull Island, even though there'd be no taking my shoes and stockings off and running around on the sand today. (That's another thing Ma wouldn't like – me even *thinking* about taking my stockings off in front of a boy.)

'So,' said Peter, 'how's your strike going? I saw about all that kidnapping business in the paper – it looked like a frightful mess'

'There wasn't any kidnapping!' I said hotly. 'The papers got it all wrong.'

'So what really happened?' said Peter. He sounded as if he really did want to know. So I told him. Somehow it all seemed even worse when I said it out loud – the screaming, the way the men blocked our path, Ali getting hit. I never cry in front of anyone if I can help it, not even Samira, and I didn't cry in front of Peter Lawlor, but some water did come out of my eyes, just for a second. I wiped it away with the sleeve of my coat.

Peter tactfully looked away while this was happening, but he did say, 'Oh dear, Betty, I am sorry.'

'It's not your fault,' I said. 'I mean, not you personally.'

'Still …' he said.

We had reached the sand dunes now. A sandy path, worn by the feet of countless beach visitors, led through the dunes and down to the beach. It was more sheltered there, and we walked through the waving grass in silence.

Then Peter said, 'Betty, what would you like to do?'

Right now, I just wanted to look out over the sea, but there was something in Peter's voice that suggested he was asking a bigger question.

'What do you mean?'

'When you're older,' said Peter. 'I mean, I don't suppose you want to work for my father forever …'

I was pretty sure I wasn't going to be working for his father at all, even if the union got what we wanted. Lawlor's weren't going to let us strikers back, not ever. But I didn't say anything about that to Peter. Instead I said, 'Well, what I'd *like* to do is go on to college, like the girls who go to Eccles Street. But there's not much chance of that.' I spoke more sharply than I'd intended.

'I didn't mean …' Peter began.

'I know you didn't,' I said. I sighed. Sometimes talking to Peter is like talking to an ordinary friend, but sometimes talking to him makes me go all spiky. 'I suppose I'd like to work somewhere … somewhere I cared about. Doing something interesting.' I nearly said, 'Like writing', but I stopped myself.

Before Peter could answer me, Earnshaw jerked his lead right out of my hand and bolted across the dunes in the way we'd just come.

'Oh, no, he's spotted a hare!' I cried, and pelted after him. Luckily I was able to grab hold of the lead before Earnshaw managed to kill any helpless wild beasts, but as I did so I heard the ringing of church bells and realised I'd have to head back home for dinner.

'You got him!' Peter ran up to me.

'And now I'd better take him home again,' I said.

'I should be getting back too,' said Peter. 'I'll be late for lunch. We're going to my aunt's house.' When he says lunch he means what we call dinner.

We didn't talk about strikes or future plans as we made our way back across the bridge and down the seafront. We talked about books. Peter said he missed his school library and I said he should join our public library in Charleville Mall. It's not that far away from him, after all.

'One of the bad things about working,' I told Peter, 'is that it's harder to get to the library. It was right next to my school, so me and Samira used to go in practically every day it was open. Now I have to get Ma to go and get books for me, and she gets the wrong ones sometimes.'

By the time we reached the road in Clontarf where Peter's aunt lived, I felt much better than I had before I went out.

'Goodbye, Betty,' said Peter. He leaned down and rubbed Earnshaw's shaggy head. 'And you too, Earnshaw.'

'Bye, Peter,' I said.

'And good luck,' said Peter. 'With, you know, everything.'

I was singing a little song to myself when I got home.

'I was going to send out a search party!' said Ma. 'Where did you get off to?'

'Just the beach,' I said.

'Well, the beach certainly agrees with you,' said Ma. 'You've got roses in your cheeks.'

After dinner Eddie hurried away to see his beloved Mary, Ma went back to sewing the nightdress, and Da went off to meet some of his union pals. It was nice and peaceful, for once. I sat by the remains of the fire with Earnshaw on my feet and looked through the latest copy of the *Irish Worker*. There was an article by Mr Larkin in it, written from his lonely cell. It made me think a lot about my conversation with Peter. Mr Larkin wrote, 'This great fight of ours is not simply a question of shorter hours or better wages. It is a great fight for human dignity. For liberty of action, liberty to live as human beings should live'.

# Chapter Twenty-Six

I haven't written anything here for a few weeks, because candles are so scarce in the house that none can be spared for me to squirrel myself away on my own to write my memoirs. But I have to write now because something strange has happened. In fact, strange might not even be the right word to describe the conversation I had yesterday. Surprising? Shocking? Exciting? Unsettling? I think it was all of those things, and I don't know what to do next.

The day started like an ordinary day – though Samira had some extraordinary news. I called into McGrath's last week on my way to the picket and found her sitting on the counter with a familiar moony look on her face. As the door opened I heard her say, in a rich and booming voice, '"Now I see that an injury to one is an injury to all!"'

'Nice of you to say so,' I said.

Samira was so startled she nearly fell off the counter, but she managed to keep her balance. 'You frightened the life out of me!'

'What are you doing?' I said. 'Surely you must know all your words by now. It's not like you're doing a one-woman show.'

'Of course I know my words!' Samira looked outraged at the very idea she wouldn't. 'But I'm practising my projection.'

'Your *what*?' I wrinkled my nose at her.

'Projecting my voice!' Samira clasped her hands with excitement. 'We found out at the rehearsal last night. The show's going to be in the Gaiety! It's definite!'

'Samira!' I grabbed her hands and pulled her off the counter. 'That's marvellous!'

'It's true!' Samira twirled around the tiny shop floor. 'In just a couple of weeks, I'm absolutely, definitely going to be singing and acting on the Gaiety stage!' She laughed. 'So you'd better get a ticket, I don't want to be saying my lines to an empty theatre.'

'No chance of that,' I said. Money may be tight, but I couldn't miss this concert. Even before they moved it to the big grand Gaiety there was a special rate for union members, and I'd already been saving a few pennies. Even Rosie was going.

'Ali and Maisie and Da are going too.' Samira was practically glowing. 'Maisie wants to use her connections and get a box but Da wouldn't hear of it. "What would my pals think," he says, "if they saw me in a box!"'

'It's a fair point,' I said.

'Anyway,' said Samira, 'the concert is to raise money, so they should be saving the boxes for the people who are going to pay full price. Which isn't any of us.'

'True,' I said.

'I thought the Majestic was fancy, but this!' said Samira. 'Speaking of the Majestic, do you want to come to the dress rehearsal of Auntie Maisie's pantomime? It's on in two weeks and we can watch from the circle.'

'What about that old Mr Farrell?' I said. 'Won't we have to see him?'

'Mr Garland will sneak us in so we won't have to see him at all,' said Samira. 'And I have to say, I do want to see Auntie Maisie in all her glory.'

'So do I,' I said. 'Of course I'll go. First we'll cheer for her, and then I'll cheer for you. The Gaiety! Oh, Samira, I'm delighted for you.'

'Thanks, Betser.' Samira's face grew a little grave. 'I think the news cheered Ali up a bit too. He hasn't been himself since that day with the kids.'

'I haven't seen him since then,' I said. I remembered his face as the Hibernian's fist slammed into him. 'Is he all right?'

Samira sighed. 'He's grand. Tired of it all. You know.'

I did.

'Anyway!' Samira brightened. 'In just a few weeks I'll be up on that stage doing the family proud. And you never know,' she added hopefully, 'the strike and the lockout and everything might all be over by then.'

I wish I felt so sure about that, but I didn't. A few weeks ago some of the big shipping companies brought in hundreds and hundreds of men from England to work as scabs in the docks. Most of them are sleeping on ships in the port because their employers know the working people of Dublin are so angry, the scabs wouldn't be safe if they tried to get lodging in the city. And if the employers can afford to bring over six hundred men, I can't see them giving in to us any time soon.

Not that the union wants to give in either. Mr Larkin's been out of jail since last week, but just before he was released Mr Connolly, who took over in his absence, called out all the Port and Docks workers on strike. You'd think this would have been enough to close down the port, but they had lots of scab workers to take the places of the striking men. Da says Mr Larkin wasn't very happy about this, because he didn't want to call out the dock workers until he *really* had to. Anyway, it means even more people needing strike pay, which means more pressure on the union.

We were talking about all this at the picket that morning when Annie dropped by to say hello to us, for the first time in weeks. It turned out she'd got a job.

'It's in a big house in Sandymount,' she said, smiling weakly. 'Working as a maid in the kitchen.'

'I hope they feed you well there,' said Rosie severely.

'Well, it's not too bad,' said Annie. 'The cook says they have to economise, you know, and there's four other servants …'

'*Five* servants?' I said. This household sounded like something out of a book. Even the Lawlors only had three.

'Six if you count the chauffeur,' said Annie. 'He's the fella who drives the car.'

'They have a motor car!' I shook my head in disbelief.

'What are the hours like?' demanded Rosie.

Annie shrugged. 'Ah, you know. It's longer than Lawlor's 'cause I've got to be up before everyone to light the range and that, so I'm working from six to, well, it depends what time they finish with their suppers.'

Rosie and I looked at each other, and then at Annie's hands which were even more raw and red than those of the girls in the washing-up room.

'Annie,' said Rosie, as gently as she could, 'they're taking advantage. You shouldn't have to work that long.'

'She's right,' I said. 'That's not fair.'

'Maybe it isn't,' retorted Annie, and I'd never heard that much fire in her voice before, 'but I couldn't find anything else! At least this way I'm not crossing a picket line or signing that pledge. And the cook's all right, she let me off this afternoon because the family are away for the week. I'm going to see my ma and da.'

'Sorry, Annie.' Rosie sounded genuinely contrite. 'I'm glad you found something.'

I was glad too. Annie's a nice girl, and a brave one too. She lost her job because she wanted to stand by us, despite not being in the union. But it's not a very cheering thought to realise that the best a girl can hope for in Dublin right now is working from six in the morning until midnight. I was thinking about that a few hours later, after I'd said goodbye to Rosie and Kitty and headed for home. In fact, I was so lost in thought that I didn't notice Peter Lawlor standing at the corner of O'Connell Street.

'Betty! Didn't you see me? I've been waving at you!' He bounded towards me through the November gloom.

'Sorry, I was miles away,' I said, pushing my hair back from my face. It wasn't raining today, but it was sort of misty and drizzly, the sort of weather that means you never feel totally dry.

'I'm going to a friend's house out in Rathgar and I'm late already so I can't stay long,' said Peter. 'But I have something to tell you. Something I think you'll like.'

'What's going on?' I said.

'Let's get some shelter first,' said Peter, and we moved under the portico of the GPO.

'That's better,' said Peter, running a hand through his damp hair. His smile was broad. 'Betty, how would you like to be working again?'

'I'm not going to break the strike.' I felt a little wave of disappointment. I thought he understood I would never abandon the picket and return to Old Wobbly. 'You know that.'

'I don't mean at Father's place,' said Peter. 'And I don't even mean starting work straight away – though it'd be ideal if you could start as soon as it's all ready.'

I was too tired to pretend I could understand him. 'What are you talking about?'

'A cousin of mine – well, he's my mother's cousin really, I suppose that makes him my cousin once removed or something – came around for tea the other day,' said Peter. 'His name's James. He's a jolly nice chap, actually, he's only about twenty-five and he's very good at rugger. Anyway, he was talking to Father about business matters, all very boring, and then he said that he'd just acquired premises on Nassau Street and he's opening up a little bookshop. He wants to sell lots of popular books, and books for kids. Nothing stuffy about it.'

'That sounds very nice.' I tried not to let my weariness show. It had been a long and damp day and I just wanted to get home. I didn't want to be hearing about bookshops. I've never been in a bookshop in my life, even though I'd often imagined going in and buying whatever I wanted. I'd never be able to afford a book of my own, I'd always told myself, so why should I taunt myself by looking? I did sometimes stop and look in at shop windows though.

'At the moment they're just ordering the books and finding someone to paint the walls and make shelves and sort out the plumbing and all that sort of thing, so James doesn't have any staff yet, apart from a manager who's his housekeeper's sister or something,' Peter Lawlor went on. 'He says she's a very nice young woman.' He put on a gruff voice to imitate his cousin. '"She's got a sense of humour, Peter" – that's what he said. "Very intelligent girl." Apparently she wanted to be a teacher but had to leave the college because of lack of funds.'

I could relate to that – sort of.

'Anyway, it's not going to be a particularly big shop, but it'll be too much for this girl all by herself,' said Peter. 'So she'll need an assistant.' He beamed at me. 'And I recommended you.'

I stared at him.

'You did what?'

'I said I knew a hardworking, polite and intelligent young woman who used to work in Father's business and had read all the books in her local library,' said Peter happily. 'And that I thought you were the perfect shop-girl for a bookshop.'

I barely registered the fact that Peter thought I was intelligent.

'But isn't your cousin in that Employers' Federation? The one that made everyone sign that pledge against the union?'

'No!' said Peter. 'He's not in anything. He's only starting out. He came into some money and he wants to invest it in a new business.'

'But if he talks to your father and mentions me …'

'I told you, he's my mother's cousin,' said Peter. 'He and Father don't get on particularly well. He certainly won't be consulting Father about his staff. And anyway, he already said he'd be happy to give you a chance.'

'But girls like me … I'm sure they don't work in bookshops.' I could feel myself blushing.

'Why not?' said Peter reasonably. 'You've probably read more books than most people. You said yourself you've read half the novels in the library. And I suspect you've read even more than that.'

'But …' I said, feeling as if I were in a daze, 'when is the shop opening?'

'If all the painting and shelf making and so on goes according to plan, they're opening in the middle of December. But you don't have to decide this very moment.' Peter glanced across the road at the clock hanging outside Clery's. 'Dash it, I'm very late. I'd better run. Think about it, won't you? You've got a few weeks. Why don't I meet you under the bridge near the Howth Road …' He took out a little diary from his picket and flicked to the last few pages. 'The afternoon of the seventh? That's a Sunday. You should be free.'

'The fundraising concert is on that night,' I said.

'Well, let's meet in the afternoon. Three o'clock. You must be able to get away then.'

'Peter,' I said. 'Is this serious? You're not joking with me?'

Peter stopped grinning. 'Of course I'm serious. I wouldn't mention it if James hadn't said he'd give you a try.'

'Oh,' I said.

'It really would be marvellous,' said Peter.

'All right,' I said. 'I'll think about it.'

'So you'll meet me on the seventh? Three o'clock?'

I nodded.

Peter grinned and rushed off in the direction of O'Connell Bridge. And I stayed there under the portico of the GPO for what felt like a very long time.

When I finally started for home, the drizzle had eased off. I passed a small bookshop on Talbot Street that had just closed for the evening and looked in the window. The walls were lined with books with brightly coloured spines, and two young men were bustling about, tidying things away and reshelving books that had ended up in the wrong place.

Imagine spending your days surrounded by books, I thought. Imagine selling books instead of overpriced cakes and expensive buns.

I could do that. I *know* I could.

And I'd be good at it too. I would remember the sort of books the customers liked, and I'd find other books they might enjoy too. If someone came in looking for a book for a ten-year-old, I'd tell them to read E. Nesbit, and if they wanted a book for a schoolgirl I'd recommend *Jane Eyre*. I'd read all sorts of books I haven't even heard of yet. And instead of tea urns, there'd be books, and instead of the sink room, there'd be *more* books, and instead of horrible Wobbly as my boss, there'd be a nice funny girl who knows what it's like to give up on the future you hoped for but find something else good instead.

Of course, I know it wouldn't be perfect. I know I'd be standing up all the time, and I know some of the customers would be rude – just because they like reading doesn't mean they'd be saints. But it would be working with something I care about, like I told Peter I wanted to do. In comparison with any job I'm ever likely to get, it's perfect. Except …

Except, unless the strike ends in a few weeks, and there's no hope it will, it would mean leaving the picket. It would mean leaving Rosie and Kitty and Joan and the others. It would mean leaving the Jacob's girls and the Savoy girls in the kitchen at Liberty Hall. I wouldn't be a scab, of course – I'd never even consider taking this job if it meant breaking a strike – but I'd still be … I don't know. What do you call it when someone abandons their comrades in the middle of a war? A deserter? And of course, I don't want to be a deserter.

But at the same time, maybe I wouldn't actually be betraying the others, or my principles, not really. I mean, we've been on strike for months and months now, and the employers keep saying they won't submit – which is how they see it – to the union's demands. And the police have been attacking meetings again. So where's it all going to end? *When* is it all going to end? And what are we going to do when it does? Don't we have to make plans? It's not like I'd be leaving the union if I took a new job. And surely I could work in the kitchen on the mornings I wasn't working in the shop. Or even before I started work in the shop. Nassau Street's not that far away from Liberty Hall. You could get there in ten minutes.

I haven't said a word about any of this to anyone. Not to Rosie or Kitty or even Samira. And definitely not to Ma and Da. I know Ma would be absolutely delighted and tell me to take the job straight away. But this is something I have to decide on my own. And at the moment, I really don't know what to do.

# Chapter Twenty-Seven

It's been nearly two weeks since Peter Lawlor offered me that job and I still haven't made up my mind. But I have to do it soon, because time is running out. There's only a week to go until my appointment with him and I don't know what I'm going to tell him. Maybe writing about it will help, I don't know. I should be exhausted because it's so late, but I'm so worked up I can't sleep.

In fact, I've been in a strange state all day long. I slept very badly last night, and I was working in the Liberty Hall kitchen this morning making breakfast for the kids which meant I had to get up even earlier than usual. It was freezing when I gingerly put my feet down on the linoleum floor of my room, and I had a brief memory of Lavinia Lawlor's room, with its soft fluffy carpets and big fireplace. I grabbed my clothes and dived back under my bed-sheets to get dressed in the warmth of the bed – it's a bit awkward getting dressed this way but it's worth it. You'd freeze standing in my room in your shift in winter. We've stuffed old rags along the bottom of the window frame to stop draughts getting in, but they manage to get in anyway.

Once I was dressed, I hurried down to the kitchen, which was slightly warmer than the upstairs of the house.

'How was the pantomime?' said Ma, pouring me a cup of tea.

I yawned and took the cup in my chilly hands.

'It was like magic,' I said. And it was. Last night me and Samira went to see Auntie Maisie in the dress rehearsal of Cinderella. It turned out that strictly we shouldn't have been allowed in, because dress rehearsals are meant to be for the cast and the stage crew only, but apparently Auntie Maisie has charmed everyone at the theatre, including all the doormen, so they'd turn a blind eye to her sneaking in a couple of smallish girls into the darkness of the upper circle. That is, if the girls wanted to go.

'You know, you're only to go if you actually feel like going,' she said to Samira a few evenings ago. 'I don't want you to have to feel like you're supporting his lordship Mr Farrell.'

The three of us were crowded around the fire in their kitchen, drinking cocoa. Ali and Mr Casey were out at another meeting, as were my da and Eddie. The union is forming some sort of group to protect the workers from attacks by the police, and both Eddie and Ali want to get involved. They're calling it a Citizen Army.

'I'm going there for you, not Mr Farrell,' said Samira. 'And besides, this way I don't have to pay him any money to see you.'

Auntie Maisie put her arm around Samira and kissed the top of her head.

'You'll show him one day, Sam,' said Auntie Maisie.

And I bet Samira will too. It's only a week until the big show – it's the day after my meeting with Peter – and you'd think she would be getting nervous, but actually she isn't. She's all calm. She's even stopped being giddy about it, now there's only a week to go.

'I need to focus,' she said after Auntie Maisie had gone to her room to rest. ('My feet,' she said, 'are going to fall off by the time this pantomime's over!') 'I know it's only a little part, but it's still important.'

'What was it Auntie Maisie said?' I said. 'There are no small parts, only small actors!'

Auntie Maisie's part isn't small, though, and I was really looking forward to seeing her on stage at last. Or at least I would have been, if I hadn't been thinking about Peter's job offer all the time. Because Samira's been concentrating so hard on the play, it hasn't been that difficult to hide my worries from her, but Rosie is another matter, not least because we're together for long periods of time every day. Yesterday afternoon we were on the picket line and she leaned over and rubbed Earnshaw's head.

'Earnshaw, my old pal,' she said, 'it's clear Betty isn't paying either of us any attention. Why don't the two of us run away to sea and become pirates?'

'What?' I said.

'Oh, you're awake,' said Rosie. 'I was starting to get worried.'

I sighed and rubbed my eyes. 'Sorry Rosie,' I said. 'I'm just tired. I'm worried I'll fall asleep at Samira's auntie's show this evening.'

'Are you sure that's all that's wrong?' Rosie's expression was shrewd.

''Course I am!' I said. I looked up and down the street. 'I just wish we had more handbills.'

We'd run out of the printed sheets of information about the union's activities a few weeks ago, and money's so tight at the union that we don't want to ask them about getting more printed. That's another thing that makes me seriously think about taking the job in the shop. What will happen if the strike pay runs out? There are families going for months now on just five shillings a week.

'We don't need paper when we have our beautiful voices,' said Rosie. She grinned at me and then turned to the passers by.

'Up the workers!' she yelled. 'Don't go into Lawlor's!'

A young man coming out of a nearby shop raised a hand in solidarity.

'See?' Rosie turned to me, beaming.

I wish I was as brave as Rosie. The worst things you could imagine have happened to her, and she keeps on getting up in the morning in that horrible little room and coming out to picket or to work in the kitchens all day. I know I should be able to do the same. But I'm just so exhausted all the time. And when I'm most tired, and wet, and hungry, that's when the idea of working in a cosy little bookshop seems like, well, it seems like heaven.

I hoped Auntie Maisie's dress rehearsal would stop me thinking about the bookshop, just for a little while. Samira met me at the picket and we arrived at the stage door at the side of the theatre about a quarter of an hour before the rehearsal was due to start. Mr Garland wasn't working there that day but the other doorman had been told to expect us.

'Ah, Miss Casey's guests,' he said. 'Which one of you's the niece?'

'Me,' said Samira.

'The guest of honour!' said the doorman. 'Well, you're both very welcome, but remember, yiz have got to be quiet.'

'Of course,' said Samira, in her most dignified voice.

The doorman led us through the winding corridors and up a flight of stairs before opening a door. We were at the back of the circle, looking across the rows of plush red seats to the stage. The heavy curtains were drawn. In the stalls below we could see a few men in shirtsleeves, talking to each other in low voices. One of them was probably Mr Farrell.

'Sit wherever you like!' whispered the door man. Then he tipped the brim of his cap, and slipped back through the door.

'Come on!' said Samira. 'Let's get seats right in the middle.'

And that's what we did, just as the orchestra began to assemble in the pit beneath the stage.

'What an old racket they're making!' I whispered.

'Shh!' said Samira. 'They're just tuning up their instruments.'

Just as she said that, the musicians all stopped playing. There was a hushed silence. And then a big beautiful melody filled the room, fiddles and flutes and all sorts of instruments I don't even know the names of, all coming together to make a gorgeous big sound. The curtains drew back and I gasped. It was the kitchen of an enormous castle and you'd think it was real – it was so perfect. There was a pretty girl on her knees in front of a giant fireplace with a real fire in it, scrubbing the floor with a giant brush. I felt the weight of all my worries and thoughts slip off my back and relaxed into my comfortable seat.

I hate to say anything positive about Mr Farrell and all his works, but it really was a wonderful show. Cinderella danced as gracefully as a fairy, the ugly stepsisters were awful funny and the effects were so good they really did feel like magic. When the Fairy Godmother appeared in the kitchen I gasped so loudly I was worried one of the people down near the stage would hear. She popped up from nowhere with a beautiful lavender light shining on her, and someone above the stage must have been throwing down some sparkly stuff because the air around her was glittering.

But the best thing of all was Auntie Maisie, who appeared in the very first scene in a black and glittering gown. Mr Farrell hadn't been lying when he said he wanted to make the stepmother young and beautiful as well as wicked. But what we didn't know was that Auntie Maisie would make her funny too. She'd say something to

Cinderella and then raise an eyebrow and look out at the auditorium in a way that made you feel that, despite her wickedness, she was having a lot more fun than Cinderella and her angelic godmother.

The cast and crew ran through the entire show with just a very short break for the interval, and even though it was two hours long the minutes flew by. And I really did manage to lose myself in the magic of the stage. I didn't think about the picket or the kitchen or the bookshop job. Until, at the very end, when Cinderella had just married Prince Charming – and the Wicked Stepmother had, with a wink at the audience, managed to marry a handsome general – and the Fairy Godmother stepped forward, in a sparkling lavender haze, and made a speech.

'So Cinderella has found her prince, and with it her heart's desire,' she said in a silvery voice. 'Once a humble servant, now a princess. For anything is possible, when you believe in magic.'

As the curtains swept back across the stage, I snapped out of the wonderful sparkling world of the pantomime. Suddenly I found myself thinking, well, no, anything *isn't* always possible. I'm not going to become a princess just by believing in magic. The only way I can better my circumstances is if I do something about them myself. I kept thinking about this as me and Samira slipped out of the door at the back of the circle and down the stairs and the corridors to the stage door.

'Wasn't Maisie only marvellous?' said Samira as we walked along the frosty pavement, our breath forming clouds in the cold night air. 'You'd think she'd never left the stage for a minute, let alone been away for fourteen years.'

'She was the best in the whole show,' I said truthfully, but my mind was distracted.

Samira was talking enthusiastically about the set and the costumes and of course the acting ('Cinderella was a bit too quiet in the transformation scene but her dancing was very good'), so all I had to do was say 'Did you think so?' and 'That's true' at intervals, but by the time we were on the quays Samira had noticed I wasn't saying very much.

'Are you all right, Bets?' she said. 'Did you not like it?'

'Sorry, of course I did,' I said. 'I'm just worn out from the picketing, that's all.' Being tired is a good excuse for being distracted these days.

Samira put her arm around me. 'It won't go on forever, you know. Even if it feels like it will.'

But that's the problem, I thought, though I didn't say it. It *does* feel like it'll never end. And if that's the case, then what difference does it make if I take that bookshop job? After all, it's not like a fairy godmother is going to come along and turn me into a princess.

I was still thinking about this this morning, as Ma gave me my tea, and I thought about it as I walked through the rain to the kitchens, and as I buttered bread and poured tea and cocoa for children who were even colder and more miserable than me, and I thought about it after Kitty fainted from tiredness and it turned out she'd been up all night looking after her neighbour's sick baby, and I thought about it this evening as Lily told us about her latest attempts to get Little Robbie to breathe in some eucalyptus-smelling steam.

And I'm still thinking about it now, as I write by the light of the fire, trying to ignore the sound of my mother and father talking in worried voices about the price of coal and how bread's got much more expensive because the union mill workers understandably won't deliver flour to bakers that are scabs (or as the employers call them, 'free labour'). And the more I think about how miserable and unfair and hungry everything seems, the more I keep asking myself the same thing, again and again and again. Would it *really* be so bad if I took the job in the bookshop?

# Chapter Twenty-Eight

I'm writing this by the light of a little candle stub I found a few days ago in a drawer in the Liberty Hall kitchen. I was looking for some more spoons and there it was at the very back. Of course, I went straight to Miss Larkin and told her about it. You'd never even *think* of taking home anything useful you found at Liberty Hall.

Miss Larkin was her usual brusque self when I approached her. She was busy checking the day's food deliveries and didn't look particularly happy to be interrupted.

'Please, Miss Larkin,' I said, 'I found this.'

'What's that you're bothering me with?' She looked more closely and then looked up at me. And something about my expression seemed to strike her, because she said, 'There's barely half an inch left in that. You might as well keep it yourself.'

'Thanks, Miss Larkin,' I said, and I put it in my pocket.

'What was all that about?' said Rosie, when I returned to the table where we were gathering the morning's cutlery.

Suddenly I felt bad about keeping a candle stub. If anyone needed it, it was Rosie.

'I found this,' I said. 'Do you want it?'

'Ah no, you're grand,' said Rosie. 'We've started going over to the Murrays of an evening. Saves fuel and food for all of us. And candles,' she added.

'That's a good idea,' I said. I was glad to think of Rosie and her sister being surrounded by a family, not sitting in their tiny bare room.

'We're sharing our resources,' said Rosie. 'What was the line from that book of yours? "One for all and all for one"?'

'That's it,' I said. But I looked away from her smiling face.

I hadn't made my mind up yet. Not then. There were still a few days to go before I met Peter. But I kept turning the question over and over in my mind. Would I take my ideal job? Or would I stay with the girls? Every time I thought I knew what I should do, I'd think of some reason to do the other thing. If I took the job, I'd be leaving my friends. But if I took the job, I'd be one less person who needed strike pay. And so on, and so on.

The only times I wasn't thinking about it were the times when the kitchen got so busy you couldn't think of anything at all but handing out bowls and mugs, or when I was in Samira's house in the evening, helping her run through her lines. She knew them by heart, of course – there aren't even that many of them.

'But I want to make sure I'm as good as I can be,' she said. 'I don't want to have to think about the words or anything at all. I want to let it all flow out of me and not worry about my voice going wobbly or my mouth going dry.'

Auntie Maisie's pantomime had opened to the public to great acclaim, so she wasn't home in the evenings – though luckily the pantomime isn't on on Sundays, so she knew she'd be able to go to the Dramatic Company concert. Mr Casey and Ali were often out too, at meetings and suchlike, so I'd often come over to keep Samira company.

Just a few evenings ago we were sitting by the remains of the kitchen fire, wrapped in Auntie Maisie's old shawls, the ones she'd never wear outside the house ('Me! In a shawl! No thank you'), but likes to wrap around herself when she curls up by the fire. I was telling Samira about Little Robbie – those steam baths seem to have had a good effect on his chest because he's practically back to his old roaring self at last – when a familiar and cheerful voice behind us said, 'Janey, you look like a pair of auld ones.'

'At least we're warm,' Samira retorted.

'Fair enough,' said Ali. 'Any room near that fire for me?'

We budged over and he warmed his hands on the smouldering coals.

'Da still at the meeting?' said Samira.

Ali nodded.

'So was Eddie, and your da, Betser,' he said. He glanced down. 'Sorry, I mean Betty.'

'Ah, you can call me Betser if you want,' I said. I meant it too. There's something nice about the way Ali says Betser. It doesn't sound like he's doing it to make fun of me. It sounds like he's doing it because he likes me.

'Well thank you, your ladyship,' said Ali, and winked at me to show he was only joking.

'How's your nose?' I asked. 'And the rest of your face.' His bruises had taken a long time to heal.

Ali shrugged his shoulders. 'Ah, you know. It'll be all right. Worse things happen at sea.'

'Speaking of the sea,' said Samira, 'you haven't been thinking any more about that stupid idea of yours, have you?'

'What idea?' I said.

'He's been talking about becoming a sailor,' said Samira. 'When the strike's over.'

'You want to go away?' I said. My stomach felt a bit funny all of a sudden.

'Not forever!' said Ali.

'But you want to join the navy?' Wasn't the navy dangerous? What if there was a war? And besides the danger, I couldn't imagine Ali fighting for the British Empire.

'The merchant fleet,' said Ali. 'Working on cargo ships. Like my da used to do.'

'But ...' I couldn't think of any objections. Of course Ali could go wherever he liked.

'See!' said Samira. 'Betty thinks it's a mad idea too.'

'Sam,' said Ali, and his voice was suddenly more gentle, 'you know it'd only be for a year or two so I could earn some money and see the world. And maybe I'd get to go to India. You can travel anywhere on the cargo ships – Da went all the way to Siam once. You never know, I might be able to find our granny and granda in Bombay. Say hello to them.'

Samira caught his eye, and something changed in her face. I knew that she didn't want Ali sailing off around the world, but I also knew she wouldn't stop him.

'So when would you go?' I said. I kept my voice as even as I could.

Ali shrugged his shoulders. 'Whenever the strike's over. We've all got to plan for the future, don't we?' He nudged Samira. 'Like my sister's planning her life on the stage. She'll be in the West End of London before we know it and she won't be thinking of her poor old brother at all.'

'Shut up, you!' said Samira good naturedly.

'I would miss you, believe it or not,' said Ali. He looked at me. 'There's a lot I'd miss. But, like I said, it wouldn't be forever. Just for a while. And then I'd come back to Dublin.' He leaned back against the side of Auntie Maisie's armchair. 'So tell us, Betser, how are the kitchens now you've got the breakfasts to look after?'

It was like old times then, the three of us sitting around the fire – even if the fire was smaller than it used to be, and Auntie Maisie wasn't there to regale us with songs and stories, and according to Ali Tom was off practising his musical number with some members of the Dramatic Company. While I was there, I didn't think at all about the bookshop offer.

But later, when I was lying in bed, I couldn't stop thinking about it. Ma had put a heated brick in my bed and I pressed my feet against it to try to warm them up. Ali and Samira were looking towards the future. So why shouldn't I? Surely it was the sensible thing to do? Cargo boats might wait a few months for Ali, and the stage might wait for Samira, but this job in the bookshop wasn't going to wait for me. Maybe they'd agree with me, I thought, as I curled my toes around the edge of the warm brick. After all, they're making their own plans.

But somehow I couldn't bring myself to tell them, or anyone else, about Peter's offer. For the rest of the week I served up breakfast in Liberty Hall, and helped Ma pin patterns in the evening, and chatted with Rosie and Joan at the picket, and all the time my mind was somewhere else. It was in a cosy little bookshop, with bright glowing electric lights and comfortable chairs and books as far as the eye could see. Luckily I was so used to the work I was doing that I could manage to serve porridge and operate the tea urn while thinking of other things. Which is why I was startled one morning in Liberty Hall, two days before my appointment with Peter, when the lady who owns the vegetable restaurant on Henry Street said, 'Why, hello, Miss Rafferty.'

I still haven't found out her name, but it'd be too awkward to ask her, so I just said, 'Hello, missus,' as politely as I could.

'I just wanted to say I'm impressed by how hard you've been working,' she said. I was on cocoa duty that morning. 'You haven't spilled a drop. And you've been very patient with the children.'

'Thanks, missus,' I said.

She smiled. 'Keep up the good work,' she said, and went over to help Miss Larkin sort out a milk delivery. If Old Wobbly had been that kind and encouraging, I thought, we might never have gone on strike. But a good boss was hard to find. The last few months have taught us that.

Looking back now, I think that was when I made up my mind. I was very quiet on the picket the next day, so quiet that Rosie stopped making a joke of me and said, with real concern in her voice, 'Are you all right there, Betty?'

'I'm grand,' I assured her. 'I'm just tired.'

'Well I hope you'll be more lively at the big show tomorrow night,' said Rosie. 'We're definitely sitting together, aren't we?'

''Course we are,' I said. 'And sure, we'll be up in the gods, so as long as we arrive together we'll get places together.'

'See you outside the theatre at half past seven, then!' Rosie patted Earnshaw. 'Bye, Earnshaw. I wish you could come to the show with us.' And with a wave, Rosie was off, hurrying down Henry Street in the evening mist.

This time tomorrow, I thought as I crossed O'Connell Street, it would all be done. In the middle of the road I glanced towards the pillar, and saw the newspaper boy who I met on the first day of the tram strike huddled at its base. His bare feet were filthy and he was shaking with cold. I put my head down and kept walking.

I was very quiet that night, but luckily nobody noticed because Mrs Dickson has asked Ma to make an evening dress for her Christmas parties and the material got delivered today. When I got home I had to help Ma lay it all out on a sheet on the front room floor and then help pin it down before she cut it out, and she was concentrating so hard on getting it right that she wasn't in the right mind to chat. To be honest, everyone was a bit tired and silent.

The next morning there was Mass. When we left the church together Samira's eyes were shining.

'Just a few hours to go now!' she said. 'And then I'll be up on stage!'

'Are you nervous?' I said. Focusing on Samira would stop me thinking about the big conversation I was going to have with Peter in just a few hours, and about the step I was going to take. 'You don't look nervous.'

'I don't feel nervous anymore,' said Samira. 'But maybe I should be. Maybe this is the calm before the storm.'

'It's the calm of knowing you've worked very hard,' said a firm voice behind us. It was Auntie Maisie. There was something different about her since she started acting again, I realised. She'd always been beautiful, and she'd always had more flash about her than most people around here, but since her success as the Wicked Stepmother she positively sparkled. And it looked like Mr Garland agreed – there he was standing a few feet away from the door of the church, a bouquet of flowers in his hand.

'You won't be back late from your walk with Mr Garland, will you?' said Samira.

'Of course not!' said Auntie Maisie. 'As if I'd miss my niece's debut!' She winked at us, kissed Samira's cheek and hurried off to join the cheerful Mr Garland.

'Are you coming home now?' I asked Samira.

'I am,' she said. 'But I've got to be at the theatre in a few hours. Do you mind if I go through my lines on the way home?'

''Course not,' I said. In fact, I was relieved, because as long as Samira was going through her lines I didn't have to say anything. I didn't think I could behave like my usual self for more than a few minutes, not today. My mind kept going over and over what was going to happen later. I knew that once the words were out of my mouth there was no going back.

I said goodbye to Samira outside my front door and told her I'd see her after the concert.

'Good luck!' I said. 'Not that you need it, of course.'

'You don't say good luck in the theatre,' said Samira severely. 'You say break a leg.'

'Break a leg, then!' I said.

'I'll do my best,' said Samira. She grinned at me and I smiled back.

'I'm awful proud of you, you know,' I said. 'You'll be playing Juliet before you know it.'

Samira hugged me fiercely. And then she positively skipped down the road towards her house.

We had breakfast and I helped Ma pin some of the bits of Mrs Dickson's frock together and before I knew it, it was half past two.

This was it.

'I'm just going out for a walk,' I said.

'Where are you going?' said Ma. 'Remember we've got to leave for the show before seven o'clock. And you'll have to have some tea first.'

'Just down to the seafront,' I said. 'I need some fresh air.'

Ma looked at me closely. I wondered what she'd think when she heard about my decision. I had a feeling I already knew. 'Are you all right?' she said.

'I'm grand,' I said. 'I'm taking Earnshaw with me.'

'Well, don't be long,' she said. 'And wrap up warm.'

I wrapped an old shawl of Ma's under my coat and opened the front door.

'All right, Earnshaw,' I said. '"Once more unto the breach". As Samira would say.'

And off we went.

I had left far too early, of course. It didn't take long to reach the big bridge that ran over Clontarf Road. So I stood there and waited in the cold. I was glad to have Earnshaw sitting on my boots, but I found I was trembling a bit anyway.

I thought I'd see Peter coming from the Howth Road, but I didn't notice him until suddenly he was standing right in front of me, smiling warmly and wearing a heavy woollen overcoat and a soft red scarf.

'You're here!' he said. 'Does that mean you've made your decision?'

I nodded.

'I think so,' I said.

'Well?' Peter's eyes were bright with anticipation.

I took a deep breath. I let it out again.

'I think I'd like the job,' I said.

There. It was done. I'd made up my mind.

'Caloo callay!' cried Peter. 'Oh Betty, that's marvellous. I was just talking to James – my cousin, you know – about you this afternoon. I can't wait to tell him the news.'

'Good,' I said.

'The shop's just about ready, you know,' Peter went on. 'I went to see it yesterday – the shelves are all painted, and the first books have arrived. It looks wonderful. And I met Miss Moriarty, the manager – she's just as charming as James said she was.'

'Janey,' I said. 'When's it going to open, then?'

'Tomorrow week,' said Peter. 'You can start then, can't you?'

'I … I think so,' I said. Everything seemed to be happening very fast. 'Peter, I have to check something with you.'

'Ask as many questions as you like!' said Peter cheerfully. 'I am but your humble employment registry.'

'The kitchen in Liberty Hall – I'm still going to work there when I'm not in the shop. Like, in the mornings first thing. It opens very early. The crack of dawn, practically. That's all right, isn't it?'

'Oh,' said Peter. His smile seemed to freeze for a second. 'Well, actually, Betty, I was going to talk to you about that. That's not so important, is it?'

Something big seemed to shift in my stomach.

'What do you mean?' I said nervously.

'Well, all the union stuff,' said Peter. 'It doesn't matter so much now, does it?'

'I thought your cousin wasn't in that employers' organisation,' I said.

'No, he isn't,' said Peter. 'But … you know, you wouldn't need to be in the union if you worked for someone like him.'

'How do you know?' I said. I felt peculiar all over now.

'Well!' Peter shrugged his shoulders. 'He's a jolly decent chap. I mean, you wouldn't have any complaints.'

I bit my bottom lip nervously. 'Didn't you tell him I was in the union?'

'Oh yes.' His cheerful tone was definitely forced now. 'But I sort of said that … that you'd been, you know, led into it by your pal Rosie.' He laughed awkwardly. 'I'm sure she'd find that amusing, the imp!'

'You said *what*?' The feeling in my stomach was now a horrible churning.

'I didn't want him to think you were a troublemaker!' said Peter. 'I mean, what's the point? So I said you'd just gone along with the union business, but it wasn't, you know, terribly important to you. Which is true, really, because it *won't* be when you're working in the shop!'

'Why won't it be?' My mouth felt dry.

'Well, like I said,' said Peter, 'you'll be treated well there. You won't need the union!'

I stared at him. And as I did, I realised that although I liked Peter very much, and he was a decent fellow, and his cousin might be too, they didn't understand. And right now, I wasn't sure they ever would.

I took a deep breath and plunged in.

'I'm sorry, Peter,' I said. 'I've changed my mind.'

'Betty!' Peter stared at me. 'You can't be serious.'

'I appreciate you going to all that trouble,' I said. 'And it sounds lovely, the job. Of course it does. But I can't take it.'

'But why not?' Peter looked completely baffled. 'Betty, it'd be perfect for you. You know it would!'

'Be honest, Peter,' I said. 'Would your cousin be happy to let me work in his shop wearing my red hand badge? Or if he knew I was going off to the kitchen on my day off? You've more or less said that he wouldn't!'

Peter looked down at his feet. 'I don't ... Look, you could help your pals in other ways! You'd be able to afford to buy them a few buns from that bakery you like!'

'It doesn't work like that,' I said. I felt wobbly inside, but my voice was firm. 'I'm sorry, Peter. I think I'd better go home now.'

'I ...' I had never seen Peter quite so lost for words. 'I'm sorry too. I just thought ...'

'Say thanks to your cousin for me,' I said. And before he could say anything that might change my mind, I turned and started to walk as fast as I could back towards the North Strand. Earnshaw barked as if to say farewell to Peter and trotted after me. I didn't look back. I just walked faster and faster until I was almost running, then *really* running. And as I ran, thoughts swirled around in my mind.

What had I done? *What had I just done?* I had turned down the chance of a good job, a better than good job. A job surrounded by books, with a 'charming' manager. The job of my dreams – or at least, as high as my dreams could go at the moment. I ran across the bridge with Peter's apology ringing in my ears, thinking of the moment his smile froze.

'What's wrong with you?' said Ma, when I stood shivering and red faced in the hall, hanging my damp coat on the hook. 'You're not coming down with that cold again, are you? Because if I see one sign of a sneeze or a cough, you're not going to the concert.'

'I'm grand,' I said, hanging up my hat. 'Just cold. And tired.'

'I was going to ask you to help me scrub the sink,' said Ma. 'But if you're not well …'

Housework would keep me busy and maybe even stop me thinking about Peter. 'I'm grand, I said.'

'All right,' said Ma, looking at me suspiciously. 'But let's get a cup of tea into you first.'

I was right about the distraction. I never thought I'd be grateful for Ma's lists of household chores, but helping her clean the taps and scour the sink did keep me from brooding about what had just happened. In fact, it seemed like hardly any time had passed when the six o'clock bells rang. After we said the Angelus, Ma ordered me to wash my face and hands and get ready for a quick bit of bread and butter.

'We've got a good long walk ahead of us!' she said, and she was right.

We made a fine parade on the way into town. Samira had gone to the theatre hours earlier, but there was me and Ma and Da, all in our very best clothes (which, thanks to Ma's clever needle, look much more fine and much less shabby than they would without her skills) and Eddie, his arm as good as new (though whenever Ma asks him to do some heavy work around the house he moans that he still 'feels a terrible twinge where the break was'), and his sweetheart Mary. There was Lily and Robert Hessian (not Little Robbie, thank heavens – he was being looked after by his Hessian grandparents for the evening). There was Mr Casey and Auntie Maisie and Mr Garland, who had gone back to the Caseys' house for tea after he and Auntie Maisie went for their big Sunday walk. And there was Ali.

'What's troubling you?' Ali asked, falling into step behind me. We had reached the quays now, and the pair of us found ourselves walking a little apart from the grown-ups. (Eddie and Mary had fallen behind all of us.) 'You look like you've lost a shilling and found a penny.'

'I wouldn't mind finding a penny,' I said grimly. Then I pulled myself together. 'Ah, don't mind me. I'm just in a bit of a mood.'

'Anything I can do to help?' said Ali.

For a minute I thought about telling him everything. But instead I said, 'Ali?'

'Yeah?' he said.

'Do you ever want to give up?' I said.

'Give up what?'

I shrugged, helplessly. 'I dunno. Not the strike, but … you know. Do you ever get tired of fighting all the time, the way we've been doing? Do you ever get tired of feeling like you're going into battle every single day and not getting anything for it because the battle is going on and on and on?'

Ali laughed. ''Course I do!' he said. 'Everyone feels like that sometimes.'

'*Really*?' I said. I felt a little lighter. 'I thought it was only me. Do you really think so?'

'I know so,' said Ali. 'We're only human. But we keep going, because …'

'Ali! Betty!' Auntie Maisie was standing at the bridge. 'Hurry up, the pair of you! We're going to be late.'

'Well, we don't want to miss the start of the show,' said Ali. 'Samira would never forgive us.'

We needn't have worried, of course. Auntie Maisie was just

being careful. Even with the evening crowds promenading down Grafton Street, we arrived at the theatre with plenty of time to spare. Rosie was standing outside, looking uncharacteristically nervous.

'I thought I'd be left all on my own,' she said, with a laugh.

'Never!' I said, grabbing her hand and bringing her to join the others. I felt a spark of warmth inside. Auntie Maisie showed us where the door was that led to the gods. I know she could have wangled herself a proper seat if she'd tried, but she wanted to sit with her family for this special performance.

'You've got to be in the gods nice and early if you want to get a decent seat,' she said, as we settled ourselves in the front row of the section, looking right down on top of the stage. I felt a bit dizzy for a minute, we were up so high, but I wasn't going to complain. I wanted to see Samira's big stage début properly. Ali was on one side of me, sitting next to Maisie, and Rosie was on my other side. Ma was beside her, sitting next to Da, who was next to Lily. Below us we could see people crowding into the circle and the stalls.

'Look at her hair!' Ma was entranced. 'And those frocks!' All the others in the gods were clearly working people, but down below you could see that quite a lot of the audience were fine ladies and gentlemen too. Ma looked from them to me and Da, her expression a mixture of surprise and, well, awe I suppose. 'And they're all here for that union of yours!'

'I told you before, Margaret,' said Da, amusement in his voice, 'a lot of people in this city are on our side.'

'The lights are going down!' said Lily, her eyes wide. I couldn't remember the last time she'd been in a theatre. I've probably been more often than her, I realised, because of me and Samira getting in on Auntie Maisie rates. Lily gazed around her with so much wonder and pleasure on her face you'd think she was sitting in a red velvet box instead of the hard benches of the gods.

As for Rosie, you'd think she was in fairyland.

'Look at all the gold!' she whispered. She was so awestruck she couldn't even make a joke. Somewhere below us you could hear a band tuning up – not a full orchestra, this time, like at the panto-mime, but enough fiddles and flutes to make a fine sound.

Then a young man walked out on stage, in front of the rich red curtain. He was wearing what they call 'faultless evening dress' in novels, by which I mean a black suit and a white shirt with a butterfly collar and a black bow tie. It took a minute for me to realise that I'd seen him in the kitchens, dishing food out of the cow boiler. I think his name is Mr Connolly, but I don't think he's any relation to the Mr Connolly who called all the dock workers out on strike.

'Ladies and gentlemen,' he announced in a fine booming voice. 'The Irish Workers' Dramatic Company welcomes you to an evening of drama and song!'

There was an enthusiastic round of applause and lots of whooping and cheering from the gods. 'All the money raised here this evening will go towards the hungry women and children whose brave husbands and fathers are on strike or locked out.'

There was another round of applause from the audience. Someone behind us cheered loudly. Mr Connolly bowed his head in acknowledgement. 'We will begin with a song by the great singer Mr Seán Costello!' And with that he bowed and walked off stage. The crowd clapped wildly as the curtain drew back to reveal a neat man with a fine head of hair, and as the band struck up a rousing tune his rich voice filled the glittering theatre. He was wonderful, but even after he left the stage and the next artists, the Brendon Trio, came on, I couldn't get as lost in the music as Lily and even Ma clearly were. I was waiting for Samira's play.

I wasn't alone. 'When's she on again?' Ali whispered as the Brendon Trio walked off to much applause. He looked down at the printed programme in my hand. We'd got one programme between the lot of us.

'There's two more singers and then she's in the first play,' I whispered back. I noticed that his hands were tightly clasped. 'Ali … you're not scared for her, are you? She'll be grand!'

'I know,' said Ali. 'I just … oh, the next one's on now.'

As a woman called Bean Uí Conghaile took to the stage and sang a song in Irish, I found myself feeling nervous too. I knew Samira didn't have a huge part, but I also knew how much it meant to her. Her first time on a proper stage, and not just any little theatre but the Gaiety itself! I barely heard what Bean Uí Conghaile was singing, and I didn't notice the next performer at all. It could have been a juggling dog for all I knew. I glanced at Ali and Auntie Maisie beyond him and they looked like how I felt.

Then Mr Connolly was on the stage again.

'And now, ladies and gentlemen,' he cried, 'it is time for the first of tonight's two plays, a labour play in one act. The Irish Workers' Dramatic Company presents …' He paused for dramatic effect. '*The Dispute* by Cecelia Harrington!'

'Here we go,' said Ali softly.

Auntie Maisie was biting her lip and leaning forward in her seat.

The curtain drew back to reveal a simple set, just some tables and chairs and a lamp that made it look like an ordinary kitchen, and there was Samira sitting at the table with a mousy-haired woman next to her. A dark-haired man was standing next to the table, a defiant expression on his face. Samira's head was in her hands and the other two didn't look much more cheerful.

'We're ruined, husband!' cried the mousy-haired woman. 'Ruined, I tell you!'

'As long as I'm a member of the union,' declared the man, 'we're not ruined yet.'

The play was about a working man who had gone out on strike. His wife didn't approve, and neither did his daughter, who was played by Samira.

'Why did you do it, Father?' she said.

I'd heard her deliver that line a thousand times (at least, that's what it felt like by this week), but it was very different watching her say it on stage. Her voice was clear as a bell, not wobbly at all. As the play went on, the man's friends turned up (including a young worker played by Tom – Ali and I exchanged a quick smile when he walked on), and their discussion of the strike changed the mind of his wife and Samira too. 'Now I see that an injury to one is an injury to all!' she cried, her voice full of fervour and passion, and I felt so proud of her I could have cried. In fact, Auntie Maisie actually *was* crying, quite unashamedly, barely bothering to dab away her tears with her spotless white handkerchief.

When the curtain went down to wild applause I saw Ali quickly brush away a tear from the corner of his eye. I clapped so hard the palms of my hands were stinging. Next to me, Rosie let out a loud whoop.

'Hurrah for Samira!'

Below me, the whole theatre was clapping too – all those fine ladies and gentlemen, applauding Samira and her fellow actors! Applauding the union, supporting what we were doing! We really weren't fighting alone, even if it sometimes felt that way. And as the audience rose to their feet, still clapping, the confusion I'd felt since turning down Peter's offer started to clear away.

Because this feeling of togetherness was what Peter and his cousin didn't understand. They didn't understand that for me, joining the union and going on strike meant standing up for fairness and hope. It meant standing with Rosie, and Kitty, and Samira, and all the Jacob's girls, and the Savoy girls and all the other girls I'd never know but who also believed that we needed to stick together and look after each other. It meant hard work and wet feet and tired legs and an empty belly and it's the best thing I've ever done in my life. And I could never, ever deny it. No matter how long the strike lasts.

'Well!' said Ma, looking quite emotional herself, as the lights went up for the interval. 'That was … That was marvellous.'

'Did the mother remind you of anyone, Ma?' I said.

'Don't tease your mother,' said Da, but he was laughing too.

And as for me, I didn't know whether to laugh or cry.

'I need to go to the lav,' I said, and I squeezed past her and Da and a dazzled-looking Lily ('I never knew Samira could sound like that!') and out into the corridor and down some stairs, where a long queue for the jacks had already formed. I was standing there, my head full of the play and the audience and what it all meant when I realised someone was talking to me. I looked up and saw the lady from the Liberty Hall kitchen, the one who ran that vegetable restaurant on Henry Street, just down the road from Lawlor's.

'Miss Rafferty!' she said. 'I was looking for a friend of mine in the gods. Are you enjoying the show?'

'Yes, missus,' I said. Then I added, 'That was my friend Samira in the play. She was the daughter.'

'Indeed!' said the lady. 'Well, she was very good. Did she work at Lawlor's too?'

'No, missus,' I said politely. It all felt a bit more formal here, away from the kitchen. 'She works in a shop.'

'Well, now you've mentioned Lawlor's, you've reminded me that I have a proposition for you.'

I hadn't expected to hear this. 'You do?'

The lady smiled. 'You remember I told you about my shop? And its restaurant?'

'The vegetable one,' I said. 'I do, yes.'

'It's vegetarian,' said the lady with a laugh. 'But yes. Well, how do you feel about coming to work for me there, once the strike is over?'

I stared at her. 'Work for you?'

'In my tearoom,' she said. 'I've seen how well you manoeuvre that tea urn.'

I almost burst out laughing. Imagine, me getting a fine new job because of my old enemy the tea urn! But the tea urn reminded me of Kitty getting scalded, and Rosie too. I couldn't abandon them. Not now.

'What about the other Lawlor's girls?' I found myself saying. 'They won't get their old jobs back either. I don't want to leave them behind.'

'Well, actually, I'm opening a new branch on the south side of the river soon,' said the lady. 'So I'll need a lot more girls with experience of serving customers. There'll be work for all of you.'

'Oh,' I said. And then, as it struck me that not only had I been offered a new job, I had been offered a job by a lady who was so supportive of the union and its quest for fair play that she helped out in the Liberty Hall kitchen, '*Oh!*'

'So?' said the lady. 'What do you say?'

'Yes!' I said. 'Yes, thanks very much!'

The lady laughed. 'Excellent,' she said. 'Call in to us on Monday and leave your full name and address. Just make sure I can find you when the strike is over.'

'I will,' I said. 'Thank you. Thank you!' Then I thought of something. If I didn't ask her now I could never ask her. 'I'm terrible sorry, but what exactly is your name again? It was too loud to catch it the first time we met.'

The lady laughed again. 'It's Mrs Wyse Power. It really was very noisy in that kitchen, wasn't it? I'll see you soon, Miss Rafferty.'

As the lady walked away, still smiling, I felt like I was floating on air.

I spent the second half of the show in a glittering haze of happiness. There was another play, more serious this time, and more songs. As the audience applauded one of the songs and the performers walked off, I glanced down into the circle and saw two familiar figures waving gleefully up at me – the suffragette girls, Mollie and Nora.

'Would you look!' said Rosie, delightedly. 'Howiya, girls!'

'How do you know those girls?' said Ma, as Rosie and I waved happily at our schoolgirl comrades.

'They were in the kitchen helping out,' I said.

A girl sitting next to Mollie who, by the look of her, was clearly her older sister, whispered something that must have been an order to stop wriggling in their seats. The girls shrugged apologetically and turned around to face the stage.

'Young ladies like that?' said Ma.

'I told you,' I whispered, as the next performer appeared on stage. 'There are a fair few young ladies who support the cause.'

All too soon, it was time for the last song. What seemed like all the artists in the programme marched out on the stage. The women and girls had red roses pinned in their hair. There was a moment of silence that felt almost reverent, as if something big and important was going to happen.

And then the song spilled out into the auditorium.

*As we come marching, marching*
*In the beauty of the day*
*A million darkened kitchens*
*A thousand mill lofts grey*
*Are touched with all the radiance*
*That a sudden sun discloses*
*For the people hear us singing*
*Bread and roses, bread and roses!*

And as the words rang out in the beautiful gilded theatre, I felt more than ever like I was part of something big and something marvellous. Something that wasn't just about fighting. It was about *hope*. Joining the union, going out on strike, working in the kitchen, standing on the picket, handing out leaflets – it all meant believing that even if things weren't going well now, they could get better someday. That someday *everyone* would have a fair wage and a decent home and enough to eat. That even though I couldn't go to school now, in the future girls like me would be able to go to school, and maybe even college too.

And it meant knowing that when you see something that isn't fair, you can always stand up and say no, this isn't right. You can always do *something*. It meant all of that, and it meant bread and roses too. The work and the music. The picket and the kitchen and the theatre full of cheering, happy people.

And whatever happens next, I'll make sure I never forget that.

None of us will.

One for all and all for one!

# HISTORICAL NOTES: FACT AND FICTION

## The Lockout, the Irish Citizen Army and Liberty Hall

The lockout ended in January 1914 when the workers began to return to whatever jobs remained open to them, while still remaining members of the union. The employers claimed victory, but the Irish Transport and General Workers' Union survived, becoming part of Ireland's largest trade union, SIPTU, in 1990.

The Irish Citizen Army, which was founded during the lockout, played a crucial role in the 1916 Rising. Its founder James Connolly was one of the leaders in the Rising and was executed in 1916. The original Liberty Hall was destroyed in 1916, but its skyscaper replacement still stands in the original location.

## Irish Women Workers' Union

Betty, Samira, Rosie and their families, friends and employers are fictional creations, but the Irish Women Workers' Union was a real union. It was founded by Delia Larkin in 1911 and it played an important role in the 1913 Lockout. This isn't a history book, and I used my imagination to tell Betty's story, based on real events and set in a number of real locations.

## Places and events

Strandville Avenue in Dublin's North Strand, where Betty and Samira live, is a real street, and four generations of my family have lived on it. Two policemen were lodgers in another house on the road in 1913, and they really were chased by a horde of people who were returning from Croydon Park, only to be saved by a man called Mr Gregory. Mr Gregory's grandson Tony would become a well-known politician.

Lawlor's cake shop and tearoom is not a real place, though if you want to picture it, I imagine it being about a hundred metres from O'Connell Street, on the right hand side as you walk down from the Spire! I based the shop on the description of a tearoom in Amber Reeve's fascinating book *A Lady and her Husband*, recently republished by the wonderful Persephone books (www. persephonebooks.co.uk).

The Savoy Café strike was real, however, and there are detailed reports of it in the union newspaper *The Irish Worker*. According to the *Worker*, one girl really did break the strike just to pay for music lessons! I don't know if the Savoy Café strikers always had hand-bills to give to the public, but there are reports in the *Irish Worker* newspaper of strikers handing out such leaflets.

The Irish Farm Produce Company, where Betty eventually gets a job, was also real, and was situated at 21 Henry Street, with another branch later opening in Camden Street. It was owned and run by the activist Jennie Wyse Power, a suffrage campaigner and Sinn Féin member, who also volunteered in the Liberty Hall kitchens during the lockout.

Betty's dramatic experiences of the weekend of 30–31 August are based on real events. There are multiple detailed first-hand accounts of the horrors of Bloody Sunday and the events of the day before, and I closely based these scenes on those accounts. The fair-haired girl injured in Earl Street was Florence Monteith.

The Church Street house collapse on 2 September 1913 was a real and terrible tragedy, in which seven people died. They were Hugh Sammon (aged 17), Elizabeth Sammon (aged 4½), Nicholas Fitzpatrick (aged 40), Elizabeth Fagan (aged 50), John Shiels (aged

3), Peter Crowley (aged 6) and Margaret Rourke (aged 55). Hugh, a locked-out worker at the Jacob's factory, had already bravely carried out three of his little siblings before returning for his sister Elizabeth. They were both killed by falling masonry. All the real-life victims of the disaster shared a funeral.

There was a union drama society founded by Delia Larkin, which went through lots of different names. In 1913 it was called the Irish Workers' Dramatic Company. The company put on a lot of concerts and fundraising events in 1913, including a big event in the Gaiety in December. I included some of the real acts from that show, although the play in which Samira performs is my invention, as is the performance of 'Bread and Roses' at the end!

'Bread and Roses' is a real song, written by James Oppenheim in 1911 and inspired by the banners carried by striking millworkers in Lawrence, Massachusetts. I love that song and Delia Larkin printed all the lyrics in the *Irish Worker*'s Women Workers' column on 11 November 1912, so we know Irish women were familiar with it.

The union really did organise a food kitchen, and my accounts of Betty's experiences there and on the quays when the food ship the *Hare* arrived, including the woman sharing her parcel with another woman, are based on reports in the *Irish Citizen* (which tells of the little girl looking for 'the right lady'), the *Irish Times* and the memoirs of Sean O'Casey. Although there are a few accounts of individual days in the Liberty Hall kitchen, I had to use my imagination a lot too, so always remember that this is a made-up story and not a history book! Some people disagree on how much work Countess Markievicz actually did in the kitchens, for example.

The Save the Kiddies scheme was also real, and Betty's account of how it all unfolded is based on Dora Montefiore's own memoirs as well as Karen Hunt's essay *Women, Solidarity and the 1913 Dublin Lockout: Dora Montefiore and the Save the Kiddies scheme*. There were several attempts to get children onto various boats that week, all of which were thwarted by various priests and greeted with physical force. I combined details of all these separate events to create the scene in which Lily and Little Robbie try to leave. Everything in the scene happened that week, just not all at the same time and in the same place.

## Family history

I was partly inspired to write about the lockout because of my own family history. My great-grandfather Robert Carey worked on the docks and was an ITGWU member who was out striking in 1913. The word 'striker' is written in red ink next to his name in the Dublin Port and Docks Board book. The same book records that he returned to work in January 1914, when the lockout ended. His son, my grandad Peter, also worked in the docks. In the 1940s he married my grandmother, Frances, and moved into her family home in 24 Strandville Avenue – Betty and Samira's road!

My nana lived in number 24 all her life. She was born Frances Connolly and she was about six at the time of the lockout. Her father worked in the customs yard on the docks and she is the neighbour 'little Frances' mentioned by Betty.

My dad, Robert, and uncle, Tom, grew up in that same house. Later, my uncle moved into another house on Strandville Avenue, number 48, where my cousins grew up. This is the house I gave to Betty and her family. It really did have an outdoor toilet at the bottom of the garden, which was still being used when I was a kid. And like Betty, I loved hearing the trains when I had a sleepover there. The shop where Samira works is just around the corner on the North Strand road and is, at the time of writing, empty. It was called McGrath's when I was a child.

Like most working class children of her generation, my nana left school forever at the end of primary school. Free secondary education wasn't introduced in Ireland until 1967. All five of her granddaughters, however, went to Dominican College, the girls' secondary school that Betty longs to attend, which became free in 1967. And all of us have university degrees.